D0404638

WHAT BOOKS PRESS

AN IMPRINT OF

THE GLASS TABLE

COLLECTIVE

LOS ANGELES

ALSO BY KATHARINE HAAKE

The Origin of Stars and Other Stories

That Water, Those Rocks

The Height and Depth of Everything

Metro: A Sourcebook for Writing Creatively,
with Wendy Bishop and Hans Ostrom

What Our Speech Disrupts:
Feminism and Creative Writing Theory

No Reason on Earth

THE TIME OF QUARANTINE

KATHARINE HAAKE

WHAT
BOOKS
PRESS

LOS ANGELES

Copyright © 2011 by Katharine Haake. All rights reserved. Published in the United States by What Books Press, the imprint of the Glass Table Collective, Los Angeles.

Slightly different versions of "The Time of Quarantine" and "One Soupy Day" have appeared online in *Corridors* (Spring 2011).

The author also wishes to thank the Cultural Affairs Department of the City of Los Angeles; California State University, Northridge; the Virginia Center for the Creative Arts; and Mesa Refuge for their generous support of this project.

Publisher's Cataloging-In-Publication Data

Haake, Katharine.

  The time of quarantine / Katharine Haake.

    p. ; cm.

  ISBN: 978-0-9845782-1-4

    1. Quarantine--Fiction. 2. Environmental disasters--Fiction. 3. End of the world--Fiction. 4. Orphans--Fiction. 5. Science fiction, American. 6. Apocalyptic fantasies. I. Title.

PS3558.A145 H22 2011

813/.6   2011914292

What Books Press
10401 Venice Boulevard, no. 437
Los Angeles, California 90034

WHATBOOKSPRESS.COM

Distributed by Small Press Distribution, at spd.org

Cover art: Gronk, untitled, mixed media on paper, 2011
Book design by Ashlee Goodwin, Fleuron Press.

THE TIME OF QUARANTINE

For my family

All three were dreaming the same dream; indeed, they loved each other
tenderly and, like proud mirrors, always dreamed similarly.

Raymond Queneau

CONTENTS

PROLOGUE

THE TIME OF QUARANTINE

THEN PETER BECAME AWARE of a dull sound in the distance, something mechanical, a kind of whirring, and let go the green plum he'd just plucked from the orchard. The sound grew louder, rolling in on him like thunder, louder and louder and bringing with it a subtle darkening of sky, an almost imperceptible cooling of air and corrosive scent of metal just before it hit with a ferocious electrostatic hum that ripped through Peter like a wind and knocked him one more time to his knees. Had Peter known that this would mark the exact moment of the world's end, he might have offered up a little prayer for grace. But although he'd been following its demise on his father's portal for years now—its plagues and its famines, its widespread brutalities, its wars, its religious strife, and ruined air and water—Peter, hardly out of boyhood, could not yet take it in and, whipped by the wind at the end of the world, went—mind and body—wholly porous, like a sieve, as if the very molecules of his corporeal being—the cells and atoms and tiny strings, just as those of everything around him, the downy new bobbin of fruit in his hand, the rocky soil under his feet, the canopy of branches above—had ceased to spin or hold together, their essential magnetism momentarily discharged, so as to create a rupture that splintered matter itself into a web of microscopic schisms with a pulsing wave or throbbing that was not quite—or no longer—sound but something else, something that swelled into a dreadful crescendo and then went out in a long, slow exhalation that Peter would remember his whole life as the saddest sound he had ever heard, while all around him the world deflated, losing dimension, flattening out, like water, into a low and final formlessness.

Really, Peter was powerless to do anything other than fall. But his actual thought as he knelt on the slab of rocky dirt until his bent knees knotted and throbbed with pain was that he would never again kneel—not like that—as long as he lived.

Whatever happened now, it was going to hurt.

Peter knew hurt.

And he knew kneeling.

And he had been waiting for this, he saw now, for so long—years, it seemed, years and years, although he had lost all sense of time—ever since his father had died without crossing over, just died in his body and lay there to rot, with Peter beside him hinged on his numb nubs of knees and bereft of his last companion on earth. There was work to be done—the final ablutions, burning the last of the quarantine huts, scattering lime on the ashes. But just for that one abject moment Peter had let himself put it off a while more, as if, in putting it off, he might somehow change what had already happened, until dark descended at last. Then he had stood and, limping a bit at first, walked up the path that had once been a road to where it ended at a bend in the highway and where, just as he'd promised his father, he raised the black flag.

For days after that, a sour smell persisted and Peter's throat felt raw and seared as, item by item, he moved what remained of his family's possessions into the high stone building that had served, since he was three, as the center of his community and world and where now, according to the contractual obligations by which the children had been bound by their consenting parents—in Peter's case, his father—he would live out the rest of his natural life, a boy alone in the woods. This, too, he had promised his father, for he'd have promised anything in those last days when it had almost seemed they might both be spared from the rapidly mutating plague that had wiped out the rest of the compound.

Peter had been so relieved, so desperate to please—and save—his father, that he'd made a great number of other promises as well—to brush and floss his teeth two times a day, to work the garden and preserve its produce, to study the school curriculum all the way through to its end in the low double digits, to remember the dead, to keep fit, to maintain the solar power packs but avoid direct sunlight, to learn a new word every day, to nurture the trees, to honor their history but forget what did not need to be remembered, to get plenty of sleep, to move into the primary shelter where it would be safer, to take inventory and keep careful records, to ration the drugs, to treat each small cut or abrasion as a potentially life-threatening infection, to respect his body and practice good hygiene (wash behind your ears, between your toes, all the way down your long, lovely back—and then his father wept, but privately, as if Peter could not hear), to continue the observances and perform weekly acts of contrition, to use proper posture, to speak aloud, to eat a balanced diet, to clean the flue and flush the pipes, to take pleasure in small things, to kill only what he ate and use all the parts—tan the hide, crush the bones, knot the sinews, collect the claws, stuff the intestines—to sing, to shave (but be careful when he did), to wear shoes, to make soap, to follow the seasons and chart the moon and keep the time and cherish the language, to mourn and celebrate (in equal measure), to maintain the periphery, to practice humility, to drink the wine in moderation, to map the elusive circle, to have patience, bear witness, be a man. And always, his father said—always, Petie, always take care of the computers, and they'll take care of you.

Then his father said, who loves you? And then his father died.

These were the things that a boy must do, the things that he promised his father, and Peter, a boy, did them all for a while, as if in doing them he might still somehow make his father proud. But it was a lot for a boy to keep track of, and there were other promises as well, promises he'd written down and promises he'd promised to commit to memory and promises he'd forgotten almost as soon as he'd made them, the promises of a boy to a father and leader whom he had assumed (the way boys do) would be around forever.

Between the moment of his father's death and the moment, some years later, when Peter would discover his father's monumental deception in the byzantine computer loop that came, in its own time, to its end, looping back to its beginning (the way loops do) and exposing so much of what he had believed as false, Peter tried not to feel sorry for himself. Accept with affection, his father had taught him, what fate had given him, and of course Peter wanted for nothing—save for companions like him. But otherwise, everything was nice in the primary shelter, which he'd helped his father build—the large community building at the center of the compound where he lived now—alone. Still, Peter understood its principles—the apex of its loft rising up in aspiration from walls of river stone; the deck that wrapped its four sides in a sturdy square, for integrity; and on the inside, the round center room, for continuity. Who would not be comfortable—*at home*—there?

But Peter also took a guilty pleasure in the storerooms to which he now had unrestricted access and which had once been intended to sustain the Intentional Community for a period of time not less than one hundred years. It was wrong, and he knew it, but he'd sometimes spend hours in them, among the grains and utensils and tools and shoes, surveying inventory and feeling, inexplicably, rich. Then, flushed with shame at how his basic trait of human weakness had showed itself again, he'd go out to survey his real wealth, the land itself, with its steady, spring-fed creek that ran for most of every year; its solemn and sheltering hills; its few stands of living trees—pines, some cedar and fir, the young graceful orchard, and here and there a dogwood that flowered in sporadic bursts, its delicate blossoms snowy and startling among the pervasive dead foliage.

In this way, Peter grew from the boy who had promised, above all, to be obeisant and true, into the small, wiry man he was destined to become, a man with a sturdy constitution and complex cerebral patterns, and without a single hair on his body.

In later life, Peter would remember these remaining years of childhood as years of stubborn labor, of watering and hoeing, of mulching and weeding and pruning and occasional atavistic praying. Peter did neglect the vegetable garden, letting the tomatoes go to seed, the carrots and potatoes, asparagus and broccoli, the beans and beets and butter squash run wild all over the woods. In that, he remained like other boys. But the discipline he'd mastered as a talented young arborist and maintained through the demise of their once flourishing community, he now turned to the orchard, tending so devoutly to its trees— for Peter, above all, was a lover of trees—that all save the pomegranate thrived and produced even as the last ancient pines in the surrounding woods continued to fail, rising dead toward the flat, gray sky.

Peter didn't blame himself for that—no one could save every tree. Still, especially at the start, he did suffer from random bouts of inattention and sudden rushes of panic—when he couldn't find his toothbrush, or forgot to change the irrigation flow, or found the fish lines knotted, or let himself be tempted (no Peter, you mustn't) to turn his father's portal away from its bead on the failing outer world to one of its fantasy modules, the games he had played as a boy.

When Peter was very small he'd had a mother and a father. He'd had a house, like other children. He'd had a street, a bowl of languorous goldfish, a best friend, a school, a future. Then the viral gene swapping took hold, the plagues came in waves, and all modest hope for the future grew lower and dimmer until at last a new government formed on the Intentional Community mandate and hope was restored to the nation. With its lucrative package of free land, tax incentives, IT support, and unconditional amnesty, the federally sponsored volunteer quarantine programs were among the most sweeping reforms since those of the mid-twentieth century had, once before, pulled humankind back from its own barbaric brink. Many still resisted the idea, loathe, even then, to cut themselves off from all others in the slim hope of merely surviving this bad time in the history of the world—and for what? Others weighed their options carefully, adding up the pros and cons and banding together, for the most part, in the urban IC's—vast condominium complexes with converted ventilation systems, whole suburban blocks suddenly contained by prefab domes sprouting up all over the place. But Peter's father was among the very few to embrace the moment with revolutionary fervor.

Peter's father was, like that, a man of vision.

Peter knew this, had always known this, from the first heady meetings at his parents' apartment, to the late-night murmurings between his mother and his father, and in his toddler memory bank there's a whole intact memory of the night the first Central Committee convened, called together at his father's behest. In it, the settlers arrive two by two, stripping down in the decontamination foyer and presenting themselves to Peter's parents—to *both* Peter's parents, his epidemiologist father and his violinist mother—with a certain sceptical interest, as if maybe, just maybe, they could be on to something here. But in the blue irradiation of the foyer, their protective gear turns as green and luminescent as their glistening purple teeth.

Looking back, Peter will be able to catalogue them all, not just from the meeting, but from his later years of living among them in their IC— the distinguished mathematicians, the artists, the scientists and medical professionals, and even the philosopher, although once he had entered the compound he'd lost interest in his thoughts—in thoughts, Peter thinks he remembers, at all—and had spent his final years exhorting others to empty their minds, be at peace, tend to the earth. But at the time Peter sees the meeting as a party, and watching the closed-circuit security screen from the darkened safety of his crib, can't stop his toddler self from wanting to come out, to be part of it too, which is wrong, he's supposed to be asleep, but of course this is impossible because what he's witnessing now, what is happening right there in the next room, what he can *hear*—with both of his parents attendant—will turn out to be the birth of the most remote and ambitious IC ever imagined, the one that is going to be theirs.

In the mountains? someone says.

Look here, here's a map, Peter's father says. See how far away it is from everything? Who would find us there?

No one in, someone says, and no one out?

That's the IC compact.

But a hundred years?

A full, round hundred years.

The other IC, there's a Right of Return. Why should we give up that?

Peter's father laughs, his incisive bitterness giving way to everyone talking at once—all but Peter's mother, who says nothing—and the air going charged and electric and maybe a little bit dangerous. And Peter's father lets it. Anyone could see that. He lets it until they know he is right.

In the quiet that follows, Peter's father says: once, long ago, the last wild Indian walked out of those hills. Now we'll be walking back.

By now Peter has managed to wander into the room and his mother's lap, cuddled in the place that smells of violin and resin and a little bit of fear, such that what he will remember, later, of the evening is the cup of his mother's hand on the crown of his head, how it tenses when his father speaks, the catch in her throat on the lullaby she hums, her fierce embrace, then the warmth of her nipple and sweet rush of milk as he turns to her breast to nurse.

You can't remember that, his father said. But Peter does.

It is, in fact, the one thing he remembers on the day the world ends when he is in the orchard tending fruit—a taste almost like milk but not milk, and with something not quite right about it. But it was a taste that would persist all through the months that would follow that first founding meeting. Peter was only a toddler, so it comes and goes, the memory of the idea of the taste of it, a sour, soothing trickle down his throat when his father came to wake him for the site-finding excursion and tuck him in to a nice, soft box in the back of a government van with the small beginnings of the orchard—the one he is kneeling in now—swaying in their tubs all around him and smelling of mulch. As decreed by his father, there were two of each—apple, pear, peach, plum— but only one fig (that failed) and the stubborn pomegranate that never would bear fruit.

Go to sleep, his father said.

And then again, go to sleep, but in his mother's supple voice, the softness of it folding around him, his thumb in his mouth and dreaming the dream of the last wild Indian as they lurched along over ancient dirt roads that led to the end of the world. In this way, his first horticultural lesson would be linked forever to the day they found the place where they settled—the small flat clearing between two steep hillsides beside a creek that ran west toward the river that flowed from the single snowy mountain to the north.

Peter's father got out of the van in the gray morning light and slowly scanned the old forest, the rocky earth, all the living things it still supported. Then he turned back to the others.

These hillsides will shield us, he said. That mountain will shelter us from storm. And whatever contaminants the river still holds, the creek will always be pure. Who, he said, repeating like a mantra what he'd said from the beginning, will find us here? What can hurt us?

But Peter had already bounded out of the van, his mother crying after him no—no Petie, be careful, it's dirty—even as his father turned to take him by the hand and show him where to dig, and how deep, and the gentlest way to tamp the earth around the first trees he would plant and among which he was kneeling now.

And so they had come to leave the outer world one dark morning in another time, the three of them together, and this had always felt so precise and true in Peter's memory that he could sometimes feel the small rocks beneath his knees, the cool, loose mud in his hands, the fretful sound of his mother pacing behind. Yet his father had insisted to the end that his mother wasn't there.

She never came with us, he would say. You must remember that.

And then his father would reach out and tousle Peter's hair, or place the big paw of his hand on Peter's young shoulder, and say, who loves you?

Over time, the orchard had flourished, and of all the chores he'd promised he'd do, Peter had pretty much kept up his end of the bargain there, for he'd always been a conscientious guardian of trees, and as regularly as anything could be said to be regular in a world with everything going out, Peter had worked to keep this one small orchard alive. He'd irrigated, mulched, and weeded, he'd pruned, composted, and sprayed, and sometimes, he'd got out the hot pots, and sometimes, he'd harvested little fruits. Although the pomegranate seldom even flowered, today he was munching the apple; tomorrow there might be a pear.

Instead, the low hum that had marked the end of the world, taking everything down—Peter, himself, included.

Peter knelt there a long time, the taste in his mouth that is not quite the right taste and trying to capture a distant thought, but the thought, like the moment, remained remote and stubborn, drifting just beyond the capture of his mind. He could stay as long as he wanted, he knew, for he had all the time in the world now, against which a century meant nothing.

Maybe the hum would come back and take him out too.

Bliss.

Maybe the moment hadn't happened.

But when Peter looked up to the dead fringe of forest, the once living mantle of earth, he saw it was singed at the top to a new burnt ash which could maybe account for the wrong taste in his mouth, neither metal nor milk.

Finally, there was a word. Well, he thought. And then, that's that.

But like his toddler self who couldn't stop himself from wanting to crawl out of his crib and into the meeting and his mother's lap, he could not stop himself from wanting, now, to look. All Peter had been doing for years now was looking, what could it hurt to look a little more?

So Peter returned to the primary shelter. He rose to his feet and he walked.

There, he made tea and turned on a recording that wasn't his mother's recording—those were all gone—but someone else's, like his mother's, but not—and climbed the stairs to the loft where the IC computers were housed.

Peter climbed the stairs, but the loft he found was not the loft he'd left only hours before to tend to his chores, and at first he couldn't take it in, what had happened, couldn't even begin to sort out the physical parts of what he was seeing—the sinewy ropes of cables that linked the computers to each other and the world all fried and knotted; the long curved bank of silky-skinned screens fading in and out, its images garbled and diffuse; the high, arced rafters filled with a streaming light from the narrow slots of windows that was really no light—not a light of day or night or sun or moon or hope—just a dull flat light he'd never seen before. Dazed, he started doing things he was not supposed to do. First, he touched himself—here, there. Then he touched the switches, even the red ones. Finally he entered the portal and tried to make out what was there, but all he could distinguish in the descending gloom of the outer world looked like nothing so much as the shadowy figures of people going down in the streets where they were, people going down and out, like lights. The last thing Peter did that he could remember was pressing himself—his whole bereft body—against the membrane of portal as if he might press himself through it and go out with them too.

What Peter feels when he wakes some time after is not exactly mourning. Peter knows mourning from the first time he'd awakened on the compound, a small boy in a blanket on a bed of piny mulch, and understood his mother was not coming. Nor is it outrage, though there is plenty of that. What he feels, right at first, is disoriented and he's hot—so hot—with his body, knobby now in awkward adolescence—wrists, knees, ankles, the bony protrusion of his prickly Adam's apple—all askew beneath him, his voice strange and ragged, having cried out.

Peter does suspect it's his voice that's awakened him, his own voice crying out, and now that he sees he is not in his bed he feels as though he were emerging from some unfamiliar place inside his body—a living place—but not entirely familiar, more as if the body—his body—has been reduced to separate, discrete parts—face collapsed into shoulders collapsed into chest. All the different parts of him lie in a hapless clump. The chest heaves; the mind floats somewhere above.

And then he hears that sound again (but where has it come from—from him?), one less of grief than—impossibly—defiance.

Fully awake now, Peter cannot tell how long he's slept, nor if it was really sleep that he'd been in, and he's only just piecing together how he came to be here, in this soiled nest of pillows, when one of the promises he had made to his father was always to sleep in his proper bed and always to make it in the morning, for a man who was careless in his personal habits, his father had said, was a man of doubtful moral fiber.

Rational habits, his father had said, ensure a most rational mind. You will appreciate this when you are older.

Trust me, his father said—who loves you?

Now, Peter's eyes hurt, his heart pounds, and his face—his whole body—feels painful and puffy. Momentarily he hopes he's getting sick, but no, he suspects the truth—that he has been crying—and he finds this thought so intolerable that, although an adolescent on the cusp of life, he considers crossing over, but almost as soon as he has the thought—a thought that includes both the thought of his own self-immolation and the thought, *who better to set the last fire?*—the shame of his human weakness, again, passes through, then out of him.

This is going to be the last time Peter thinks like this, for the next thought Peter has—his thoughts are coming on fast—is the memory of what's happened, followed by the clear and simple thought as he unfolds his body from its limp clump of sleep (or whatever state he's been in), that, okay, it's not just his father. They're all gone, he tells himself firmly, but without satisfaction. That—the satisfaction, cool and purposeful—is coming, like the sudden taboo urges running through him now—the urge, for example, to burn down what remains of the compound and wander out into the dying woods, the urge to return to the outer world and ride the empty subway cars and play the empty concert halls and make multiple radiant MRI images of his own internal self, the urge to destroy the computers.

Peter looks around him at the blank and darkened screens, the inert control panels, and in the absence of the whirring of fans, what he hears is silence. As far back as Peter can remember these computers have hummed in the loft. They were supposed to have hummed for all time. And now at last Peter thinks: for what?

When Peter was a boy he'd had the secret hope that his father was working to bring his mother back. He would do this with the beauty of the world he would create—for her—as if everything he did, he did to make them whole again, a small, intact, and loving family unit. As Peter grew, he learned to imagine that the archive they were building of the history of the world—an exact replica of everything that humankind once had achieved, everything it did to self-destruct—was the one thing on earth that might ever convince her to let go of her hold on the actual world, even as it failed around her. Peter thought this as long as he could, but even as he thought it, he knew the day was coming when he would have to wonder where he had figured in.

But not with Peter's father who, although a man of vision, had a limited capacity to express emotion, despite certain guarded moments of affection, coded and opaque. Still, even from the time that he was very small, his father let him in to the archives, the only child—of all of them—allowed there. The others had bats and balls to play with, and jump ropes, and drawing pencils, but Peter had his own handheld processor and was allowed to wander freely in the loft, to pry among the portals and recursive databases—to *play* there. Later, his father would teach him about information and how to service the machines, to troubleshoot and program, things he would need in the future. Still later, he'd had lessons on the motherboard itself.

A time will come, his father said. I'm not saying when, I'm just saying you've got to be ready.

In this way, as Peter grew, little by little, his father introduced him to the outer world, the one they had left but would now attempt to salvage in the vast computer memory banks as replicas, or copies, that would, like them, be sheltered from storm by the mountain to the north and protected from disease by the creek that buffered them from the river that ran through contaminated cities to the south. And so they began their endless compilations of music and art, architecture, science, philosophy, literature, history.

Everything your mother loved, his father said, more than she loved us.

Ok, Peter said, but it was all so strange and difficult to parse. The wars in the actual world blended into his fantasy modules; Beethoven sounded like his mother. And how could he ever be sure what was real, what was not? In the loft, away from other children, he felt so thirsty and acute, so connected and disconnected all at once to everything, so—Peter did not quite know how to think yet—human. Sometimes being up there with his father amused him— the lights and the images, the complicated sounds and information, data. More often, he was bored and restless, anxious to be done, to go out and play, instead, with the other children.

Released, sometimes he would be allowed to join in the games—the things they did with sticks and how they chased and hid and laughed with each other. But sometimes, like all children and out of jealousy and spite, they formed vicious child circles against him who only wanted to kick the ball and run— with them.

Years later, after his father completed his work and shut down their interface with the outer world, Peter alone was privy to the one remaining portal, the single real-time feeder of the world's sad demise that continued, throughout Peter's time alone, to stream data back at him with maddening neutrality, forcing him to *see*. It was the seeing—the unrelenting animal consciousness—that he hated most and would have deleted if he could have stopped from wanting—needing—it too, the watching—the *knowing*.

For knowing, Peter also knew that somewhere deep inside a hidden database his father had encrypted the file of his mother that contained not just her music but also the last image of him and of her, the two of them together—of her on her knees and him sprinting toward her, a boy with flexed legs on the run—an eight-year-old, nine-year-old boy—and her in the dirt, her violin thrust in the weeds to the side and her arms spread open and wide—for him.

But there was also this: that somewhere deep inside his own skull, his Brain Computer Interface had been expanding all his life and no one—not even Peter's father—had known what would happen if he disconnected it.

For this reason, although the moment has come at last when he could, if he chose, walk away from the computers, abandoning them to malfunction, he finds himself driven instead by the surprisingly compelling need to repair them. It is tricky, exacting work, and although Peter is young yet, his father's lessons, which he'd often only half attended, already lie so far behind in a long-ago world that the problem seems hopelessly beyond him—the motherboard fried, the programs scrambled, his own organic unit numb and unresponsive in his head. Sometimes there's still a little static in his left cerebral cortex and, more infrequently, a stabbing pain, but mostly, the place where, shortly after his birth, his father had implanted the experimental cluster of synth-ethic cells just beneath the second layer of meninges wrapped around his brain where they could take root and grow into his body as surely as they grew into themselves just feels blank, a total loss, and this, more than anything, drives him, for in the absence of a working BCI, Peter finds that he no longer knows how to know himself, as though he were somehow complicit in what he understands now as his father's betrayal.

You did what? his mother cried, blanched above him and holding back something—something fierce, but also wounded. Her evenness of tone and clinical detachment alerted Peter, the mewling infant in her arms, who instantly quieted himself. Weeks old, his tiny hand flailed before him, grasping at the white skin of his mother's breast, the coarse black hair of his father's fingers.

Of all the memories Peter can't be said to have, this one is the most improbable, but yet it persists, troubling and insistent. Above him, his mother's bloodless lips hold back the words they might release at any moment while another unspoken struggle plays out between the adults, each with one hand on the infant.

You don't understand the simplest facts, his father said. It doesn't replace things; it replicates them.

But no, they were in the kitchen, where his mother had been cooking, the room soft and moist with steam and the dense scent of garlic. And Peter was older, sitting in a high chair, banging with a spoon, but when his father spoke, the infant Peter stopped and looked instead to his mother, her furious hands chopping at some green and leafy vegetable for stew. In the silence when she should have responded, Peter's father scooped him up and tossed him playfully over his head, but his hands were rough and unfamiliar, and Peter just wanted down and already, a bit, also out.

Finally Peter's mother said, so what do they do—copy him, double him? How does it work?

You don't have a thing to worry about—the BCI is entirely organic. His father sounded almost ecstatic. You'll never know it's even there. I grew the cells myself.

But Peter's mother shakes her head, slow and determined. Nothing's happened yet, she says, taking Peter carefully and giving him a breast. It's like a zygote, even I know that. There's a lag time after implant, and you can still get rid of them. Then she paused. I'll assist.

Although that's where the memory ends, Peter has always believed it to be the precise moment that his mother turned away from his father in her heart, and sometimes he wants so much to change what happened next that he tries to imagine it different, tries to believe his father would have done as his mother asked, tries to imagine his own infant body anesthetized on a soft flannel blanket, his tiny arms and legs strapped to a board, a bead of infant sweat swelling in the tiny cleft of his upper lip. Someone's hands—his mother's—hold his head steady, two warm clamps on his cheekbones and temples, as his father, poised above him, guides the laser that will kill the synth-ethic cells already multiplying into the BCI that will link him forever to his father's computers.

But that's not what happened.

In the part of the memory Peter can't access now, his father would sigh, as if he already knew that the choice was coming down between Peter, as he'd made him, and Peter's mother, whom he believed he loved. However much her resistance confounded logic, he knew he could defeat it.

The procedure, he would claim, wasn't even invasive. We just threaded the cells from the inside of his thigh—look, there, you can see the tiny bruise—up through his femoral artery all the way to his beautiful brain. He'll have more capacity is all. He will grow into a better, more versatile boy. Inside himself, our boy will be huge.

And then he would toss Peter up toward the ceiling again with something like an enthusiastic grunt.

Put him down, his mother said. He doesn't really like that, you know.

Later, rocking Peter in her arms, she would whisper sadly, *you are perfect just as you came. You are the most perfect boy in the world.*

But Peter can't remember that, and now as he works to rebuild the motherboard and recuperate the copy of the outer world from the space where, if he fails, all human record might vanish forever, he is reduced to the single, savage hope that if he can get things running again, he will restore the part of his brain he needs to feel himself again—to feel *alive*. As he works Peter finds himself oddly stripped of curiosity, suspended in a subtle state of mind that keeps him focused on the idea of the one hidden image of his mother he knows he must salvage to prove to himself that his memory is real. But how can it be? In his heart, Peter knows he was three and sleeping soundly the night his father took him, bundling him up in the back of the van and leaving her behind forever. Knowing this, surely he must know the other image of her on her knees in the dirt and him sprinting long-legged toward her is just as unlikely as the image of him clutched to her breast while his father primes and programs the laser that will keep them from splitting apart. But Peter, who's had plenty of time to think, secretly believes it must be like this for all boys and mothers, ripped from each other forever through all time.

And anyway, his father said, it's just a dream. Go back to sleep. You know your father loves you, yes I do.

In the aftermath of the world's end, Peter stays up in the loft a long time, working to salvage the computers until at last they are repaired, booting up as suddenly as they had shut down in the first place. It happens without warning, a sudden whir, a click, and then the long sinuous skin of screen floods with a brilliant blinding light even as Peter's own dormant BCI sputters with the low familiar thrumming that is him. Finally he stirs, a bit stiffly, and reaches up to run his hand over the back of his head, which he finds to be sticky with sweat and shockingly bald. Proceeding a bit gingerly, he tests out the various parts of the rest of his body—curling and uncurling each of his fingers, flexing his knotted calves. All the joints in his body ache like those of an old, old man, and then a cooling numbness surges through him, followed by another blinding flash and a series of deep, wrenching jolts as, one by one, the computers blink back on to reveal the world made over again and already healing.

That can't be.

But as Peter settles down to the portal to watch, he *sees*—already, and at once—signs of every kind of life except what's human coming back— water, flora, fauna, weather—the earth restoring itself, healing over with the toughness and resilience of a scar. Ruptured mountain ranges knit themselves whole, while deep in their valleys newts and frogs and iridescent dragonflies appear out of nowhere, fish and opossums, skunk and quail, wolves and weasels and hawks and sloths repopulate their native landscapes. Peter has only to turn his eyes away from a barren swath of desert to find it verdant and lush when he looks back again. Black water turns blue before his eyes, rippling and dense with new growths of giant algae and vast schools of glistening fish; glaciers reappear; high water rescinds; rainforests spread back down denuded slopes, replete with bright-plumed birds and delicate orchids; meter by meter, the ozone hole closes. And even the vast infrastructure of human construction is rapidly going down to decay, with strip malls and housing developments, suburbs and slums, going out in cleansing waves of spontaneous combustion that give way to native grasses instantaneously. Pit mines fill back in, garbage dumps recede into nothing, toxic waste sites disappear in radiant blasts of purifying heat. Soon, very soon—Peter sees now—all that will remain of human history are his father's archives and Peter himself.

Peter watches as long as he can take it in, and then shakes his head and reaches up to touch it—still bald. In the absence of hair he thinks he can feel a tiny indentation just beneath his lambdoid suture, the place where the cells attached. Well, and why not, he thinks as he rises from the soiled nest of pillows where he has been watching the world restore itself. And now he is standing again. He's walking down the stairs, touching different parts of the world—the banister, one stone wall. He's opening the door. He's breathing the air, hearing the wind in the trees above, the water in the creek below.

Beyond the compound, Peter knows, the world—the human part of it, anyway—is gone, but inside the sealed borders of his father's vision, Peter and his little plot of planet earth continue spinning safely through the galaxy and time. It's an odd feeling, really, but one that Peter rather likes. There will be no leaving now, he knows, not now and not in one hundred years, for why would he leave when he's already here?

Out on the deck he discovers that his own immediate world is strangely unchanged, with maybe a bit of the glare gone out of it, the air dry and tinged with musk, a few green shoots showing, here and there, through the old piney mulch.

And then, because this moment—this precise moment—has been coming forever and is finally here, a sanguine feeling spreads through him, like water, as Peter hears himself speaking aloud in a voice he does not recognize: *in the history of the world a time came when one boy alone remained.*

THE OLD, SAD MOON

ONE SOUPY DAY in Peter's lonely adolescence—all the days were soupy in those days—he is startled awake by the strangest feeling in his body—an unfamiliar lightness that he paradoxically experiences as a heavy weight pulling at his chest even as the rest of him languidly floats, and when he gets up his hair is tousled and damp. Peter has the momentary feeling that he is not alone, almost as if he can feel a breath on the nape of his neck, as if he might know what a human breath would feel like.

Peter is up now, walking around. Is it possible—has someone come for him?—and a catch rises up in his throat. But almost at once he forces it back down, for he knows well enough that what his father said was true: no one could find them here. And now Peter has to force down a little bit of bitterness too, not at his father's choice of so remote a place at the very edge of what had once been the habitable world, but at the dogged stubbornness with which his father had ensured they would escape even infrared detection by scrambling their coordinates and installing the defensive cyber dome. In the first days of his time alone, Peter rued this most of all, for a body put off heat and if he *could* be found, or if he could even breach the dome's encryption and reach out himself, why wouldn't his mother come for him now? In those first days, Peter longed so intensely for another human being—someone he might talk to, touch, someone *breathing*—for *her*—that he felt no compunction toward their IC compact, for although he had been bound to it by one consenting parent, Peter's mother never signed. It was bad there, in the outer world, and he knew it, but what was there to keep him here save for his trees? And how could one boy, alone in the world, hope to protect even this one small plot of living earth?

Nor at his times of bleakest loneliness did Peter feel the least apprehension about his own contamination—whatever he might spread, if he went out, for whatever he had introduced to the compound in his person had come—and this, Peter knew, he would live with his whole life—from *out there*.

But then the earthquakes struck, rupturing all the old faultlines at once and splitting his part of the world off into its ruined patchwork of landlocked archipelagos, and now, even if she'd wanted, how could his mother cross the fissures that cut him off from the outer world, some of which intruded so deeply into earth's outer mantle as to threaten the integrity of the planet itself? And then cities started to crumble or go up in flames, just like in his fantasy modules. Elsewhere, the oceans rose. In Peter's dreams, sometimes the earth would shrug him off, flinging him and the rest of human detritus out into space; sometimes, he'd be sucked deep into its molten core.

In this way, Peter lost his desire to be rescued or to leave, for as he kept his steady eye on the outer world's collapse, he never felt afraid. Out there, anything could happen, but inside the compound, his father was right. Inside, he would always be safe.

By the time the outer world finally came to its end, Peter had embraced himself as a full citizen of the IC compound, even if he was the only one. And although he took great joy as, improbably, the earth restored itself absent of humans, he understood and accepted his sole purpose in life as restoring it *here*, where his father had brought him.

But on the day Peter wakes with his unfamiliar feeling that someone else has lain beside him, none of this has happened and he is still a boy, lonely in his adolescence. And he shakes the feeling off and tries to laugh: of course, he is truly alone.

And yet it persists, a subtle unease that provokes him to try to flush this imaginary other out—spinning abruptly to effect surprise, or leaping out from behind a wall or a tree, but each time, nothing—another tree, a rock. Even in the shower he's bothered, but when he emerges, again, nothing, or maybe just a bat, its eyes peering beady through the overflow hole in the sink.

Oh you, Peter says, tapping the basin. You don't belong here. Go on outside.

Which, because it's time to work, is just what Peter does, but not without taking some extra protein element to clear his head and donning his protective outerwear, gone a bit short at the wrists and ankles and maybe wearing thin, but good enough, he decides, to protect him from the sun on such a day. First, the irrigation channels; then the perimeter traps; probably there will be time for the trees.

Busy hands, his father said. Think of someone other than yourself, his father said. And this time, Peter really does laugh, a hearty guffaw from the belly.

But in the silence after, he does: he thinks of someone other than himself, imagining the feel of breath on his neck. He's alone and can't leave the compound—would never leave now, for what is there to go out for? But the thought Peter struggles not to have is already there, and although he knows that he must fight against it, he can't stop, on this day, from beginning to wonder what might happen if someone came *here*.

Peter has been growing—several inches in what seems like only months—and his chest and genital area look strange, even foreign, to him, with their new curly tufts of dark hair. His shoes have long grown too small for his feet, but he can't bear to break new ones in and even though there are plenty of left-behind others already softened and formed to human feet, there's no telling who they might once have belonged to—his math teacher, the compound electrician, his own father—and so Peter prefers padding barefoot on thick and calloused soles, and in thinning pants several inches too short.

And this is not the only way he disobeys his father.

But on this day, the unsettling sensation of another lurking presence makes him acutely aware of his exposed wrists and ankles, his knobby and blackened feet, his knotted hair, and when he closes his eyes, an unfamiliar smell—some heady musk—hovers nearby.

In the afternoon, his chores complete, Peter sits down at the portal to check out the world's demise. He does this with keen anticipation, for although he doesn't like seeing the large mammals go and the human face of famine is uncomfortably close to that of their own plague, the wars, which so closely resemble the games he had played as a boy in the fantasy modules, are normally a source of distraction and excitement, and Peter has looked forward to this moment all morning. Somewhere in the world it is night, and the glow of missiles slicing through black sky has always seemed so beautiful to him.

But everything is quiet in the outer world and Peter gives in to a momentary feeling of pique.

That night, at last, he takes himself in his own hand, closes his eyes, and with another unfamiliar feeling—a feeling of lightness—he imagines the sensation that has plagued him all day as a lying down thing beside him, as if the space taken up by the mass his own body has somehow been increased by the size—and the heat—of this other presence. And this, he will think years later looking back, is the first time in his life he has truly felt alone.

Now, and in this way, Peter begins to develop what will turn, over time, into his insatiable need to hear the sound of another human voice. But it comes to him first not as a desire, but as a memory, for his favorite times had always been the evening story hour when all the children gathered at the fire where an adult would read to them from prior tales or what they called the future. As one of the youngest, it was easy for Peter to find a larger body to snuggle up against, girls, for the most part, with new, emerging breasts, and so pretend he still had a mother.

But if he did, she would not be like this.

His mother had argued, she'd fought to the end.

You've got to be crazy, she'd said to his father. You're no better than the redneck survivalists of the last century or the mad teapartiers that came after. She had put her violin down and was facing off against him from the straight-backed chair where she shut herself off against him to play. It doesn't work like that, and you know it.

Mormons stock provisions for—what, seven years? You're not saying they're crazy, are you?

We're not Mormons. Peter's mother lifted Peter to her lap. And seven years is not a hundred, and if you say another word about this I will take him and leave and you'll never see either one of us again in your life, and I mean it.

This is no place for a boy, and even you know that. How would you even survive?

There are places, there are ways.

Peter's not sure he remembers this, when he was still so small, downy-headed and loose-limbed, clutched against his mother's chest, and when she had spoken so softly at the end it was never clear to him she had spoken at all. He does remember her body, the fierce tension of it and the heat, the musky underscent of salt (she always sweated like a horse, she said laughing, when she played), and he remembers the mineral taste of her neck.

But, from his crib, he would listen to the argument continue.

You will not, his mother said, take that boy into bitterness like that. And after the silence that came next, I won't let you.

And how do you plan to stop me?

It's barbaric. He'd be better off dead.

They had argued on and on until Peter really did fall asleep, and in the morning their faces were worn and bruised looking, and Peter had paced between them, working his way up onto their laps or into their arms and then slipping off and padding to the other, first his mother, then his father, using his body to comfort and keep them together.

In later years, Peter would sometimes remember the softness of his mother, the swish of her clothes and the plant-like smell of her, but not a real plant—something sweeter, cultivated—and the smell underneath of resin, a smell of hope. Peter knew hope. Hope came from the land, from the tiny sprigs of new trees that sometimes, even now, pushed up from below the mass of decaying mulch, the great green stalks of food-bearing plants in the garden, and the shared community memory of vernal equinox, despite the gray, depleted climate of the time.

There was never any real equinox, of course, for the late climatic volatility had destabilized earth's orbit and knocked it off its axis. But there was a kind of change, a subtle lightening, and then both air and light would soften for a while and initiate a period of keen anticipation. The near freezing weather would warm a bit, the murky skies lift. And this was what would count for a season, as children and adults together awaited the turn, which could not be predicted, no more when it would come than how long it would last, but then, like that, it did, arriving on the cusp of a bright, white, crystalline dawn as the temperature rose in an hour on the blast of a hot wind from the south. And Peter would rouse from his sleep with his young pulse racing even before he was quite conscious. Everything smelled if not new, then on the verge of being new, the long fetid air tinged with sharpness and the sky outside blinding.

On that day, the first day of new light, everyone sweated and suffered from headaches as preparations began for the Celebration of New Life.

People accepted this, even the children who, despite their keyed-up impatience and inability to understand why they must wait—again—performed their tasks with subdued obedience, although inside they could hardly be contained. Adults, too, went about the business of the week—airing out their homes and turning the soil of the community gardens, strengthening the fish lines, taking careful inventory, preparing their minds to accept both ritual and work with equal grace, just as they accepted their reduced circumstances and all the rest of the proscriptions of the IC compact with affection and obstinate hope, for hope was what remained of human memory.

And so they watched and waited for the signs—the almost imperceptible lightening of sky, the rising heat, the barely longer day—in keen anticipation of the first meager promise of new life. And then they went to work, for hope was also everyone's responsibility, including the youngest of children as soon as they could navigate the woods and find their way back, on the seventh day, alone. Every child knew this, knew too that they'd be judged—their community value assessed and ranking established—by their ability to find and nurture new trees.

And every child also knew that this would be their measure of success: those whose trees did well would receive special treats and recognitions throughout the coming year, while those whose trees did not would be shamed. Maybe not overtly but in subtle ways, ways that would cause the child to feel less than cherished or suspect about herself what others had concluded—a pathologic laziness or organic lack of empathy for other living things. No one knew how such children were going to turn out, and so it was a matter of palpable relief and no surprise to anyone that when the deaths began, these small failed children were among the first to go, like their own trees before them.

Peter looked forward to the tree-hunt all year and counted it among the happiest and most exciting times of his entire childhood. Unlike other special days—Christmas, for example, or the Day of the Compact—Celebrations were mercurial and could not be predicted or fixed on any calendar, but came instead on the wing of an auspicious wind that marked a new season of growth. During the endless final week of preparation, Peter slept poorly and was plagued by frequent thoughts of his mother who, in his over-stimulated mind, would urge fortitude and patience and promise to help him if he would just be good, just for another moment, another hour, another day.

Until at last Peter's father came to wake him in the pale darkness of the seventh dawn.

Feel that? he would say, brushing Peter's cheek with the barest stroke of the rough, dry back of his hand.

Do that, oh do that again.

But his father, so reticent with feeling, would not, and Peter knew it, for his father was a stoic who had already taught him to investigate and analyze, with understanding and logic, right principles to live by. And not to display anger or other emotions, but to be free of passion and yet full of love. Not, above all, to show the trait of human weakness.

This was Peter's catechism, and he'd try to make it last, the morning of the tree-hunt when his father came to wake him, the tenderest time of the year for them and both of them pretending just a moment longer that Peter was asleep, both honed to the touch of father's hand on the downy cheek of the boy.

Feel that, the father would whisper, stroking gently. Come on Son, wake up.

And then Peter would be up and off, out into the woods, always among the very first and intent, the whole day, on his search for the tiny vegetal breaks in the mulch that promised, with diligence and love and luck, to grow into trees.

Some of the children were greedy and thoughtless, and would run from tree to tree, making claims without thought for the work that lay ahead. And of course, it was always too many trees, and these children, flushed and over excited, would later kill most of what they had promised to nurture, and there would be shame. Others were lazy and stayed close to the compound shelters, content with a tree or two, and here, too, there was shame. And of course there were those who were already failing themselves.

But not Peter, who thrived on this rigid calculus, this stubborn alchemy of love and labor, and who remained throughout the day as cool and analytical as he was resolute. For neither greedy nor lazy, Peter already comprehended the dying-off of old growth forests as a greater harbinger of things to come than even the IC itself. And Peter also had the secret part of him, his growing BCI. And so, between his natural temperament and his synth-ethic adaptation, Peter would grow over time so preternaturally gifted at sensing viable life that he became the only child who never lost a single tree.

One tree at a time, they would reclaim the world, if they were only good enough to do it.

So Peter tried to be good, and he worked hard, going out earlier than other children and working a systematic grid through the compound, from its farthest reaches at the ridge of the first hill, back and forth across its steep slopes to the pristine waters of their sacred creek, then up the other side. This marked the full breadth of the compound—the two opposing ridges north to south, and east to west, the old road that led to what had once been a highway on the one side, and on the other, the glacial creekbed, from its spring-fed source on the western edge of the outer perimeter to the culvert beyond which the outer world lay—and Peter always tried to finish his first surveying by noon so he could enjoy a little rest and nourishment before going back to mark the trees he knew would flourish with his care.

Peter's trees flourished. They grew and grew, slender and strong, daily thrusting their roots ever deeper down into the soil, their crowns ever higher toward the light. And as they did, Peter's skill and reputation grew as well such that by the time the tree-hunts came to their natural end, Peter would have cultivated what, grouped together, might have counted as a small successful grove of hardy indigenous pines.

And these were to be known as Peter's trees.

Until, one hunt, two things happened to change everything.

First, Peter had a dream, a portent. Or maybe it wasn't a dream—for when had he slept?—but the idea of a dream, something that took place in his BCI. Either way it was as vivid and implacable as any other portent, for in his dream, or not-dream, Peter found a tree already living, and it wasn't a pine but a fir, the only living fir he'd ever seen, silver-tipped and glistening in the sun and already as tall as himself.

And second, he was followed. She didn't even bother looking for her own trees. She was just following him.

But of course, Peter didn't notice, because he was distracted by his dream and searching so intently for its resplendent fir that he lost track of other things as well—the grid itself, his father's reasoned instructions on passion and love, and all indications of the girl's presence which, if he'd noticed them at all, he'd attributed to something else—her clumsy cracking of twigs behind him to the general excitement of other children, her breath to the careless panting of boys, her acrid smell to his own excited sweat.

To Peter, it would always seem as if both things had happened at once: the tree appearing before him, not so big as in his dream but still silver-tipped— and a fir!—in the first healthy stages of life, and his own heart pounding with excitement, and almost in the same breath, the new uneasy sense that he was not alone. Maybe the twig snapped too close this time, or the smell spiked too sour and flat to be him, but as he bent to part the mulch around the seedling, to examine the soil and look for other signs of promise—a smooth and shiny bark, many buds of branches, good color—his hand closed involuntarily around the small plant as, suddenly aware of—*something*—Peter froze.

Then he turned and, momentarily blinded by the sunlight in the clearing against the gloom of the forest behind him, shook his head to rid himself of the strong, unpleasant feeling that he was being watched. No, it was ok, he was alone. So Peter turned back to the seedling, already lightening at its tips, and knelt to offer up a quick prayer before staking his claim upon the only living fir he'd ever seen.

But the something persisted, edgy and distracting, such that Peter could not stop himself from checking one more time, staring long and hard until his eyes adjusted to the darkness behind him where at last he could make out her shadow, motionless beside a dying cedar.

What, Peter called, hunching over the fir to protect it. Go away. This one is mine.

Now the scent sharpened, turning acrid, and the shape made a sound, the sound of the catch of a breath drawing in. So it was human after all, a child like him, but a girl, he thought, as he thought she might be crying, but why should she cry on this joyous day—unless she had given in to despair, or else was cheating. And once he thought all this, the only thing Peter felt was annoyed.

Until the shape stepped out of the shadows and, brushing lank hair from her face, revealed herself to him.

Go away, he said again. Find your own trees.

I'm not after trees, she said. Mine always die. You know that.

And she took another step closer to Peter, smiling uncertainly and showing him discolored teeth. She was smaller than he was, but with a broad flat face, and the deep widow's peak on her forehead lent her face a troubling heart-shaped appearance. Peter was still kneeling, still shielding his small fir with his own small body, but her teeth confused him, gleaming in the sunlight like wet yellow stars. Of course he knew her at once as one of the pallid, failed children, the one who lived with two fathers—skilled technicians both—in the last remote yurt. The girl had two fathers, Peter knew, more than anyone, but no mother, and it was for this reason, the lack of a mother, that his heart had gone out to her when she began to fail. But were her teeth the cause or result of her failure? Beneath the light gauze of her shirt, soft mounds of breasts moved up and down with her shallow breath. She was older than he was.

If you're afraid for your tree, she said, I'm not going to hurt it.

Oh, Peter thought, staring at her teeth.

I won't hurt you either, she promised.

Peter's knees, in the mulch, were damp and suddenly cold as the girl started moving slowly toward him, but doing something with her hips, something sinuous and strange, and because he really was afraid that she might endanger, by her proximity, the miraculous tree he had dreamed, he rose from his knees to meet her halfway through the clearing.

When the girl sickened some weeks later, Peter had felt shocked, haunted by the memory of the softness of the breasts he had felt that day, her wet mouth—the mouth with bad teeth—on his body, and the outcome, what they had done. Also, the fir died, or maybe never even was, for when he went back to build the net enclosure, the tree was gone. Peter found the stake easily enough, and the clearing itself, no longer bright, but nothing inside it was living, and so he had knelt there again, his knees lodged in the very depressions they'd made the day before, sifting through the mulch as if he might find something there and wanting to weep.

But what he told himself was that this—his first failure—must be nothing to him now.

Peter's resolve was going to have to last a long time. For between the first sickness—the girl's—and the last—Peter's father's—the Community would go through all the stages of grief—from the first stricken sense of denial, through brutal panic, to grim acceptance, ending finally with serenity and grace. By the time it was over, everyone would know what to do and how to do it.

But it began when Peter's father found the girl.

Maybe he was looking for her, Peter never knew, but when he found her, she was curled beneath a mound of leaves in the outer reaches of the compound and already so diminished even he might have missed her had she not made a sound. The sound was hardly human, but he knew it. He knew it, and he brought her back.

Everything happened so fast.

One day, the girl was kneeling before Peter, whispering, I'm not going to hurt you; the next, Peter's father—his own father—was unfolding her like a piece of shredded fabric from underneath the mulch where she had hidden, hoping never to be found. But there wasn't going to be any hiding now, and *you poor thing*, Peter's father murmured, brushing the dirt from her face and hair as tenderly as he could manage, *you poor thing*. Then he lifted her shivering body and carried her across the creek where he built a little yurt for her and gave her food and water.

Peter's father did all this.

Then Peter's father kissed her and left her there. That was protocol.

But between that first moment, when she and Peter touched in the clearing, and the last, when Peter's father left her, shivering and alone, there had been so many others. In them, they had gone willingly down into the mulch, the two of them together, whenever they could, over and over, undone by their need and careless as children will be. They were both so small—any strong wind might have blown them away. But there wasn't any wind, only dank emanations rising from the earth.

Only the warmth of her mouth on his body, only that and nothing more.

Until they'd grown so absorbed by what they were doing that neither of them heard Peter's father crashing through the brush, saw his jaw twitch above them. At his father's side, one white hand hung, opening and closing, like a threat. The other took the girl by her scruff of yellow hair, pulling the two apart. All his life Peter will remember her face, stunned, and the arc of his own sperm spewing above them.

Oh, Peter cried, don't hurt her. Please.

Peter covered his face with his hands, trying to hide, but he couldn't stop from hearing the sounds the girl made, not like the ones his father heard later, something else. Then, as he reached down to button his jeans, rolling tentatively to one side, he became aware of another sound, the sound of his father, massive above them, somehow apologetic.

You don't know what you're doing. You're just children.

To the girl, he said, go home. Let's never speak of this again.

Then, like his son, he put his own face in his hands, as if to keep them from hearing, we don't need any more children, not like this, no more.

And then he took Peter to the creek.

We were just, Peter said, shivering in the water, his small body shrinking from cold. But of course he did not know what else to say. Beside him, his father crouched to scoop up a handful of sand.

Come, he said, rubbing grit on Peter's back.

In his memory Peter can't ever sort out how long they stay in the water, his father's hands on him gentle but firm, scouring—caressing—every inch of Peter's body—the knob at the back of his neck, between his little toes, in the crack where his spine ends, the deep round dimple at the back of his ear. But he does know what is going to happen when his father finishes and—Peter can't ever forget this—kneels in the rocky shoals, bringing his own body down to the height of Peter, and turns his bare back to his son.

Now, he says, you.

Two things sustained Peter through their time of plague, but only one of them was honorable. The first—the steely fortitude he discovered on the day the fir was gone—would serve both to steady and to solace him.

The second was harder—the second was his ravaging guilt.

For what troubled Peter was not what he had done with the girl—Peter, not yet twelve, would have kept on doing it if they hadn't gotten caught—or even how often they'd done it or what might have happened if she hadn't gotten sick, but what he'd been doing on his own and for months.

Peter would have stopped himself if he could. That was one thing he knew. But the work he did tending his trees took him out into the compound every day, every day, circling its perimeter, every day walking the creek.

It was a rocky little creek, mostly running shallow in its bed but with a few pools deep enough to swim in, clear cool water for drinking that came from the earth. And Peter knew the terms of their compact—no one in, and no one out, not for a period of time less than one hundred years. Everybody knew this, it was how they lived.

Maybe if their world hadn't ended with a culvert, but once an old freeway had crossed their creek there, and under the freeway, the culvert.

Maybe if the culvert hadn't seemed so much like a portal, or a threshold—a passageway to somewhere else, beyond.

One night, before they'd walked out of the world to here, Peter lay between his parents in their bed. In this memory, they're not fighting anymore, but wrapped instead together, Peter's small body tucked tight between their large, hot ones. Both have a hand on him but he isn't what they're thinking about. Why do they seem so sad?

What's wrong, his mother said, with an urban ic? The buildings are sealed—they're safe.

No place on earth, his father said, is going to be safe from the next part in the history of the world.

There'd been a pause, and then his mother sighed. I just don't see why it has to be so far away. You might as well take him to the moon.

Peter had followed the creek. That was the easiest way.

He broke the IC compact. He went out.

In later years, Peter would remember only fragments of this first transgression—the sound of the water, needles dropping, the smell of something pungent just beyond. He would remember, but not in any choate way, the simple improbable lure of what he had heard. And by the time he had threaded the culvert and followed the creek all the way to the river that flowed through the rest of the world, the only thing Peter could say about what he had done was that he would do it again.

And so he had, just as he'd lain with the girl, over and over, although at first the one part of his mind—the human part—wasn't even sure it was a violin he'd heard. But nothing else—nothing—could ever have accounted for the sudden charge at the back of his neck, his boy pores opening to release a startled sweat, the pounding of his heart that came from the outside, not in. And even before the first note had settled into his ear and worked up the length of his auditory nerve to make itself known in his synth-ethic lobe as the sound of a violin, the other part—the natural part—of his vast frontal lobe had known it as his *mother's* violin, though Peter had no real memory of his mother. That, the memory, came later—came now—swept in on the arc of his expanding BCI and his mother's music, which, as he listened in the woods, streamed around him, like air, like water, like breath.

That can't be, Peter thought, as a limpid feeling ran through him.

Who loved him? Peter thought.

But when he tried to tell his father later, his father said it was a dream.

Dreams can do funny things, his father said, his hands clamped firmly on Peter's boy shoulders. They can seem more real than reality itself.

Peter looked down at his own hands, the stubby nails black with dirt, the delicate skin of a pine needle lodged like an eyelash under one, and wanted, for the first time, to squirm away from the grip of the man who determined what was possible—what could be imagined—and what was not.

Peter found the embarkation camp he remembered from the time of their leaving, where they had all gathered before coming here. He found the camp, but he didn't find his mother.

It was getting late and he knew he should get back, shouldn't even be here, but with his trait of human weakness, he could not stop from exploring the paths he'd crossed so many times as a very young boy—here, the old tattered yurts where they had slept; there, the cottonwoods beneath which they had played; and over there, the wood deck where his father once sat in the shade of an oak to process the people who came or turn them away.

In this moment, Peter's father is right, and his brain feels huge, the BCI primed and acute where his father had been, and where now, as if the wood itself remembered, Peter remembers his own arriving, the taste of dry dust cleaved in his mouth and his own hot stupor. He remembers the sticky bulk of his father body beside him, and he remembers the hot rush of air as the van comes to a stop and the door swings open to a broad shallow shoal of the river. He remembers tumbling out, rushing toward the water.

But, *don't*, his father cries. It's dirty.

Peter, not yet four, slips in the dirt and looks thirstily on.

Stay away from the water. It will make you sick.

But there's enough going on in the new outdoor bustle of the embarkation camp to distract him and his boundless toddler energy—each day, all over, supplies and equipment arriving in crates, and all the packing and unpacking, the assembling, the people who wait in small yurts to be cleared and released. Among them, a trenchant air hangs, and there is an almost frenetic energy to the renunciations that take place every day at five o'clock in the afternoon, followed by evenings of music, all kinds of music, and the people, both happy and sad, for in the morning there would be the ritual shavings, and then they'd go naked into that new world, stripped even of hair that might carry disease in with them.

And where was his mother now? When was she coming?

Peter lived in this camp as long as it was camp, his father in charge of final processing and all the pertinent procedures and records—medical, financial, familial—to be reviewed and expunged in the final protocol of Withdrawal. It was a lot for one man to keep track of, and what with the boy all over the place and the contaminated river—all the rivers were contaminated then—the drug he used was perfectly harmless, just something to slow the boy down and keep him safe from the dangerous world. But of course Peter can't remember that. He can't remember lying on the dusty floor at his father's feet while, one by one above him, his father deleted each settler from the outer world's database.

If Peter remembers any of it, he remembers thirst, an overpowering sleepiness, and a sudden eruption of rage one day above him.

But the wood remembers.

You can't, the words fly, hot and angry. I'm filing suit.

And then his mother's face and hair floating like a moon in the blue sky above his sleepiness.

How did you get in? his father, looming huge.

I could have you arrested, there's a court order.

It can't touch us and you know it. Now get out before I throw you in the river.

What part of the rest of what actually happened next Peter can't ever know, and he was so sleepy anyway, but through the stupor came the feeling of hands on his body—his mother's hands, his father's hands—the clench and the tug of them, and the noise of the still rising anger.

What have you done to him, his mother cried. Then: what makes you think you have the right? as she was dragged forcefully away.

You can't remember that, his father said. It must have been a dream.

But what Peter did remember, as palpable and persistent as the memory of her touch, was the sound of her violin drifting through the woods, and though others were sent out to find her and to stop it, no one could, no more than they could stop Peter's dreams. Those dreams lasted a lifetime, leaving him gasping, hooked like a fish.

Now, having followed the sound that should have led him to her on the deck that remembers, Peter stands gasping on the deck, for no, he's completely alone.

Maybe his father was right.

Maybe Peter never had a mother. And in fact, it seemed to him now as he considered the other children, the ones who did have mothers, whose faces showed signs—arch of eyebrow, purse of lip—of the faces of parents—the *two* parents—who hovered about them, he supposed that he ought to, but never really did envy them. There was something incomplete—something hopeless—about the way they were divided, split between a mother and a father, for how could such a split ever be resolved?

What had he been thinking anyway?

So Peter did what any boy would do: he renounced his mother in his heart and went off to swim in the river, wandering up the railroad tracks that followed the river to the great high rocks from which he would leap, time and again, into green pools far below.

Don't touch the water, it's dirty.

And then, two days later, he did it again.

Asked, Peter could not have said why. He knew where the river ran, knew, too, the threat of plague, neither viral nor bacterial, but something altogether different, with innate abilities to mutate into anything it needed in its relentless search of human hosts. Knew, too, as well as anyone, had learned as catechism in his father's loft that the compound's most sacred compact was to remain apart for a full, round hundred years. This was to protect them, to ensure the survival of humanity itself. Peter knew this too, knew full well the importance of it. For Peter had stood at his father's side, had watched the elegance of his algorithm grow until even he had been satisfied the cyber dome could not be breached, neither from within nor without. This, too—*don't touch the water*—was for their protection. Once the dome was installed they would completely disappear from the outer world, as if they were not even there.

Then his father turned to him, now you.

And so it was Peter himself, although still a young boy, who had keyed in the code that set off the dome that would keep them hidden, and safe, for a hundred years.

But yet here he was, having willfully transgressed it the only way he could, through the galvanized culvert that channelled the creek deep enough in the earth to deflect the dome, and so violating both the compound perimeter and its most sacred compact, and without remorse. For the only thing he really knew now was that he would do it again.

In fact, Peter went because he wanted.

He went because he was a boy.

He went because he had a mother.

He went because there was a violin and there was a river.

He went because he could not be contained.

He went because the culvert was a conduit out into the world.

He went because there was an outer world.

He went because where they were might as well have been the moon.

And though Peter would remain in all other respects the most obedient and praiseworthy of sons, against the lure of the river, its cold rush and phantom violin, he found himself completely powerless against what proved to be the pleasure of transgression and the lure of the music that persisted, drifting through the trees from somewhere over—*out*—there.

Of course he was careful. He made certain no one saw him and removed all his clothes before leaving the compound, folding them neatly and hiding them beneath a dry rock overhang. On the way back, he rinsed the river water from his body in the lower creek and rubbed himself all over with sand to scour away any possible contamination, scrubbed his hair. For good measure, he did it again once he'd re-entered the compound, letting himself completely air dry before getting dressed. Then he performed the ritual ablutions so as to return purified in both body and spirit.

In his mind, he did everything he could to avoid contagion, except— inconceivable—not going out at all.

But of course he had no way of knowing then what peril was.

When the day came at last that his mother stopped playing in the woods to draw him out and came for him instead, Peter was weeding in the orchard, hard at work on his bony knees. There were flies that day, swarming and crawling all over him, and he was the only one working. Peter won't remember and will never really know why he is alone—perhaps he's being punished? But what he does know is, he knows she is there even before looking up. First, the sudden charge at the back of his neck; then his hands clumped with dirt, digging involuntarily deep.

The road she's walking down—the dirt road to the highway—has been sealed since Withdrawal, but she's walking down it anyway, heading straight for him, a red violin case flung over one shoulder and wearing a bright yellow cap on her head, with a long ponytail down her back. The only thing wrong is her too-red mouth. It's smiling too hard; it's showing her teeth.

And then Peter's running, and *she's* the one kneeling, both arms opened wide for him who flings himself into them, knocking them both to the dirt.

It's okay, Petie. It's all over now, and everything's safe. Her words go into his hair, his neck. Is that really you? How big you have grown—such a big, strong boy.

Sometimes, what Peter remembers is the smell of pomegranates, sometimes that she lets him bury his small, dirty face in her neck. Sometimes, her jeans and white t-shirt, the clutch of her hands on his back.

Sometimes, her words, and I'm here to take you home.

But sometimes the men come to take her while Peter is still running. And sometimes Peter's father grabs him before Peter even starts, a hand clamping down on his shoulder from behind.

You and your big imagination, his father says. It must have been a dream.

At first, a plague among them seemed impossible—how could that have happened? But Peter knew. Peter, alone, knew that it came from the river—from him. He'd known the river's dangers since he was a tiny boy, and yet he'd gone ahead and swam in it, leaping gleefully from high rocks to the deep, green pools below. Peter did that.

But the others blamed the first failed child with the heart-shaped face, instead, for bringing down on them what they had forsaken the world to escape.

And then, because they had seen it before, they drew up plans for quarantine as calmly and efficiently as if this had been their purpose all along. Then they built the gate and bridge, from the one side of the creek—where people were still healthy—to the other—where people crossed over.

While Peter, who would, in this time, come to *know* watching, could do nothing but watch.

Some of the crossings were deeply wrenching—the goat woman, for example, who had long provided them with butter and cheese and yoghurt and whey and sometimes big vats of her rich, sweet cream, proudly left at the first signs of sickness, hardly even pausing as she offered her best bell at the gate for the ritual pyres. To Peter, she'd seemed almost luminescent as she'd bypassed the gate and, abjuring the bridge, splashed through the water to the other side where she sang for a while, as if there were goats.

For several nights after, Peter watched her in the moonlight caring for the others who were already there. Buxom, she moved lightly, making frequent trips to the creek for water to quench their thirst and cool their unbearable heat. When newcomers crossed, she'd be waiting to embrace them, holding them close to her chest. And when it was time, she torched the yurts, each going up in a blaze, until the blaze was her own.

The librarian downloaded files, one story for each surviving member of the compound.

The potter, pots and vases and beautiful bowls, each with a name and instructions: break before crossing. Peter's was blue.

Then she shattered the rest of her work and scattered the shards.

One whole family crossed together as soon as the youngest child fell ill.

More often, people waited until near the end, eking out the last drops of pleasure—time spent with loved ones in the comforts of home. Some were so diminished that their crossings exacted a terrible toll, and still Peter watched, hidden in a rocky knoll where stones cut painfully (but not painful enough) into his body and where some nights he slept.

Until one night Peter watched a father rip a child from the arms of a mother to send the child off alone across the bridge. The mother clung to the child and argued, but when she tried to go too, the father grabbed her by the forearm and would not let her go. There was yelling—mostly at the child, who hardly even whimpered. A frail, moon-faced boy with a clump of yellow hair, he waited with terrible stillness. And when the parents finally left him all alone on the bridge, he just stayed there waiting for the mother to come back.

So Peter went instead and took the small boy by the hand, which he found to be electric in its heat, and tried to lead him gently to the other side. But still the boy resisted, wanting his mother, so they stayed for a while in the middle of the bridge, sitting companionably side-by-side with their four legs dangling over the side of the bridge toward the black water below, and swinging, swinging back and forth like a pendulum or single organism. At the end of the boy's legs, half the length of Peter's, the boy's bare feet shone unnaturally white.

Finally, Peter said to him: a mother loves her child. She does it in her own way and the best she can. You know the way your mother smells? Close your eyes and tell me what you see.

When Peter opened his own eyes, the boy's long lashes threw spidery shadows down the length of his pale cheek.

No matter where she is or what she does.

The boy seemed calmer now. Are you coming too?

Not yet, Peter said. But don't be afraid. It won't hurt, I promise, even though he knew this might be a lie. And I'll help.

The next time, it was Peter's teacher, who had waited too long, and who, when she knelt at the gate to leave her schoolroom whistle, found herself too weak to rise again. As Peter watched her struggle, he thought about the boy he'd finally carried over only nights before, the sturdy line of the librarian's back. What did they know? What could they see over there that they couldn't see here?

Could they see, Peter thought, did they know what he had done?

And then he imagined his own teacher's shame at being found there in the morning, on the wrong side of the creek. She had always been a complicated woman, who had taught him several languages and complex algorithms and, in the absence of his mother, had kept a careful eye on his diet, prepared plasters for his childhood illnesses and flues. Why had she waited so long, Peter wondered—was it hope, or indecision, or some intractable nostalgia for the dying human race? Maybe she had just not wanted to cross over alone, although she had always been alone and now look at her—prostrate at the gate and making small, helpless noises, like a cat.

It hadn't been that hard with the boy, crossing over and returning—no harder than threading and rethreading the culvert.

But oh, yes, please, she whispered when he offered to help.

First he found a yurt no one was using and he settled her there, taking off her wet clothes and helping her into one of the white, passing gowns. In the yurt Peter smelled something sweet—like moss in the river or the big leafy plants that covered its banks. Then he felt his own mother's hands guiding his as he went to smooth his teacher's back and forehead, and she smiled broadly at him and said, you won't believe the light. Pale as new wheat, her body itself seemed to shimmer. Still, she could not stop smiling, and there was something else about her too, something serene—and much, much younger, her breasts, the small mound of her stomach beneath the white gauze, warm and firm, like those of the straw-haired girl. Peter sat beside her, his hand on her forehead, watching her eyes dim, even as the rest of her grew brighter. Her teeth beneath her parted lips glistened like wet stones. Then, just before the final moment, she grabbed Peter's hand and moved it from her forehead to her breast.

There, she said, now.

And then she was gone in a final flash of radiance, brilliant and fleeting, and the body still and vacant beside him.

That night Peter broke all the taboos. He went to the creek to replenish the cisterns, entered the yurts, and tended the sick. He fed them. He cleaned them, wiping their pale and attenuated bodies until they were as new and clean as when they started out. He held their hands and listened to their final stories, the sounds they made not so unlike those he had made with the girl in what already was a prior time.

And he kissed them: one by one, he kissed them all—their foreheads, both cheeks, their lips.

Some years later, at the end of the soupy day on which Peter had awakened to the feeling that he was not alone, the feeling that had grown throughout the day from the first unnerving presence to the absence that made the presence present and expanded all the space around him, filling it with loss and the overpowering need to assuage it, Peter took himself in his own hand for the first time since his father found him with the girl.

Peter knew this feeling, this relentless wakefulness.

This, what he was feeling, once again, was shame.

No, not shame, human memory itself.

And as much as he tried not to, Peter was unable not to think, on this night of all nights, about how his father must have known. For if his father had known where to find him that first time with the straw-haired girl and what he would find them doing when he did —what Peter was doing now—what had ever made him think he could hide anything from him?

And so he thought about his father's face, which had looked, when it had looked on them, not stricken—stricken was what the others looked like—but momentarily defeated. And then something else—something frightening.

No, Peter, no, his father had said, his hand moving to stop them and Peter's sperm spilling on all of them.

And then his father sent the girl home.

And then his father wept.

Now, as he does again the thing that made the girl sick and brought his father to his knees, Peter lets himself remember the girl herself, the silky wet warmth of her mouth, her failed teeth—what she wanted. For long before she'd followed him on his hunt she had been following him to the culvert.

Look what I'm doing for you, she had cried later. Please, take me with you.

The way she said it shocked Peter, her little moon face pale and urgent.

I want, she had said, to go away too. Can't you see what it's like for me here?

They were standing at the bend in the creek beyond which Peter could see the culvert and so, he thought, could she. He could see the rock where he hid his clothes. He could see the light at the other end. But although he could see all that, could almost already feel the roughness of the corrugated metal and wind inside the culvert swooshing past his naked skin, the words she had said—her *words*—had not even made sense: how could *she* go out? She was good, Peter thought, thinking of the taste of her, and going out, he also knew, was bad.

Inside his head, a desperate clicking as he found himself transfixed by her teeth. In all the times he had been with her—and Peter feels himself flush with a different kind of shame—he had never once imagined her as a separate person with her own desires.

Where did she think he went anyway? How far did she think she could get?

But Peter had his mind on the other thing—her mouth, the goodness, himself—and so he told himself that it was just a river, the same as any river, as he placed his hands on her head to bring her to him.

Sometime later in the night—the night Peter acknowledges his own hand as the last hand on earth that will do this for him—he gets up to vomit. He does not use the bathroom or any of the sinks but goes outside and walks into the darkness of the woods, instinctively tracing the path to the place where he'd found the fir and met the girl, and when he gets to where he thinks it might have been, he digs a hole and vomits into it, and then he, too, lies down in the mulch and weeps, his face turned toward the pale part of the sky where he knows, if the clouds would only part, the old, sad moon still hovers.

THE SUSTAINING POWER
OF THE PIONEERS

IN THE YEARS that followed the end of the world, Peter lived simply and with such clarity of purpose that by the time this ended too, he'd achieved a kind of grace and inner luminescence that would enable him to embrace his own knowing.

How amazing, the adults used to say, the human capacity for adaptation really is. You could, they said—and sometimes these would be the last words they would utter before crossing over—get used to anything. *Anything*, they said, and the word, in their mouths, could sound graceful and forlorn.

But wasn't it ironic, Peter's father said, that human beings would turn out, after all, to be the lowest form, the basest of all animals, because they *knew*.

He had taken Peter out to tend the fish lines where they'd gathered a small pile of trout to gut, writhing on the sand before them. Everything we do, Peter's father said, slicing open one shimmering, still shuddering belly and pulling the entrails out, we do with comprehension, we *choose*.

Then he threaded the fish through its gills on a stick and handed it over to Peter.

Then he died.

Ten-year-old Peter lay down beside him, curled up like a cocoon, and willed himself to go too.

But, mortal in the end, he could not bear the stink.

It wasn't like that when the world ended. When the world ended, there wasn't any stink. The people lay down, like everyone else, but then they just faded, like dying stars or shadows, dissolving back into the earth, expunged. This fascinated Peter, who had seen so many people cross in different ways, but this was so final and so strangely comforting that although Peter could not stop his watching, he didn't feel guilty anymore, maybe only inured to the tangling of fish traps or rotting of carrots deep in the ground and the rest of his untended chores, because he understood that all of human history had been leading to this moment and now it was here.

In this way, Peter grew, sublime with his knowing, and in this way, he watched, for watching was all he knew how to do now, all that was left for him in the world, and because he knew that it would have to last him his whole life, Peter watched with the same diligence he'd once used in tending his trees or brushing his teeth.

Time was harder, and him moving through it, like water.

One day, he woke in a crumpled heap of disarray in front of his father's computers.

One day, he woke to a trenchant loneliness.

One day, he combed his hair.

One day, he put on shoes. One day, he took them back off.

He stopped chewing ragged the inside of his cheek.

And grew haunted by the presence of someone else's absence.

The headaches came on without warning, blind punitive pain that forced him to his knees, his face in his hands and sweat pouring out all over. Later, he would rise, weakened and light-headed, and it was in this state that he began to do again the act his father caught him in when he was still a boy.

And then the computers crashed a second time.

What Peter remembers from the moment he awakened to the silence, a heavy and threatening thing—on the outside, no lulling roll of sea or hum of mainframe fan, but on the inside, no, not silence—*something else*—is that it *was* sleep he'd awakened from, a deep and natural sleep, though he could not say how long it had lasted.

And he remembers whales. That was the last thing—waiting for whales.

Peter had been watching for some time now, and as the planet healed, remaking itself coherent and lovely and whole, he had seen so much already—on land, the large mammals—elephants and tigers and the golden grizzly bear—and the birds—flamingos and owl and albatross, hummingbirds and parrots. He'd seen newts and snails, butterflies and yaks, a goat, a marmot, a shrew and axolotl. And in the water, so much life—seaweed and kelp and coral and fish, crustaceans and squid and sharks and manta rays and eels. But not a whale yet, the largest mammal on the earth. Surely there were whales—just, there.

It was hard work, really, all this watching: what if he missed something? If he missed it, would it cease to exist?

In the absence of whales, Peter focused intently on the calm blue surface of the rolling sea, with maybe now and then a flying fish or porpoise, but mostly just nothing—the blue sea, and the sky, empty, blue too.

A calm sea, a quiet, soporific sea.

Another thing he remembers from his awakening is panicky disorientation, for how could this have happened *again*?

The last thing he remembers is knowing, with both certainty and fortitude, that this, what has happened, is his doing, for unlike the last time, this crash does not mark some grand external event like the world's end, but only his own sloth and carelessness, his trait of human weakness, his neglect.

For this above all, his father had said, take care of the computers, and they'll take care of you.

And now, in their most resplendent moment, he had not.

Peter will never know how he could have let it happen, but there is something else he doesn't wonder yet, because he is still young and can't quite bring himself to think about his father's role in things, but one day he will. One day he will wonder: had the first crash been mere accident, something that could not be predicted; or had it, somehow, been willed?

How much of what he'd seen was real?

But in that first moment, so unlike the first time when he had gone as limp and inert as the mainframe and could not even think until he brought it back, Peter can feel the steady synth-ethic thrumming of his own BCI inside him.

Impossible, his father would have said. It's a link.

Impossible, Peter knew as well, but yet he could feel it, the difference inside him, completely unfamiliar but as thrilling as transgression, and for a moment the sensation of it, like the river that had closed in a cold, green fist around him, hit him with a jolt of temptation. What could this possibly mean? Did this mean he could leave, just walk away now, down the creek to the river—*out*?

Then Peter remembered whales.

And maybe it's his trait of human weakness, or maybe something else, but the idea of whales just beneath the rolling surface of the blue sea somewhere hit him with the force of what it would be years before he knew to call desire.

So Peter did what anyone would do and just as he'd been trained as a boy, he went to work to analyze the problem and repair it. And now he saw that there was dust everywhere, a thin white layer that covered everything and hung in the air like a mist. How could he have let things come to this, he thought, on his knees with his vacuum, sucking dust from inside the computers where he, their only guardian, had let it pile up? Where could all this dust be coming from?

And when they were clean, Peter rebooted the computers.

Once he'd been a boy. He'd had a father once, and before that, a mother. Once he had watched for whales in blue seas primed to receive them. Before that, there *had* been—he had *seen* them—herds of wooly mammoths lumbering peacefully across green valleys and headed north, toward him. Later Peter will be full of plans for everything, but if he'd had one before now, it would have been to wait until the mammoths came, massive beasts out of the past, and to ride them away.

Peter remembered that.

He remembered waking to the silence, heavy and threatening the *glitch*, so small a thing—dust in the fans.

Breathe, Peter, *breathe*.

Momentarily, he couldn't—no breath, no breath out—but not from what he was doing but from what he was trying not to do, trying not to look, looked instead down at his black and calloused feet with toes turned to the claws of an old, old man. How strange time is, he thought, see what it's done to this man.

But then, because this is who Peter is and what he does, he looked.

Breathe, Peter.

Not whales.

Only this: other men and women all around and not so unlike himself going on about the daily business of their lives. They were eating and driving and buttoning coats and hunched over desks in offices that rose high up into murky skies. They were tending children, walking dogs, singing in choirs, preparing for battle. A woman flapped white sheets out in bright air before bringing them back to her body and folding them up into a tight, precise square. A man tenderly wiped bloody surgical tools. Boys were repairing machines, solving math problems, camping, touching themselves. Girls were making love, being born, flying airplanes, tying shoes. In a glass and steel tower, one stood pressed to the window, face flushed, her whole body taut with longing. Elsewhere, in a library cubby, a messy-haired man with long fingers crunching a pile of numbers. All over the world, people were sleeping, their breath rhythmic and calm, or wrapped in the arms of their lovers or children. They wore shirts and shoes and stockings and clips in their hair. They had such beautiful teeth.

And this was how it happened that Peter's father's loop came finally to its end in a single stunning reboot that delivered Peter back to the time of Quarantine—or *just after*.

In the aftermath of the second crash that had, like the first, taken down the computers without warning, Peter had gone out to lie on the deck, naked and pale as a worm and away from his watching. He had lain there for a long time, living on air and the mean inner hope that what remained of the sun might take him as it had so many others. But although every hair on his body fell out and would never grow again, Peter did not even burn.

During this time of waiting, Peter had felt himself paradoxically yearning for *things*, and what he missed most were the things he had burned in the quarantine yurts—deliberately burned—along with the bodies of the men and women, the children, who had been his only family. He missed the physical remnants of them—one man's cashmere socks, or another's pipe or flannel shirts, his teacher's chamomile tea bags, a boy's toy truck. Beneath his thinning skin, the map of his vascular system was becoming more and more marked, but he'd have given anything for the goat herder's bell, a tiny pair of earrings, a clay bowl, the string of what he knew to be a violin.

It was ritual, of course, but it was also protocol to burn personal belongings with the body in what would be, and everybody knew this, a failed attempt at containment. But dutiful to the end, Peter kept it up, even when they knew it did no good, even with the remains of his own father, and now it was all gone. There was nothing in his world, no physical object—scrap of fabric, bristle of brush— that had known any other human touch than his, save for the shoes, for shoes had always marked the planting of feet on this sacred earth.

Maybe if he'd burned them too, but it's too late to think that now.

And anyway, his father made the rules.

But what was he to do with all those shoes?

Here, now, and in this way, Peter began at last to consider his father. He did not do this in thoughts, for his thoughts had grown dim on the deck, strange amorphous things floating somewhere half inside his consciousness and half outside it—or *elsewhere*. But he couldn't stop himself either, for it would seem to him now that if the world hadn't ended—if men and women were still out there somewhere, working for wages and having ideas and making love and brushing hair, if children had homework and pets—there must be a moral lesson in the story that it had, written only for him. But had his father written it in anger, to keep him there forever? Or had he done it to protect him, out of love?

Pete did not suppose he would ever know now. And as he took this in with a kind of subtle outrage, something like a separate will or self formed inside.

Or *something else*.

Because sometimes, drenched with his own essential fluids in the fierce blast of sun, late in the afternoon just before the evening came to wrap around and cool him, Peter remembered something else from the rebooting, not the image and not the words either, so much as the sounds of what might have been words before they were words, the idea of words organized into a kind of syntax he had never seen or heard before but so utterly familiar as to suggest the intimacy of physical touch. And then there was a surge inside his head— neither in the BCI, nor the other, the natural part, but somewhere between— that was pain and not-pain at once, and his left ear clicking loudly, or skipping.

A thought would be coming to Peter on the wing of time.

Somehow Peter knew this, knew too that for the thought to come, there was only this one way and he must wait the moment out, the way his father taught him, and with it, his strongest, most visceral urges—rage, each acute curiosity, desire and despair—until he was as cool and systematic in his thinking as a cipher.

He must wait for the mind of his father.

By the time he stood again, using the body that had lain for so long dormant and useless to him, Peter had grown lean to the point of translucence and all the knobbiness of his ragged adolescence had softened up a bit, his limbs hanging loose in their sockets, with a breadth of head and chest that wasn't there before, and his skin as smooth and white and poreless as an egg.

At the back of his head, just where the skull rounded down, he could feel a new ridge pulse where the plates had opened up around his BCI and fused into a single, subtle segment.

Peter went down to the creek to wash, shedding a pale crust like ether. As his father had taught him, he washed. First he put both hands palms down in the water to start the cooling process in his wrists, and then he splashed it on his forehead, mouth, and chest. Then he lay down in a shallow pool and let it run around him, soothing the place at the back of his head where the new plate was and letting the coolness run through him until he had recharged himself. Then he squatted in the water to scour. He used sand to do it, rubbing and rubbing the dead skin away. And when he was done, he was as fresh, as clean, as perfect as any new human being.

And as Peter finally turned his attention once again to the world, slowly he began to take it in: water rushing over rocks in the creek below, as it had always rushed; wind soughing in the trees above, as it always had soughed; pine needles dropping to the forest floor, as they had dropped through all time; his own heart pulsing with the current of his altered BCI.

Who loved him?

Take care of the computers.

Be a man.

Then Peter wasn't thinking anymore because Peter, who was once a boy, had never not been failing his father who knew everything but what his son was doing.

When his thought came at last, Peter hardly recognized it, not right away, rising as it did first as a desire, and then very curiosity that had consumed him as a boy, like other boys, at play on the banks of the river, the conduit out. And there it was at last, and Peter grasped it, not even a fully formed thought, but only the words—*the river, the conduit out, the river, the conduit out, the river, the conduit, conduit, conduit out.*

Or, *back.*

As soon as Peter thought this he is already going.

But how could he go?

Maybe if there hadn't been a BCI he would have done this at the very first, before the faultlines ruptured and cut the compound off. Maybe if there hadn't been a cyber dome, they would have marked his body heat and come for him.

Now as he worked on his thought, that would in time become a plan,

Peter gave himself over to a first small thrill of pleasure as he understood with stunning clarity that he would have to make them come for him *there*.

Some time a long time later, although he cannot say how long, Peter will again be standing in the creek, just at the edge where it rises to his ankles. He will stand there leaving. It is time.

Between that moment and the moment he determined to head there and only there, Peter had worked in the loft long enough that he'd forgotten what it felt like, this water, the rocks. The work he had done in the loft had been the hardest work of his life, and he'd done it without conscious thought, peeling back the rigid layers of his father's parenting and portal with his mind detached from his body but wholly engaged. Once he'd started, Peter found he could not stop. He worked without respite or hope. He worked on blind faith and the hapless intuition that, even now, at the end of time, everything remained not just possible, but necessary.

Despite terrible headaches and a plaguing sense of doom, Peter worked until he grew keen and sufficiently incisive to locate the node between the motherboard, his BCI, and the neural cyber knot of his father's making—and that was when he understood his father's one true genius was to turn the portal inward and let it write it itself.

All Peter had to do was reverse it.

Now, in the creek, Peter pauses one last time to review the pathetic history of his own small life, a boy raised alone in the woods by computers at the end of the world. The water is cold enough to make his feet throb, and Peter, who has never seen ice, wonders idly if it could freeze and trap him here again. It had never seemed so cold, when he was a boy. He had never even noticed its temperature then.

Momentarily, he regrets that the drugs did not last.

And then he lets it go and starts off down the creek toward whatever lies ahead for him now.

At the back of his head, where the skull plates meet, his BCI pulses. It's yet another soupy day, and as Peter works his way down the creekbed, stepping, sometimes jumping, from rock to rock, he's aware of a pungent stench of decay he never noticed before, and here and there—impossible—an animal carcass or snakeskin, new leafy plants with a urine-like odor. Peter's balance is off and the rocks are slick, so he falls, more than once, into deeper pools than he'd expected, but the bank is thick with mulch and if he tries to walk along it, he sinks to his ankles in rot. Peter has tried to dress nicely, wearing old jeans and a fine-wale corduroy shirt he hopes will be presentable, but now he is wet, and what does he know anyway?

What does Peter know about anything at all?

When the portal finally opened, it opened with a slight click, or a beep, certainly a sound he'd never heard before, and then a series of them, fast and imperious, making him turn, dust cloth in hand (for Peter, at that moment, had been dusting), toward the motherboard itself as it untied the final knots of encryption and reconnected Peter's BCI to the one true portal from which his father—his own father—had cut him off long ago.

Peter would remember his whole life the futility of the dust cloth hanging hapless in his hand, the powdery dust he'd raised all around him, the flat and luminous light it reflected back at him—the exact same light he could not keep from leaking out of him—until it seemed he could no longer tell the difference between him and the radiance that blanketed him and then, in an instant, went out as the portal opened to a dark, blank emptiness, like a hole or a burrow, and with nothing at all written on it.

Then Peter put his cloth down, went back to his soiled nest of pillows and, pausing for a moment—was this what Peter wanted?—uplinked his BCI link and was in, as seamless and as fluid as destiny itself. Peter entered the portal like water and let it enter him, a viscous sea of code for the idea of everything, and him the capacious receptor, expanding exponentially—becoming huge.

Peter made a small room in the portal. He furnished it with things he could imagine—sofas, pillows, sources of light. He arranged things in the room so that he might be comfortable and could come and go. And then he went back to his watching, content with the knowledge that what he was watching was finally real.

At first, it was the dailiness of so much human activity that amazed him, all those people ratcheting around in so much empty space. How busy they were at such ordinary things—making love and eating and misunderstanding each other, driving their cars, washing their bodies, tying shoes for their children, making beds, walking dogs—*dogs!*—riding in elevators and being subjected to medical procedures, making love, buying produce, suing and leaving each other, reading books and writing and making love, doing laundry, putting on clothes and taking them off, going to movies, going to work, going to war, singing, mourning, laughing—*ha ha ha ha ha*—making love. There were not so many of them as there had once been, but there were plenty. They made such incredible noise.

All but the Remainders (among whom Peter suspected he might count as one), who were not so much silent as reduced, for while some few had proved capable of resuming prior lives, most had emerged from their disparate Intentional Communities pale and listless as moths and strangely *depleted*. As Peter moved through and among them, it seemed that something had gone missing from their memories and bodies that left them somehow *insufficient*, drifting here and there and in and out of other people's houses, using up what remained of their personal effects—their canned goods, their *beds*—wearing their *clothes* and reading their books and drinking their tea and using their whitening toothpaste, taking their drugs, developing their neuroses and disorders, their hopes and memories, but not without a kind of slippage, almost molecular, in which the space taken up by the mass of their own bodies never quite filled up the spaces of those who had lived there before. They would do this as long as they could in one dwelling—a home, an apartment, a dormitory room—and when they had exhausted it or run out of toothpaste, they'd move on to the next one, exchanging other people's lives as capriciously as people once had changed shoes.

In all other respects, Peter's strongest impressions from those first miraculous forays into the idea of a real outer world would remain completely visceral, as indeterminate and open-ended as any present moment. He had no initial system and no real control, going out to wander randomly among others and then falling back, stunned and exhausted. The link would just go suddenly inert, and he'd find himself gasping in the loft, dust swirling around him, the sound of the creek, the smell of him, his heart—his own heart—and BCI pounding, and him wanting nothing more than to go back in, to do it *now*, to miss nothing at all anymore for the rest of his life.

Slowly Peter's plan came into being.

This was going to take time, but Peter had that. All the time left in the world was his.

Yet now, when even that is over and everything is ready—the portal primed, the replicant virus he's written as confounding and omnipotent as his father's loop and designed to do only one thing—to let the world know he's here and make them come to him—Peter slows himself, wanting paradoxically to put off a while longer the moment when he will cross again through the forbidden culvert and find out if his plan will work, or not. In his mind the virus has to be perfect, and he knows that it is, eloquent and vital and so very simple, one continuous wave of the code for him released beyond the sheltering shield of his father's cyber dome to pass through everything in the outer world, from the simplest domestic devices to the most secure corporate networks to the archives of the transcripts of her. This will show his power. And then it will go out before anyone is quite sure what has happened. And this will make them curious—a Remainder from where?

Peter is shocked—truly, viscerally shocked—to discover how close the culvert is, just beyond a few bends in the creekbed, under the ragged rope bridge from *before*, past the scattered ruins of trailers where people once lived, and between the dead Ponderosas. But now that he is finally here he cannot stop himself from giving in to the luxury of small second thoughts, for has it always—all this *time*—been so close? Not even a mile, he calculates, when once it had seemed as far as the moon. Stunned, he runs one hand over the orb of his baldness. A train could fit through the old culvert as seamlessly as a boy. Slick with algae, its corrugated surface still frames the algebraic problem of his boyhood thinking, with x being the spot beyond which he could not turn back.

Touching his head again, Peter notes the curved dome of the culvert to be black with bats, their dark wings folded, silky and precise, across their trembling bodies. The water at his calves no longer feels so cold, more neutral. A wind rises up at his back.

Today, he fixes x at the center—the 147th ridge.

Then he clasps the small computer in his pocket with which he will release his virus and steps into the culvert, which roars from the rush of water.

This is the moment the headache should come, but no—just the steady pulse of water parting at the backs of his calves, the pounding of his heart, the heat of the sun dissipating as he moves deeper into shadow. Maybe it is just a culvert after all. The remnants of freeway still pass overhead, the water still flows through, the fish, if there are fish, still swim in great loops on its other side where the green pool gathers.

But the sound of the water still sounds like transgression—a sound that courses through him, pulsing and hypnotic—and Peter drags his feet, relishing the feel of the rough and rusted metal, each corrugated ridge of which marks the measure he'd used as a boy to fix the space between the inside and the outside of his world. Now, as then, he counts them, gripping their cusps with his toes. Just broader than two inches at their apex, they cup the animal soles of his feet as precisely as his memory. Before him lies the center, Peter thinks, a thought that brings a certain sanguine dreaminess and subtle acquiescence.

Whatever happens now, it is already happening.

Maybe the loop is not so bad. He's been through the worst of it already— he *knows* what happens inside the loop—inconsolable memories of the future. And maybe the next time it comes to its end, the world really will be reborn whole and coherent—all the animals but those that are human springing up where they should be alive, the flora restored to its proper colors—green, ochre, riotous pink—the seas and the sky reflecting each other once more, even the hole in the sky knitted closed to nurture them all.

 But maybe not.

Maybe everything would turn out different the second time around. Maybe the loop, like his BCI, is organic, self-evolving, capable of producing a world of tremendous joy and optimism where there might be children—and mothers.

Wouldn't it be lovely to think so?

And now Peter really does hesitate, for beyond what he will do at the old embarkation camp to activate the virus and call out *come here, come here*, the rest is mere hypothesis and hope.

Maybe that world already exists, and maybe Peter, in choosing to go out, is choosing not to choose this benign and perfect world.

Peter looks for all intents and purposes, like a wild man.

This is madness, Peter thinks.

No, madness would be waiting, forever, for the mammoths.

Madness would be watching.

Peter's heart is pounding and it occurs to him that he should be afraid. For here he is already—the center of the culvert and 147th ridge, across which sometimes, as a boy, he had dashed, afraid that it was there, in the culvert, that he was most vulnerable to discovery, his shadow stark against the round of light on either end. For this reason, too, sometimes he had crawled or slithered like a snake through the cold water that wasn't dead yet.

The next thing that happens surprises him when in a single moment of involuntary action, an impulse he doesn't anticipate and can't believe he still possesses, his body, as though with a will of its own, acts, his feet stepping over the 147th ridge to plant themselves on the other side as Peter chooses to be human after all.

EPISODES

FUTURES FOR HER

WHEN HELEN was a girl, Helen had a rabbit.

Helen did not, so far as she knew, have a mother—only the memory, the idea of a mother. But she did have a rabbit.

Of course, the rabbit wasn't really hers, but it was a real (not a simulated) rabbit, a living pet with real fur, real blood red rabbit eyes, long rabbit ears and a furtive rabbit manner that made her the only one who could take care of it, so in a sense, it was hers. One dewy morning—all the mornings were dewy in those days—Helen went out to the back where it was her job to water the plants her father grew in rotting half tubs of old whiskey barrels and to check them for aphids and other dangerous insects or fungi, and there it was—the rabbit—just there in the backyard, crouched motionless in a patch of what had once been a lawn but was now reduced, like all the residual lawns, to weeds and voluntaries, the plants that moved in when the watering stopped.

Helen stared the rabbit down, forcing herself to seem calm. Her hand went over her mouth. I wonder if it's real, she thought. Then the rabbit's nose twitched and its red eyes turned on hers, two glistening ruby jewels of animal apprehension.

Where could such a thing—a *rabbit!*—possibly have come from, she thought, taking in both the rabbit and the ruined vats of lettuce. Oh, Helen thought, her father was going to be mad. But this thought, as it formed, was a slow, dull, not very urgent thought, surprisingly depleted of dread, which Helen attributed to the force of the opposite thrill she felt at the idea of what might be a pet. And it was only lettuce, the limp winter planting, and not her father's beloved, if failed, tomatoes: lettuce in the winter, tomatoes in the summer. You could get anything in cans, but not lettuce. So her father grew it, and she watered it—and now, this rabbit had eaten it.

Oh, Helen thought again, oh no.

Helen had never had a pet. Helen had never known a single other person who had had a pet (though she did know plenty with mothers). Helen was barely even familiar with the concept of pet except as something they studied in school. People had owned dogs for pleasure—*before*. They'd owned cats and gerbils and resplendent talking birds; some people had even owned large animals, horses and pigs. No, pigs were for eating, and horses—utility or sport? Sometimes it was hard to keep things straight, what things were like before the plagues changed everyone's allegiances and habits, with survivors split between those who had chosen quarantine, giving everything up, and those who had not. But of course, like Helen's father, they'd had less to begin with to give up. Hence, the paucity of animals, but here it was again, and now the rabbit's ears twitched. What a savory stew it would make, but what Helen thought instead was how did one even care for a pet, much less a rabbit, which had just eaten up all her father's lettuce, all three five-gallon tubs of various edible leafiness, new and tender and green. All gone.

Between then and when Helen grew up to be a court reporter, a woman adept at effacing herself, calamitous world events would include such drastic changes in the weather that no one had backyard gardens anymore—a sad time in the history of the world. But in the beginning, when the fat and furtive rabbit had first appeared to Helen, a remote child with all the regular dreads and yearnings, the rabbit triggered such a visceral animal recognition that, despite the twin dangers of disease and disappointment, Helen felt something like hope.

Helen did all the right things—the things her mother would have had her do, if she had had a mother. She went door-to-door in the neighborhood. She posted signs: rabbit found, please call. She fed it, first carrots, then proper rabbit pellets she ordered off the NetZ from somewhere in the heart of the country, and she occasionally cleaned up and collected the other round pellets of rabbit refuse her father regarded as good for the soil. What Helen loved about this rabbit was not the warmth, or affection, a pet might have provided—the rabbit, in fact, was not at all cuddly and Helen almost never touched it—but its quiet randomness and the surprise of it, looking back at her, or not, each of its moist red eyes glistening and alive.

Helen liked to have it there, crouched among the tough shrubs in the backyard where she would often sun herself in secret, reading long tragic novels from prior centuries. Sometimes, Helen and the rabbit would just sit staring at each other, and sometimes Helen would find herself falling into the animal gaze, falling and falling like Alice, she thought, which would sometimes be her last thought as she sank into a kind of zen-like reverie, detached and wholly serene.

In other respects, the rabbit was inconstant, disappearing for weeks and leaving the back yard emptier, by its absence, than ever, until it would reappear again, as random and as unexpected as at first, if a bit scruffy-looking and reduced, to munch on some bit of opportunistic sage or wandering horsetail or broom.

This went on for years.

As much as Helen could be said to love anything, Helen loved her rabbit.

Helen was the only child she ever knew to have a living pet of any kind. Well, maybe fish. Some children had bowl fish, but they didn't last long, rotting in their water with fatal bloom-like extrusions that were almost pretty if you didn't know.

Then, when she was twelve, a raw-edged bundle of girl misery on the ragged cusp of adolescence, the rabbit disappeared. At first, Helen hardly noticed—that rabbit had been disappearing for years—but then week after rabbitless week had gone by and a kind of desolation set in that made Helen feel as if some essential part of her were splitting off forever. Soon her hair fell out and a sort of high-pitched whistling started in her ears. Also, Helen stopped growing.

Well, puberty can do that—make a fat child thin, or a thin child fat. But Helen suffered more from a kind of late onset failure to thrive, a slow, insidious wasting so persistent that by the time—years later—like the rabbit, Helen disappeared, she had become the thin, almost child-sized and thoroughly bald adult she would, for the rest of her life, remain.

The first sign that something was wrong was random clumps of hair appearing, like the rabbit, out of nowhere—in the bristles of her brush, on the nap of her flannel pillow, around the openings of the necks of her sweaters— until her scalp had developed a pattern of female baldness that resembled nothing so much as a map of the world that was coming.

One day she went into the bathroom and shaved off the rest of her hair, and when she emerged, her father (who had so wanted a normal child) poured himself another drink and said, you look like a failed Remainder.

By this time, Helen was deeply worried. More and more it seemed as though she would never grow again, and the whistle that had started in her deepest inner ear just kept getting louder. And although she had hoped that removing what remained of her hair would release it through the channels of her open roots, her bare head had only grown more sensitive, picking up such a startling range of aural acuities—registers beyond the range of human hearing, sounds from all over the world, things she never wanted to know—that she fell into deep adolescent anguish. Helen blamed her father. If she only had a mother, she might even still have hair. A mother would have bought her medication or herbal salves and other treatments. A mother would have *noticed*.

Her father, instead, had her adapted, waking her early one morning in the summer of her fifteenth year.

It's time, he'd said. Pack some things.

And when she came back two weeks later, he'd shrugged. Well at least your head is shapely, he had said, clasping her in a clumsy embrace.

Awkward, they'd walked down the street, her hand swallowed up in his hairy paw. Almost grown by then, Helen knew this wasn't right—people would *see*. But he was trying to make it up to her, she knew, the missing weeks. And maybe he was trying to hide his own disappointment—had he expected her to come back with hair?

Looking around, she saw that, indeed, some of the others had come back with breasts, or biceps, or uncommon intuitions. But because she also knew adaptees were designed to blend in, developing as though they were normal, she understood with stunning finality that even her father's hand, hot on her own, the rueful tenderness of it, could do nothing to stop or undo the implant inside her he had bound them both to.

I'm just thinking, he had said, about your future. Someone has to. You will thank me, he said, when you are older.

Everything Helen touched felt new and strange, her whole body ached, and she wanted to sleep for at least another week.

From now on, he had said, we will call it your tattoo.

And the hearing had only gotten more acute.

Not all the adaptations took, of course, and later, Helen knew, there would be more tests and training, but for now she'd be allowed some little time to heal as her implant got used to her body and took root inside her.

And so it was that in the night room of Helen's lonely years of adolescence, she'd lain awake listening to the nearby Remainders, as clearly as as if she could somehow see them too. Helen hated the whole process of Remaindering, but now she could not shut it out, and even though she could hardly remember, she knew she'd known them once, the people who had lived by their natural rights in the houses that echoed now around her, or at least her father had, her *mother*. Once they had been neighbors who had borrowed things like sugar or downloads for movies, who eaten had her father's tomatoes and baked cakes or knitted socks to thank him, or children like her. Helen imagined she'd played with those children, and squabbled over things like candy or toys. She imagined there had been birthday parties.

Not all, of course, had crossed over in the plagues. Some had simply wandered off to embrace the end of time, but when the plagues ended instead and the IC's reopened, the people inside them, pale and listless as worms, had to live somewhere. Some lodged futile court battles to reclaim what they'd once freely turned over to the government in exchange for sanctuary, but most of these left-over survivors, known as Remainders, had simply drifted aimlessly among the empty houses—there were so many anyway—as though they might make themselves at home there.

And this was what kept Helen up at night, their awkward missteps and anxious attempts somehow to fit, but underneath the wrongness of their racket, she also heard the lost love and laughter, the fears and vulnerabilities, the rage and confusion and longing of those who were gone, like her mother, before them, and underneath all that, the poignant misalignments of the Remainders themselves—in the infant's bassinette, the soft padding sound of the feet of the child who would have been growing by now; in the solitary bed of a sole survivor, the murmured endearments of men and women bound forever together; the clicking of phantom computers.

And in Helen's silent home, always, the lack of a mother's tongue, which might at least have provided some comfort or counsel for her dreaded voyage out into the world. Because after what her father had had done to her, there was nothing for it but to wait out the remaining time of childhood, which would end—there was no stopping it now—with the summons she'd receive on her eighteenth birthday. Helen was not going to be able to avoid it coming any more than she could have avoided her hair falling out, but a mother might have helped her find a mate instead, and although Helen knew it was useless to hope for, there were days, whole days, when she'd imagine that, if things had only been different, she might have gotten a husband instead of a chip, a man who would share both house and labor, and who would take her to his bed at night, the both of them filled with hope for an undoomed offspring.

But because Helen also knew this hope was wrong, she spent much of the rest of her final days missing her rabbit and trying to memorize the world she'd soon be leaving forever—the softness of her childhood bed, the old aluminum window that framed the shadowy street below, the floor with the paths where her feet had crossed—here to the bookshelf, there to the closet, and there to the door that led out into the world.

When the day came at last, Helen lingered a little too long in her bed. One last time she imagined that her father might have had a change of heart. For years she had nurtured his futile plants. She had watered them and weeded them and picked them when it was time to pick them; she'd distributed surplus to neighbors, when they had neighbors; and when they had Remainders, she gave them food too. Her father, who never noticed anything, might yet be waiting in the kitchen with two mugs of coffee steaming—Helen was grown up now—and a little gift of seed money, something to help her start out. Well, times were hard all over. She mustn't be bitter.

Instead, what she found at her place was a glass of pulpy orange juice and a piece of dry toast with a boiled egg, cool and serene. Aside the glass, a small medical cup, and in it, a memory capsule designed for ingestion with two shiny halves, one red and one black, and two metallic tips at either end glistening, like the juice, in the morning light. And beneath it a note: forgive your mother, sweetie. She—we—loved you very much.

Helen was delivered to a moldy cubby on the fifth floor of an ancient boarding house where most of the other residents, well past training days, were closing in on fifty and noisy with phlegm. The tightly made bed in one corner lay close to the ground with a rudimentary panel set into a ledge beside it and, on the opposite wall, a yellowing screen. Otherwise, the room had few adornments—a closet with four or five hangers, a washstand with toothbrush and paste, ceiling lights, a fan, one bare rug by the bed.

That first night, Helen sat on the bed until lights out, listening to the old ones drag oxygen tanks down the corridors just beyond, their lungs scarred and useless from—*before*. Sometimes Helen wished she and her family had crossed over back when times were bleakest, or if they'd had the means, to have joined an IC. But no, for people like them, the world would end, or not; they, too, would go on, or not. Either way, what did it matter?

By the time the first crude adaptations came along, people were so desperate to protect their chilren they'd do anything to get them, and soon a vast illicit trade was booming.

And look at her now.

Helen sat and listened, not daring to hope things might be different here, but if anything the noise was worse than at home, with sounds coming at random and from everywhere now—the hacking just beyond her own door neither more nor less pronounced than those of men and women making love down the block, or parents wailing in the streets below, or whole species expiring on the far other side of the planet, the last exhalation of the last of each animal—sphinx moth or tiger or clam—as clear and immutable to her as the sound of her own heartbeat or breath. Helen heard it all—the fluttering moth, the thin winds of dying forests, a mother instructing her children on how to find freedom in their closest major vein—when all she ever wanted, starting from that moment, was not to hear anything at all.

In the morning, she welcomed the distraction of the pull-down training menu, for now she was here, the only thing to do was complete the adaptation. But really, it was all so confusing, the lists and lists of occupations for which she might be suited and range of training options—futures for her—and a private torment, for Helen also knew that once she started, there was never going to be a way out. If she started out as cook, cook she would be for the rest of her natural born days, and the same was true for artisan, bartender, colorist. She'd be good at what she did—that was what the adaptation was for—but once the circuits started integrating into her natural capacities, that was who she was going to be. If only she had a mother to tell her what to do, but between belly dancer and beautician, how could she possibly choose? For days, Helen tried, but the menu kept shifting, opening or closing whenever someone else chose or finished or simply went out, their adaptation having failed, but although she found herself unable to get past the letter C, she developed in this time the unusual serenity and fathomless reserve of placid patience that would be such an asset later, for it marked her, almost to a fault, as a model of discretion, a woman detached, the old people rumored, from basic human interaction.

Helen waited three weeks before taking the capsule. She didn't really want to—didn't trust its metal tips, never mind her father's note. But it was there and she was here, stuck and unable to decide, until finally it began to seem a quid pro quo. The capsule, after all, had been her father's parting gift. Perhaps there had really been a mother.

The instructions said to take lying down with eight ounces of water and twelve hours to devote to the memory that was coming. There was also a powder to be mixed with the water and a cracker to settle the stomach. The water, slightly fizzy, left a sour taste in Helen's mouth that lingered only long enough to signal the tingling that passed with a rush from her head, down her neck and spine, and all the way out her limbs, the tips of her fingers and toes. Vaguely recursive, the current rippled through her, electric and liquid as, little by little, Helen felt the capsule release. Seconds later, she was gripped by a wrenching wave of nausea, and then her skull exploded with pain and not pain—the idea of pain—then nothing at all, just blankness, a dark, soothing silence.

The man who enters through the door in her skull is not her father but an official looking man in a white coat, with a young woman trailing behind. Beneath her tingling skin, Helen can hear something—the man's coat crackling, but maybe also the woman, pale beside him and visibly trembling. Reddened by rash, the man's Adam's apple bobs up and down excitedly as he bends over Helen to prod her here and there—first her temple, then her throat, then her wrists, her groin.

But she is not fifteen—she is three or four, hardly more than a toddler. She is small and white and her body looks pinched.

It won't hurt her, will it? the woman says.

Pretty, the man says. What does she like? His blunt fingers on her wrists smell of antiseptic.

She likes to read, the woman says, her voice vaguely familiar. Words, you know, and pictures. She'd like an animal—could you arrange for that?

In time, but the man sounds distracted. He sounds, Helen thinks in the tingling part of her brain, strangely hungry. Everything in its own time.

In the boarding house, Helen's larger body lies pinned to the whiteness of her bed, watching with a separate part of her brain her child self on the other bed. In that room, in that bed, everything is white—the man, the sheets, the woman who is handing her over. Now, as the man examines her feet, each toe and each translucent toenail and the spaces between, Helen tries to squirm away, but something holds her down there too.

Finally, the man stands and straightens his shoulders. She'll do, he says.

Do you have the consent papers signed? Then he turns to the woman and adds in a lower, hardly audible voice, good luck. You've done the right thing.

Helen doesn't see the woman go—she is there, then gone, forever—but she's alone with the man now, who is rubbing ointment on her neck, down the inside of her arms, all around her wrists, along the rounds of her palms and each finger, one by one. Still and white—every bit as white, she thinks in the separate part of her buzzing brain, as the room itself—the child Helen lies immobilized, her arms bare and open to the man. Beside him, a tray of cruel instruments gleams.

Relax, he says. I'm not going to hurt you.

Then he lays one hairy ear on the arc of her shivering chest and listens for a long time to the thumping of her tiny, child heart. Helen can feel his breath going in, going out, the rasp of his chin on her icy skin, his hands as they continue their examination, and then a strange savage sound comes out of him. Seconds later, he straightens himself up, takes a gleaming scalpel, and makes two tiny cuts, just there in her neck, on either side, and carefully threads the implant down the length of her arms.

By the end of the following morning, Helen will have chosen court reporter and begun her training in the oblique encrypted language of transcription. She'll have done this with no further thought to the future, telling herself it was a c—after Chef and before Courtesan. She'll have done this without even looking at her hands, which lay inert at the ends of her arms, as if waiting to be activated. Helen couldn't really look, but she knew they were there, strange and translucent and with new indentations at the backs of her wrists that shimmered from within, like mercury or silver tattoos—like the tips of the memory capsule.

But it wasn't like that, she would think. My *father* sent me to that camp. Some of the girls came back with breasts. It wasn't like that at all.

What Helen really wanted was a way to let the noise out. She'd have done anything to quiet the world.

Thus, in time she will look back and wonder was it accident or fate? True, she had had to choose something. One after the other, the people in the hallway were beginning to go out, leaving little holes of silence where they'd been, and whatever was leaking from the center of those holes formed a dangerous vortex for her. Still, she could have chosen nurse, choreographer, semiotician, or something regular, like data entry. With her steady mind and agile fingers, she'd have been good at that, recording live births, gene mutations, extinctions. Even inventory work, keeping track between the claims of those returning from IC's and Remainders taking up their sqauatting occupations here, there. She could have been anything, really. People still could.

Or could she?

The ten years between Helen's induced memory and her natural one was such a long time in the history of the adaptations. Helen wanted to know but she didn't suppose she ever would now what, exactly, had happened to her, but it didn't really matter anymore, for as the diodes she'd ingested took hold at the base of her wrists, already they'd started to glow, like tiny ancient stars, and sometimes they ached, and heat came from them too—both heat and speed. Flushed with the shock of it, Helen worked her way through the training modules in such spectacularly record times that rumors were already starting before she was fully licensed—the fastest court reporter on record, and utterly discrete, who could take down anything every bit as if she were not there.

But while another person might have taken pride in her achievement, Helen turned, inside herself, ever more remote and sad, for she could not help but look at her hands as somehow alien to her and wanted nothing more than to get rid of them like an old pair of gloves. Nights, she would thrash, unable to sleep, flailing at her pillow, hating her father—the one who stayed behind, for her. Her mother, she would wake up crying. Why had they taken her mother and not him?

Helen so wanted to have been like the others—two parents at home and only moderately altered. Helen tried not to, but she couldn't help from envying their openness of destiny, what still remained of their capacity for human interaction, for choice and change, for intact memory. She'd heard the black-haired boy who came back buff had quit the fighting cage and started teaching, the girl with exceptional recall had managed to mate as well. Helen wouldn't really have minded a less noteworthy skill that might have left her, like them, with a more resilient remnant of her purely human self. It was possible, she told herself bitterly—every bit as possible as that the rabbit had been real or that her hair might one day grow back.

But even as she told herself this, Helen's talent for transcription was evolving into something wholly different, a new and multivalent system that even in the moment of its coming into being had already begun somehow to deepen. For underneath her perfect record of the court proceedings, another record lay, and another, as Helen began, in her own way, to transcribe a greater field, one that transcended even language to include the very thing she most longed for in her life—human intimacy itself. In layer after layer, Helen peeled story back, beginning with the courtroom, its assembled body and each of its participants, then burrowing into the lives played out there until her transcripts began to replicate the visceral experience of having been not only at the trial, but also at the crime scene, and before that, at the conflicts that preceded, layering and layering with such subtlety and nuance that, like ancient photographic negatives, each layer could be superimposed, one on the other, until taken together at once they could be said to contain not just the telling but also the told, an uncanny post-verbal replica of that time in the history of the world.

And so this was how it happened that Helen, a small bald woman of impeccable discretion, began her meteoric rise from the obscurity of her father's failed tomatoes to her curious renown as a court reporter, a profession she'd selected just because it was a c.

Equally sought after for high profile celebrity cases and classified government work, she soon became known as the woman in gray, perpetually dressed in a neat charcoal jacket and mid-calf length skirt and a delicate pearl gray blouse. Modest and reserved, almost diffident in person, she hardly ever spoke, and when she did, it was in the same low, modest tone she used to attend to basic needs—to request certain foods at the market, or to arrange for sundry items of clothing to be laundered and delivered to the small room where she lived, as parsimonious with spoken language as she had grown expansive at the stenograph machine.

And, true to her profession, Helen had started not so much to disappear behind her gray uniform and discrete appearances in court as somehow to fade. Her own father, passing her on the street, would never have noticed, though anyone who really looked could make out the contours of an actual woman, especially the hands. But no one did because in Helen's perfection of craft, she'd so utterly effaced herself as to become, in some true sense, imperceptible.

When Helen had exhausted the literal capacities of all existing stenograph machines, she set out to have one built for that would transform the trajectory of human discourse itself, for on it she would soon begin not just to represent the moment, but in some heretofore unimaginable sense to *recreate* it. And in the recursive logic of her system, Helen began finally to exceed the limits even of writing.

For Helen at work (or at least Helen's hands), could be said to perform intransitively, so completely porous that all things passing through her, almost at the molecular level, would be transformed to public record, up to and including the judge's asides and distracted inner thoughts, the defendant's remorse, and Helen's own sensitivities to the long, sad exhalations of the world going out. The effect was so stunning that it soon began to alter the actual course of events, with prosecutors and defending attorneys responding more to what they read in Helen's transcript than to their own courtroom exchanges. After that, it was only a matter of time before there were junkies among them, addicted to the rush of being other than themselves, and then the journalists, and before long a vast underground file-swapping network had sprung up for Helen's work fueled by people all over the world who craved the trial records more real than their own lived lives.

As for Helen, who remained oblivious of the following she inspired, she'd begun almost from the moment she'd chosen court reporter to live fully and only in the cusp of her own capacities. From the first heady moment of jury instruction to the last of final verdict, she would be caught up by the competing versions of the truth that circled fiercely around her, addicted to the fluid charge that started each time her new stenographic apparatus began rising from the floor to unfold like a flower on a slender stalk. It began, just there, at the place on the pale underside of her wrists. It began with a terrific *zinging*. And Helen knew herself to be as powerless to circumvent it as she had been to circumvent the charge of her father's potent capsule, for after the *zinging*, a kind of bliss, or coming down of silence which carried with it no further obligation than accuracy and speed. In the subsequent wash of syllable and syntax, Helen's fingers found their rhythm and their purpose, linked to the steady beating of her heart, the extraordinary sensitivities of her inner ear, and the immense juridical database to which they were uploading even in the instant of their coming into being.

In this way, Helen's transcripts passed from record to reality to lore, with her the still, small conduit that fixed and stabilized events—the final arbiter of what had happened and had not.

Until one day she turned out to be at least partly human.

Later, much later, she would hope it was the human part of her that had grown impatient. For anyone might have gotten bored, she would think, in that tedious haze of corporate corruption and general bleariness of greed.

Anyone might have intervened.

It wasn't like her, really, but after that first time, she couldn't stop herself, and whenever the clicking started inside her, she knew it was futile to resist, first the clicking, then the will-less acceleration of her own hands beyond the capacity for human thought or speech. But oh, they were beautiful hands, long fingered and finally free, so quick that no one, watching them, would have guessed they were now subject to the hot and radiant pain that from that first day on would accompany such moments, a pain that ran all the way up the length of each bony metatarsal and back to its source at her wrists. For this was the moment, the exact moment, that Helen began not just to record but to *anticipate* things.

After that it didn't matter, nothing mattered, really, as she could not stop herself from entering an even subtler state of mind, her fingers flying over the silky membrane of her apparatus and, independent of her body, faster and faster, spinning and flying toward the sound only she could hear which, if she could only get it out—get it down—would stop. But like the spinning center of an elusive circle, Helen never could, until finally she'd exhaust the sudden burst, bow her head, cast her eyes demurely toward the floor, and with a barely perceptible sigh or flush, let her hands finish. And it was this, not any sign of irritation from the judge, or hesitation from the witness, or rustling in the jury box, but Helen's sudden stillness that would signal the attorney he was flagging, that he'd better hurry now to catch up with the recorder and find out what was going to happen next.

Helen, the slight one, ever discreet.

PETER WAKES TO A ROOM
STRIPPED OF HUMAN TENDERNESS

PETER WAKES TO A ROOM stripped of human tenderness, a white room hovering high above the earth, with four small windows cut, also high, and facing each direction of the compass. Peter wakes with a feeling of vertigo and a deep, throbbing ache in his back, but when he tries to move, he finds himself tethered, curled tight on a bed and clutching the tender part of his belly, which also aches. In his whole life, Peter has never felt such a sensation—a sensation of being actually, physically constrained. The humming is much louder than it ever was on the compound, and a bitter, stinging smell clings to the bedding.

Peter scans the room again and decides he is wrong about the windows, that what looks like small panes of glass high up on the walls are really just flat sources of light—the light in the room, an artificial light that glows with a regular underlying pulse, the source, perhaps, of the humming.

The bed opens on a hinge from a white wall and hangs suspended above the white floor. Aside from the small white commode, a white service bowl, also bolted to the wall, and a folded white chair, there is no other furniture in the room, which also lacks any visible ingress or egress. And as Peter takes in that the room is hermetically sealed—an idea he's only ever imagined in his fantasy modules—a long shudder passes slowly through him.

Is this what he wanted?

Peter's head hurts, too, and he tries to soothe himself by reviewing, yet again, how he got here, and why, but as always, even just the thought of the idea of the three he has culled, like his trees, from the portal fills him with such anxious tenderness that Peter can't help but release the electronic tether to pace the white room.

For no one, he tells himself with some satisfaction—not even his father—could keep him encrypted forever.

By the time the men came for him out of the sky Peter had grown calm, not even sweating, a man on the banks of an ancient river awaiting redemption.

But whose?

First the low hum in the distance, a rising crescendo. And then a noticeable thrumming and a strangely familiar physical sensation just before the palpable sound burst over and through him with a force so violent it knocked him to his knees.

The men who came for him descended from a vessel that hovered in the sky, sliding down a long rope in sleek contamination suits topped with clear bubbles for their heads to see.

Don't, he tried to cry out, *touch the water.*

But it was so terribly noisy.

He knelt and he lowered his head in what he understood to be a gesture of submission. *Come*, it would say, *come here, to me.*

But stay away from the water—it's dirty.

For Peter well knew what the water could do.

The men who descended were not gentle, but they were careful not to damage him or get too close as they circled him warily before finally approaching, awkward in their yellow suits and so cautious that Peter, who had waited so long, found he could wait no longer and couldn't stop himself—he *could not*—from looking up, turning his radiant hope toward them and for all the world to see. But it was he who saw something he had not expected and had never seen before.

On the inside of their helmets, faces vexed with dread and stuffed with hair.

Hey, he cried out, for the first time afraid, I'm not going to hurt you.

But even to him his words sounded garbled and strange.

Just beyond, the river ran, clotted with algae and warmer, perhaps, than when he was a boy, but still the same forbidden riffle over rocks, still flanked on both sides by small stands of live trees, and among them, Peter saw now, a bird, poised, like himself, for flight. In that instant, just as he turned to catch it take off, wings spread to a warm draft of wind—nothing, just a sudden, inexplicable blankness—and then he was dangling in a net above the earth with his shadow leaving traces of him far below, like the bits of his replicant virus, broken off in the world as a harbinger of him.

How did they do that, he wonders now in what has turned out to be the last of a series of sterile white rooms where men with guns and women with hair spreading filth to their shoulders had prodded and probed him and pestered him with questions, all the while fussing with that hair—shaking it out of their eyes and pushing it back from their foreheads, sucking and gnawing its ends—until finally even that had ended and they had brought him here, alone again at last.

Peter looks down at his tough little feet, which have hardly seemed to age at all, and for the first time considers the possibility of failure. When he was very young and there were others on the compound, it had never been like this. On the compound, people had been so distinct. Their hair grew back, sure, but it grew back clean. They had their separate minds and bodies and filled them, entirely, up—husbands and wives, parents and children, the two dads and the librarian. No two among them were interchangeable. They possessed things—pictographs and combs and baby teeth and prayer shawls—their own private thoughts and memories, their desires. And when they were gone, Peter had burned them, body and things, leaving gaping holes where they'd been that sometimes took years to close up. Peter had lived among these holes for years, avoiding entire areas of the compound, sometimes so loaded and acute not even the drugs could assuage him. And yet in all that time, he had never assumed another person's space or used another person's thing. In this, he had been as his father had taught him, discrete.

Now, in the white room, Peter considers the bed in which he has just been lying—his bare skin pinned to sheets that have known other people's skins. He breathes air that, despite advanced filtrations systems, cannot filter out the molecules shed by other men and women in rooms and floors contiguous to his. Peter considers all this, but does not know quite what or how he is supposed to feel. When he'd thought about it in his loft, settled in his little nest of pillows all his own and exploring the world through the safety of his portal, it had always seemed so right and so simple. By now, the state of things out here was in such demise that demands for moon colonization had grown and it should be easy to lure the others back to his little spinning plot of spaceship planet earth. And really, he only needed to convince the three he had selected, who had shown so much promise for natural adaptation, who might work.

But now, Peter didn't know. Peter could offer them—what, trees? A few old growth pines had survived, and there were those he had found as a child, which, solicitously tended, had acclimatized and flourished. He could offer them fresh fruit from the orchard, the creek, which still ran over rocks with fish, his own loft, so distant and cosy, and the portal it housed. He could offer them hope.

In the white room, Peter tries speaking out loud. Help, he says, working hard at the difficult blended end consonant sound that makes his tongue feel furry and fat.

And again: I'm not going to hurt you.

And then his head explodes with something not pain, and he's stumbling back to the whiteness of the bed where he curls up into a knot again in an attempt to regulate his own inner mechanisms. But it's hard to breathe, and beneath the pungent mix of ammonia-based disinfectant and artificial scent—lavender? plum?—another, more terrifying odor lingers, ancient and decaying, centuries of bodies, layers of unabsolved bones at the end of time. Peter sucks hard at the bad air and holds it in his chest before slowly letting it out as if this might purge him of its toxins, but nothing can rid him of the feeling of exhaustion and wasted inertia that this old, used-up world has brought upon him.

Forced now to lie in someone else's bed and brush his teeth at someone else's sink and walk the steps of someone else's feet, Peter suffers from a terrible impatience and another kind of urgency, for he knows that where the present moment of the world meets history, all remains open-ended and could change. Peter knows this, just as he knows—acknowledges and accepts—that his project could fail, for certainly his father's most egregious error had been to think he could control things. The dome itself, supposed to be impregnable, had revealed its one weakness to a boy; the boy, supposed to stay put and live out his natural life free from harm in dead woods and sustained by computers, now a man released in the world.

So far Peter's own computer virus had gone off without a hitch, but it could be unpredictable in its final stages, prone to splitting or breaking off in partial vestiges, a shifting of particles each one over from the next, in a vague distortion, not entirely unpleasant but nonetheless persistent, that he'd never been able to account for. If that happened now, the entire cyber-structure of the outer world might overload somehow and implode, going out, or—this was possible—*ignite*. And yet, like his father before him, he'd gone ahead and acted. What else was he meant to do?

Lying on the white cot, Peter calculates the days of his life spent in a waiting room of his own making. The high white squares of artificial light in the four walls of the room pulse, but there's no sound, not even a hum. One must have a mind of my father, he tells himself again, but again—as ever—he does not know what to think next, any more than he can imagine, exactly, what his father did, and when he did it, or why.

If you take the idea of a human body, Peter thinks now as a kind of somnolence comes over him and he finds himself stumbling back to the bed through a thickening scent of acorns.

Peter knows to be a sieve. He knows that desire is dangerous and can crush him. But like his father, too, in the long days he had coded his complex computer virus, Peter had begun to understand that taking information in could hardly be distinguished from the corollary function of creating it.

Still, he cannot say—for no one can do that—what is going to happen next, and in the weariness of bones and unrelenting whiteness of the room it occurs to him at last that his father's loop might in fact have been intended as a kindness—one small measure of safety for him, then only a boy. Homesick already, Peter longs for the recursive code that, like an endless bedtime story had, indeed, taken care of him and served as his mindful and constant companion throughout the long years of his childhood and adolescence. Both mother and father to him, it had kept him safe and entertained and warded off his loneliness and deepest moments of despair, consisting finally, for Peter, of nothing less than everything, the only solace of a boy who, alone in the world, had watched it end and be reborn again, cleansed of human consciousness and suffering.

Bliss.

Even if that never really happened.

THE POET

When Peter was a boy, his father gave him lessons in the loft, stringing large-font algorithms across the skin of screens, codes for almost everything, remaining water tables, moral principles and ethics, their own corporeal selves.

Here is the code for *you*, his father would say, uploading a small file, when you are here with me; here is the code for you when you're playing outside. See, his father said, how close it is, how very nearly identical—but also how different! And then here, his father would say, is the code for your BCI.

Even then, when he was very young, Peter's primed mind would take it in, the similarity and difference, and the commingling, how year by year, the BCI code would weave itself ever deeper into the code of him, until Peter would find it in concept—in its *idea*—so seductive as to render the other material world, the world of people and things—the actual world, before and maternal—somehow pale and vapid.

Good, his father had said, his hand like a paw on Peter's head, that's right, he'd said. Rational habits of thought, he had said, a rational mind. Then he'd squeezed the back of Peter's neck, only in part affectionately.

The first one Peter found in his portal was a poet, although not a poet yet, just another restless adolescent rebelliously trolling the NETZ. She wasn't supposed to be there, of course, any more than Peter was, but there they were together in the small room he had made full things he could imagine—sofas, pillows, sources of light—whatever he could extrapolate from the outer world that might still resemble the private nest of pillows where he worked and, familiar, anchor him. She was small, freshly budded, but adventurous, trying out the nuances of her new body the way his mother might have tried out a new string or bow. This appealed to Peter, who felt her urgent thrumming before he ever came close to her actual coordinates, the moment so charged and illicit as to feel as though she were there with him.

For there was nothing rational or orderly about the poet's mind.

I'm not going to hurt you, she called after him. Hey you, it's me.

Me? Peter thought, intrigued—his first other.

Wow, she had said, your room rocks, so much cooler than my box. Where did you get it?

If my mom finds out, she'd said. Then, faltering a bit, or my dad.

But god, she'd said, you're just so dark. So what are you, anyway—some other race?

And then she was gone, leaving only the trace of what seemed like her scent and a pink glow, and Peter himself breathing so hard, the code of his own body radiant and pulsing, and maybe a little panicky. She was so terribly young.

I'm not going to hurt you, the girl's words floated in and over him, again and again, setting off a kind of thrumming at his inner core that was not entirely unfamiliar.

And, from almost nowhere, disembodied, she called to him again, I'm at the window now, standing in the light. It's the time of falling—wow, you should see me now.

Peter got up to pace the length of the loft, thinking it over, before going back to the portal where she had returned and was waiting for him.

Hey, what's your name? Who are you?

I know you're there, why don't you answer me?

Answer, she said, and I'll take off my clothes.

Sometimes the obligations of Peter's body seemed so bothersome, so unnecessary, but with this girl everything was different.

I'm fifteen. They're already off.

He's not going to remember any of this, he told himself that first night, a warm night, warm enough to take off his own clothes and imagine himself falling outside her window, to imagine the body of another human being beside him in his pillows and what he was going to do now, to his own body, thinking of hers, which was not so unlike, after all, the body of the other small girl with the straw-colored hair who had liked to lick him clean. It's a small, shared memory of basic human need, and as easily as he could delete it, he never will: her hands, his body; his mouth, her.

But the poet was so erratic, pulsing on, then off, and off with such static that her words, in his ears, seemed strangely unintelligible. Yet still she insisted on words, refusing to appear to him—to let him look—until she had told him her story.

First, she said, listen.

No one listens to me—will you?

Peter was listening, but she didn't make sense.

Then she laughed. Who is there to listen anyway?

Do you remember, she said, the time of quarantine?

And now Peter was listening and now she made sense, for what else in the world was there to remember?

Well, she said, me neither. I'm only fifteen, but that's how old my mother was when the IC mandate came. What kind of sense did that make, to shut yourself off?

I'm just trying to make you understand.

My mom was just a girl, but you know, without her parents—they went fast, in the first wave—what could she do anyway? Even if she had the money, she was too old for an adaptation, and for the IC's you needed a family. Did they put you in an IC? Well, it wasn't like an IC for my mother, where she ended up, just apartments somewhere on an inner courtyard, just people taking refuge together. But at least she had the others—females like her, some children, and the noise of their being together.

I'm not going to hurt you, Peter said.

Who said anything about getting hurt? I'm just telling you what happened—first me, then you. That's what you should want.

Then she detached, leaving Peter alone with his longing. He knew where to find her, the fixed coordinates of her box, but she wouldn't always respond. Peter hated that, finding the box dark and inert. Worse, sometimes she did show herself, pressed up against the window where she lived in the sky but refusing to speak or to listen, just standing there watching. And *that* Peter did understand.

Because, you know, it was safe for her there, or it felt safe. If anything happened to one of them, it happened to them all.

But then, it never did. They just went on and on together, until the end.

The poet (who was not yet a poet) talked and talked. She wanted, she said, to make it real for Peter—the candles her mom used to light, even during the day, to ward off the people who lived in the walls, the endless cans of soup they ate with the shining silver that must, her mom said, once have been part of someone's trousseau. She said the word *trousseau* the same way she said *hope chest*. Her mom, the poet said, loved the wall more than she loved her. Her mom said it would be their savior and their warning.

But nothing ever warned her when her dad came. Not even her mom.

You can't remember that, Peter managed not to say.

I wasn't even born yet, just going to be born, but you know, between going to be born and being born, how much difference is there anyway? What do you think: if your mom had to choose between you and her, which would be better, which worse?

The poet talked and talked. It was what she did, what she was—all words, words.

But really, that was not what Peter wanted.

You should want this, the poet said. You should maybe even try it.

Then, for no reason—do you remember this?—things quieted down. Everyone who was crossing had already crossed, and those who were left—my mother—had anything they wanted—food from cans and clothes from the empty apartments and, you know, each other. They slept together in their beds, three or four at once, and told each other stories. They combed each other's hair. When they cooked, it all smelled like garlic. And there was always someone looking out.

I'm looking out now, but it's not the same. Who would come for me here?

And this is how the world doesn't end.

Maybe you remember this.

How when they promulgated amnesty and shut the IC's down, all over the world, people danced and sang in the streets. They did this until dawn. Later, when all the women were pregnant, they touched each others' bellies, smiling to think of the future now. But even though nine months is long, the future is longer, and most of those people couldn't go through with it.

But my mom—my mom, what was my mom like before? Why did she miss all the clues?

Stop talking, Peter thought, and touch me. I can change things back. If you want to live among others, four to a bed, I can do that. Tell me what you want to be happy. I'm not going to hurt you.

There was so much accumulated desire in him—for the smell of a woman's neck, the color turquoise, someone else's breath. Anything could set him off, and although the poet's crude device was so primitive that she often appeared only half articulated, rattling around in her box without defined form, he still wanted her.

But as soon as she sensed this, she was already gone.

And my dad, she would say the next time, my dad. My dad, had work to do—census reports, climate variations, rates of Uprisings and Area Closures. That's what my dad did—he kept the facts. And tried to keep us safe.

The poet said this, then for a long time she said nothing, her breathing ragged and sentient, until finally she made another sound, with a catch in her throat like glass. Oh fuck, she said—is that how you say it? It wasn't his fault they had to move into the highrise, it was mine. Even before I was born, I made them vulnerable all over again.

Much later she said, we were safe all right—that was one thing we were. Then her voice went all the way low and distant, stretched to the point of disappearance. But isn't that the strangest thing? They weren't like that at all, before I was born.

After that, she didn't say anything for so long Peter was afraid she was going to disappear on him again. But then her next words knocked him for a loop.

Here, she said, *touch me, right here.*

MATH

The mathematician, by comparison, calmed Peter down.

A scientist by temperament and training, his was a perfectly rational mind, with its tendency to gather information and work hypotheses and testing so consistent, so coherent—so *familiar*—that from the very first encounter, Peter already depended on him. Sometimes he used this male bond to cool off from the poet, going straight into the think tank to debate the latest recursivity theories, or new water table technologies, or the pros and cons of adaptations and Remaindering.

But sometimes he would go in for a fierce game of chess, or to wrestle around in the pillows, testing arm strength and other forms of bravado that included shared fantasy sexual conquests and hopes for saving the planet.

Even their bodies still somehow matched, part for part, except the hair, such that in time Peter grew to love the mathematician the way he would have loved a brother or best friend when he was ten.

He loved him as though they were ten.

NOT TEN

Peter could never really say how long he trolled the portal, looking for others like them. He did it for a long time. He would have kept on doing it. Maybe, trolling would have been enough.

But then one day his BCI encountered something strange, a kind of swirling vortex, that knocked him for a different kind of loop and undid all his cool detachment, his calm and rational mind, with both a rising and a falling, an ascent and a descent paradoxically one and the same movement, like breath, and held together by the force of the desire that they should.

And that was the court reporter.

From that day on, Peter would begin to develop his separate sense of purpose that would evolve over time into his plan and this white room. But at the start all he wanted, like anyone else, was more. And it wasn't so much the story she told Peter wanted as it was the telling itself, the multivalent act of transcription like an echo of his own synth-ethic mind. Oh, Peter still wanted the others—the small electric thrills the poet still sent through his physical body and the complex knots of the mathematician's problems, but nothing was as mesmerizing as the reporter's strange transcriptions which wrote over Peter like a fist and rendered him inchoate, a palimpsest that was no longer—and yet wholly—him.

Peter did not yet suspect that whatever it was in this that triggered whatever it was in him that might count as desire would forever mark the moment that he turned away from his father in his heart. But having once entered, like this, the consciousness of another human being, Peter could not now un-know it.

And yet, for the longest time, the only way to her was through trial itself, his first complete connection not even a real juror, but just a second alternate, a frail aging man in a shiny green suit whose wife was preparing to leave him for a woman she had met in another transcript. Neither woman was especially attractive, both overweight and with affectless voices, but the man had loved his wife for many years and grown accustomed to her oily salads and tough roasts of canned meat, and as the world rallied around the contours of his sadness, Peter, maybe for the first time, did too.

It could have been anyone, really—the black market entrepreneur on trial for hoarding solar battery packs, or the blousy back-row spectator whose children, one by one, had gone defective, or the slack-jawed judge herself. For it was the idea of order, the world itself made choate in the construct of a single human consciousness, that Peter craved.

What did it matter whose?

Peter had no interest in the crimes, which he found to be both tedious and banal, but only in the transcripts, which made the world readable, knowable—as though *present*—in a way it never was before, suggesting a kind of substitution and replacement so exact and nuanced as to collapse, in a single line of code, every permutation of a shared lived moment—a *human* moment—and then another, and another, more real than reality itself.

And so it could be said that Peter had finally met someone like him.

But unlike the poet, there was nothing sensory about the court reporter, who did not appear in her own transcripts and existed only as an absent origin, opaque and seductive. Sometimes, Peter tried to imagine her—the *idea* of her, body, the shape of her head and elegant fingers, the sinuous curve of her back—but there at the center where the writing came from, only the blank space of her.

But in the curious paradox of his desire, Peter restrained himself here and held off from looking. It would have been easy enough. He could have followed her home to watch, to listen—with her—to the dying over again—the perpetually dying—world. He could even have stayed through the night, lain beside her, stripped of gray, in her small gray bed. But he didn't. He didn't because the humming inside her so perfectly matched his own that although he could not yet let himself imagine physical love—with her—already he longed for something else, a kind of kinship, maybe, or affection, or just her capacity to know him—and him her—all the layers of body and self, concept and code they might uncover in each other.

And as nothing else in the outer world had begun to approach so powerful a suggestion of a possible mate, Peter almost welcomed her disembodiment, as though it were enough for her to hold not his head, but his mind in her lap. Peter did imagine her fingers—if she had fingers—there, just there on his overheated temples. Peter imagined them stroking him gently—*you poor thing, you poor thing*—as if by her touch she might somehow soothe the endless agitation of his BCI, and as if he already knew she alone in the world was going to be capable of doing this for him.

THIS STUBBORN ALCHEMY

THE RUMORS ARE ACCURATE—the defendant is bald.

Recuse yourself, Helen tells herself.

But as Peter enters the courtroom for his trial and pins his gaze on her—fixed, penetrating, ancient—something shifts inside her and she knows it is too late.

Already, she's been brought from where she's sequestered above. She's been seated at her chair. But the light in the courtroom is not the right light, but strangely opaque, the opposite of light, and priming has never been like this, and as she moves to depress the pedal in the floor, which meets the ball of her left foot with a satisfying click, she knows she won't recuse herself because she wants as much as anyone to understand this monstrous by-product of history gone wrong.

Just like now in the courtroom and the thing inside Helen that has shifted, before it shifts back.

But when Helen thinks about this later or reviews the records, that part, the glitch is not there. He had paused in front of her, shackled in his loose gray prison sack and so close she could smell him, or smell something, something metallic. And then he'd looked at her—that potent gaze—as though he had *recognized* her. Helen is as sure of this as she has ever been of anything.

But it was more than recognition—it was personal. And that, too, was not in the record.

Do you swear, the clerk had said.

Peter swore, his hand on a book.

All this happened, exactly as it happened in countless other courtrooms. But different.

And this, too, Helen wants to understand, to know how he has done it—how *he* has done it. For the first time in her life as a reporter, she is curious, but already so disregulated that she can't quite dissolve, as is her habit and her talent, into the moment, her apparatus opening out on its pneumatic tubing and her trying—trying hard—not to think, to wipe her mind clear for these most important proceedings.

Helen straightens, reaching out for her machine. This should steady her, but when her fingers meet the silky surface of the pad, she startles almost visibly, finding it hot where it is supposed to be cool, cool where it should be hot, and setting off, by her touch, what appears to be a subtle shimmering. Or perhaps the disruption comes from her, who alone seems to have retained some vestigial trace of the computer virus he released. At least she thinks that could be it—bits of his unruly code that manifest themselves in her as tingling, and now heat.

Then Peter winks. Helen is sure of it. But it is not a normal wink—it's a link. And she can't stop the flush that rises in her with a kind of subtle thrumming, between molecular and electric, and with something so familiar, so intimate about it that, although Helen knows she shouldn't, she does the thing she mustn't—she lifts her eyes to look at this defendant.

And regrets it at once, for having looked, she will see him looking back, see too that he's distinguished not so much by what he is—the last Remainder and sole survivor of what had once been the most remote and ambitious of all the ic's—as by what he lacks, some internal coherence that leaves him paradoxically both diffuse and intense, and neither boy nor fully formed man. Seeing that, words will come to Helen—*you poor thing*—that have nothing to do with the proceedings, but she can't stop them either. For despite the smallness of his stature and utter hairlessness, his body is so muscular, so defined, that it seems completely out of context and him—*you poor thing*—misplaced inside it. For Helen also knows that only the body remembers and sees at once how, unlike ordinary Remainders who can't accommodate the spaces they have chosen, this defendant, by comparison, is huge.

Inside her mouth, Helen's teeth bite her tongue, for Helen, who has long since emptied herself of human desire, wants something now.

But what space could contain him, if not this?

In other respects, Helen notes a smallish male of indeterminate age, with a glistening bald head and large steady eyes. She notes this and accepts it, for in those respects, she is only, as ever, a conduit through which everything—everything—that happens in this courtroom is going to pass.

And then it does, her fingers flying over the membrane of her apparatus, still almost imperceptibly the wrong temperature, not the temperature of Helen's skin, but someone else's. And again, the strange, disregulated flutter at the tips of her fingers.

His gaze, she thinks, her hands, a dizzying feeling.

Later, she's returned to her sequestered room.

It's not a very big room, and it's not a small room, but a medium-sized to largish room which seems to float many stories in the air, and in it, four small windows with four sofas facing each direction of the compass. But because this is not possible, the hovering, Helen registers it as the idea of the hovering.

Still, unconvinced, she finds that if she stands on the back of one sofa near the room's northwest corner, she can peer out a window to what might be sky, or water, or trees. Either way, it's not the right color, the surface a dull steel gray or desiccated blood rust, and beneath that, here and there, a bit of ocher. At certain times of day, this scrap of element that can be glimpsed from the back of the sofa remains glassy and smooth, but at others—especially the cusps of the day—night sliding into dawn, dawn into day, day into dusk—it's violent and choppy, with little peaks of puce-colored foam like pockmarks.

Helen will note all this as the trial progresses. But the strongest sensation will remain one of hovering—detachment.

Each of the windows is high and round, like an eye. Or a portal.

But strangely flat.

Otherwise, it's a bland-looking room, mostly beige, a bit worn-looking—institutional.

In addition to the sofas, there's a smallish metal table with an old desk chair, but no lamp and no clock either. No electronics at all, Helen notes, nor even any wires—another dizzying moment—and the feeling that runs through her as she understands that the room is fully sealed is a kind of shock—or zinging—then nothing at all, a cool numbness and, incredibly, silence.

Helen has been sequestered before, but never like this. Usually, there's a bit of luxury—a downy bed, wood furniture, an artificial view of seaside or mountain, with, often, special features to the bed. This room, by comparison, is stripped and rudimentary, and without apparent function. A kind of waiting room, she thinks, but waiting for what?

The sofas are old—very old—and worn to the nub in places, and they smell of something pungent that reminds her of her rabbit, the living thing she once had tended to.

Helen goes from one to the other, running the tips of her fingers over the coarse upholstery, then, uncertain where to sleep, begins to undress in the middle of the room, peeling off the gray skin of stockings, unzipping and then stepping out of the out of the modest gray skirt, removing the jacket, the shimmery blouse, until finally just her underwear remains—the stiff bra, the practical panties, the slim elastic bands at the knobs of her wrists. When they are off too, she stands there naked and alone, but strangely self-conscious—as though someone were watching—and then raises her arms to the nape of her neck to untie the gray knot of scarf and reveal her baldness.

At once, a stinging blast hits from behind, and the light goes milky, as if to lull her.

But Helen doesn't feel lulled, she feels stimulated, unable even to choose a sofa to sit on, never mind sleep. Back and forth, she paces through the light, thick here too, as in the courtroom that morning—as it seems to part around her with another kind of sound, fused to odd fragments of memory that break over her in waves—the sleek green seats of the bus that took her to camp the summer she came back altered, the last meager remnants of hair she had shaved off clumped in lonely patches at her feet, the sound of moths going out on the far other side of the world, the vast pull-down menu in her boarding room that had defeated her by its very excess.

Soon, Helen's wrists are the brightest things in the room, and as the warmth of the light of their glowing eases through her, a stupefying drowsiness takes hold. In her room things are the same as she left them in the morning, but somehow also different, the sofas shifted slightly from where their feet left indentations in the bleak, gray carpet, their pillows turned, the windows murkier. And the scent is muskier, with a heaviness to it, and she knows she should sleep, but she can't. There is almost a noise, a humming, as if— almost—it comes from somewhere outside, beyond the walls, or from inside the walls themselves.

Helen is very sleepy now, so maybe she'll just choose one of the sofas—this one, with floral brocade that faces what must be east. Maybe she'll just lie down and sleep.

There's going to be more but it's not clear yet what more there is going to be.

When sleep comes at last, it comes with a voice: Do not ask me who I am, or how I came to be here.

Then the voice sighs, like a man translating himself from a portal.

By the time my father died, we were the only ones. I was twelve. When you're twelve what do you do—brush your teeth, tend the garden, change your socks?

I'm just trying to make you understand—isn't that how these things happen?

Then I did what anyone would do: I burned him.

You would have too—he stank.

All this happened. It was real.

But of course you already know that.

By the time I was fifteen, I'd seen it all.

In the not-dream, Peter chews on the inside of his cheek until it is bloody, listening to the saddest music he has ever heard. Helen listens too, her own cheeks wet with tears, and wakes to the taste of his blood.

Do you want to know what happened to your rabbit? Your mom?

The headaches came on without warning, blind punitive pain that forced me to my knees, and sweat pouring out all over.

On the couch, Helen sweats, face buried in her hands with something like a current running through her.

You see what I mean? Peter says.

And Helen does. She sees and shares—his pain, and memory, and stubborn alchemy of love and labor that has wrought—and then, because she does not know what else to think, she thinks—all this.

Helen can't tell from the light in the windows if the night is ending or just beginning, but it feels old—ancient—to her. And it's not so much that her head hurts as it is that it *has* hurt, leaving her dry-mouthed and disconsolate. In a few hours she'll be back in the courtroom. The defendant will be seated inside his plexi chamber, and she will be seated in hers. She will be telling and not being told.

But when Helen awakens, she is filled with the strangest feeling and does something she hasn't done in years—she thinks about her rabbit, and then, like that, she thinks about the defendant—about, Peter.

It is very early now, neither night nor morning, though she doesn't really trust the light in the windows, which might be a lie. But she's up anyway, up and thinking—*shh*, Helen, *no*, but she can't—she *cannot*—stop thinking about how one day Peter must have been, like other boys, a boy. He must have had a mother and, probably, a father. Helen's own father had grown lettuce, what would Peter's father have grown?

Helen does not like to think like this. She knows it cannot lead to any good. Her uncanny empathy—her capacity to transport herself through code—has always been just that, a linguistic phenomenon, as neutral as it is arbitrary. But this is not neutral at all.

This is her imagination taking root.

And so already Helen also knows a time is coming when she will smile shyly and take off her gray scarf to show him how closely they match. She will transfix him with the large irregular patch of roots spread out like a map or a bruise, tracing a sinuous arc up the contours of her skull—her delicate skull— and curling finally into itself just behind the spot where her left temple throbs.

You can touch it, she will say.

But what she won't know in the courtroom—for how can Helen know this?—is how difficult the defendant will find it to endure the noise of others, their crush and stink, nor how he will regulate himself by honing himself to her stillness into which, despite the rapid fluttering of her fingers and steady beat of blood beneath her skin, she almost seems to disappear. Peter will fight it, but he can't help himself, and there will be moments, plenty of moments, when he almost stumbles free of his restraints and ruins everything, for nothing in his life has prepared him for the curve of Helen's thigh, beneath her gray skirt, beneath the gray stockings that sheathe it.

For surely his strongest memories of people have always been of their shrouding— the coarse gray muslin, the crude stitching, the thick needle itself—in and out, in and out. Peter, alone among the living, had stitched the countless shrouds. And then he had torched them, one after the other, until his alone remained. Of course he had fitted that one too, and he'd cut the small hole he'd crawl into, he had laid out the various relics of his own life beside it, and he had waited.

He's still waiting.

Everyone thinned at the end, and it shocks him now to note how sheer Helen really is beneath her layers of gray, her skin on the verge, like theirs, of dispersing. Hold on, Peter thinks, amazed by the reality of this present moment—his trial, the reporter, their breathing, her blood. And as he again imagines the idea of that blood coursing through her veins, the gauzy filigree of her capillary system, the throb of the stem at the base of her wrists, he can't help but imagine an invisible network pulsing and throbbing around them, the blood of all the others in the room pulsing as a single organism, the human race itself to which he still belongs.

Peter will look at the reporter, who sits small and unobtrusive at her stenograph machine. He will watch her breathe. Beneath the taut fabric of her stockings, there is more—*much more*—that he wants to see.

Your body, he will think, as they rise for the judge, his own body stirring—*my body*.

Then he will think, *your machine—mine*.

But as Helen can't know any of this yet, her other feeling remains one of anticipation and—what, curiosity or hope? For night after night, he visits her room, or the idea of him does.

One day, Peter, like any other boy, had a father.

Oh, Helen thinks, *oh. Oh*.

One day, he made promises—to rescue the fish and swallow the lies.

No, Helen thinks, that's not right.

In her own world, when the dying had come, it had been managed so discreetly that, walking down the road, no one would have noticed. The people were simply gone, efficiently removed from public view in an orderly subtraction that simply reduced things—people, neighborhoods, schools, places of commerce and work and play—as life all over the planet contracted. How different it must have been inside the compound, Helen thinks now, where each going out—each subtraction—had been so personal.

Immediate, she thinks, and visceral.

And then she weeps. She weeps and weeps, unable to stop. How long has it been since she wept?

Nightly, Peter visits, moving from sofa to sofa, perfectly at home but yet with a certain urgency that spills out in his words, spilling into Helen, all his memories of the straw-haired girl, the teacher, the herder of goats and boy with toy truck, the absent mothers, his father. Sometimes, Helen takes them in so fully formed it is as if they have been part of her forever, but sometimes they startle her awake, contracting on the sofa, for sometimes it begins to seem that the sound of someone going out in the not-dream is the exact same pitch as the ringing that had started in her inner ear when her rabbit disappeared.

Then, in the murky light of the room that is unlike any light she has ever seen, Helen thinks of the defendant as individual and human, and this will make her vulnerable to him.

Returned each day to the courtroom, Helen will be learning more of the history of the world than she has ever wanted, but already she has learned it will never be enough. Meantime, the other story, intact and immutable, of the boy raised alone in the woods by computers and what he wants now, remains a small, shared narrative of need and desire, and as it accumulates night after night, the trial progresses by day through its long tedious jury selection and various rulings. Monstrously thirsty, Helen suffers an increasing alienation from her apparatus, which looks so odd to her, even alien, on its slender pedestal, the minimal scoring she wrote herself—white lines on a thin gray membrane—as archaic and arbitrary as—but she doesn't want to think this either—any dead language. Although her fingers continue to record, she feels herself reduced, over time, to a dream—or idea—of herself—of her in the courtroom honed to the man who transmitted the replicant virus and walked out of the woods in its wake.

Why are you doing this to me? Helen thinks, a tic at her wrist where the pulse has been thrown out of sync with her very own pulse, as though pumped by a separate heart.

What would happen, she wonders, if she just refused—put her hands in her lap and stopped?

But she can't stop, and neither, she knows, can he.

Some nights she finds her room strangely altered. One of the sofas—a bland, beige, late twentieth century design—looks crumpled and is turning pungent with a new smell, not a bad smell, but something rich and earthy, and with one end freshly soiled, as if someone's head—someone's bald head—has lain there. Often, she doesn't really want to, but she gets up and crosses over to this other sofa and carefully lays herself on it, placing her head, uncovered for the night, just there where the soiled place is, where the smell of the earth is strongest and the chenille flattened.

Like earth, Helen thinks, and sweat.

But it's so quiet here, just here. Almost no noise at all.

And then Helen thinks, *don't sleep.*

When sleep comes at last, it comes with a story:

Which begins when you are a child and your mother—you still have a mother—is prepping your father for work. She does this every day, and mostly—you're young yet—you don't pay much attention. She hums; he grouses. It's a complicated business, this fueling of the body with morning nourishments, this donning of protective gear—the yellow suit, the bubble hood. But because you are so young, you go on playing with your blocks, you sneak some glistening cubes of sugar from his coffee service.

But it's not the same today, and sucking on the sugar, you crouch behind the couch to watch. Already you are good at this, watching. Your mother is just being so solicitous and kind, strapping your father's gear on, sealing the seams and taping them off, attaching the hems at the boots. Now she kneels—*kneels*—before him, kneels and smiles and hums in her special, soothing way.

Shh, your father snaps. Stop that. I'm trying to think.

There now, your mother says, you're all set, latching the visor and patting it gently. Go save the world. It needs you.

I'm just trying, Peter says, to make you understand.

But now you see—you can't not—that there is something wrong with this, her cheeriness, because it isn't for your father, it's for *you*, so you are not really surprised when she spins around to you the very moment your father leaves. She spins as if there's a secret, which maybe there is because the first thing she says, and she says it in a whisper, is: *don't ever tell, don't say a word.*

And you don't. You never do. Not until now.

As it happens, your mom—you see this, too—is happy, and now that your father is gone, she's humming again but not the low, soothing—the placating—hum she used for him, but something quicker and lighter, something excited. If there were words, you would call it singing. But there aren't words, just a kind of high-fluted trilling.

How radiant she is, almost luminous, as she gets out your own protective gear, just like your father's only smaller. Suddenly she's on her knees before you, doing *for you* what she just did for him—polishing your visor, latching your latches, sealing your seams.

All this is happening fast.

What I mean is, Peter says, this was not a drill.

You are going *out*, your mom and you. You really are.

By the time you're in the elevator, you're hopping up and down because nothing—*nothing*—like this has ever happened before. You're so excited. Until finally you look down and notice her feet.

What about you? you wheeze through your tubing, suddenly a little bit afraid. Don't you have to suit up?

Oh me, and you know, she just sounds so happy. You should have known then, but even though she's completely bareheaded and practically barefoot, you don't. Even then, you don't know what is happening.

Never mind about that, she says.

And she's laughing, you know—*ha ha ha, ha ha ha*. So you do too. You laugh and laugh, like her, but it's hot inside the bubble and you can't help yourself. You whine to take it off. And you stare down at her beautiful red-painted toes in her little silver sandals and you whine to go barefooted too.

But this isn't going to happen because already you are outside, underneath a gray sky, and although the street is full of water, it's so long and open-ended that you try running. You know the concept, anyway, the idea of running, but in all that space it's harder than it should be, and you get winded and keep tripping and falling, but your mom catches you every time. That's what moms do—they catch you.

Then you're both splashing in dark puddles—pothole lakes, she calls them—skipping and kicking water at each other as though it were clean, which once you get the hang of it is what you do all the way down the long deserted glass and steel canyon to the statue of a man with his face half eaten by rain.

Years later (but how can Peter explain this, even in the not-dream where anything is possible? Helen, he thinks almost bitterly, should explain it to him) what he will remember of the dome of the concert hall where his mother does not take him is its gilded opulence, marbled and decaying. He'll remember the box, suspended just to the right above the stage. He'll remember the worn red brocade of the upholstery, sweetly scented of the past, and the light that floods the stage where suddenly his mother appears in a long velvet gown, still shining, before the heavy purple drapes, with two gold pillars on either side upholding the roof of the world. He'll remember the catch of recognition in his throat. He'll remember his delight at the burnished gleam of her violin. But of her playing—that miraculous concerto, the last one on earth—he'll remember nothing, for how can he remember something that could never—not in a million years—have taken place?

What Peter really remembers: because none of this could happen, it did not.

You can't expect me to understand, Mom, he'll cry out forever. It doesn't work like that. I have to lose you first. I have to grow up. It takes a long time for a boy to grow up, and in that time, anything can happen. Really, Mom, it happens all the time.

But to Helen, only this: of course you think she's taking you to the concert hall, even though it's been closed for months, because that is the one place you remember that is not the inside of your apartment. You think—you hope—she's going to play there, the fingers of her left hand flying over the neck as her right hand eases the soul from the belly of her instrument. You hope this because she is beautiful and because she plays beautifully. To you, she's the most beautiful woman in the world, the music spinning around her, the brown drape of velvet revealing her lovely body beneath, the look on her face saying no, no, there's not going to be time for any of that, this is all the time we have, I wish there were more but there's not and this will have to last you your whole life.

Also, you're hoping for others—children like you—to be listening too. You're hoping for a stage filled with musicians in black and their wondrous bassoons and basses and horns and violas and shining trumpets and thunderous drums. You're hoping for rafters filled with birds, a hall flooded with light, your mother at the very center of it all.

Who would not hope for all that?

But that's not where you're going.

Where you're going, instead, is to a door with a guard. But you don't understand that at first. At first, your mom just stays in her gray skirt and yellow sweater and little silver sandals, and although you pass right by the great marble stairs to the concert hall, you could still go back. You see the man ahead. Your mom is rushing toward him. But you could still go back, even now.

But the man has already given your mom a key that she's clutching in her bare, white hand. And that's that.

All this happened, Peter says, but of course it isn't all that happened.

Just before you go inside, she turns to you and says, *I don't expect you to understand any of this, but maybe someday you'll remember.*

Then you're in tunnels, miles of tunnels—who could ever have imagined tunnels like this, a whole world of tunnels underneath the failed city, guarded by doors and men with guns who sometimes lead you through the darkness with their flashlights and sometimes let you go on ahead alone, your mom with the key that opens every door. Where tunnels come together, sometimes there are stairs, and soon you've gone down so many you've completely lost track. It's hot on the stairs, and dim, and you're clutching your mom's hand, the same way she clutches the key, wishing you had stayed on the wet streets above or gone, as you had hoped, into the concert hall, that she had played, or even that you'd never left the apartment at all—wishing, even, for your father, who would never have allowed this.

But you don't really want that.

You don't have your bubble anymore—but where has it gone, did you leave it with the guard, did you *lose* it?—and when you try to breathe your nose fills with soot and bad smell, choking you a little. Your legs hurt, going down so much, your footsteps echoing in the stairwell and your wet hand slipping in your mother's. You're not whining anymore—you understand that would be pointless—but you do whimper a little, sniffling. And still you're going down—down, down—so long and so deep you're convinced you are headed to the center of the earth.

Then, like that, you are out. With no warning at all, your mom unlocks the last door, and then you both take one last step into a chamber—a vast, wide chamber filled with other people, like you but not like you.

I mean, Peter says, hundreds of them—thousands—thousands and thousands of underground people.

This whole enormous space is completely filled up with these people, more people than you could ever have imagined.

Around them, the oil-stained concrete floor stretches out forever.

And here and there, massive pillars hold up the roof of the earth, like the gold ones in the concert hall above. But you can feel it pressing, pressing down.

Another amazing thing—even though it's so crowded in here, it's quiet, stunningly quiet, the only sound being the sound of breath, and maybe some rustling as the people feed their children or go about the other daily acts of life—picking nits from other peoples' hair, folding up the soiled rags they sleep on, nibbling at the little cubes of compressed nutrition wafers that scatter down through the air shafts like rain, performing somber cleaning rituals, preparing for sleep. The stench of urine and hopelessness is so strong that your eyes water and you feel dizzy. Giant fans are blowing, but really, they're only blowing this terrible stench around, and you bury your face in your mom's thigh trying to breathe in her scent instead.

This isn't what you wanted. This isn't it at all.

Except for the fans and the rustling and the breathing, it's as if sound has been stripped from the world.

Suddenly, something whooshes by and you cry out and every one of all those people—all the scabbed children and mothers, the men with their faces blown off—turn to look. They are looking at you looking at the bird that's just whooshed by. And now you see that there are other birds, countless other birds, swooping high in the yawning eaves. That can't be: white birds swooping everywhere above.

You'd have thought it was a bat, if you knew, then, what a bat was.

Later, when what is going to happen happens, you recognize but don't understand it. You recognize and accept it, just as you accept the birds and the underground people and even your mother's red-painted toes, which you know are going to fall off from what she's been walking in. They're going to rot and fall off like the face of the statue in the square or the noses of these underground people.

But maybe, Peter says, not.

Because what happens next is as unexpected and wondrous and impossible as everything else in this strange day—another violin resonant in the cavernous room. And now you see that your mom has been waiting for this. You see her smile and relax, her hand going gentle on the top of your head, stroking your hair—you have hair then—and parting it with her fingers, just stroking and parting, stroking and parting, but not absently at all but with focus and intensity, as if she were the one playing.

Listen to those runs, she says, isn't it amazing! *Shh*, she says, let's just stay here and listen, right where we are.

So that's what you do. You listen and listen, and it's so beautiful it hurts.

After a while your mom tells you they were friends in the academy, before. But he won't remember, she says. All he remembers is what his hands remember, her breath going in and out like the music, like bliss. *Shh*, did you hear that— something like eighteen or nineteen notes in a single pickup? Good lord, listen.

She kneels then, your mother—for the second time that day—going down in all that filth to bring her whole self to you. She kneels and hugs you and takes one of your hands to press it against her hot face. In her face, there is something, but you can't tell yet if it's tears or, stranger yet, happiness.

Please, Peter tells Helen now, *you have got to understand.*

Then she says: please, you have got to understand. You're just a little boy and I'm sorry for that, but my god doesn't have any special name. It's here, though, all around us, in the world. It could be Beethoven or Glass, Peter, or those puddles in the street—and yes, they're toxic and we'll just throw your suit out when we get back and never say a word, ok?—but the water, Petie— the *water*—that was once *rain*. Who'd have thought of that, the rain? Do you understand what I am saying to you?

But you don't—you can't—and she already knows this, so she does what moms do all over the world. She puts her arms around you and pulls you into the warmth of her body against the softness of her breasts where you can feel her heart thump.

Oh, you are just so little, but listen—pay attention—to those runs.

Around you, the others are listening too, tuned somewhere to the single violin, their pasty faces rapt.

I would give my life for you, your mother says, but not this. She sighs. Look around you. This is where these people, frail as moths, will live out the rest of their lives. But they will listen—look at them listening. Remember that, ok? If anything, of all of it, you should remember the listening.

But really you're just a child. You wish you weren't. You wish you could listen like her—like them—but you can't do that either. And you're worn out by all the excitement and just want to go home. So you, who know nothing yet of promises, tug and whine, and you promise.

I promise, you say. *I'll remember forever.*

Ok, she says—and you can tell this is it, the last chance you're getting. You're going to get it now or not, but either way it's all there's going to be—just these words, and the underground violin, and her and you, and the listening.

What I want, your mother says, but you're too young and tired now even to wonder why, is to be with my god and not worry about the far-off stuff, just get through the day and be grateful for its common beauties. All these people, I just want for them to be ok—to sleep and to dream like human beings do—all of them—the musicians and gardeners and mathematicians and teachers and seamstresses and fishers and storytellers and pharmacists and archaeologists and librarians and rodeo riders—to sleep and then to wake, just like you and me, in the light, with the birds and the music.

Well, your father doesn't think so, but a day will come when we will have to do what they do and die. Until then, just do your best, and accept it, with affection, what comes. In the meantime, I hope they rest well.

I hope, Peter says now, *the whole world rests well.*

———

In later years, Helen will think about what begins to happen not above, in her room, but below, in the courtroom as an interruption, or a more sustained glitch. When it does, she is simultaneously aware and unaware of it, like a charge that passes through and out of her, like the virus itself, marked only by a momentary hesitation in her fingers, a subtle arrhythmia, the briefest second when—for that single instant—they somehow go blank. A careful study of the records would reveal nothing, but in the courtroom even the most casual observer might have noticed the faint sheen of sweat on Helen's forehead, her upper lip. That was it—the discreet and modest sweat of a much older woman—that was all there ever was. And yet for Helen, it would be everything.

For although again and again she will tell herself not to, she can never stop from looking up at the bald defendant, who will neither return the glance nor not return it, but just continue to look clear through her with his opaque, inscrutable gaze, his glistening animal eyes. On the inside of Helen, the feeling is oddly delicious, a milky touch, but on the outside nothing—just the slight sweat—as she struggles to maintain her decorum. But this is hugely difficult because the feeling, loose and fluid, continues to increase, growing stronger and more difficult to resist. Helen doesn't really need to listen to the proceedings to be able to transcribe them—that's not how it works—but still the interference from the bald defendant exerts such a pressure on her that finally something gives with a small electric charge that is him uploading himself to write over her.

And for the first time in her public life, Helen looks down at her own hands and lets them go with a serenity that approaches detachment because she does not yet suspect that her own susceptibility to being hacked goes all the way back to the rabbit that had not been hers, the ringing in her ears, or the look on her father's face as he waited for her to get off the summer camp bus.

Helen does not yet suspect this because Helen has discovered how much she likes the feeling, and by the time she realizes he can do it at will, replacing the record of her hands with the code of the thought of his mind, she will have passed beyond pleasure to need, already dependent on the thrill of relinquishing both body and mind to the little bald man who is still part boy and not—the sudden rush of the moment when he makes himself present in her, and of what she will do later to recover it in the room without electric current.

For of course not even Helen has any way of knowing that the time is coming when he'll look directly into her startled gaze and delete the proceedings altogether.

Now, for the first time, Helen is about to find herself delivered whole into the present moment, the future blank before her. Like the feeling of being hacked, this feeling is a bit heady, increasing her thirst, but not for water. Momentarily confused, Helen feels both cut off and entirely connected, and strangely acute. Maybe not yet, looking back at the defendant's singular gaze, but soon the moment will come when Helen won't care, when this is what she'll find herself willing to accept:

That night, Helen will awaken on one of the sofas in the unwired room that hovers high above the surface of the earth with a sensation of tingling that begins at the base of her wrists spreading now throughout her body, as if she were being touched, but from the inside. On the sofa beside her the defendant will sit, his bald head glistening. He will be smiling kindly. His body, removed from its sack, all animal sinew and muscle, is not much larger than Helen's, but it is powerful. In his hands, he will hold a white cloth, and he will be rubbing Helen with it.

You don't have to, you know, he will say.

Helen won't be able to stop herself. How do you do it? she'll say. You're not real, you're not even here.

He will smell of musk, earthy and bitter.

He will place his hand over her mouth, but she will not be afraid, not even when what is going to pass between them passes between them, something familiar and—not.

And then he takes her by the hand and opens a window and helps her climb out. It is such a long, long way down the cliff of the building, then out through the tops of trees and into the world that awaits them. There will be familiar things about it—soda pop, terror alerts, traffic. But they will move through it with impunity and grace and every bit as if they were not there.

THE FUTUROLOGISTS GATHER

ANY MINUTE NOW, the sun would be blasting over the tops of the mountains, filling the long low valley below with the scorched desert light of this first edge of day, which was going to be hot, like all the others. Will was drinking his coffee with ice—the only way he could stand it, even so early in the morning—and waiting by what should have been a pool, if there'd been time for that or any water, for that one moment that, no matter how many times he would see it, would fill him one more time with conviction. Not that you'd catch him saying so, of course—Will was a scientist, not at all religious, and light was just light, a spectrum that ranged from all color to none and had nothing to do with transcendence. But sometimes when the sun rose in the desert—even this one—it seemed to him like radiance itself.

In other respects, Will had consoled himself since boyhood with the thought—a pretty sorry thought, but a thought that yet provided some small comfort in the form of either bitter vindication or grim satisfaction—that he'd been born just in time to bear witness to the end of the world, an historical accident that turned "Fire or Ice" into his favorite boyhood poem and black into his favorite boyhood color. Still, Will rued the old days, when people like him had gathered in think tanks full of real hope, dreaming up robots and models of clean mass transportation, zoos without walls, in-home water recycling systems, solar-powered loops. Sometimes he rued the days he had spent as a boy, playing ball on green fields. But mostly he wondered if there had ever been such a time as that, and for a while it had even been exciting, with each new suitcase nuke that had gone missing, each rampant virus—human or computer—giving him a little thrill that maybe, now, things were going to get really, really bad.

In that way, his whole life had gone by, and now here he was, a hair away from middle age, drinking iced coffee beside a phantom pool and waiting for a sunrise to convince him he was wrong. Will made a vague, half-remembered gesture, and seconds later an extravagant pastry appeared before him, delivered by a small, dark girl in an abbreviated khaki dress. He could have had her too, but just then a haze blew over the tops of the mountains, dulling the sky enough for Will to consider a walk.

He had time, he thought. As much as anyone.

There were twelve of them gathered together for this Desperate Measures Seminar, not counting the bland-looking leader with his wreath of gold hair and perfect white teeth. Some of the others were women and some, men, but each had been selected through a rigorous national process, complete with intensive psychological testing and multiple-stage interviews. Will, himself, had had three face-to-face sessions, followed by a complicated sequence of physical and mental endurance tests that included three day wilderness isolation simulations in both mountain and desert terrain during which he'd sucked water from cactus and eaten bugs—things he enjoyed—but in the end, he believed he'd made the final cut the same as anyone—not for his ability to go without water for long stretches in extreme heat or to scale the sleek-skinned faces of rocks, but for his naïve belief things could still change.

And each had arrived with a sanguine disposition, an impressive curriculum vita, and an end-of-time portfolio loaded with predictions for catastrophe and last ditch proposals for salvation that ranged from new historical models, to theoretical physics, to (Will had heard this, but did not yet believe it) poetry. Will's own work was in numbers, page after page of complex algorithms by which he could predict the end of almost anything—species, fossil fuels, human days on earth. They were futurologists, after all, the last of yet another dying breed, who believed, to a one, their own genes to be part of the solution.

In the meantime, a little high-end living wouldn't hurt.

This was the lure of the Foundation DMS, which offered luxury in exchange for work and hope. But despite the promised opulence, things were stretched a little thin, and this group's last-minute change of venue had them all on edge.

Not that Will quite wanted out. Will wanted, in his own way, to prevail. It had happened before. There'd been that whole long epoch of nuclear disarmament, the Climate Change Congress, world government attempts. Before that, the Cuban Missile Crisis, peaceably resolved; Hitler, defeated; Mars, too. Most of the scourges had been wiped out—malaria, polio, Alzheimers, AIDS, the common cold, bird flu, smallpox. History was full of reversals like that and the future could be too, Will believed.

Although, lately he hadn't been so sure.

Saving the world was turning out to be a big responsibility—it was huge.

But of course, things had been bad Will's whole life, beginning in the year his parents had conceived and chosen to keep him, all the while making their private preparations for release. Will's father, a low-level politician and early architect of the Intentional Communities Movement, and his mother, an acolyte in one of the helping professions, suffered no illusions, and although his father had been instrumental in drawing up the IC provisions and incentives, he'd declined, in the end, to take advantage of them.

Whatever happens now, it happens here, he used to say.

And so, every year on the day of his birth, between the presents but before the cake, Will's mother would take him aside to instruct him on the private protocol of leaving. It was a solemn and intimate moment, and all his life he would remember with great fondness the flush of the knob at the back of her neck as she knelt to weigh him—oh, Will, how you've grown!—and recalibrate the formula. Always remember, she'd say, freedom is as close as the nearest major vein in your body.

Will, who was squeamish about blood, had grown instead relentlessly into his own life—no one could stop his growing—wiry and strong, and between his father and his mother, had learned to balance out the pros and cons of hope and hopelessness, and to make the necessary calibrations even before he had mastered his multiplication tables.

How else could a futurologist be a futurologist?

Still, Will was eating well and, for the first time in years, sleeping well, too, what with the luxury sheets and panoramic views of the broad, seared floor of the valley stretched below them like a warning, and if the others preferred the muted coolness of the compound, idling their unscheduled hours at the open bar, Will liked to explore, up through rocky washes toward the high lips of bluffs and honed, like a compass, to the single snowy mountain that rose to the south, the black cinder cone beside it. He was fit, fast, and strong, and already well adapted to the desert, but he also was a scientist and knew what happened to the human body deprived of its essential fluid.

Still, he'd heard there was an ice cave somewhere, deep inside a lava tube. It was quiet on the compound, but not quiet like that. Not the peaceful quiet Will was after.

Not, he thought, the quiet that was coming.

The table had been everybody's first big surprise, the table that was also a sculpture, the sculpture that was also a machine—a complicated piece of advanced computer hardware so sophisticated that only one among them would be unimpressed, and that was later. Him, and maybe Will, who had been vaguely puzzled by the extravagance of a gesture so purely superfluous. Will thought of the heavy oak tables from graduate school, battered reminders of a prior century, or the cheap prison-issue desks at his think tank. It was true, they'd been lured here by the promise of luxury, but decadence was something altogether different, and later, Will would come to trace his disillusionment to this exact moment, the moment when the table was revealed.

There'd been all that anxious chatter in the hallways that first morning, then the usual coffee, the pastries—delicate and buttery and sweet—and the leader presiding at the head of the table still covered with a rich, red tapestry. But Will, who was upset at the lack of windows in the conference room, hardly paid attention, no more than he had paid attention to the three women, as scantily clad as the rest of the servers, who came in to fold back the cloth and remove it. And even then, even after the women had gone away, it took a while for the buzz to die down.

After that first time, Will couldn't get it out of his mind. Not the technology of it—that was just engineering—but the half-buried contours of the back of the lying-down man, like the hills that surrounded this valley, a beauty in stone. Well, concrete, so smooth and lustrous as to invite—to compel—touch, and the man not even fully formed, all sinew and muscle and without even feet and only a part of the curve of the skull, just the shape of a part of the back of a man poured in this luminous substance, an inanimate form. But still there was something about it, the generous spread of the man's thick arms, the shoulders dense with muscles, the sinewy lines that ran down the torso so intricate and subtle as to seem to be actually moving.

Several layers of tiny inlaid tiles—glass, stone, metal, clay—that surrounded the man made a geometric border, ringed by another band of concrete, with thirteen computer monitors embedded just off center from each station at the table, thirteen ergonomic keyboards discreetly tucked beneath.

But it wasn't the extravagance of it—some of the stones were precious, the inlay, gold—that bothered Will so much. He'd expected—he'd desired—some of that. No, not that, and not the annoying ergonomics either. But like the equipment itself, the table felt somehow wrong and was connected, in Will's mind, to the wrongness of the valley, that, unlike the original valley promised in their contracts, had no meteor craters to amuse them, or stones that moved over mudflats at night, and could not technically even be said to be a real desert, but only the ruined remains of what once must have been a green-skinned agricultural bowl.

For when the drought had come, even Will remembered this, it came not as people would remember it most vividly, but as a premature and inauspicious spring, with flowers everywhere and broad shallow lakes where no lakes ever were.

Then, day after day, month after month, year after year, no rain at all.

The land split, blew away, peeled back to its rocky substrata, its essential desert. Will knew this; everybody did. But yet there was something unnatural about this one, not that he could say what. Just north of the compound, a river with salmon once flowed to the west, and to the south, the two sentinel mountains rose up, but none of that was down on any map, and Will sometimes had the feeling that if he walked far enough, he'd walk right out of this, or *through* it, but what could that possibly mean? All he knew for certain was that his GPS was scrambled and that no one had a clue where they really were, as far out of the world, it seemed, as a person could get—or, impossibly, farther—as if it might as well have been the moon.

And the table, with its elaborate hybrid of hardware and art, was equally distracting. Will was still trying to figure out how to release his keyboard that first day when a tiny 3-D figure appeared in their computer screens, a young man with delicate features and expressive hands, to talk about Art.

I make, he said, my sculptures into furniture—and here he gestured at the table itself, thirteen tiny images reflected thirteen times around the table in thirteen intimate computer screens—so it becomes the art of daily life. He spoke without irony or self-consciousness, and he was wearing a smock. I will spend, he went on, one year, or more, on a sculpture. Maybe, in my whole life, I will make twenty sculptures, or thirty.

Annoyed, Will moved to cover the image with the palm of his hand, but the Artist ducked out from under, calling Will bizarrely to attention.

Don't you like it, he said. Don't you think it's beautiful, my work. I consider them my gifts to the world—to you.

That, the leader chuckled, as if he had amused himself, was before he started getting our Foundation checks.

Will tried not to blanch—they were all receiving Foundation checks.

But already the screens had shifted to reveal an ordinary refugee camp somewhere on a flat expanse of dirt with tall grasses waving in the background, and then, in rapid succession—tracers of bombs arcing through inky night skies, drowned cities with new tides ebbing in and out of second story windows, the fiery walls of volcanoes spilling red on towns below, pest houses, dead zones, black water, Remaindered neighborhoods—like nothing so much, Will thought bitterly, as postcards from home.

In fact, Will had come to get away from that, and now the only thing he felt was bored and irritated. For the first time in his life, he was sick to death with endings, and if history was about to throw them for another loop, it seemed to him he might just as well watch from here.

Will had not always felt this way. Even now, he could almost remember the original sense of purpose the call for papers had evoked in him, the unexpected thrill that had lured him from his cinderblock think tank and recharged his waning commitment. Well, and why not? Will could almost remember this, now, the same way he could almost remember playing stopper in soccer, his childhood fiddle, or the beached baby whale he'd rescued as an adolescent, the quivering mound of sad-eyed slick-skinned lost and dying mammal that he'd rolled back into cold blue water, over and over through the hard packed sand, using only his own bony shoulder and an unsteady fulcrum jerry-rigged from driftwood, and stroking the whale's rough head, speaking softly to it as it rolled, cushioning the impact as he could, and just at the edge of the deepening water, momentarily laying his own face next to the eye of the whale, cheek to cheek, before giving it one final shove. The whale's cold skin stank of something acrid, like semen, and that night Will got drunk and made out with a girl, and in the morning the rest of the whale pod—twenty or so massive adults—had beached itself on that same strand, lying down where they were, the baby wedged securely among them.

After that, Will turned to numbers, which he thought of as particular and personal, and loved the way a poet might love words, or a musician, sound. He loved their complexities—their twinned irregularities and predictabilities. He loved the musical feel of them in his mind, like the places his fingers found on the neck of his fiddle, their points and counterpoints and elegance of pattern. Maybe it wasn't the right way to think, but Will also loved the discipline of them, the way that, first thing, every morning, over coffee, he'd review the long strings of numbers he'd gone to bed with the night before, splayed across his bedside table, on the bathroom counter, in the kitchen. Sometimes he'd dreamed them, and sometimes things broke open in the light of day, and sometimes he could tell exactly where they were headed and why, and sometimes they made no sense at all.

But like an automaton, he'd go at them and at them, between runs and classes and stints at his fiddle, working and worrying their confounding logics until he'd spread them, once again, on his bedside table and sleep.

In this way, and during those initial years, Will lived for little more than his numbers, though he soon lost track of what he hoped to find there, what he'd even started looking for in the first place, what drove him. Will lived alone, and the numbers steadied him and gave purpose to his otherwise habitual existence, working in mysterious ways to hold together what remained of his contradictory desire to patch the ozone rifts and watch things fall apart forever.

You had to do something, he thought.

And now he'd signed on to save the world in exchange for little more than three good meals a day and maybe down the road a sinecure.

Almost as soon as he'd arrived, Will had begun to hate it, the feeling it gave him of being somehow adrift in the world, or misaligned. Will was pretty sure they'd flown north instead of south, but all he really remembered was the helicopter circling for a while, its windows blacked out for "security reasons," and then flying low and for a long time until, one by one, the futurologists slept.

And when they woke up, they were here, which really was no place at all—the desert all wrong and the complex itself not even finished. Will, who had signed on for an ancient historical spa, hated the constant reminders of this—the slide-away glass walls of rooms that opened onto empty space where balconies should be, the bar that served the dirt pit of some future pool, the markings of rock and string that fixed landscaping plans. All the carpets and textiles had been installed, and the beds were as posh as promised, but here and there empty corners of hallways lacked settees and reading lights, as the lobby lacked a piano and the rooftop its garden and guardrails.

Now, after so much time, they gathered, more and more, at the bar after dinner, and sometimes in the morning as well, beginning with their breakfast Bloody Mary's and throughout the day, giving Will plenty of time to walk. Every morning and during lunch breaks that extended well beyond the double martinis, Will went out to push the limits of his pacing and endurance, farther and farther into the desert and without protective gear, driven to explore the indecipherable world which, even allowing for recent devastations, could not be made to cohere with any available topographic data or accounted for by any known science.

In his most dispassionate moments, Will liked to imagine just walking away, disappearing out beyond the limits of his human body and leaving it behind to be scoured, like the earth, to bone. He liked to imagine his deliverance not as the opening of any major vein but instead a kind of flowering as his blood inside him, deprived of its essential element, would swell and thicken into a viscous paste. And then Will imagined his mother, bent on her knees to his child self, the steady gray light of her gaze. Like her, Will thought now of these final moments before his body burst open from within as a state of grace and subtle frame of mind more like divinity than madness.

But madness, surely, it was, and even as the planet failed around them, the futurologists continued to work their inbred theories over cocktails, for if every calculation ended in heartbreak, the general feeling went, the only thing to do was just to keep on drinking, which they did with such regularity and purpose that Will at last began to join in.

Meantime, as the seminar stretched beyond the standard three-week format, no one seemed to notice they were losing all sense of time or connection to the world as if they, like the moon, were drifting away. Three weeks, months—years?—and still they soldiered on, although sometimes—when the heat was really bad—desultorily, with sessions being cancelled for no reason or seeming oddly familiar, as though they'd been recycled.

How many ideas could a futurologist have anyway?

Had Will's portfolio always been blue?

Each time he opened it, he half expected its contents to have turned into something altogether different—French, molecular physics, musical notations, stoic philosophy.

In fact Will hardly cared, and although the numbers lay there, his most precise calculations, they seemed oddly disconnected from himself and as flattened and inert as they were meaningless, for nothing, in this time, seemed to matter but his walking.

And then the storms began, rolling in without warning and turning the night sky white, the lightning so close that the thunder erupted simultaneously in deafening waves that left the air charged and electric. Sometimes, the storms continued for hours, and when they finally stopped and the velvety dark came down like a heavily ionized blanket, the stunned quiet of the night would be so acute that Will couldn't sleep. No one really slept, and in the morning, the bruised-looking haze that hung over the valley suggested nothing so much as that the world had ended without them.

At the center of the compound, a generator hummed, but it was not a pleasant or a soothing sound.

Until that, too, went out.

Will heard it fail, with a little click, as if someone had deliberately shut it off and said enough of that for you. Outside, the wail of elements howling, but inside, a quiet nothing—their last link to the world extinguished. Sleepless, Will got up to press himself against the glass wall where there should have been a balcony but where, if he stepped out, he'd step into a void instead. Maybe the lanky physicist was right. For in the violence of this most spectacular storm, it began to seem to Will as though the very molecules of matter were being rent apart, opening minute spaces between them.

Will stayed at his window watching almost until dawn, when he was overtaken by a wave of vertigo, followed by an overwhelming lethargy and sleep, and in the morning the world had been cleansed. But something inside him had been wiped clean too, for when he tried to remember the prior night—howl of storm, click of generator failing—he found himself grasping at nothing, maybe a blur of sound and light, a sensation of dizziness, but then again *nothing*. Will had slept, he was pretty sure of that, so what was he doing sitting on the floor, his wall wide open to the glistening world outside? And as he struggled to unknot himself, the pain felt strangely unrelated to the idea Will held in his mind about the mechanics of his very own body.

Will had needed a drink—he did remember that. He needed a shower, but could not remember if it was his day or not. He needed—Will could not recall what it was he needed, but the need was so urgent that he managed to sort out the problem of dressing—flip-flops, shorts, a loose stained tee—and stumble down to the patio for coffee where he now found himself taking pastry from the girl in abbreviated khakis and waiting for the sun, staring bleakly at feet that seemed not entirely his. Well, the valley was still wrong, though this was not yet a fully formed thought, any more than the bits of partial memory that plagued him—the smell of dry whale skin, the CFP, the fiddle that came from his father and from which music once slipped off the tips of his fingers just as numbers once slipped off the edge of his mind.

But here was the girl, his coffee and pastry. And here, just the suggestion of her touch on his shoulder—was there anything else?—although as soon as Will turn to say no, she was already gone. But Will could still smell her. Or he could smell something. Underneath the fried motherboard smell of the compound, a strange new smell he'd never smelled before.

Will took a bite of his pastry as if that might focus him, and then everything went low and still as he noted *something* in the dying stand of cottonwoods below. *That can't be.*

But now he was standing, peering out into a distance already wavering with heat.

And there it was again, unmistakeable—the trace of a movement.

But nothing moved here, nothing lived. In all Will's explorations, he had seen no evidence of animal life—not a turd, not a track, no husk even of insect, skin of snake. But yet, and he saw it again—something was moving below, and it appeared to be human.

Impossible.

No one else was even awake. But there, Will was quite certain now, there it was again, something—no, *someone*—what appeared to be a small man, hatless and utterly bald, walking barefoot toward the complex in the brutal morning sun. The man carried a satchel in his left hand and a parrot on his shoulder, and he might have been whistling—the last thing Will would remember before something seared his brain dull and inert as the man approached the first of the checkpoints, then the second—slipping by unnoticed, as if he were not there.

And in this splitting off of consciousness, it will seem to Will that he is other than himself, as though it were *he* walking out of the desert. Will remembers rising up from the earth to follow a striated fissure down a flank of rock, smooth as the curve of a woman's thigh to the shade of a green, green tree. There, Will kneels—has *knelt*—on the wet—*wet*—ground, and there's a sound—*water*— then the movement of some small animal, a rodent, the light above stippled by foliage—*living* foliage. Will doesn't really mean to, but the smell of this place, the black earthiness of it, is overpowering. And he's kneeling and digging his hands into what he thinks is rot but it's not—it's time.

Ok, Will tells himself: ok.

Then the feeling passes and he finds himself literally on more familiar ground, as though he were actually taking the walk he'd been thinking of taking only moments before—except that now he seems to be following the footsteps of this other, impossible man, up the dry spring bed from the stand of dead cottonwoods, across the old ranch land on what remains of an ancient road, to the stony wash, and past the first, then the second checkpoint, which he, too, slips by.

And by now, Will is late—he is really late. The session will have started without him, and there may be drink rations tonight.

But instead the leader hardly acknowledges him as he slips, flushed and winded, clumsily into his chair, knocking his portfolio to the ground. It takes that long—dropping the papers, fumbling to sort them—before he lets himself take in that the lanky physicist is gone.

I'm not saying, the leader is saying, we're completely on our own.

And in his place—in the very place where only yesterday the physicist had argued that everything from molecules and strings, to planets and tectonic plates and lovers all the world, were losing the attraction by which they once had held together—the bald man grins slyly back at Will, as if they shared the most intimate of secrets. There is something unsettling, almost hastily assembled about him, small where the physicist had always been tall, and with his bald skull rising heat-flushed above what turns out to be a mild, almost benign countenance. The room smells like the rot Will was just digging in, but also somehow burnt from last night's storm, and more than usually stale, with all the expectation drained out of it.

Will glances around at the others, who seem listless, almost petulant. At the head of the table, the leader is droning on with his usual storm damage reports—the last of the land lines down, another disabled transmitter.

Look at the bright side, the leader concludes, at least the table still works.

Across from Will, a woman in white puts her head in her arms and weeps, and the bald man winks. And that is the moment, the exact moment, that Will looks down to find someone else's research displayed on his own monitor in a shocking security breach. Immensely curious, Will can't stop himself. One of the others, he knows, dreams in algorithms, another can visualize seventeen dimensions. And as he begins to devour this one illicit paper, he finds it, this reading, to be the most exciting experience he's had since the seminar began, and the most disturbing—the moon, he reads, the moon is almost gone.

Will looks up to see the bald man press his hands—his small, graceful, and thoroughly calloused hands—on what Will knows to be the physicist's portfolio as something like a charge again passes between them.

Get out, Will thinks. *Get out now.*

But go where?

The bald man is barefoot but no one seems to notice, and his shirt is so thin Will can see the skeletal lines of his chest. Still red, his almost translucent scalp stretches taut over the bony plates of an unusual skull, a little light leaking from its sutures. Despite its large, disproportionate size, the rest of the man seems smaller close up.

Who's the new guy? Will whispers to the botanist beside him.

What new guy? the botanist whispers back.

THINGS THAT FALL

AN OLD CALIFORNIA GRAY pine stood like an ʟ by the side of the road, and around it, tumbling sagebrush and mounds of ashy dunes. In the belly of the valley where Lyda was headed, low land spread for miles along ruptured faultlines that split the surface of the earth. And wasn't this what she had wanted? Wasn't this what she had always wanted?

Lyda had been waiting so long—her whole life, really—to descend onto a horizontal world across which she could walk—forever, if it came to that—one with a horizon and perspective and space, but now a hot wind blew grit at her ankles and the light was growing murky, and even though it wasn't that late, it was plenty late enough to be nursing a slew of second thoughts.

What good was a horizon if you couldn't see five feet ahead of you? Who'd want to walk into this?

Lyda wasn't really a poet. She'd lied about that, just as she'd lied about everything, to get in to the DMS, and now, at last, she was on her way, plucked off the waitlist for—this? Lyda knew all the other participants had all been ferried in on luxury corporate helicopters, but that had been weeks, maybe months ago, and nothing could fly in these storms. Still, the driving logistics had been complicated, arranged around a kind of relay, but here the final pick up was late. Not as if she'd been given any choice—the last driver was clear about that. He'd take her as far as he could and still get back on one tank of gas, and as long as the light held out. After that, she was on her own. Their guy would show up soon enough, a big redheaded guy with a full beard and enormous feet—but overland was tough up here.

By the time they'd arrived at the drop-off, Lyda had been glad enough to see him go. But now, the emptiness—the aloneness of it—seemed more threat than relief. The drive out had been long, whipped by a fierce wind down the old canyon, and Lyda had gripped at her seat and managed her nausea by trying to track the road ahead, but most of the time it was obscured by this dust—or ash, or whatever it was from deep inside the earth that blew down from the north and stank of sulfur.

That is, the driver had said, if he can get through. And why the hell hadn't she flown in with the others? Those corporate copters are nice—lap of luxury, he'd said.

Oh, Lyda said, I'm just a second alternate, didn't you know? The others have been at it for ages already. Then she grinned. Besides, I'm the poet—I wanted to *see.*

Well, the driver said, look around you. Used to be a river here. Hell, used to be three.

But it's not just the drought, you know. Lyda tried to sound like she knew what she was talking about. It's the volcanoes.

The driver reached over and opened her door. If you say so, he said. But this is as far as I go.

And then, like that, he was gone.

Had the desert always been a lure, soft and enticing on the edges of dusk?

But no, it wasn't soft, and right now, it wasn't enticing at all.

It wasn't even a real desert, not like the ones they'd been promised in the CFP, just one of the new dried out valleys to the north, only recently changed. The Foundation move of venue notice had described it as dynamic, but dynamic did not mean things were going to be changing back.

How long, she thought now, after pulling you in did the desert turn deadly?

Then she surveyed her surroundings, what she'd been told was once a county park at the headwaters of an old river. Sure enough, across the playing field where he'd dropped her off, Lyda could make out the old log community center, low slung and rectangular, its shutters flapping bleakly in the wind, and just beyond that, the headwaters shrine where water still rushed from the base of the mountain, although it disappeared again a few hundred yards into its bed and Lyda knew not to drink it. The building looked empty and was at least shelter, but you never knew, and while rural Remainders had mostly just faded away, going feral in their hills, Lyda wasn't taking any chances.

But she couldn't stay out in this wind for long either. Already her skin felt abraded and burned, her eyes clotted with a sticky residue, and if the other driver didn't show up soon, Lyda knew she would have to take cover somewhere.

There were still coyotes, she had heard.

How easy it would be to disappear.

Lyda shook her head, as a small pain lodged itself just behind her left eye.

And then she took off through the murk for what appeared to be an old Little League dugout at the far side of the park, half hidden by trees, and three sides protection from the wind.

But unused to distance itself, even this was hard going, and she had already come so far. Between where she had started out and where she was headed, Lyda was left fragmented and dizzy. She hadn't expected any of it—the smells, the tastes, the unimpeded movement of a world without walls and windows—although she wasn't really sure what she *had* expected. She *did* have a map—an old forest service topographic map illegally boosted from the NETZ—although with her bootlegged BCI it was difficult to read, and nothing on it correlated, anyway, with what she had seen, the rivers mostly gone now, the mountain ranges so transfigured by earthquake and eruption that all Lyda really knew about where she'd ended up was that she'd long since passed the point where she could change her mind and turn back.

But now, as she tried to imagine the rough distance ahead along ruined not-roads and across the backs of lesser ridges, down the flank of the new desert valley, suddenly, for no reason, she missed her mother. Who was there to watch her now?

Then she thought: well, sure, her mother watched her, but how had that ever helped?

She thought: poet, that's a laugh, wondering what had prompted her to put down poet in the first place. True, she'd wanted out—all her life, she'd wanted *down*—and lacking any other skills, to speak of, poet might do. But although Lyda might pass for a poet, she could never pass for an adherent, and this was maybe going to be a problem. The Desperate Measures Seminars, like the IC's before them, had shared a single mandate, but what earthly good was language, anyway, for saving the world?

You couldn't feed a child or repair an ozone rift with a word or metric. Even Lyda knew that.

What else did Lyda know?

Crouched now in the dugout, Lyda placed her hands upon the earth as if that might steady her somehow. It smelled of something old—minerals and lichen. Next she tried counting—floors in her building, beats of her pulse, home runs once hit from this plate.

Was this a test? The others had been tested, she knew.

On the other side of the mountain, a parched world waited; behind her, the old community center at least appeared to be empty, but the wind carried a bad smell from that direction and, from time to time, a plaintive cry—a young child or, perhaps, a coyote. Lyda thought again about disappearance, a thought that filled her—inexplicably—with peace. It's possible, she thought, hunching over bent knees and covering her face in her hands against the sharp metallic taste of what might be a poisonous dust. Anything was possible, she thought, as an unfamiliar drowsiness began to pull at her limbs, weighting her down, bone by bone, not just the major bones—her tibias and ulnas—but all the minor metacarpals, the tiny nub at the top of her spine on which her whole body was balanced, until finally, despite her efforts to resist it, she slept.

Lyda will never know how long she sleeps—hours, or minutes—but, sprawled on the floor of the dugout in an even denser brownout, she awakens to what might be the sound of a motor. But how can she tell in this wind? She can't even tell one direction from another, hardly up from down, but there it is again, a kind of whine. And although her next thought has not come yet—that in this blast of grit and dust how will this driver find her?—when it does, it comes with the full force of the wind, its toxic dust, and her keen consciousness that this is it.

And in the panic and disorientation of storm and sleep, Lyda jumps up shouting, but because she knows this to be futile and also that she doesn't have much time—no vehicle can wait long in this, whatever this is, this dust, this sand, this ash—Lyda starts—she can't help it—to think again about her own disappearance, how fungible she is, and then Lyda runs. Or, ducking her head against the fierce maw of wind, she at least *tries* to run, but mostly stumbles forward, gasping and choking. But she's had so little practice, it's the best she can do. And she can't stop anyway. Nothing can stop her now that she's running and waving and trying to make herself big and loud enough to be heard over the screech of wind, although the sound that comes out is puny and Lyda is small and so obscured by the grit—if she overshoots the vehicle, she knows, she could end up lost forever, wandering alone in the desert until she goes out. But it's hard, this running, so hard, much harder than she'd have thought—*before*—a kind of gritty flailing against an unstoppable force and already exhausted, unable to breathe, and then, like that, dizzy, so dizzy that Lyda feels herself going down—feels herself *falling*—when a blindingly bright arm appears out of nowhere and pulls her up into the stillness of a cab where everything is white.

Except it's not the big, redheaded driver she has been told to look for, but a small and neutral-eyed man in a gray knit cap who is offering the whitest, the cleanest and most soothing towel she has ever seen and muttering something unintelligible.

He's talking, anyway, Lyda can see that, but she can't hear a word. Or maybe she can hear but she can't sort it out, whatever is coming from this small man's mouth—get out before the fuel lines clot, or hold on to her hat? He might be telling her something important, but no, now his mouth stops and he's looking right at her—almost as if he is trying to assess, or *memorize*, her.

Then, with no warning, he moves, raising a hand, his left hand, to touch her forehead briefly, before turning away to put the vehicle in gear and pull it out onto the road, as casually as if he already knows that in an instant they will drive out of the storm and into a bleached, white world.

But when Lyda turns to him again, he's got his eyes on the road ahead and nothing about him reveals a thing.

Lyda doesn't really believe in the Desperate Measures movement. What was, was, she believed, with your own life raveling out from the moment you were born, and you couldn't change a thing about that. In a different life, things might be different—she might have had dreams of a husband, or a world without Remainders. As a bitter adolescent, Lyda even tried fixing her thoughts on the planet, as if that might heal things. And then she had fixed herself.

Still, it's surprising, the ease with which she has gotten this far, for what she doesn't think, because she doesn't think like this, is that she's attractive, in a physical way, with a slender build and delicate, even features, that give her a general appearance of frailty and belie the other startling fact that she's strong as a horse and inclined toward a frankly animal sensuality at appropriate moments.

Then Lyda sags. She's never going to carry this off.

But the driver just drives. He drives and he drives, not on any road but just cross-country and without any discernible pattern but yet as if he knows exactly where he's going.

After a while, he nods toward the several large canisters of gas strapped to the back of the truck and says, in case the electrical assist goes out.

That much gas, on any market, is impressive, Lyda knows, but why would there be a problem with the electrical assist?

The driver has a little smile, more about the eyes than the mouth, and even with the cap there, Lyda can see veins pulsing in his skull. On the outside the world flows by, but on the inside everything is—*altered*.

Looking back, it all happened so quickly—her mother going vapid and speechless, her father's rage, her own panic, and then the service elevator responding to the imprint of her thumb for the first time in her life. But what else could she do? Her father already was coming, ascending in the other elevator and the middle of the day, as cupped in the miracle of her own descent, the two elevators passed each other in the shaft somewhere near floor seventeen and *nothing happened*, only her own continued descent toward the surface—the actual surface—of earth, the great revolving door in the glass and marble lobby going round and round and round, the vast urban canyon outside. There was a breeze, Lyda does remember that. And she remembers running down the darkened street, buildings close on either side, and the concrete hard and cracked against her feet. Finally, she remembers the plain pine plank of the other door at the end of the canyon, the one that was waiting—for her.

After that, nothing.

And now, as the ruined world glides by on the outside, she finds she doesn't really care, one way or another, what door she used or how she had passed through the known borders of her world. Not with the other drivers so much, but with this new one, this small opaque man who has handed her one white towel and a glistening blue bottle of water—it's different with him—and something already is shifting in her. And as they follow the west contours of the valley, edged by small hummocks that break off again and again in clay-colored cliffs, Lyda reminds herself that there is nothing natural about it, however beautiful it seems, a world stripped bare to its bones.

Until with no warning, it stops. Or the Ranger does anyway, coming to a sudden halt at the edge of oblivion. And even Lyda, who does know up and down, is confused, for nothing about this—*rupture*—can be imagined or even taken in. This—what is it? A wash or a faultline—a gap that opens here to transect the planet, separating them, on this part of it, from there, on the other, where they're going.

The vehicle shudders above it.

And there isn't any bottom that Lyda can see—just empty, open space, with no end.

Stop, a voice cries, and it's hers. But they are already stopped. I mean, let me out.

Slowly, the driver blinks, beginning to back up. It's not safe, it's almost dark. But he's not really arguing.

From the other side of the chasm, a shadow folds over its depths like a shroud; while traces all around of yet unruptured faultlines remind Lyda that a moment will come when they, too, split apart, when the earth, like the built world, will also collapse. It's a slightly thrilling thought, but she doesn't know where it comes from, and now she is running again, running and running along the split open lip of the world as, behind her, the driver calls something about danger—snakes, or water, or UV radiation, or just time passing, getting on now, swiftly, toward night.

There's a buckled roadway up ahead, he is calling.

Watch out for falling rocks, he calls.

But it's not a warning but a song, and still Lyda runs, away from the sound of the driver's song, running again, as if running were the most natural thing in the world. Lyda is running alongside the—*rift*—but it's different this time, the running, physical and full of need and graceful—like something she's been doing her whole life. The shale at her feet spits up warm and loose from the ragged edge of earth that drops off into nothing and goes on and on. And still Lyda runs. Lyda runs until she can't run anymore, until her mouth goes dry and her tongue cleaves to its roof like an alien thing, and when she goes down, she spreads herself, chest up, to the sky.

Ok, she says, to no one in particular, the driver too far behind to hear, even without the wind that whips her words away.

Ok, ok.

Hey, the driver says right behind her, but how did he *get* here? Be careful. Then he is laughing, we wouldn't want you falling in.

Toward the west, Lyda strains to see, and maybe, in the distance—far, far away—it might broaden somewhat into a real wash, but how far down does it go? So she kicks a small stone over the edge, just to find out. Then another.

Don't do that, the driver says.

Lyda kicks another stone in. Why not? And another, and another, until she understands—they're not landing. Hmm, she says, ok.

After that, they stand for a while, side by side—Lyda, out in the world for the first time since she was a toddler, and the driver who is not the big redheaded one but the small neutral-eyed one—still listening for the stones to stop falling. The driver has his hand on her shoulder. Depending on their depth, Lyda knows, some fissures—if that's what this is—emit toxic vapors, but the air that rises from this one doesn't feel dangerous, but tender, almost sweet. It feels, like she does—*alive*. This is probably the wrong way to feel, but Lyda smiles anyway, kicking a small shower of stones off the ledge.

What's so special about poets anyway?

And for the first time she lets herself see that there's something not quite right about this man, who is only in part present, only partially a man. Crouched on a rock, he looks up at her now, moon-faced and humming. She's not even sure she has spoken aloud, but she knows he's not going to answer. For some reason, he has removed his cap to reveal interlocking plates of a beautiful skull fused along cranial faultlines that look to be as potentially unstable as the earth itself. At the back of his head, beneath its cusp, there's a small gap where Lyda can see the pulsing inside. The gap is big enough for someone to put a finger in, or something else.

Ok, she says finally. Now what?

Well, there's water, and all the regular emergency stuff. We'll do ok—we can sleep in the back of the Ranger, or—he blushes—you can.

That's fine, she says, feeling oddly chastened. She hasn't meant to be an inconvenience. No, really, I'm done now. I just got carried away. We can go on now, that's not a problem for me.

The man runs his hand over his head and shrugs. There isn't any point in pressing on now, he is saying, and as Lyda understands—slowly, because of the way he parses his words, terse and deliberate, but not, she realizes suddenly, as if he were angry, but as if there really is something he's hiding from her—another little thrill passes through her and she thinks there never was, or he never had any intention, of pressing on, not today—or, ever—they are there, where they are, because *he* has willed it. Because, she thinks again, he has *willed* it, and the little thrill jolts her again, like a charge. But why would he have brought her here when anyone could see that the wash only appears to be endless?

But no, the Ranger is hung up, behind them, he says.

There's a problem, he says, with the electrical assist.

Up ahead, there's a landslide on the road.

But even as he speaks Lyda knows these to be lies—crude, transparent lies—that paradoxically evoke a certain tenderness in her, who turns her full attention to him, finally—this small, bald *man* who has driven her here to the edge of the known world and with eyes so neutral, so absent of any intention as to seem somehow wiped clean, or to burn right into her, burrowing deep, as though she were a hole. The gap at the back of his head, the fine webbing of bluish veins spread out beneath the sweaty, stretched layer of scalp still pulses visibly—a living, subcutaneous map.

On the other side of the rupture and a little to the south, Lyda can make out what appears to be an unobstructed road curving sleekly through the valley.

But the driver is holding out another bottle of water—blue, blue water— his teeth, behind his labored smile, yellow and meticulous, and Lyda takes it.

A map, Lyda thinks, but not of the world—*something else.*

In that moment, it suddenly occurs to her to wonder, for the first time, what had happened to the large redheaded man with big feet, even as she studies the seductive darkness of the nothing before them. How easily, she thinks, they could be crushed by a geologic shift, another shift of tectonic plates. Here and there she can just make out what might have been the faint markings of trails where other people once had walked. And at the far end of the valley, lights blinking on in what must be the DMS compound.

All her life she has dreamed of escaping the glass and steel tower where she grew up away from other children and sheltered from the world, but now that she has—truly has escaped—she feels, oddly, like weeping. But the tears aren't for her and they aren't really sad. A wind is rising from the inside of the earth below, a faint, gentle one, just enough of a wind to make her eyes burn and crust. Just that, her tears dried by the soft breath of earth, like the breath of the man crouched beside her, a breathing man, his breath another wind, bald and forgiving. There is something so elementary and particular about this moment that Lyda does not want it to pass.

And then, like that, like all moments, it does.

Night's coming, he says gently. We'll just stay here for now.

Oh, it's all so utterly exhausting.

Or, he says, but perhaps he has *already* said this and she's only just now hearing it, we could stay up there. And as Lyda follows his gaze up a rise behind them to a round, dark opening in the earth, a hole or a burrow, he adds, it will be cooler up there.

WHAT LYDA DOES NOT REMEMBER

In the weeks that follow, Lyda will remember almost nothing of her night in the desert—not the depth of the wash, not the small round opening in the earth where they sleep, not the smell of water—but only the metallic taste of waking to the sound of the Ranger humming back to life, and the smell of gas, as if there really had been a problem with the electrical assist. And she will remember the big redheaded driver, and his *anger.*

Last time I drive a damned poet around. He really was mad.

Also, she'll remember the medical exam on her arrival, the IV hydration, the soak in the deep clay tub, sleep.

But she won't remember the dreams she has that afternoon of falling, again and again, into the earth in the arms of the man she does not remember who drove her to the place where the earth split apart. Oh, she will think in her dreams from the touch of the man who's not wholly a man, or maybe only the wind, or the sound of them falling together. But no, it's a hand, which does not feel entirely human, more like the memory of something that once, long ago, had been human, which if Lyda *could* remember she'd find every bit as improbable as the dream of the hole in the earth, or the man who is crouching beside her.

Lyda will remember waking and wandering down through the complex to a conference room where a chair was waiting for her, still warm from someone else's body, at an elaborate table, carved to look like the back of a man who is almost familiar. And she'll remember the others, scientists and scholars—geologist, historian, biologist, mathematician. *Mathematician.*

From that moment on Lyda will accept her new insufficiency of memory as a more or less permanent condition, although she retains enough of the world to appreciate the luxury of small things—the downy softness of her bed, the icy martinis at the end of the day, the rush of the wind through the valley that feels, for the first time in her life—Lyda remembers enough to remember this—natural and wild. But a good portion of the rest of what she should remember is just gone, so efficiently erased as to deliver her, intact and full of promise, to the present moment.

Among the things Lyda does not and will never again—or not for some time—remember is the glass and steel tower where she grew up, high above the world, as if this would protect her, nor the pale pair of her reluctant parents, twinned at either end of a long, blonde table from another continent and era. She won't remember the meals, the glistening cans from which they're prepared, nor the luminous sheen of the polished wood, the glass wall of window behind her.

Don't look, oh don't look, oh don't look, her mother would say.

But Lyda won't remember that, no more than she will remember her scurrying mother, working the perimeter of their white world, ear pressed here, there, to the walls.

This is not my place, her mother would say. I belong in there, with *them.*

Shush, her bent-over father would tell her at night. It's not like that at all.

Lyda won't remember the moan of unnatural wind wrapping the building, nor the whoosh of elevator doors, or her father stepping out, calling, *I'm home.* She won't remember the floor-to-ceiling windows that formed the boundaries of her world. She won't remember the white upholstered box at the foot of her bed—what her mother called a "toy chest"—where she made her little nest to hide in and play. And she won't remember the primitive BCI she ordered off the NetZ and sutured to her scalp, working backwards, in a mirror.

Lyda was just fifteen when Peter found her in the portal, but she won't remember that either, no more than she'll remember how easy he'll claim it was to find her, standing so high—no static at all—pressed like a tree to the window.

Of course, Lyda did have two parents—she'll remember that, but what good were the parents she had—the mother who clung to walls, the father who descended every morning to disappear inside the Department of Records, which Lyda knew to be huge. At night, when he returned—*I'm home*—of course he was depleted by the day, all those meticulous notations—whole bodied live births, Remainderings, crossings over. Anybody would be, and maybe Lyda remembers that. But how can she remember that he came back with two needs—the need of a woman's body to grope in the softest, the most mysterious spots, and the need of food?

Of that there was so much to choose from—can after can of soft white asparagus tips and bright pink ham, juices squeezed from all over the world, anchovies, capers, tuna in tins.

Every night dinner would be waiting—wine glasses sparkling, silver set out, round white plates with shiny gold rims—while in the kitchen all the cans would already be rinsed out and crushed. Everything ready for him—Lyda's mother was efficient like that. Often, she'd have music playing, candles burning, Lyda plugged into a narrative or game. This would satisfy the one need well enough.

But as to the other—*I don't belong here, but in there, with them*—Lyda's mother's body was fading so soon, and although she sometimes tried to help— *here*, she would say, *no here, here*—Lyda, already, was growing.

Almost, but not quite, Lyda can remember how the mother—*her* mother— had been young and lovely once, how in that time—before they had risen to live above the world, before Lyda had even been born—they had lived, the two parents, among others rejected by the IC Commission and clustered in a stand of old apartments on an inner couryard where fear should have made them feel so acute, but somehow it didn't. They took their supplements and breathed their filtered air and hoped to stay well, but in the meantime, they cleaved to the present and each other, a small community of hangers-on who, as time went by, drew closer to one another, three couples reducing their space to a single apartment.

And then to one bed.

All but Lyda's father, who had never really liked this, all crowded and high-strung and close. But because he did believe in safety in numbers, he'd let the mother do as she liked, sleep askew among others, wrapped in their monstrous comfort. Sometimes, from the sofa, he would watch them sleep like a great multi-limbed organism, and sometimes he would pull her from it, ravenous, in the middle of the night. But during the day, he felt so completely reduced in the thriving hum of their little enclave that he resented everything—the happiness she found preparing food with other women, or staying up late exchanging memories, or even just reading, looped in the arms of others.

Thus, when the plagues ended as suddenly and arbitrarily as they had begun, he was unprepared for her euphoria, which took the form of hope, of dancing in the streets and having real sex again. How happy they had been, how fervently they'd believed that everything—*everything*—was going to change. Person to person, neighborhood to neghborhood, nation to nation, declarations were made, and for a brief time all the young women were pregnant and glowing. Most came shortly to their senses, but not the mother—Lyda's mother—who remained, for nine months, obdurate and beatific.

If not us, she said, who?

She had really believed that.

And Lyda's father went along because she had grown so much rounder and softer, because of the new residential dispensations an intact family unit would provide, and because he had the dream of only her.

But of course neither one of them had known—couldn't possibly have anticipated—how completely Lyda's birth would change things. That part wasn't even gradual. How one day the future lay before them, a challenge and a promise, and the next, a terrible threat, and it made the optimistic spirit with which they'd gone ahead and carried the child to term somehow cavalier and shameful.

Lyda won't remember any of this, not her mother, ear pressed to the walls, nor her father, the bent over civil servant and tracker of statistical anomalies.

Shh, he would tell her when he tucked her in at night, his hands clamped firm on her body. Your mother doesn't think so, but no one can hurt us here.

These were the tenderest words her father ever said to her when she was a girl.

They loved her, Lyda's parents. Lyda never doubted that. But Lyda's mother had been happy below, in the ground-level apartment where Lyda was born. Below, she had thick, safe walls and neighbors—people to talk to. A girl needed that, Lyda's mother said—the companionship of others, to laugh with and for help with preparing the food and to share children and chores and ideas with.

It's not so much to want, her mother said. You'll understand when you are older.

But Lyda's father wanted something else. He wanted Lyda and her mother to be safe, sure—any man would want that. But mostly he wanted only them.

Lyda's first and only real excursions out into the world were when she was a toddler and her parents had finally received their housing allocation, complete with its generous bonus for the new child. Nights, her mother would weep and plead, but in the morning, as often as they could, the three of them would suit up and take off with maps and transportation tokens and long lists of available buildings. This is what Lyda will not remember as the time of going out, a time in which her yearning for the world would take seed, even though she was still so small.

But maybe she does remember her mother's lament—we'll be all alone, who will help me with the child, if I'd known you were going to do this, I'd have got an abortion, like everyone else.

Lyda, by then, was two or three.

They looked for months.

Once, a small, white dog followed them, slinking along just behind and nosing his way in at the buildings where Lyda's mother, with visible relief, quickly unwrapped the child to let her explore. Once, they trudged up three floors of worn marble stairs, edged with mahogany banisters, only to find the apartment burned out from the *inside*. Once, the transportation grid broke down and they'd had to stay the night in a stale apartment crammed with antiques. Lyda ran around, endangering once priceless possessions, while her mother slept on the floor by the window, curled up in a knot of despair.

What Lyda can later retrieve of this failed memory will not be the knot of her mother's despair, nor will it be the grid of leaded window—Lyda *knows* windows—but her mother's rising from it sometime in the night and wandering through the apartment looking for Lyda's father, and how when she finds him, she lies down next to him, the both of them pale as pot worms and uncertain how to proceed, until Lyda's mother takes Lyda's father in her mouth in an act that astonishes them all.

Shortly thereafter they go up into the building from which, until now, Lyda will never again descend. On that first day, when the elevator doors swoosh open for the first time and her father steps out into the blinding whiteness of the vast apartment to pronounce his first and final approval—*this is it*—Lyda's stunned mother can do nothing but unwrap the small child once more and put her down on the bleached pine floors. At once, Lyda is off, careening breakneck toward the floor-to-ceiling windows—*don't look, oh Lyda, don't look*—as if to catapult herself into their airiness, pressing against them until her small child body fills with milky radiance.

Lyda would never have remembered this—her pink beginnings—even under ordinary circumstances, but in the desert later she will not remember either the subsequent years and years of pressing herself to that same window, longing for release, nor the things that fall outside, as if others have climbed to the top of the building to throw their belongings over its edge and to watch them go down—first their treasured things, and then, them.

This is the window where Lyda grows from chubby toddlerhood to bitter adolescence.

Don't let go, her mother said. You'll fall. Everything—everyone—falls.

But of course Lyda wouldn't mind falling—she *wanted* to go down.

It was the one thing Lyda wanted, the only thing she ever wanted, and it remained the single thing her parents would deny her—her mother, because, having left the women who'd been with her when she bore and kept the child, she'd turned into a fraught and timid woman, terrified she'd lose her daughter too; and her father because, after everything he'd done for his small female family, he now found himself at a far greater remove from the woman who had taken him in her mouth one night, and for this he blamed the daughter and wanted—blindly wanted—to punish her. Still, there were times when the small girl moved him bizarrely, a feeling like pity rising up in his mouth and filling it with a sad, salty taste.

More than anything, as she grew, Lyda wanted to escape the flatness of her father's smell that marked the rooms he had claimed as his own, along with the artificial musk her mother used to mask it, mask, as well, the smells that drifted in from the walls, traces of those who once lived here, and up from what rotted below.

It will be a long, long time before Lyda can remember any of this.

What she will remember, what remains part of her enduring consciousness—even later, in the desert, when she will have forgotten almost everything else—are her nightly dreams of falling, sometimes of herself, falling either toward or away from the earth in an endless wind-whipping plunge, but mostly of others, plummeting or drifting past the window where she spends her days watching them fall. Maybe, Lyda dreams, these are the people from inside the walls, but maybe they come from above, the top of the building, higher even than the apartment. Lyda dreams them there, replete with their things—their beautiful things—which they let go before going themselves. But not from despair, *something else*—people released into the dailiness of life, and as fully engaged in their routines as though they might go on forever—bending over bathroom basins and brushing their teeth, playing their pianos and shooting their basketballs through hoops, sitting in imaginary lounge chairs deftly reading crumbling books, kissing and making love and peeling vegetables and fruit to eat fresh and raw with each other, feeding each other, singing songs, calculating receipts, holding each other, and all of them falling together in such blissful oblivion that, over time, even during the day when she is awake, Lyda wants only to join them.

Of them all, only one—a small boy struggling to tie his white shoes—seems aware of Lyda, and each time he passes, he glances up from his task, catching her eye almost casually and opening his mouth to say something—maybe, *teach me how to do this, show me, please.* But though she tries to read his lips, to imagine all he might be saying—and to her—he falls—always—away and too fast.

Then one day when Lyda is twelve, she puts her hand to the glass just as the small boy flies by, as if to reach for him or stop him or tell him what he wants, how to loop the lace like the ear of a rabbit and thread the other ear through—anything at all to intercept his endless fall and make him tell her why he, alone among them all, looks back at her. But this is the first time he doesn't. She presses her palm flat to the glass and calls out to him, some sound that is not quite a word. She calls it again. But still, he refuses to look, his slim neck bent in a delicate arc, brow furrowed, so engrossed in his task—the tying of shoes—that he can no longer be bothered with her.

And when he is gone, Lyda looks down at her body and sees it is changing—her body—and this breaks her heart a little for the boy because she knows his never will.

THE WOMAN IN GRAY

IN THE DAYS THAT FOLLOWED the bald man's arrival, Will would sometimes reflect on how different things might have been if the Foundation leader had been a tired academic, not so unlike the seminar participants themselves or the mentors they had left behind, another extraneous man with drooping hair and stained collar and cuffs. In the presence of such poignant cuffs, every one of them, he'd think, would have rallied to defend him. But the opulence had skewed things from the start.

God, Will hated academics.

Maybe if they hadn't all been so hung over, but the bald man was subtle and so effectively strategic that each time the leader tried to rein him in, the bald man—who said to call him Peter—would just lower his head to wait the opposition out, and in this way deflate it. And then they'd return to their topic— the progressive extinction of fifty percent, plus or minus, of the world's plant species, or new viral gene swapping threats—but with something gone out of it somehow, the urgency lessened. Really, it was ironic. All that power and control and the leader could not do one single thing to shut the bald man down.

Will's first reaction was to be entertained.

And for a while—a long time really—he had been.

A man walks out of the desert to set in play an act of substitution and replacement so exact that no one even notices—really, who would not be impressed? Of course Will did not know—could not have known—that his own connection to the bald man's arrival was not going to last, that in time he, too, was going to forget that there had ever been a physicist, lanky or not. He couldn't have known this, and even if he had, there'd have been no way to circumvent it. For even as the next presenter launched into her research on famine trajectories, the memory of the man walking out of the desert was starting to fade.

And then the two women appeared, not together but simultaneously—the long-awaited poet, who arrived one morning in the midst of great commotion, and an otherwise phantom woman in gray, apparently manifest only to him. Everyone gathered to welcome the poet, who'd survived—incredibly—a night in the desert and a trip over roads that had not been passable in more than a quarter of a century. The poet—another replacement, but for whom?—arrived with a good deal of noise, dusty but animated.

Do I have a story to tell you, she'd exclaimed just before being whisked away.

But the woman in gray made no noise at all.

Will hardly believed in either of them at first, no more than he'd believed in Peter. How did they *get* here? But neither could the scientist in him dismiss the evidence as each was clearly persisting—the one, the poet, heartbreakingly young; and the other, ageless and remote, more a shadow—or idea—of a person than a real, corporeal being. More, Will thought, a sensation, for although she appeared to him often, as soon as she knew he had seen her—a very small woman in a modest gray suit and shimmering headscarf—she'd scurry away, but not before something, Will's *sensation*, had passed between them. And then she'd be gone, as if she'd never been there at all.

At first Will had rejected the idea of her outright. Just back from his noon hour walk and late for a session, he'd been rushing, breathless and wet from dousing himself to wash off the sweat before going in, when he'd noticed her hovering just down the hallway.

Hovering, he thought, the word coming into his head as if from elsewhere.

More than usually dehydrated, Will pulled up short—a gray suit in this heat, a stranger, a woman. Impossible—he was hallucinating.

Maybe he should drink the water instead.

But no, she was still there, at the end of a corridor that led to an unfinished wing. And she was looking at him—Will was certain of that. She'd been looking the whole time—as he poured the water from the drinking pitcher over his head, then shook out his hair and wiped his face with the hem of his t-shirt. She'd watched him until he looked up, and then she had slipped away.

That was the first time.

In the days that followed, she was everywhere—or, there and then not, over and over, disappearing into areas of the complex that, like the balcony of his room, had yet to be constructed. Sometimes, she'd be waiting at the bottom of stairs that led nowhere, or beside a limp agave in blistering heat, at the bar when no one was looking. He'd seen her through windows, her face a transient moon, or poised on a stoop he knew for certain was not there—outside, was that Peter's room?

Two things about her were constant: that she hovered and always wore gray.

The poet had her place at the table and was already everybody's favorite. But the woman in gray appeared only to him, and if he wasn't going mad altogether, seemed also to appear as if *for* him.

Soon, Will came to like it—*her*—or the sensation of her, that glimpse out the corner of his eye when he knew he'd been followed, the tiny agitation of the place where she had just been that stirred something deep in him. Not love—Will had never been in love that he knew. But maybe a little bit like love, the way she would be present all and only for him, the sly curve of her shoulder as she turned away, the shimmer of gray that persisted even when she was gone. How could Will say what it was? He had been to some parties as a boy or young man, had even kissed a girl on occasion, and had learned to imagine the bodies of women in his solitary acts of love. He had experienced *desire*. But in the end, he'd chosen numbers, which he'd found every bit as abstracted and provocative as the woman who haunted him now.

Will came to think of her as the woman in gray—all and only in gray, so utterly out of place on the compound as to seem imported, her charcoals and steels, gunmetals and pearls working, somehow, to contain her, not in the manner of Remainders, but yet so profoundly misaligned as to suggest that the body—her body—had its true location *elsewhere*. And in certain light, Will would have sworn, it left an afterimage, something he could almost—but not quite—touch.

Meantime, the bald man—Peter—persisted, unruly and undisciplined, challenging their protocols and reason. Sometimes all it took to derail an afternoon's session was for him to look at the presenter, turning his gaze—sometimes hot, sometimes cool—toward whomever might be speaking, glancing skeptically from person to data. More often, he'd launch in himself, his voice cracking open and his skull throbbing weirdly, as keen for argument as Will was for walking. Then it wouldn't matter who had the floor or how much time remained, Peter would go on and on, the torrent of words spewing out in tiny, sizzling surprises. Really, it was dizzing sometimes. Peter did like to talk—that much was clear—but it all came out in a rush, as if he had to say everything at once, and it sometimes seemed to Will that he'd never heard language used quite this way before, with little gaps between, urgent and loose with association, and ever more expansive as, unable to contain it, Peter himself grew huge. But not with meaning—*something else*, something old.

Others suspected him of being in collusion with the Foundation, but what kind of sense did that make? Since Peter arrived, nothing made sense—Peter, the one-man resistance team, but resistance to what?

Do the math, he'd say, grinning across the table at Will, the Foundation is screwed.

The Foundation, the leader countered acidly, is us.

Well, sure, Peter said, and that vain little artist you keep in your computer. How much did you pay for him anyway? Or them? Peter waved at the others. How much did you pay for all of them together?

Saying this, Peter smiled, but with something so beatific about him as to make the rest of them seem crudely stuck to their hypotheses and algorithms, their hapless, pedestrian facts, their sloth. And yet Will knew—he had looked—Peter had no research to share, nothing written on the pages in his portfolio, no data. Instead, he seemed to be there only to disrupt things, although, like the rest of them, he drank, and relished the tender, the succulent meats they were still served every meal with unabashed pleasure.

Sometimes, a blue parrot sat on his shoulder. Sometimes, his bald head pulsed.

And sometimes he plied Will with vodka, and sometimes the poet called Lyda drank with them.

Will liked that, liked having the poet around, who, unlike the woman in gray, was utterly corporeal and short on facts, although she had a certain knack for words. It wasn't the words Will liked so much as her body, as solid and grounded, as frankly sensual as the other's was fleeting, and when sometimes after dinner they stayed late in Peter's room, he could not help but touch it—touch *her*—as furtively and often as he could, brushing her shoulder as he passed by for more ice, reaching out to pat her hand for added emphasis, helping her with her sweater when the night got cool. Each time, the body—the poet's body, Lyda's body—startled Will with its warmth and palpability, and he'd flush the same flush just the thought of the woman in gray could provoke in him now.

And Peter let them. More and more he let them touch and be touched by each other while he sat back holding forth—and watching.

Think of me as your token post-humanist, he told them one night, the glass wall of his room opened out to the world. Think of a rock as a rock; a shoe, a decaying remnant of something *before*. Imagine, he'd said, the archaeology of it—red spike heels, steel shanks, Vibram soles forever.

Will twisted the stem of his glass and forced himself not to look down at his own Vibram soles, worn to a smooth patina.

Shoes, Peter said—that's what will be left when we're gone.

Numb from the vodka and fatigue, Will looked out on the desolate valley that, emptied of people, was achingly beautiful—until the phantom woman appeared among the rocks.

Peter speared the fat stuffed olive in his drink and popped it in his mouth, clearly savoring the moment before adding, almost as an afterthought, what would you do if you were the last man on earth?

Or woman, Will thought, on the verge of asking Peter about his apparition, but what could he possibly say—look there, the one dressed in gray only I can see? Instead, he just bent to kiss the top of Lyda's head and left for bed.

Not that Will could sleep these days, preoccupied and baited.

And so he took to walking more and more each day, harder and farther and deeper out into the washes, up the ravines, down to the floor of the valley where he would set a punishing pace across the parched crust of earth and try to imagine it green, with trees. But it never mattered where he'd gone or how late he was getting back, the woman in gray would be waiting for him, poised like an animal and set to dart off. Sometimes, he tried to lure her out, leaving sessions early or following traces of jasmine through unused portions of the compound. It got to where even the idea of her was enough to excite him.

Oh, Will thought, ok. But it wasn't, because he could not—he *could not*—stop thinking about her, wanting her, the delicate knot of gray silk at the nape of her neck, the discreet turn away at his glance.

A few times, he tried to engage her. He'd wave, calling out, hot enough for you? He tried to be friendly.

The same grave regard, the same subtle evasion.

Once he tried to grab her, just the wrist, to see if she'd stop. It wasn't a violent gesture, only impulsive—*stay, who are you?* But then for several days she didn't appear at all.

Will knew he'd have to say something soon, but when he did, it only made things worse.

Her? Peter said, when Will finally asked. She's just a court reporter, what did you think?

A what? Will didn't know quite how to respond.

Oh, you know, a person who writes down what other people say.

They were sitting, all three of them, in Peter's room again, their six legs slung over the ledge where the balcony was supposed to be, and Peter was giving them vodka again much better than the vodka they could get at the bar, although where he managed to get it, Will didn't even want to know. He didn't want to know now, either, about the court reporter. That Peter saw her too was not so surprising, although it could make him jealous if he thought about it too much. But he found the idea of her transcribing their words deeply unsettling for no reason he could say. The concept of a personal privacy was so obsolete by then it would have been naïve to assume they were not being recorded, down to their asides and hems and haws—he'd probably signed consent forms even before his initial application was complete. But the idea of a human mediation, which he knew to be fallible, was archaic, and it bothered Will. It really did.

Until he considered her hands—the clots of the sounds of the syllables that formed in his mouth moving through the tips of her fingers—and something not entirely unpleasant shifted inside him.

But where were they keeping her anyway? Where did she go?

Beside him, Peter was wearing a worn gauzy shirt and shorts as brief as the play clothes of a child, revealing thighs as smooth and poreless as his scalp, the little round knobs of his knees pulled taut and white. Not a hair on his body, Will noted.

You spent too much time at that think tank of yours, Peter said. Didn't they ever let you out?

Will shrugged, looking up uneasily. Isn't that what the sensors are for?

Have you even talked to her? I know she wants to talk to you.

Saying this, Peter looked strangely restrained, as if he might go on, but then did not.

What I'd give for a fiddle right now, Will said.

Lyda placed her warm hand on his thigh. What reporter?

As she spoke, the moon eased from behind the last clouds, flooding the valley with light and Will with a sanguine feeling. Right or wrong, for just this moment, the woman in gray was nowhere and the world was peaceful and lovely. Just for the moment, hardly more than a heartbeat, Will could accept, be content with, all this and only this—the heat of the vodka inside him, the moon, Peter benign to one side and Lyda, hot, to the other. Then Will emptied his mind even of that as a powerful serenity flowed through him that left him feeling keenly—unnaturally, perhaps, but nonetheless potently—alive, made both conscious and coherent by the ever diminishing space between two points in which everything remains not just possible but necessary.

Maybe, he thought from nowhere, they should just take a Ranger and go.

Not yet, Peter said.

What?

He means, Lyda said.

Stick with me, Will said. I'm in charge of the variable.

She won't hurt you, Peter said.

The olives had a peppery bite—jalapeno?—the vodka, smooth and icy. With nothing else to do, Will kept on drinking until Peter seemed, again, a man like other men, and Will's vision of him walking out of the desert no more unlikely than this new one of them walking back into it.

By the time Will finally found her in the tiny inside corner of his computer screen, it seemed to him he'd looked for her everywhere—behind the diaphanous screen on which they projected their presentations, inside pocket walls, just above or below the last finished floors. By now, he'd grown attached to the idea of her, everywhere and nowhere, the woman and her stenograph machine, a blur of precision on the arc of the sound of their words—*his* words—as they worked their way into her perfect cup of ear—spiralling through its outer shell and dark inner chambers, over the miniscule bones, up the throbbing auditory nerve to her cerebral cortex, then back down her slender neck and arms to hands that transcribed the world. Will had imagined all this, but he had never, not once, imagined her so close—inside his small computer screen where she'd replaced the little artist just as surely as Peter had replaced the lanky physicist no one remembered.

The woman's sudden appearance there, just to the left of his hand in the corner of the image—but only his—reduced the proceedings to a distant murmur. *That can't be.* But there, indeed, she was, sitting erect in her tiny chair, legs primly crossed at the heels, and with a tiny table before her where she typed on a tinier machine. But she wasn't really typing, Will knew—something else. Will tried to imagine what it might be like, taking his own words apart in his head, disassembling them into their different parts, but stripped of cogent sound and meaning, they were nothing but noise. How did she do it, he wondered?

Seeing her there, it was hard not to touch her—to lift his smallest finger and place it on her body, but she was so small he didn't want to hurt her. And, on the other side of the table, Peter was watching.

You don't have any idea how lucky you are, the leader was saying. Things are bad out there. Use your sunscreen, wear a hat—by law, you're Foundation investments.

Below, the woman smiled, but the smile seemed to belong to another time and world. Now Will could see how easy it was to have missed her, reduced to such a tiny node of light and motionless save for the flutter of her extraordinary fingers across the surface of her miniature machine, reducing their proceedings—Will himself—to nothing more than insensible syllabic code—*dth, uunnng, phlaat.*

But it wasn't like that, Will knew. It wasn't like that at all.

Then she did move—such a slight movement, maybe not even a real movement. But no, she'd uncrossed and re-crossed her ankles, realigning her body into an exact mirror image of its prior self, and in that moment another image came to Will—not the image, not even the idea of the image, but the thing itself—of him on the inside of the computer screen touching *her.*

And this was how it happened that Will found himself kneeling before her at last as she continued her transcription oblivious of him, his hands on her knees, sheathed by the sheerest of stockings, and then on the collar of her gray blouse, and then—so softly it barely even counted as a touch—on the snaps at the bands on her wrists and what lay beneath.

Afterwards, he could not wait for this to happen again.

In the days that followed, Will like to imagine her in a real court, her posture perfect, her demeanor as fixed and unobtrusive as any court reporter, but with her extraordinary fingers doing to the outer world what they had done, already, to him. Will imagined her head bowed discreetly toward the floor, her eyes averted, demure but determined as the flutter of her hands pressed ever forward in a kind of duet between her and the attorney, the one the silent partner to the other who was speaking, or a call and response, that must have sometimes felt a little bit like sex.

And then, because now he could not stop himself, he would slip back to find her.

At first, their lovemaking had been confined to the small computer screen embedded in the sculptured conference table, made ever more extravagant and poignant by the dire presentations going on above and the severity of Helen's gray wardrobe. They began without words, using, mostly, their hands, the uncanny movement of skin against skin, like another language altogether. Neither one of them had ever encountered such articulate hands, and while their tongues would grow swollen and clumsy inside them, their bodies trembled from the fluency of a single touch—one finger—so delicate it hardly counted as physical touch.

Still it broke something open inside them.

Their skin felt like glass. The scarf stayed on.

But they were also small, inside the computer.

Will knelt before the woman in gray, who continued, as if impervious, to work while he ran his hand underneath her skirt. His fingers met her underpants—gray, no silver—tugging urgently. His face went into her lap.

But was it even typing, what she was doing on her keyboard? Will didn't know what to call it. The proceedings went on above, and her fingers—those most remarkable digits—went on doing something, taking down what they were saying, or what they were about to say, or—Will had the strangest feeling—what they *should* say if they meant to save the world. And it was this—this complex palimpsest of the reporter's overlay—that drove Will crazy with desire for what her fingers did, as well, to him.

Nights, Peter kept plying him with expensive vodka. I hope you know what you're doing, he said. You keep this up, you know, and something is going to happen.

Something, Will thought, already is.

Later, Will would remember the drinking. He would remember Peter. He would remember a real woman lecturing on climate change above them, her years of work spread across the demonstration screen where Will had once imagined the woman he now held. Pay attention, the real woman was saying, to what happens when I manipulate the data only slightly. And if Will had only looked, he might have given pause to see the dramatic effect, less organized than chaos, like a child with tempera paints stirring them all together at once. Now, watch again, the presenter said, as I change it back. And a low murmur went through the room, but not Will, whose tongue was tracing the arc of the small woman's thigh, for this only increased the agitation, whirling the continents and seas and atmosphere more frenetically together until, finally, they spun into darkness.

Be careful, the woman in gray pressed her lips to Will's ear, there's no going back.

But before Will could turn for his kiss, Peter shuffled his papers above, straightening them with a thump at the side of his screen, and already the woman beside Will was dressing again, repairing one gray layer after another, gray piece by gray piece by gray, methodical piece.

———

Her name, she would tell him, was Helen.

But she would not tell him this until they had exhausted the small, distracted space of the computer screen and moved their lovemaking out into the ruined world. Will had planned this carefully, as if the idea were his own, making thorough preparations for their first real encounter. He found a sheltered place above the compound with a flat rock large enough for bodies; he brought pads, a blanket, a bottle of Peter's best vodka. He rehearsed with his body and tongue.

He planned words he might say, places he might touch. But on the night they finally met, full-sized in the world, the haze lifted—one last time—to reveal a sky softened by the light of half a moon and countless stars, and no amount of planning could have prepared them, or even accounted, for this.

That night their lovemaking so surpassed anything they had experienced in the computer that when they fell apart at last beneath the stars, a word came into Will's mind—*resplendent*.

A word came to the Helen—*pulchritude*.

Then she giggled—she was human, after all.

Another word—*amphibious*.

And another—*consanguinity*.

They were, Will noted with the one part of his mind that was still rational, being forced into speech even as the reporter put her hand over his mouth, her eyes imploring, making her own small sound, like a breath, like *shhh*.

Later, she said, you can touch me, here.

When the meteor shower began, it was breathtaking, really—whole segments of sky falling into blankness with no possible explanation beyond the imminent failure of the paradoxical laws by which things held together. As long as it lasted, Will buried his face in Helen's neck and refused to watch the universe betray them.

Then, almost guiltily, he let his hand reach over across the small space between them, to stroke her warm thigh, to touch the sharp ridge of her hipbone, but she shifted unexpectedly, like the thing inside him, and Will withdrew his hand.

Ok, he said, but Helen, again, placed her hand on his mouth.

No, I mean it, the word like a body between them, a star.

Now the woman put her hand over her own mouth. Everything, they both knew, was about to be changed by what Will was doing—by Will speaking.

You don't have to, you know, she said.

At first, Will said, when I was a boy . . .

No, she said, I mean it.

. . . we were the same as everyone else. My father did something for the government, my mother taught music in school.

Helen stirred. When were you ever a boy?

This was up north, during the rain. It rained and rained, so my mom would bring home instruments—oboes and violas and fiddles, and even once a tuba that took up a whole corner of my room. After a slight hesitation, Will added, my mom, you know, she really wanted me to be happy. She gave it her all. And isn't that an odd thing—the very thing she never wanted for herself?

With her back still curled toward him, Helen sat and pulled her own knees to her chest, tightening her whole body against him. When she spoke, her voice was small and sounded lost in the dry desert air, like a tiny shudder, and then nothing.

No.

But Will couldn't stop. All my dad ever wanted was for me to play baseball, like him. If I disobeyed, he took away my computer. He got better scores than me on his college entrance exams, but I got into a better college.

Helen shrugged. All fathers compete with their sons.

But I did have a fiddle. I really loved that fiddle.

See what I mean, she said, suddenly smaller and more distant. She sounded *removed.* One last time Helen tried. She turned and placed the tips of her fingers, then the flat of her palm, then the back of her wrist, to his mouth, close enough that Will could feel the pulse.

Peter says you choose your own destiny.

Then she let go and reached up to take her scarf off, for the first time fully naked before him, and as she worked at the knot at the back, her arms crooked graceful above her, Will felt a tenderness he'd never felt before and, for some reason, wanted to stop her.

No, he said, surprised by his own urgency. *You* don't have to.

But Helen had already started and by the time the scarf lay between them, revealing a baldness as smooth and exacting as Peter's, Will's tenderness had turned into a small kernel of knowledge, and for a single lucid moment it seemed the desert where they were was just another screen, and that somewhere at the heart of all the screens, like the layers of Helen's gray clothes strewn around them, lay something more consoling and closer to the truth.

Then it passed and Will sat up, hugging his own knees and turning toward the desert, pocked by tiny hummocks—mounds of rock and sand. Maybe he did play the tuba once. If he closed his eyes and tried hard, he could almost imagine that, his small boy frame dwarfed beneath the instrument, his cheeks puffed out like a chipmunk's. He could imagine chipmunks. He could remember rising in the early darkness of an autumn morning and scalding his tongue on his mother's cocoa. He could remember his fingers, numb from cold or nerves, inside his father's gloves, too big for his hands, and inside those, inside another set of gloves with the tips of the fingers cut out. He was riding in his father's pickup into another flattened world, stretched out beyond the cab of the truck—the one with the gun rack in the window—in a hurt-looking gray that would turn into a sheet of blinding white when the sun finally came up. And it would—it would be coming up.

Think of the gun, his mother had told him when she woke him that morning, the same way you think of your grandfather's fiddle. Make your father proud. You have to trust me on this.

Then his mother had kissed him and handed him the steaming mug of hot chocolate, and he had scalded his tongue, which still hurt as he waited, jammed in the cab of the big pick-up truck, to kill his first deer and become, in that way, a man.

Will was wearing the gloves that were too big for his hands, and inside the gloves he had special mittens on, mittens with the tips cut out of the fingers. Soon they would stop at the end of the road, then trudge a long way up a trail, and then they'd hunker down in a little hollow where dawn would finally come, a bruised dull light in gray autumn sky, and they'd wait, snow falling around them, clotting up their eyelashes and his father's beard, Will's already extra-long limbs knotted up into little balls of pain, waiting and waiting, until what Will would hear—the broken twig, the rustling branches, the snow turning icy and crackling where it settled on his cap.

Helen shrugged. You're not the first boy whose father ever made him shoot a gun.

But Will didn't tell Helen this, because by the time he was telling her anything the stars had started crackling overhead, and he didn't want to give her that kind of satisfaction.

I didn't say anything about guns.

Ok, Helen says, but you're going to.

But maybe his mother just cut out the tips of those gloves so he could play the tuba on the football field in the marching band. Or the fiddle in the freezing house.

Or maybe they really were batter's gloves. *Batter up. Batter up. Batter up.*

Will doesn't suppose he will ever know now because by the time he was ready to tell Helen the rest of the story the stars had started crackling overhead—crackling and going out.

What do you think it means? he said.

I know what it means. But then she didn't say anything else.

That night, the night in the desert, with the stars crackling and going out, was not the last time Will and Helen made love, but it was the one he remembered.

THEY LEFT IN THE
MIDDLE OF THE NIGHT

WILL AND LYDA

They left in the middle of the night, blacker now that so many stars had gone out, and quieter too, with the *crackling* over. That had been the saddest part, the crackling, and now the memory of it would be forever connected to the memory of the night that stretched before them, flat and luminous, the fissures they would follow, and Peter—Peter taking them away.

See, Lyda said brightly to Will as they worked their way through one of the dark compound hallways, no one is trying to stop us.

Will looked at her dully. She couldn't be more than eighteen or nineteen, a child poet with the slenderest feet and a close-fitting top that really, when he had been in school, would not have been allowed. It was nice, though—maybe she was older. They were leaving together, he could see that, but something was wrong with Will's mind, something missing, and the leaving they were doing felt strangely incomplete.

How could they just leave, like this?

It was the oddest feeling, like something inside him snapping in two, or as if the ringing that sometimes had troubled him here, *inside* his head, had slipped to the *outside*, an ominous echo that followed him all the way down the dark corridor he couldn't quite fix on the map in his mind. Peter was waiting, they both knew this, somewhere in the desert beyond. The world rang loudly, and Will's head had started to hurt—pound.

Stop, he thought, and they did, in the hallway, just there, as if he had said it.

The girl, the poet—Lyda—stopped too, but seemed anxious, in a terrible rush. Will scanned his memory, trying to parse a narrative that could hold, something more convincing than this child's insistence that Peter said it was time, that they must go, *now*.

No, really, she'd whispered when she'd come for him that night, Peter said.

Said? Will thought. Peter told him something, but not that.

Hurry, she whispered now, Will. He won't wait forever.

Will had his own sense of urgency, and a part of him wanted, obliquely, to touch her, but another part of him saw her as altogether dangerous, a stranger, and so very young. The way she showed up after all the rest of them, her night in the desert—she could be in collusion with the Foundation, a trap. But wasn't that what others said about Peter?

Stalled as he was in this inchoate moment, the hallway—this hallway—like a path in a maze he had never seen before although he'd been housed in this compound for—months? Will turned once more to the girl as if to say something—but what?—and something split inside him. Well then, he thought, we'll just have to wait it out, as though he could do that forever. It would be a little bit like death, this waiting, a thought that somehow calmed him without stirring any curiosity as to what in the world they might be waiting for.

A part of Will's mind knew it was his idea, to slip away with Peter, to escape. They'd planned it together, it was what they all wanted—to ditch the Foundation, nab a van, and take one last journey out into the world, an idea—a plan—that had worked its way into their consciousness and left little deposits of desire inside them, like spores. Now he was choking with them. For if Will had lost his drive to intervene—if he no longer saw himself burying time capsules or stuffing notes in interplanetary bottles or tagging crumbling walls of dying freeways, making his mark—he did want to be there when the world ended. He wanted to watch—to *see*.

And Peter had promised—he had *promised*—to take them. He had stolen a Ranger. He had water, a map. Then he had winked: not *that* kind of map.

From here to there, he'd said, and off we go.

In this way, Will knew, they had planned and plotted and waited for this exact moment, and now it was here. They had been clever, discreet. Earlier that same evening, like always, they'd taken dinner with the others. And then all the usual time-passing activities—drinks, word games and numerical problems, debates over data or hypotheses, the nightly wagers—they had done these too. Will gave himself the pleasure of one final bet on how long before the southern hemisphere went dark, and Lyda read a poem about water. Then the soft settling all over the compound, the murmurs and sighs that preceded sleep, the tamping down of everything—breath itself—until *quiet*, and then they had slipped out of their luxury beds and into the muted hallways. They were going and soon they'd be gone.

All this felt so precise and particular in Will's mind.

But then the split, as though he'd forgotten something crucial without which he could not—could never—leave. Stalled in mid-flight, like a glitch, Will spread one hand against the coolness of the wall and felt so helpless.

Come on, Will, Lyda said, her voice barely more than a whisper, hurry.

Both knew what would happen if they were caught; both knew if they waited too long, the desert would kill them by day. And Peter was out there, waiting for them: how long would Peter wait? But Will wasn't budging. In the dark hallway, heavy with the smell of curing concrete and something lemony, like wax, he'd planted his feet in a place that was nowhere at all.

Will, Lyda said again, more gently, there isn't much time.

But even as she said this they both felt themselves fighting off the other, the corollary thought: *time for what?* Leaving felt both dangerous and sad.

And somehow inevitable.

In that exact moment Will's will collapsed entirely within him and was replaced by another will rising up against it. All around, the corridors, flat and distorted, seemed to have aborted their small attempt at leaving, leading them somehow not out, but deeper inside—or *between* things. And while at first he had reached out to the wall for steadiness, now the dizziness was clearly coming from it, as if, if he just pressed a little harder, his hand would pass through the surface of the wall into—or *nothing* at all. Looking at his hand against the new, white plaster, it seemed to Will the hand was holding the wall up, holding the wall—*this* wall—together.

And then a cool liquid feeling passed through him, and he smiled a smile of infinite resolve.

Lyda took his hand and tugged, but she didn't look right either. Around them, corridors floated in their maze, leaving Will immobilized by the thing—the one thing, an unyielding force against the force of Peter—he had to do before he could go.

Peter's waiting, Lyda urged. If you want out, we have to go *now*.

The words spilled around him in a barely effectual whisper, a natter of gnat, as Will thought, *we are already out.* It was a thought that would disappear almost as soon as he had it, but for the moment it was clear and unambiguous, but: *where did they keep her at night?*

And then the door came. It came in the manner of all doors in dreams—but this wasn't a dream, *something else*—drifting down the long corridor and all the way up to where Will had stalled, holding the world together with the flat of his hand. It came as if with a will of its own, but there was something wrong with it—too narrow, too blue, too dimensionless—and when Will tried to open it, it did not budge. But how could that be, when it had come for them?

Will tried again, pulling and pushing. Not a big man, but yet strong, he used all his force. He dug in with his feet for leverage, and he pulled and pulled, with something both so physical and poignant in his effort that Lyda found it hard to watch. But nothing Will did, no force he exerted or key or code he tried, produced any response in the door, until he gave up and stepped back from the door, using the keen part of his mind simply to will it to open. This required no physical but only mental effort, an effect Will only distantly recognized as the door swung noiselessly wide like a hand in a gesture of welcome.

And then he stepped into the seminar room where the great diaphanous screen was already unfurling.

Hey, and now Lyda sounded angry. We don't have time for this.

But Will, who couldn't really hear her, was nothing now but steadfast beside the table that was not a stone but that nonetheless contained prodigious heat. Here, a strange thought came to him: *it wasn't real time anyway,* more just the idea of the time of the screen coming down, of the woman in gray in the lower left corner, of him waiting only for enough of her body to emerge that he could reach his hand out in a pale imitation of a real hand to part the filmy layer of the screen and pull the woman out.

Behind them, solid and completely corporeal, Lyda watched without judgment as the woman expanded in space. She was smaller than normal, with a bland countenance and shapely head, bald beneath her gray silk scarf. Another one, Lyda thought, but what she said, after a decent pause, was, ok. Then, not unkindly, you can't go in those. And she turned to rummage in her pack until she found a gray sweatshirt and pants, which she tossed, also not unkindly, to the woman, saying, please hurry, we don't have much time.

Moments later, the three of them were running out across the grounds of the compound, the fleet barefooted woman in gray leading the way and Lyda and Will jogging heavily behind, weighted down with small packs and the parrot in a cage shaped like a bell. They wore thin, wicking garments and light running shoes but, made clumsy by the things they carried, stumbled along the rocky ground while the woman in gray ran on ahead, swift and light and seeming to hover just a hair above the earth, toward where Peter was waiting beside a Ranger—for them.

HELEN

Helen wants not to hover. More than anything, she wants her feet to go all the way to the earth, touch the dirt there like Will's and Lyda's, sending up little puffs of chemical laden dust and making small sounds—*boom, boom, boom*. Helen wants to be subject, like them, to gravity, but in her mind, there's a split that divides each moment of running—step by step—into a separate moment of hovering, along with the knowledge that no matter how closely she attaches herself to it, there will always be another layer above, beneath—a layer, she knows, and a gap—the gap between moments, consciousness, body, earth. And this—this impossible suspension—has been going ever since she left the courtroom with Peter in a kind of perpetual division, each moment separated from the moment before and after, each defined by the space that surrounds it, or as if she has entered her own moment of transcription where things can fold seamlessly together and fully be.

In fact, she imagines, it could be a state of grace, although it doesn't feel like that—not yet, anyway. Something more has to happen first.

Now, as she runs, she lifts one hand to the crown of her dusty head and tries to stop, with her singular touch, the circular thinking that begins and ends exactly here and that includes, before the screen and the man who pulled her from it, the trial, the defendant, his gaze, and before even that, Remainders, the rabbit, the lettuce, the father, the heart-wrenching sounds of the dying of the world. It's not a line but a circle, and it's cumulative, layer after layer.

But the thinking goes on and on, and after a time, the running stops instead, as Helen's pulled up short by the curious thought: she could come to like it.

Helen looks down at her hands: what would happen if she were to clap them, as if to call out, *enough, enough of this for you*. But because she also understands that nothing she can do will change the course of what is going to

155

happen now—will restore the world to what it was before Peter lured her into his portal and then, with a barely discernible shift in her consciousness, out into *this*, she does nothing. Her hands do not clap. They hang at her sides. She just stands there instead, hardly even breathing, as the others catch up and she whispers, it's just over the hill now, and then we can go.

Go where, no one thinks. They can't think this because it has already happened that for them there remains just the span of this one, long night, by the end of which there will be stars, or not. Each, in her own way, knows this. And even if the morning finds them wandering lost and alone in the desert without water, they will still have the solace of having left. Lyda is so young it can't mean yet to her what it means to the others—the going. But it means—and looking at her now, Helen sees this—something else, like falling.

In this moment, with the Foundation Ranger waiting just over the hill and the other two people beside her—new people, still flush from running—the wind in Lyda's hair, the earth thumping soundly beneath Will's feet, their conjoined breath—Helen feels more unsettled than at any time since the day her father sent her off to camp and said—his parting words—ok kiddo, you're on your own now, but you should really do something about that hair.

The hair fell out, clump after clump. Later, the noise came in.

It was a curse, Helen saw now, to be sensitive. But hadn't she always felt like this?

There were things she could still remember from *before*. She could remember her mother's hairbrush that was made from the actual bristles of boars, with bits of straw-colored hair caught in its teeth, remnants of her mother's body. She could remember a ring, a deep green stone anchored by four small diamonds that was very, very old. She could remember the shape of her mother's shoulders, the tuneless humming as she'd walked away—but that, Helen knew, was the memory capsule, still working in her. For how could she remember that, when she had been so young?

And of course she remembered her father's tomatoes. Sometimes it just seemed sad, him and his backyard tomatoes, year after year, the digging, the watering, the initial hopefulness, as though he somehow believed if he could produce even one vine that did not wither before the fruit grew plump and plentiful, where hummingbirds swarmed—he could make it up to her, the lack of a mother, who had only ever wanted to protect her. But no place in the next part of the history of the world was going to be safe, and the tomatoes did die, and Helen's mother did what she did, and all her father ever grew successfully was lettuce. He grew it and the rabbit ate it and he went on watering his failed tomatoes long after they had shrivelled and collapsed. In the wind the dried stalks rustled, the first of Helen's sounds.

If only Helen's father had not given up so soon, if he'd tasted even one of the few small tomatoes that actually did grow (she had and they were sweet), however misshapen or splotched, maybe her own life would be different. Helen did not go so far as to think her adaptation might have failed or that he might even have allowed her to have it reversed (there were ways to do that now), but maybe she'd have ended up in another, more youthful boarding house, full of people with futures and plans. Maybe she'd have gotten farther in the pull-down training menu, well beyond c to maybe "mechanic," "pugilist," "solicitor." She might have been a writer, like Lyda.

Reporting hadn't been that bad, though, for a job. It was ok, until Peter. Even Peter was ok, but seeing him now, in the desert, waiting to herd them together into the air-conditioned comfort of the stolen Ranger, Helen wonders what she's missed. There's a word that might help, if she could only call it up. It's floating out there just beyond her reach of mind, elusive in that space between being and not-being that constitutes, for her, a split of consciousness. And then it comes to her.

Apart, she thinks. A man *apart*.

It's amazing, Peter says, how great the capacity for human adaptation really is. You don't know, you can't have any idea, Peter says.

But of course Helen can. And they both know it.

Maybe it's not so long since he led her from the courtroom, down the vertical walls of the building and out through the trees. Not so long, anyway, as all those years when he'd eluded infrared detection before coming out— impossibly—whole. But if everyone else in the world found the idea of him loathsome, Helen, at least, appreciated how his body so fitted the dimensions of the space it occupied as to create a node of perfect silence. Wherever Peter was, no sound leaked out, none at all, although sometimes, Helen noticed, there was light. How beautiful he is, Helen sees now, and again the brainy light that fills his head, brightest in the back where his adaptation has attached, like a tiny jewel or decoration—or a tattoo.

No, not just beautiful—powerful—a powerful beauty.

And suddenly the night and the valley and the earth beneath their feet seem tenuous as never before, anchored by the two southern mountains—one white, one black—each the negative image of the other.

For now Helen remembers everything at once—how in the middle of the trial, her hands, without warning, had gone heavy and inert in an uncanny interruption that was not so much a glitch as a pause and that affected everyone at once. A lawyer gesticulated mid-air, another fiercely frowned. And Helen's hands—her own never still hands—lay motionless before her, stalled in the courtroom stripped of sound and motion and as if without a will of their own. Only Peter moved, and he moved like water, letting loose his restraints and rising from his plexi dome to release her, forever—to choose her, forever. Helen remembers his smile, tender and benign, just before he let loose his second wave of virus, the one that piggybacked on her own courtroom transcripts to delete all trace and memory of them.

And then they were gone.

Ok? he seemed to say, like a boy who had asked for a dance.

And now he waits at the cab of the Ranger, watching them approach—Helen, hovering, Will and Lyda—the one who threw the baggy clothes at her and the other who pulled her from inside the machine—cumbersome and lumbering, but they'll do. Will looks sturdy enough—stable—his edges finite, grounded. And Lyda is good with words. They'll both do. They are properly aligned. They fill up their spaces, not as well, as fully, as Peter but enough.

But yet, how human they look, Helen thinks with a shock of recognition, how terribly vulnerable.

THE RANGER

They drive a long time in the air-conditioned comfort of the Foundation Ranger, high above the crusted surface of the earth. They drive in silence, each avoiding the other, the world going by mile after mile on the outside, while on the inside, it is cool and muffled, like sleep. Maybe, Will thinks vaguely, Lyda's fissure will be finite. Or maybe, Peter will let him drive. Will would like that—he'd head south, toward the white mountain. He'd get them out of here.

In cup holders to the side of each seat, blue water bottles glisten—one each, and maybe some stray ones in the back. Ahead, the two bald heads rise like moons from the headrests, and in the wells between seats, two GPS modules, apparently scrambled. From time to time, Will fidgets with his, but the data remains a garbled sludge of code.

Leave it alone, Helen says at last. You can't fix it now.

Shush, Peter warns.

They drive and drive. Around them, the earth breaks and folds, the reds and ochres of it washed gray in the moonlight.

Once, long ago, she and Will had gone out together. They'd taken a Ranger—maybe this very one—and driven all the way to dunes made of ash. Helen remembers this now, remembers following him up the silky dune, digging her feet in as hard as she could to make the powdery substance from deep inside the earth fall away from her as it did from him, the whole universe shifting around him. But no, not a mark, not a single print, as if her feet had found the exact steps of his, fitting herself to them—or as if she had no mass at all.

And on that other, final night, when the stars started crackling, Helen hadn't wanted to leave. Lie here, she had thought, with me, and it won't take long. Freedom is as close as your nearest major vein. For this was still the kind of thing that could break Helen's heart—the damp crust of sand at Will's eyelids, the clicking of his teeth when he bent to kiss her, data, the thought of his bones, burnished by sun, cupped in the low bowl of this lethal place.

But now the driving seems endless, as though the valley they had once crossed on foot or in an hour were somehow expanding, the lip of its edge receding forever ahead as, all around them, a subtle darkness pulls and pushes.

Peter says that distances in the desert are deceptive.

A low humming runs through the van.

When the Ranger finally does get hung up on the bottom of a wash, they're not even halfway out.

But how can that be?

Lyda does not think at first that this is *her* wash—it's not bottomless after all, but in fact has the broad floor they are driving along now. It's been a long time—eons, maybe—since water ran through here, and the rocks that have settled are luminous and massive enough that when Peter runs the Ranger into them, they don't budge.

Want me to drive? Will offers.

But Peter says nothing, just keeps his eye ahead, driving ever deeper into what is beginning to seem more like a gorge until, finally, there's a crunching, a hapless ratcheting back and forth, followed by a shuddering stillness that subsides only slowly into the eerie recognition that this is where he's been taking them all along.

Will lets out a long, low whistle, ok.

Oh Peter, Lyda says, not again—you promised.

On the inside of the van, she presses her face against a window that's already losing the last trace of air conditioning, even as Helen reaches back to pat her hand, don't worry. Will considers the flank of the gorge rising high on either side, the moon a white round hovering above and unimaginably far away. Both of the women are pale and small, and in the driver's seat, Peter hasn't moved, hasn't shifted his hands on the steering wheel or offered reassurance or even, Will thinks bleakly, tried reverse.

I thought you said, he says, you knew what you were doing. I thought you had a plan.

Peter half turns toward Will, a strange, almost quizzical expression on his face, then blinks and steps out of the car, letting in a blast of air so hot and desiccated that even Helen lays her forehead, like Lyda, against the last cool remnants of window as though to drink it in, before she, too, gets out of the van to join Peter.

We're going to have to ditch the Ranger, and this time he really is talking, and go. The words, as smooth and fixed as stones, seem to have been here all along, just waiting for Peter to say them. There used to be a road here, huh.

You don't have to do this for me, Helen says, as now Will emerges, dishevelled and dazed, and starts to stretch his amazing—his corporeal—body. Do it for them.

The air tastes rotten, this muted world a jagged and unlikely place for four such paths to have crossed, but it seems to Helen now that she has known this all along—known it *all*—and as each part of this long night's *before* and *after* plays itself out, she welcomes it with a kind of recognition. Already everything hurts—her head, her body, her skin, but Peter looks like things are turning out ok.

You get the bird, he tells Lyda, suddenly in charge again. Will, water.

Then he turns to Helen, brushing his hand lightly over her head to pull the scarf off, and something passes between them.

You too—it's time. Let's go.

Behind them, some grumbling, from Lyda, bent over in the van and rummaging for something in the darkness, and Will is bent over her, too, speaking so softly that no one—not even Helen—can hear. But seeing her white leg stretched out behind her, something stirs inside Helen, even before Will puts his hand on Lyda's thigh, just where the muscle flexes.

Then, like that, Lyda finds the shoe she's looking for, and puts it on, and ties it, and things settle back into place.

Where are we anyway, she calls out, reaching back in for the birdcage and shaking her head a bit, as if to clear it—wash, socks, bird.

This isn't my wash, she says. My wash went on forever.

But Lyda's not so sure anymore, for it seems to her the wash is deepening and widening as she speaks, but what does it matter? Everyone is moving now, springing back into action, efficiency itself, and no one is listening to her.

Peter, too, is moving forward—moving all of them forward—already striding fast across the bottom of the bottomless wash—while Will stuffs water bottles into his knapsack, and Helen hovers between them. Inside the cage, the blue parrot squawks, as Lyda clasps its handle, worn and burnished like bones, to pull it out and come along.

Come along, Lyda. Come here, come here.

But it's heavy and it's awkward, and if only Lyda had a little more time, although already they are walking along the same path—Peter, then Helen, then Will, and finally her with the bird in its cage and the sounds of their footsteps crunching along a little bit after them. Lyda's glad she found her shoes, it's so rocky where they are, following Peter down the wash that seems deeper now than it seemed only moments before—a deepening wash that bends and curves as it follows the ancient path of water. From time to time, Peter calls something back, but no one can hear him because of the bell of silence that has closed over the world. They can't hear—only Helen can hear, but Helen can't sort the words out—but after a while they do begin to see where Peter is headed—what looks like a high, loose jumble of rocks and, above that, a shelf and a hole in the earth at the end of the endless wash.

Suddenly Helen does something strange—an impulse—and turns to cross back over the part of the desert she has already traversed, going not forward, toward Peter and Will, but backward, toward Lyda, who is trailing the others a bit because of the bird and its cage.

No, yes, wait, the words spill loose from her mouth like pieces of light.

Well now, she says, when she gets back to where Lyda is still moving forward.

And then she takes Lyda's hand—the other hand, the one without the birdcage in it—a simple enough gesture and the lightest of touch, but it stops them both.

Head for the lava tube, Will shouts back, each of his steps taking him farther away. We'll meet you at the lava tube.

And then he's running to catch up to Peter, who is moving fast now, leaving them all behind.

But that's ok—Helen's in no hurry. Lyda's got her shoes on and they can take their time. That's all that's left for them now, is time. Maybe Helen should know how much that is, but Helen's just a conduit, a thread through which everything passes. And what she's doing now—helping Lyda—isn't prescience anyway, but common decency.

That birdcage sure looks heavy.

A little rest won't hurt.

And so Helen, still holding Lyda's hand, leads her with the bird and its cage shaped like a bell away from the trail Peter has made to the level lip of a rock, like a table or a bench, on which they will sit for a while, resting, and looking like nothing so much as two women exchanging gentle female gossip.

Ahead, Peter calls out again—encouragement or exhortation.

But seated side-by-side on the rock, the women don't pay any attention, for this is what the future is, stretching out before them like a dream, and Lyda starts to laugh.

Stranded again, she giggles. Haven't I been here before?

At first, she says, it didn't seem so, but oh, she tries to tell Helen, it *feels* the same—not *like* the last time, but the *same* as the last time, exactly the same. Except for the wash. The last time, we were on the top, up above—but now look at us, we are here on the bottom.

Helen wishes there were an easier way, but instead she just uses one of her hands—her long-fingered hands—to brush the hair out of Lyda's eyes—so much messy hair. Above, Helen knows, Peter's already waiting at the hole in the earth that might be a lava tube or burrow, and even though she knows it won't, Helen can't help but wish that this moment will last, just go on and on until it doesn't anymore.

But no.

Hurry, Peter urges them forward—*hurry, hurry.*

Oh, but what is the rush—they are almost there. Or, she thinks, giggling like Lyda, *here*—they are almost here.

Helen rather likes the idea, although it solves nothing.

Well, that's where he wants them to go now—up and into the cool darkness of the hole in the earth that looks like a tube or a burrow, but could be a portal.

Still, Helen puts the moment of leaving—of finally leaving—wrapping one whole arm around the other woman's—around Lyda's—shoulders and quietly reflecting on the awful beauty of the place. Things will be different by day, she knows, and if they don't do something now, it will catch up to them, what they are leaving. She'd like to be able to offer some comfort to Lyda, but knowing her to be wholly human, imagines that this—just their two bodies touching and breathing right next to each other—is going to be the best she can do. Maybe just squeeze these heartbreaking bones a little closer to her own, maybe lay her head on Lyda's shoulder.

But when she does, it is Lyda who says, don't worry—Peter knows what he's doing.

And when Helen says nothing, Lyda sighs. It's what I want too, you know—it's what I've always wanted.

Come on, come here, Peter calls. Just for the day, to get out of the sun. Come quickly—it's almost dawn.

Looking up, they can see that Will has already disappeared into the opening of the earth, but Peter continues to wait for them there, urging them on, until at last Lyda sighs and rises.

It's not so far away, she says. And anyway, I don't think it's even a real hole in the earth—more just the idea of a hole in the earth.

I suppose, Helen says.

There's just one last thing, Lyda says even as a single shared image passes between them, and she kneels to open the cage and let the bird out.

THE HOLE IN THE EARTH

Above, Peter is both there and not there, waiting and not waiting for them, but Lyda is so tired by now that she lets herself slip from the outside of the earth through the hole to its inside without even noticing the way their little trek across the wash—which had seemed to take much longer and to have covered so much greater an expanse than the distance that remained between them and Peter—could only lead, with a kind of looping logic, to where it ended—*here, now*—in a place that was no place at all.

Maybe what Lyda will remember of this moment, this place, will be its flickering. It really is flickering, but not with light—something else.

Or she'll remember Will's words—no one will find us here.

Or nothing—Helen's hand, Peter's breath where he waits and not waits in the conduit that transects the world.

But it will be a long time before she remembers any of this, and at first, where they end up will seem like what she thinks it is: the opening to an old lava tube on a rise above a wash that never was endless at all but just an ordinary wash, with igneous rocks. These tubes can go on for miles, Lyda knows, a secret geography Indians once used to hide from their enemies or give birth. They are old, these tubes, as old as the earth, but it doesn't look old here, on the inside, but instead the pale gray of fresh, new ash.

Is this, Lyda wonders, what it's like to fall?

Then, for the longest time, just nothing—as if the tube is a blotter that soaks up everything, consciousness, even time, deleting it not just from her memory, and presumably Will's, but also from the world itself. We are going, she thinks, and now we are gone.

Still, she struggles not to disappear into the blankness of this moment—to persist, to cohere—until the last thing she remembers is the last thing she wants to admit: the other woman waiting in what looks to be a hole in the earth and holding something white in her hands with a look of acceptance, like grace, about her.

I'm not going to hurt you, she says, helping Lyda lie down in the rocks.

This means, Lyda thinks.

But how did they *get* here?

I'm not going to hurt you—pulling her *inside*, a dizzying feeling. For, in fact, it was Helen who had pulled her from the outside to the inside, from before to after, from then to now. Or—Lyda's hands are covered with a fine gray ash— did she pull herself?

But still there is Helen with the cloth in her hands that she uses to cleanse Lydan's hands. Her own hand is warm, warmer than it was when they were outside, but it doesn't feel so much like a hand anymore.

Come, she says, lie back, as she begins to wipe the rest of Lyda slowly with the same cloth, cleaning the outside off of her. It's gentle, the way she does it, slow, very slow with the warm, white cloth—up Lyda's legs and around to the small of her back, then between her breasts, then the breasts themselves—one breast, then the other—wiping Lyda clean. And it's so calming, so completely lulling that Lyda is only half aware of Peter, behind them, watching, and of Will, exhausted, already asleep. And then, she can't be sure because of the flickering and also the strange feeling in her own body—a feeling, she may later describe as her body, her own body, being rendered insubstantial, living cells pulled, cell by cell, apart, molecule by molecule, and the spaces between them filling up with nothing at all, a feeling of passage—but in her half awareness that they are not alone, Lyda sees that Peter is no longer watching her, but has turned his attention to the other body that lies, like hers, at rest among the rocks and above which Peter holds something white—another cloth—that he raises, one time, to his forehead, before beginning the ablutions on Will.

Inside the tube it is warm and dusty but smells sweet, like herbs—basil or lavender, maybe manzanita—a beautiful word, but—a shrub? Peter works on Will, just as Helen works on Lyda, both pleasant and unpleasant, and on one wall Lyda can make out some red markings—a hand, or a fox, or a bird—where long ago a man had put his hand. He had dipped his hand in something red—pulped berries, blood—and placed it on the wall. But on the other wall, what looks to be an instrument panel of some kind, and from somewhere that seems so far away, water—a creek or a spring, water falling over rocks inside the earth.

And Lyda's falling too.

From deep inside Helen's body, a steady thrumming, and this is what Lyda pays attention to—all she pays attention to—as Helen finishes work on her body and turns to her head. It's a thrumming that contains all the sound in the world, like Lyda's box. But no, it's not from Helen but the place itself, the tube where they are hiding, like the Indians before. First her forehead, then her cheeks, her chin. Helen works smoothly, efficiently, her hands like separate things, wiping, cleaning each speck of dirt, each open pore. But there is so much hair, momentarily, she hesitates: what is she to do with all this hair?

Blindly, Helen's fingers probe the back of Lyda's head.

Let me help you, Lyda says, lifting her hair up and away from her neck.

Let me help you, Helen says, finding the place just behind the left ear and wiping it clean. Lyda can feel Helen's gentle fingers probing, tracing each rough stitch, the thick scars that have formed around them, the crude illicit lump of her device.

Shh, Helen says, wiping, let me.

Lyda, like Will, almost asleep now, only catches a glimpse of the tiny gleaming scissors, so tiny that they almost disappear in Helen's hand, but she can hear them, far away, as Helen keeps on working, deftly from behind so that Lyda cannot see but only hear, only feel the snipping and wiping, snipping and wiping the blood away. At the base of Lyda's head, a kind of numbness and the sensation of tugging, or pulling, but it doesn't really hurt, just the sound of it unpleasant as the other woman works: *one stitch, two.*

Lie still, Helen says kindly above her, and I'll try not to hurt you.

That old thing never worked right anyway, but the words come out wrong, all garbled, and then a sudden rush as Helen pries the mechanism out and fills the empty space with something both cool and hot, something liquid and solid, something stabilizing and—*not.*

THE MOST PERFECT
EGG IN THE WORLD

THEN LYDA FEELS terribly sad and as though she were dreaming—
but maybe this is the real part—and then she's in a city, and it's raining—
raining—hard, and there's a bird—a blue parrot—on her shoulder, and two
wet cars shining before her. One of the cars is a sleek black sedan and the other
a little red hump of a car with new-smelling vinyl upholstery and sparkling
windows. Dressed in jeans and an oversized striped, wool pullover sweater,
raveling a bit at the hem, Lyda stands there in the rain, looking at the cars, and
does not know when she has seen anything quite so beautiful before.

HellO, Lyda, the bird squawks, pecking a little at her head. HellO, Choose.
Choose, One.

Looking more closely, Lyda sees that the black sedan has soft leather upholstery
and seems to be a new, entry-level luxury model—a manly car. The smell of the
leather, buttery and rich, drifts out into the smell of the rain.

If not now, the bird says, when?

Then it makes a sound like a vacuum cleaner or a coffee grinder, a sound
from the past that makes Lyda smile, while a sudden fierce longing passes
through and out of her, as though she were a sieve.

Lyda will stand there in the rain looking at the cars for a long time: one car
red, one car black. At the back of her head, a numb spot where her memory
once was.

Come on, the bird says. Choose, let's go.

In that moment, Lyda recognizes herself as a young woman, hardly even a woman, just a girl coming out of adolescence, with an entire life—years and years—spread out ahead. But as she imagines the spread of that many years, Lyda feels none of the ordinary hopefulness of youth but something flat and grim, for what kind of future could that be?

The bird, she thinks for no reason, might as well be a rabbit.

Then she slips seamlessly inside the red car, which fits snugly around her, and wiping the water from her face, brushes her wet hair back with a strange, nostalgic longing but nothing to fill it. In a minute, she tells herself gamely, she will look for a map. Well, she thinks, not now, but in the moment after now, she will turn on the car and blast the heat, and this will dry out her socks.

That isn't all she knows, but for the moment it's enough.

The congestion, though, is terrible, as Lyda steers the car south through narrow streets in the old inner city where mobs of people throng among colorful tents on either side of the street hawking cheap goods. Off the awnings of the tents rainwater streams on desperate bargain-hunters driving deals for coveted items—basketballs, or paring knives, or fake Armani shirts in subtle colors—but why would anybody horde fake Armani suits?

Forced to stop at every intersection and often in the middle of the block to let people cross, Lyda wonders if there's something going on, something she should know about—an event or a crisis—about to take place or already over. This thought brings a bright, mineral taste to her mouth, her throat constricting with something bitter, like tears, and then, as the crowd surges forcefully around the small car, fear. Somehow, her hand finds the horn, her foot the gas pedal, and the car moves forward, parting the people around it.

Let's go, the bird squawks from the top of Lyda's headrest, let's go—GO—its voice as familiar as that of someone with whom Lyda had once been intimate.

The red car like a bubble responds to her commands—but when has she ever learned to drive?—floating through the now thinning crowds and into a vacant business area with red-lettered signs in a language she cannot identify and a pungent smell of spice mixed with wet asphalt. There aren't very many people out here, but those that are carry flowered umbrellas and wear clear galoshes to keep their feet dry, Lyda notes with some small bit of envy. The engine of the small car has heated up now, and she can feel the blast of hot air on her own feet, but her socks are thick—possibly wool, or some cotton/wool blend—and will take a long time to dry out, so she works her sneakers off at the next stop sign and kicks them over to the passenger's footwell, provoking a sudden surge of a feeling like loneliness. Well, she's alone anyway, that much is certain, but if there were someone there beside her, who would it be?

Lyda shrugs and keeps on driving, heading deliberately south into streets that open out around neighborhoods of small, wood frame houses, anchored by commercial pods—endless clusters of drugstores, dry cleaners, and beauty supply stores, with the occasional fish market or specialty cheese store. Although most of these stores seem deserted, Lyda fights off a little pang of hunger, or not really hunger so much as an emptiness she cannot place.

Lyda really can't tell if she feels cold either, but the clothes she is wearing—clothes for keeping warm in harsh weather—don't feel right somehow, as if she has been dressed in someone else's things. She takes a deep breath and tries to remember what she would be wearing if she were wearing clothes that would feel like her own, but the only recollection she can manage is a fragment—less than a fragment, just a scrap color that might have come from a dress, or a skirt, or even a fine-gauge knit sweater, the color somewhere between avocado and chartreuse. Lyda takes those two words—*avocado* and *chartreuse*—and rolls them around in her consciousness like a sweet, hard candy in her mouth, realizing she can do this with any number of words and that doing so might help her focus, so she starts in on a long list in her head—*albatross, cinnamon, refraction, highrise*—but no, that doesn't work either.

And then even the commercial pods have disappeared, and Lyda and the parrot and the red car are sailing out onto the open road and, one by one, Lyda pulls off her wet socks with her toes and kicks them over, too, with the shoes. Far below the gutted highway, waves crash on gnarled rocks, quickening her spirits, as she wriggles her toes in the blast of hot air and hums a low tune, the bird joining in, following along with regular percussive blats and bleats.

GO, GO, GO, GO, GO, the bird squawks.

Go, Lyda says. Ok, we're going.

Hours later Lyda pulls out to a vista point, below which—far below—gray ocean waves pounds against the rocky cliffs and has a memory.

She can feel it coming, low and charged, as it works its slow and damaged way from somewhere deep inside her and into her numbed cerebral cortex, though it seems paradoxically to originate *elsewhere*, and as it rises in her Lyda finds herself walking out along a trail to the lip of the bluff where she sits on a bench staring down at the water far below.

And then it hits full on, as vivid and immediate as if it were happening all over again.

The rain has slowed to a drizzle.

The memory goes like this: Lyda's father is standing in an open doorway, his red hands hanging like meat at his side, like little, fleshy animals, Lyda thinks. If they move, she'll run. There's not so much room for running in the apartment, but she can dart around him if she needs to. The hands aren't moving yet, but they could. At any moment, her father's hands could start to move, and when they do, that's when she'll dart around him—one side or the other, she'll slip past him through the door to where her mother will be waiting on the sofa and everything is white except where the windows let the outside in. Sometimes, it's hard to see her mother for all the whiteness of the room, and the sofa, and her mother's dress and scarf that render her, sometimes, indistinguishable from the rest of the whiteness. Only the small pinched face floats visible above. Then, a white arm rises, beckoning to Lyda to nestle there beside her. As though that would change things.

Come, her mother seems to say, but there is no sound.

By comparison, Lyda's father, who says nothing, makes so much noise—his breathing, his hands clenching and unclenching with little sweaty pops. Lyda's mother's mouth opens again, her tongue flapping inside, but it's just pathetic, her silent flapping. Lyda, not quite trapped on the other side of the open doorway: should she dart or wait?

But then all the fury drains out of her father at once, his hands going limp at his sides.

But our brains, her mother is trying to say—somehow Lyda knows this, even though no sound comes out—have been expanding, haven't they? All this sacrifice is going to be worth it. Again, she waves vaguely to Lyda, a funny little smile on her face. Lyda, sweetie, come.

If only there were sound, Lyda thinks, turning away from them both to crawl into her box. Inside her box, Lyda does not have to think about any of this, not her mother's vacuous smile, not the gluttonous animal hands at the sides of her father's thick thighs. Inside the box, the world is capacious and warm, with a heat that exceeds normal heat. Inside the box, Lyda is safe.

Upholstered with a lush and satiny fabric and large enough for Lyda, the box is clearly not what her mother always calls it in her tight determined voice—she calls it Lyda's *toy* chest. And why not? That's what Lyda wants. Lyda is just a little girl and little girls want toys, no matter where they come from or if the prior child—the one who had lived here before and to whom the box once had belonged—were a boy or a girl, if the toys had been soft and cuddly or hard and complicated, with wheels—none of that would have mattered, if there had been toys. But the box had been empty and smelled nasty, of mothballs, and there were dead bugs in its corners, such that no one could ever again call it what it really was—a *hope* chest.

Lyda ate the bugs. They were crunchy. She made the box be what her mother called it. She put things in it—pillows, another small box for treasures, one laceless shoe that closed up just by pressing the two sides of it together, and she crawled *inside* it, just as she crawls inside it now, to be safe.

The miracle of the box is that it never gets stuffy or cramped. Also, when she is inside it she can hear things—cats crying down the street, motors revving up from when there were cars, her own mother's fretful voice. Inside the box, she can want things: toys, a pet, a playmate, the sky to stop dropping the things it drops, a mother's protection and love. No one can stop the want coming out of her there, inside the box.

Now, in her memory, it's coming out again, gutting her like a fish, a memory of desire.

When it clears and Lyda looks up, she is startled to see a whole small family dressed in bright fleece just getting out of a dun-colored van parked now beside her little red car. The orange fleece father is pointing out something to a blue fleece boy, something far away, across the ocean—a boat, perhaps, or the spout of a whale—but the boy, only half attending, bends to pick up a rock instead, and curls his body into a taut s just before snapping it open in the blur of boyish movement with which he hurls the stone out toward where his father is pointing.

Did I hit it? he cries. I bet I hit it.

Behind him, the features of the mother's watching face realign themselves briefly with something both rueful and tender, but then the baby—a big baby of indeterminate gender and age—starts to fuss, and the mother, looking exhausted, heads off toward the bench Lyda has just left. When they pass each other on the path, each momentarily avoids the other's gaze before turning back, as one, to greet the other shyly.

I can't see, the boy whines on the bluff. But I bet I hit it.

There, the father insists, *there.*

There, there, the mother coos to the baby, who might be a toddler already, bundled up in its little, tie-dyed fleece sack.

Well, Lyda thinks, noticing a campground back behind the vista point, she might as well sleep here for the night.

But it's an old campground, dark and wet, with some of the towering trees that grow all around between the sites and among the dense thickets of invasive undergrowth still seeming to be alive. A few, anyway, just at the top where their crowns meet the sky, maybe some green needles, a bit of sticky sap still oozing out.

Except for the little fleece family and Lyda, no one else is around—not even a ranger or host—and Lyda has to fight off that feeling again, not quite of loneliness but maybe solitude. It's a strong, unsettling feeling that brings the bitter thing to her throat again, and maybe, she thinks, she should just join up with the colorful fleece family, or at least share their good-smelling dinner cooking on the fire they built. How did they do that, she wonders, when the wood is so wet—although, of course, on the inside, it is dead.

Lyda thinks about the deadness of the wood, and realizing that no matter how hungry she is, there's nothing she can say to explain herself—who she is or how she even got there—and so she rummages around in the car until she finds some stale mints and an old power bar with nuts, enough to tide her over. Then she sits in the back seat out of the rain, munching on her too-sweet food and listening to the sounds of the fleece family settling in for the night—cleaning up their dinner, then tamping down the fire, the bedtime story demands, the dad asking and the mom refusing as, from the ocean, a new storm howls in heavy with rain.

Sometime later in the night when the storm hits hard, Lyda and the fleece mom will both seek shelter in the women's bathroom, which at least has a roof and a door. Outside, the ocean will pound, the rain will splatter, the wind will shriek. But on the inside, there's a kind of muted peace and at least they will be dry enough, if shy at the first, each of them going about their business as if the other were not there.

Then one says, some night.

And the other, I'll say.

And soon they will be huddled, hip-to-hip, on the cold concrete floor, exchanging female confidences.

I'm not kidding, the mom will say, tucking the insatiable baby up underneath her green fleece to nurse—the last words I remember saying before my waters broke were: this baby better not be born today. And then, well—babies, you know, have impeccable timing.

When the mom says this, Lyda feels something, a tiny flutter—or maybe just the idea of one—stirring deep inside her, but as soon as it comes, it is gone, and she turns to the fleece mom, so bright in the fluorescent glare of the bathroom, murmuring consolingly, why not?

Oh, the woman sighs, shifting breasts, we'd been up all night arguing. It's normal to feel upset, you know, that's what the books say. But all I wanted was a small IC, someplace safe, with other kids.

After a pause, she adds, we qualified, you know, what with the two of them and us—a whole, intact family.

Outside, the downpour increases—buckets of water pouring out of the sky—but it's late enough now for another kind of calm to have settled on the world, and what Lyda wants—and it strikes her that this is what she's wanted all her life, what is happening to her now—is to curl up into this calm, like the baby in its tie-dyed fleece at the mother's green breast, and just wait for things to be over.

But with the quarantines and all, the mom is still talking, we're kind of camping out until things settle down. That's our plan, anyway. Or, he says we might find a small town far away from everything, or just a cabin in the woods, but I don't really want that.

No, of course not, Lyda says, wondering, *quarantines*?

But she can't ask either because already the mom is nodding off above the large baby. I want, she mumbles softly, but that's going to turn out to be the last thing she says.

The rain smells so close, so edgy and metallic, that it's almost stupefying, and Lyda realizes she can't begin to pull together anything even remotely resembling a coherent thought—not anything out of the past before the red car, the driving, the bird bending now from its perch on the stained rim of sink to nibble affectionately at her ear, the woman and baby beside her.

Keep talking, Lyda thinks, *oh, keep talking.*

But they aren't going to keep talking, and in the silence that's about to overtake them, Lyda stretches out along the concrete floor, the moist, dim air flattening out above her, and it's really getting harder to breathe now beneath the press of it, almost like a mirror— *breathe, Lyda, breathe*—except the image that stares back is not her own.

When Lyda awakens, the fleece mom is gone and the baby is gone, and for an instant she panics that the bird is gone too—but no, there it is, perched on the top of the red car in the wet world, smelling earthy and clean. Well, ok, Lyda thinks. She has had this feeling before, this abject abandonment, and it organizes itself around a deep ache in her sternum, just a small point of pain that, really, now she considers it, never wholly leaves her. In its more acute phases, it's an actual prick of pain, right there beside her heart, but today, just the low, familiar ache, along with the cold.

Lyda stands in the open doorway for a long time, surveying and sniffing like a dog, she thinks, smiling forlornly at herself—but no, they really are gone, and there's nothing outside waiting for her except a world wiped clean of human habitation, wet and empty and bleak. Lyda thinks about the family, wrapped up warmly in its fleece, remembering that sometime in the night she had dreamed of going with them, finding that small town somewhere and settling in as the new grade school teacher. In the dream, Lyda picked grades 1 through 3, for certainly she loved the little children when they were new and young like that. She'd taught them things like colors and the alphabet and what happens when you put an avocado seed in water, and they'd wrapped their arms around her thighs, burying their small, hard child heads into her belly as she ran her hands through their hair in her fervent effort, even in the dream, to cushion their headlong forward rush into life.

Now, outside, the whole world drips—rocks, the branches of enormous trees, the moss that hangs from the dead trees in clumps. Lyda sniffs, wishing for the smoky smell of campfire and maybe coffee percolating, others she might join, but no, just the cold wet air that smells of nothing at all. Looking back on what has happened, she really hopes it was a whale the fleece dad was pointing out to the boy from the cliff above the ocean just the day before. She hopes this as fervently as she has ever hoped for anything—for there to be whales and dads and sons and camping trips, just for fun.

Even though she knows it's not for fun, she hopes they all slept well in the night.

And then she makes a beeline for the little car and hopes for something else: she hopes for breakfast—maybe eggs.

Still heading south, Lyda drives inland to the world's tallest trees, the road here straight and serene until it twists back toward the sea, up and over a torturous, winding pass. The emptiness inside her is beginning to feel like hunger, and she licks her lips, which are dry, from the cold, but also the hunger. Lyda has her eye out for a roadside café, but although there are plenty of painted wood signs advertising FOOD AHEAD, with bold images of coffee cups and pie, each café she comes to is boarded up or closed, and by the end of the morning her stomach is growling uncomfortably, accompanied by a dull caffeine headache and the growing concern that maybe she really should have followed the small fleece family wherever they were going.

Food ahead, the bird squawks from its perch at her shoulder. Food, food, food. Lyda's head hurts—really *hurts*—but because she recognizes the bird as the one companion she has left in the world, she clucks to it in what she hopes is a consoling way.

After a while, she reaches over to rummage in the glove compartment, looking for something to dull her pain, but the thought of possible drugs sets off such a craving for something more than food that Lyda has to suppress a sudden urge to stop the car and walk away from it forever, into the nothing out there.

It will be late afternoon before Lyda comes to a town that shows any sign of life, a town stretched out optimistically along the highway as if people might still be driving through it, like Lyda, in cars. Some of the storefronts display handmade dolls or sculptures of beach glass or homemade jam and other condiments, things you might buy in July for Christmas—things, Lyda recognizes, for tourists—but although the lids are swollen and oozing from the inside, there are other signs of people living here—a café without boards in the window, one blinking traffic light, the thin strains of radio music coming from somewhere, and a murkiness to the light that is almost viscid.

Lyda pulls off into the lot beside the café, tires crunching on ancient gravel. Hello, she calls out, emerging stiffly from the car, is anybody here?

There's a light on inside and a smell of something not completely rancid, with cheerful red-checked table cloths making the tables inviting, but then Lyda sees the sign on the outside: CLOSED UNTIL MORNING, IF WE HAVE EGGS.

Lyda is hungry, she is very hungry, and the thought of eggs, with their lambent whites and inner, golden centers, makes her even hungrier—ravenous.

But now that she's out of the car, the air feels fresh and restorative, and so she begins to wander about, inspecting storefront windows that suggest a prior time of cash registers and sewing machines, lives lived by the work of hands. At the end of one block, she pauses before a store that sells, or did, tools and feed for farm animals, closed, like the others, for business, but when she puts her hand to the glass of the window, it's colder than ice. Wandering on, she passes through a weather-beaten neighborhood of gray clapboard houses, and then a small industrial section where something was made once—something mechanical, or maybe paint—its old sludge pond black and noxious among the gentle dunes, and then all the way to where the town ends at a high, windy bluff above a jewel-toned beach, but it's all the wrong colors—turquoise and green and a deep, glistening purple—such that Lyda is already starting down toward it even before she has quite found the path where, off to one side, an old historical marker explains how, in a prior time, the beach had once served as a public dump where people had freely discarded whatever they no longer wanted or had any use for by tossing it into the sea.

Worn from wind and other elements, the marker is hard to read, but its meaning is clear, and reading it, Lyda can't help but feel a certain kinship with these people from another era who had stood where she stands and rid themselves of the junk and detritus of their lives—condiment jars and wine bottles, pesticide containers, worn out bits of broken machinery, fish tackles, crockery, spools and ball bearings and bobbins, rusted nuts and bolts, useless car parts, torn fencing, teapots and delicate saucers, medicine vials, fishing buoys, broken mirrors, split-backed banjos and busted guitars and smashed keyless trumpets, bent cutlery, fruit cans, wedding rings, crystal, perhaps even themselves—until an early environmental movement of the last century had shut it down in hopes the refuse heap below might one day be restored by pounding wave action to the natural world. These words—the natural world—are oddly comforting to Lyda as she struggles to make out the final words—last, or no, of course—*Glass* Beach.

But the beach itself is beautiful, the sand luminous with afternoon light, and Lyda already knows she will spend all the time that remains between now and dark sifting through it, finding odd pieces of pottery and bits of broken bottles, the leftover debris of lives lived in a time when the world still seemed inexhaustible. Some of the china shards have discernible writing or letters, designating, perhaps, countries of origin or mottos or patriotic slogans, and soon she is spelling words with them. Each wave overturns or carries in new pieces, and Lyda finds that if she follows them out, she can sometimes snatch unusual fragments before the water buries or reclaims them—the whole serene handle of one pink cup, a coin embossed with the image of GOD.

Lyda looks a long time, enjoying not just the finding but the looking, which she takes a certain comfort in, so charged and familiar that the memory that comes with it without warning sends her to her knees on the wet, packed sand, the back of her head pulsing.

One day she crawled out of her box convinced that something was wrong. It happened so fast—just a small explosion or popping noise inside her, and then she was on the floor in the bright white light, hugging her knees to her chest.

Mom, she cried out. Mom, come here quick.

Nothing hurt, it wasn't that. But her arms and legs felt stretched and grotesque, and on the inside, they throbbed. Lyda lay on the white carpet, pale and wrong and clutching her belly as if she might somehow change back what had already been done to her inside the box, and then she remembers her mother's bent over concern and soft, milky breath, her small and bony arms of regret.

This memory is not going to last, Lyda knows—is already receding— but she can still make out its sounds of love and solace, a kind of soothing maternal patois by which she understands that what she wants, all there is left in the world to want, is this: she wants five minutes with her father just to yell *how could you?* She would yell it a million times: *how could you, how could you, how could you?* She would leave him to fill in the blanks.

When the memory clears, Lyda is not on the beach anymore, but on the ground, curled up in the loamy dirt of a trail that loops back from the beach toward town and its café that will open in the morning (if there are eggs), and somewhere the car, but there is something as wrong about this trail as there had been about the beach. The trail, like the road and the furrows she had followed in the NETZ, is both definitive and not, and Lyda has the feeling she could follow it forever—but where?

Either way, the humped hills that surround her are covered in the same pink-flowered iceplant that was there when she walked down earlier, but it's no more right than her own arms and legs when she came out of her box. It fills the wrong space, or bends away from the wrong wind, or reflects the temperature of another day. For that matter, the *boom boom boom* of the surf below is wrong too. It's too old, Lyda thinks, not the boom of *now*.

Lyda's body aches, and however ineffectual her mother might have been—*before*—Lyda can't help but wish she were there to rock her, just take her up again into those bony arms and crush her up against her heaving chest, for how has it happened that she has come to be here, instead, sleeping in the wrong-feeling dirt and with a part of her brain excised?

Well, that's too many questions to resolve just now, and she's about to curl up and go to sleep again when she feels something in her pocket—shards she discovers, reaching in, collected from the beach and each containing letters. Curious, Lyda pulls them out and spreads them on the sandy dirt before her, arranging them like clues—B, then D—until, with a hot and sudden flush, she remembers something from the present: she remembers the bird. At first it's not panic. That, the panic, will come later. It will rise, like a tide, and maybe take her down. But now, just for now, the bird, or the thought of the bird, feels distant and vaguely abstract, a little like the journey she is on, or the *boom boom boom* of the surf, or things falling.

Lyda doesn't really know if the journey would be different if she'd chosen the other car instead—the black sedan with the soft leather seats—but she hadn't chosen that car. She had chosen the little red car like a bug, roundly waiting for her in the cafe parking lot somewhere on the other side of this long sandy path—either this one or another—that she had taken down to the beach made of beautiful garbage and to which—the little car—she is starting back now, stumbling a bit on the uneven path, which shows signs of having been worn down in the past, used by countless people, but is now, like the beach itself, being returned to a natural state, eroded and uneven.

Be careful, Lyda thinks. Don't fall.

Nevermore, the bird will say, hopping here and there. Nevermore, nevermore.

· Except, she isn't to the car yet and the bird—maybe the bird won't even be there.

The path had not seemed so steep when she wandered down it earlier, but now it stretches uphill so sharply that it's hard to climb, and Lyda is breathing hard—panting—but from—what, exertion, or fear?

Not wanting, yet, to know, Lyda stops to catch her breath, bending herself to the fog that's blowing in over and around her, stalling on the path and thinking how there wasn't anything her mother could have done, for no amount of rocking could have changed the changing in her body or the used up cans and worn nylon stockings, tossed from above the way people once tossed their stuff from the bluff that rose from the beach made of beautiful garbage. But in the absence of pounding wave action on the streets where Lyda lived, what had become of their refuse heaps? Of everything her father never told her, at least her father could have told her that. It's better, her body, now, the changing more complete or at least familiar, but like the little hummocks of hills rising in all the wrong angles around her as if they don't entirely belong in this too fragile space, Lyda's own body is strangely out of place here.

Not so unlike, she thinks, the small fleece family and the vista point with its possible whale, but the thought of the whale pierces her with regret. Once, Lyda knows, the whales rose up, breaching on ships to split them in two and drown the whole crews, but that was a long time ago. Now, like the bird, they are gone. But the grief Lyda felt for the whales is nothing to what she feels now for the missing, domesticated bird that is not even hers. Lyda knows nothing about this bird, which came with the car and talked like someone else, but as she starts back toward it again she's trying not to think, at least not with words, about how it really might be gone, hoping, instead, to find it disgruntled and noisy, perched on the back seat of the red car with the windows rolled up tight and safe, all its feathers ruffled, and something like a scowl on its bright bird face.

And this is when the panic hits, making Lyda run, but with a running made wrong not just by the steepness of the trail and the wrong-colored plants, but also the darkness that creeps from beneath and swallows up the world like fog, but not fog. What she'll do, when she gets to the car, she'll cup her hands with water and hold them to the bird, to drink. This will be her offering. The bird will drink, but to her it will feel like little bites, little pecks at the palms of her hands until, refreshed, it will hop up like always to the back of the passenger's seat and announce, let's GO. This thought, the thought of the bird's imperative, makes Lyda smile a smile that's not going to last because at some level she also understands it's not really a bird but just the idea of a bird, and anyway it's gone now, for good.

Once she thinks this, she will split again in that old way from inside her box and find herself back in the present moment, stuck in its raveling cusp, one moment after the next, and wondering somewhat bitterly how she could ever have imagined things might be different, a thought that sets off a pique of frustration and leaves her, profoundly, on the verge of hot, terrible tears.

Sometime after dawn, Lyda finds herself curled in the back seat of the tiny car with a few green feathers drifting up around her, already starving for eggs. There's not a thing about this that surprises her, but yet it's hard to uncurl her stiffened body anyway and make it take her back across the still deserted parking lot, thick with something more like real fog, toward where the café windows are lit up like beacons.

Inside, the smell of burnt coffee and pie, stacked high in a gleaming display case, causes a sudden burst of Lyda's salivary glands. The coffee will be bitter, but Lyda doesn't mind. She doesn't even mind the blue bowls of powdery non-dairy creamer. Chemicals, she thinks blandly, but without revulsion, as a neutral-faced waitress shows up wearing jeans exactly like the ones Lyda is wearing.

Got eggs, the waitress announces, boasting shyly. Then she nods to a dim back corner where another girl sits hunched over coffee. That girl brought them, fresh from the hen.

Oh, Lyda says vaguely, eggs. Oh eggs would be nice.

And pie? *Olallieberry* pie. We could even do hash browns, but it might take a while. The waitress warms to the idea. Hash browns and pie coming up.

In the temporary glitch that follows, Lyda struggles to fix things from—*before*. There is something familiar about the waitress—a bit like the fleece mother, or even Lyda's own, her gaze clear and open and—blank. Lyda closes her eyes and imagines a great dimmer switch that could cause this world to flicker—flicker and disappear—but when she opens them again, it is all still there, and biscuits would be nice, she tells the waitress even as the waitress offers her final enticement: biscuits, she says brightly. I'm starving for biscuits, aren't you?

On the yellowed counter, Lyda spreads out beach shards—s-o-e-l-g-t— beautiful blue letters from another time. Playing idly, she arranges and rearranges them like the tiles of an ancient game until they spell things—spell glotes, spell toesgl, spell: LET'S GO. And such a loneliness washes over her that she turns to consider the girl in the booth, only to find her gravely looking back. Small and startled looking, she's wearing a stocking cap pulled low over her forehead and is dressed, Lyda notes, entirely in gray—an oversized sweatshirt and jeans, both faded to gray, like the gray in her flat gray eyes. And there's something not entirely healthy about her, but frail, instead, in the manner of women who carry their frailty with them, from colicky infancies, with slow growth and limited weight gain, through childhoods plagued by infectious diseases, to wan young adulthoods blunted by emotional trauma.

She does not look, Lyda thinks on closer inspection, entirely there.

To test this thought, Lyda stands and calls, hi there, her voice as bright and determined as her step, I'm Lyda. Mind if I join you?

And in the silence after she has spoken, she becomes aware of a faint humming, almost a fluttering sound or soft and rapid tapping, like a rustling of leaves. There's a lag before the girl responds, then what might be an affirmative nod toward the dull formica of the table. The room is growing dense with the overheated smell of biscuits baking, the windows fogging from the heat, as Lyda takes a seat across from the girl, but the uneasy silence that roots between them makes her instantly regret it. Even though the coffee is scorched and the whitener lumpy, she's so anxious to put something other than words in her mouth that she burns her tongue.

A sudden image of eggs in a nest of soiled twigs rises up in Lyda's mind.

I had a rabbit once, the girl says just as the food arrives, great mounds of it steaming on their plates. Then she smiles, a bit sadly, revealing pale gray teeth. Now I have a tattoo. Moments later, she says, did you hear me?

You mean about the tattoo or the rabbit, or both?

Eat, the girl says. You'll feel better.

But Lyda is already shoveling food into her mouth. The eggs—the yellowest, creamiest eggs Lyda's ever seen—taste astonishingly rich, the biscuits are buttery and flaky, the hash browns, delicately browned and crunchy. But eating like this, Lyda will soon finish it all, and the wan girl across from her still has not lifted her hands from her lap, taken even one bite, or sipped one sip of coffee.

Excuse me, Lyda flushes with embarrassment. I must really be hungry.

The sound of her voice has the somewhat surprising effect of dispelling the awkwardness between them, freeing up a moment of inattention during which the girl picks her fork up, then self-consciously puts it back down almost at once, laying her hand beside it where Lyda can *see*. And although looking feels as impolite as staring at a defect or anomaly—something deeply private and normally hidden—Lyda does look. She looks and looks, as though famished for the sight, for they are such beautiful hands, the most beautiful hands, it seems, in the world, but like the mismatched features of the girl's face, seem not to belong entirely to her, or *here*—to belong *elsewhere*.

But not the girl, who sits with her hands turned open like a woman awaiting a transfusion, the tiny scars on the back of her wrists—the indentations—pulsing and blue until, seemingly satisfied, she lifts them again—the hands—and they burst into the somewhat ordinary mechanics of eating. One by one, the fingers unfurl, reach for a fork, picking it up and working it through the mound of yellow eggs, the eggs that steam, speared by the fork in the beautiful hand which, as it moves toward the girl's pursed mouth, resolves at last into the next part of the memory that slams Lyda without warning.

In it, they're standing, the two of them—Lyda and this girl—beneath the throbbing sky of a barren planet where any minute now, the sun will come blasting over the ridge of the wash they are in and the rest of their lives. The white sky presses down in what Lyda recognizes as a threat. Lyda does not know how she knows that if they don't act now to save themselves, they will be lost here forever, but she knows she must struggle against the lure of it, for in the absence of water—and she knows this too—their blood will slowly thicken in their veins until, like frozen sap in trees, it bursts open inside them.

Hurry, Lyda thinks, but without conviction, her pores already opening like valves in anticipation of the sweating, her own skin—the largest organ of her body—preparing to betray her, splitting open, too, beneath the ruined sun.

Lyda can't tell if it's a real desert, but it feels real. *Hurry*, she hears the girl say, reaching out one of the hands that might save them. At her feet, there's a bird in a cage and the door she's just opened, and above, a hole in the earth.

Then Lyda does run—she runs and runs.

And the bird flies out of its cage and flaps into green flight behind her.

And then the sun does blast over the mountains and the sweat does pour out of her, while just ahead, the gray-toothed girl hovers just a hair above the ground as they ascend toward the hole in the earth that's been waiting forever for them.

But the girl's not so much a girl, in the memory, as a small bald woman, hovering and expectant and holding out a damp towel as white as the shell of the most perfect egg in the world. Much smaller than Lyda, the woman has to stand on her tiptoes to wipe Lyda's face, and this close up, even in the darkness of this place that's not a place, there's a strange translucence to the woman's skin, especially her scalp and the backs of her hands, stretched so thin Lyda can almost see through its outer layers all the way through to the pulse of her blood. Her touch, though, is gentle and soothing, and Lyda hardly notices—*then she does*—that just across from them another bald person—a man—is doing the same thing to another man, wiping his face, then his neck—stroking, cleaning—the shoulders, the chest, the back—even as a feeling overtakes her, a paradoxical feeling of both coherence and dispersal, a feeling like sleep.

So that's that then, Lyda thinks, the bile of eggs rising up in her throat. On the other side of the table, the girl leans toward her, chin cupped in her beautiful hands, words forming slowly between wet, gray teeth.

Maybe, Lyda thinks, momentarily hopeful again, this is just another glitch, but already the girl is raising her beautiful hands up to remove her stocking cap, peeling it seamlessly back to reveal, beneath her perfect baldness, the unreadable map of her skull. At the sight of it Lyda reaches up to touch her own head, the place in the back where crude homemade sutures had once healed into tough little scars, but there is something wrong there too—as wrong and as absent as the bird.

Now that they understand each other, the bald woman smiles a slow, shy smile and, lowering her voice to the point Lyda can't be sure she is speaking aloud, says, *I can help you find what you are missing, if you let me help you, and if you help me too.*

THIS NEW SPECTACLE
OF HUMAN SUFFERING

BY THE TIME Will walked out into the rain, the last thing he could remember was the last thing Peter said: *I think you are going to like it.* Will was so sleepy—so dusty—and Peter, when he said it, had been bending so closely over Will, wiping his forehead with something white, and then Will's whole head had gone fat and fluffy and falling away, with only the words to buffer it.

Now the rain made things acute again, if curiously damaged and lifeless. The keen analytical part of Will's mind was damaged too, or missing, as though cleanly excised from his brain, its absence a little stab of loneliness to him, who, because he no longer knew what or how to think, turned his face to the sky and let a low shudder pass through him.

Then he shook his long limbs out, clenched and unclenched his hands at his sides, reached decisively for the handle of the black car door, and folded into its buttery smell.

The black car was the car that was left.

Will swallowed what felt vaguely like a memory of stone or a low malarial fever come on in a time of sadness. With his delicate features and long-fingered hands, he even looked like someone else's idea of him—head bent, limbs reined close to a body that, once unfolded, would be sure to reveal a tall gaunt man with a fierce awkwardness, like one of those long-legged birds you might see at the zoo. Or a wetland. If there were wetlands anymore, or zoos. Or birds.

In general, Will unfolded with reluctance, but there was something, too, about this moment—him ducking and slipping sideways into the car—that turned his many angles into a kind of grace, a beautiful thing.

Like Lyda before him, Will headed south, easing his car through mobs that surged as though there were something to surge for—supplies to horde or slogans to endorse—but unlike Lyda, Will drove with manly purpose, blindsided by an alien desire to gun the engine and head straight for the open road. Will forced himself to breathe slow, deep—it had to be somewhere around here, the road—and almost as soon as he had this thought, he came to a gap in the buildings through which he could see, down the hill and to the east, an ancient freeway.

But when he breathed his next deep breath of relief, the smell of saltiness and decay dissipated into a thin smell of absence.

The leather in the black car was soft and had a private human smell, deeply intimate, but the animal skin of it, mediated by only the unfamiliar clothes he was wearing—jeans and a soft flannel shirt—gave Will an uneasy feeling, and because he did not want to think about whose smell it might be, he turned his attention to the improbable mobs, each block a different mob, each mob like the one before—the same teeming faces, the same stink, the same disorganized seething—until a strange calm settled over him.

On the inside of his car, Will felt separate from the outside—apart and powerful. How fast could this car go? But everywhere he turned another mob surged, and the streets were blocked with rubble—smashed cars, crumpled girders, fallen street lights and power poles—and, here and there, the odd yellow quarantine barricade or gigantic concrete planters filled with replicas of what had once been native trees—redwoods or stately Ponderosas—green and optimistic in the gloom. I am not myself, he told himself firmly, as he gunned the sleek car down one alley, then another, in the hope of a freeway access or at least a thoroughfare, when he took a fast corner and suddenly screeched to a halt, rain splatting hard and beading on the car's polished surface, all his interior calm shattered.

In the street before him, a thin man pounding on the black car hood had miraculously escaped being crushed, the nose of the car having stopped only inches from the man's wasted body. Inside the car, stunned and shaking, Will watched the man, on the outside, pounding and pounding, but he couldn't hear him—heard nothing—no thump of hand, no splatting of rain, no cry of the man or what looked to be the infant or small child the man clenched under one arm, folded around it like the wing of an ungainly bird. The man was crying out to Peter —Peter could *see* that—and he was pounding hard, splashing off the water that was marbled on the waxed car surface, but inside the bell of Will's silence, all was quiet, and a good thing too because if all that sound got in, surely it would be deafening.

At first Will tried to back the car up, easing it away from this new spectacle of human suffering. He felt the knob of the gear stick round and cool in his hand, the pedals supple at his feet as he switched the car into reverse. But he wasn't moving fast enough because the man, with the child clutched under his arm, threw himself onto the hood of the car, his mouth wide open with its howl and something coming from it Will still couldn't hear. But he could see it—the gape of the mouth, the dark rows of glistening teeth. The man, thin and long, lay prone on the hood of the car, and if Will didn't do something soon, another mob would form and watching would not be all they were doing.

Will's chest heaved—in and out, in and out.

The man's legs folded up beneath him, curling his lanky body around the infant or small child to protect it, and although it seemed to Will that there had been a time when watching like this was all he had done, he felt a man of action now who told himself one sharp turn would do it. The other man, the man on the hood, had crawled all the way up to the windshield and was pressing his face against it, along with the face of the infant or child, its tiny round cheek flattened just at the level of Will's eyes. Beneath the neck of the man's torn pin-stripe shirt, Will could see the round neck of an old t-shirt in colors that might signify something—a political party or academic affiliation—but now Will saw the smooth cheek of the infant or child was not the right color, that there was also something slack about the whole small body.

One sharp turn, Will thought again, but without conviction.

The man pressed his free hand on the front of the windshield, splaying his fingers to reveal something written there—numbers or letters, a sign— but the ink had run together and Will couldn't tell. No, they were definitely letters, Will saw, even as he cranked the steering wheel of the car tight to the right—and three of them, the three in the middle, Will could read— L-P-U—although there were other letters on either side that he couldn't. But the wheel of the car was all the way cranked now and so Will did gun the engine, flooring the gas pedal to veer the car sharply in one direction, and then, just as sharply, another.

Now, in the black car sailing along the open road, what Will felt was rage, as pure and un-ambivalent as any feeling he had ever experienced, and along with it, a secondary feeling of loss. Perhaps a smaller, a less sleek —a clumsier—car might have helped contain what Will was feeling, but this car was so powerful it seemed, instead, to inflame it. Will had his hearing back, but the black car was so quiet there wasn't much to hear—just the muted *swhush* of wheels on the wet asphalt, the wind slipping over the windshield as it barreled along down the freeway heading south through dying pine forests, all that remained of a world it seemed he must once have known.

Will drove this way for a long time, swooping down inclines and around lambent bends in the road. He drove mindlessly, full of fury. But as mile after mile rolled away behind him, Will felt himself loosening and softening, little by little, until all the anger inside him had emptied, as though he had shed an old skin or self, but with the new emergent self not yet fully formed or choate. Will did not know if it was the car or the road that made him feel like this, half formed and edgy. On either side, a still-green frontage of genetically altered trees, but each time Will crested a hill to drop down into a valley, the view beyond—vast stretches of devastation, yellowed or dead, and the lowering sky, brown and fetid as smoke—served to remind him of the time when state and industry had colluded to sustain the idea that the forests were an inexhaustible commodity.

Seconds after cresting one such hill, Will made a decision he recognized as the kind of decision he might once have made when the keen part of his mind had remained intact: he would become a sponge, taking in all available data, but put off analysis until—later. As soon as he thought this, Will felt better, soothed by the feeling, remote but persistent, that there would be a theory to explain this, later. He had only to be patient for the theory to come.

The smoke, if that was what it was, smelled faintly sulfuric, and it was oozing, Will saw now, from an old lumberyard where stacks and stacks of smoldering wood suggested the presence of people and danger—for if there were people in this valley, what kind of people would they be?

Another part of Will's brain was plagued by the feeling he'd been on this road before, as a boy—a boy with a gun—but because what remained in him of memory had been reduced to something fragmented and partial, he could remember only random images—the gun, the road, the logging trucks barreling along just as he himself barreled along right now. All those trees, he thought, a great ball of grief welling up in his chest. But who could stop what was?

A man's body, as it ages, thickens, but Will's, in the car, was both thick and not-thick, and like the growth rings of a tree, each of his years was somehow marked and showing through him, layer after layer, all the way back to the unlikely boy with the gun, although the boy was so slight beneath the heavy years of the man it seemed impossible not to be crushed by the weight of them. Will wished he would be. Right now, he wished this so fervently his face began to twitch, just the top part of his left cheek, for more than anything he wanted not to remember how poorly aimed and ineffectual his first shot had been—his first shot at his first deer.

Don't shoot, his father had cried at the last second, it's only a doe.

Inside the skin of his present body, the skin of the boy constricts with remorse.

But there was another skin, a secret skin, at the core of his fingers, a supple interior sheathe that contained another knowledge—the knowledge that his knowledge of how to shoot and track a deer—somehow he knew this—was not authentic knowledge, not really *his*.

Thinking this, Will flushed and grasped again at the dull metallic absence of the keen part of his mind. They'd had to track that doe for two days in the snow, following the trail of blood to find the deer and kill it, but turning this memory over in his mind now, he found it as distorted and improbable as the faces of the man and the child pressed to his windshield, the features so bland and asymmetrical as only to appear to be normal.

Maybe it wasn't a deer at all, but just the idea of a deer, because one thing Will would have sworn to was he never had a gun. Maybe a fiddle, but never a gun.

Therefore, the memory was false.

But the satisfaction Will derived from identifying the memory of the false boy was short-lived and ephemeral, because he also knew that by the time he had reached driving age, no one had been driving anymore, making the skill his own body exhibited now—gunning the black car through the rainy city and sailing it along at high speeds down this crumbling freeway—not really his either, but just the trace of someone else's skill.

The next thought Will was going to have was that this car would not go on forever without gas, and it hit him with a slug of anxiety, for he had already noticed the signs that had once confidently promised GAS, FOOD, LODGING, were blacked out or painted over, the stations themselves darkened and empty. Will fought a surge of anxiety at how quickly this car was using up the gas it had come with, the needle on its gauge already drifting toward the last quadrant, and regretted again, but differently, not helping the man in the city. If he had brought the man along, the child might be sleeping peaceably in the back seat, dwarfed in Will's old black shirt, and the man—calm now— would be company and, Will hated to think this, reinforcement. Will tried to imagine the other man driving, his shirt, now dry, open at the neck, and a carefree look on his wide-open face. This thought—the thought of the wide-open face—produced a somewhat pleasurable sweat as Will imagined being driven, the world drifting by on the outside while, on the inside, he watched. There was something so agreeable about this idea of watching—him on the inside, looking out—that it struck him as oddly familiar.

But almost at once, something slammed shut in him and he knew he would have to pull off for gas.

If only there had been another car, at least he would have had a choice.

At that precise moment, the car rounded the bend in the freeway and an exit appeared with two gas stations—one orange, one blue—below, and choosing the orange as the more cheerful, Will got out to look around, surprised by a deep ache in the low part of his back and a loose and rubbery feeling all through his legs. Outside, a few scraggly trees decorated the stained concrete apron of the station, smelling pitchy and sharp. Somewhere a solar generator hummed, making the inside of the station glow with light. But when Will opened his mouth to call out—hey, anybody here?—the bell of his deafness descended again and a sobering emptiness prevailed.

Surely people lived here, or had—men and women, even young children— spinning out lives—their whole lives—in this once deeply wooded valley, and because their absence triggered whatever it was that remained of Will's curiosity, something quickened in him. How different this emptiness was from the teeming chaos in the city, but it felt just as wrong, as though the people here had come to the end of one ordinary day, closed up shop and faded off, leaving everything in order and ready to resume, just in case someone—Will himself—came by to fill her up and buy potato chips and coffee. What kind of people, Will reflected, would have walked away from what kind of lives—the marriages of children, the assortment of goods they could provide, the quality of their gasoline? And where would they have gone—would they have marched off together in a brave little band down the freeway, like birds, toward warmer climes, or splintered, instead, into fragmented groups, turning inland toward farms or other hamlets in search of human kindness?

Inside the part of the gas station that served as a convenience store, bottles of pain pills, bags of chips in exotic flavors, and neat stacks of cups in different sizes for drinks were arranged so precisely that Will began to wonder if the prior people might not have been expecting someone else to come along and replace them, new owners flush with cash, or Remainders.

But all this thinking was making Will's head hurt, so he went into the restroom to wash up. The hand towel looped from the stainless steel wall box, only slightly rumpled, smelled of the same green soap in the dispenser, but its whiteness triggered something deep in Will. How white and soft it was, how strangely comforting! Maybe he'd make a little coffee—coffee would just hit the spot.

Looking back, Will would always imagine the sound that split open the bell of his deafness as something more dramatic—crash of thunder or honk of horn. Such a sound might have accounted for the way his heart started pounding, his nervous system charged and his mind reactivated, without warning. But the sound was modest, hardly audible, a persistent, monotone gurgling or mewling that seemed, at first, to have no source but to come instead from everywhere—or *elsewhere*—seeping in from every conceivable angle to rise up and submerge him, like water. Will stood listening in the restroom, the white towel in his hands, and although there was nothing natural about the sound, it restored his hearing to him, even as it took him down, for he had recognized it, however distantly, as human.

There wasn't any gas here, and maybe he'd forget about the coffee. Just walk out and drive away, and maybe down the road a way he'd find a country store with actual people who might sell him gas in a can—a red can—or a motel with a flashing green Vacancy light and a room he might rent for the night from a round-faced woman eating popcorn from a bowl he could tell about the sound and where he had heard it.

Will had almost convinced himself that, at such a distance, the sound would be reduced to something benign, even hopeful, and so was about to get back into the car when he heard it again.

Well ok, maybe he'd just look around a bit. The sound of the word *ok* in his head felt distinct and soothing, as though, having thought the word *ok*, suddenly it was. But the other sound was gathering strength, and what was

Will going to do when he found it?

Will started in the back room with the mops and rodent poisons and account books, and then moved through the store aisles, one by one—cereal, first aid supplies, paper products, beverages. This part, the looking, felt fine, felt familiar, not unlike—as one hole in his memory filled—pursuing an equation to its end, the looking and listening and solving being, in equal parts, logic, instinct, and gut. Will started inside the store, although it seemed the sound was coming from somewhere else—but how could that be? Suddenly Will was laughing from a surge of relief, for if it was outside, then it could not be human—maybe a cat, or a litter of kittens.

So that was that. Maybe Will would still have his coffee.

But it was a baby after all, nestled in an oilcan box, underneath the workbench and wrapped in many layers of bright, tie-dyed fleece. Of indeterminate gender and age, the baby was big and cramped in the box, its limbs tucked too tight to its body. By the standards of the new smaller babies of the time, this baby was huge, the awkward kind of huge, being unable to crawl or even sit up and just lying there placidly, making sounds from which even Will could tell it needed something. Under the fleece blankets, the baby was dressed in another layer of fleece, a kind of zip-up sack, but without the zipper. Aside its oversized head, a sucking tube with a little nipple mouthpiece lay attached to a white plastic tank. Lacking eyebrows or lashes or even peachy fuzz of any kind, the baby looked as smooth and as hairless as an egg.

Hello, Will called out again, but louder, anybody home?

Then he stood above the baby contemplating it.

Now what?

This close, the sound, which hadn't changed, was not really any louder, only more insistent, and hesitant to touch any part of the baby, Will used a scrap of clean rag to wrap the feeding tube before inserting it into the mouth to suck, hoping this might quiet the sound. But the baby spat the nipple out, a bit of yellow drool coming out of the side of its mouth. This, the yellow drool, caused a feeling of revulsion to well up in Will, but what kind of person would it make him if, in the course of a single day, he failed to assist not just one needy child, but two?

So Will steeled himself to pick up the rag, and determinedly wiped the baby's face clean.

At no point during the next part of what happened did Will use the word abandoned. Some animals abandoned their young; some—coots, demented dogs—even killed them. But not human beings. Human beings, even in terrible circumstances—in instances of rape or where another mouth would cause starvation among others—welcomed their young (of desirable gender) as blessings or occasions for joy. Human beings loved their children, and it really did seem as though this baby had been cared for—it had its blankets and nutrition tank and its comfy box, and tucked to one side of its smooth round head, a list of instructions: keep tubing clear, rinse daily, handle with care. Will thought back to the man on the hood of his car, his arm tucked like a wing around the other child. That man had at least *looked* familiar, like a friend, or someone in whom Will might confide, or had even known once, a relation—a cousin, or closer. At least he had hair.

And now Will was on his knees on the oil-stained concrete floor beside the fleece baby, slammed by the memory of the baby whale long ago, the skanky roughness of its skin and its curved dimensions as seamless as the roundness of this fleece baby's head.

The man on the hood of the car, Will thought, he looked like *me*.

Unable to bring himself to get back on the freeway, Will strapped the baby in the seat beside him and headed east on a busted-up county road, its broken asphalt littered with rubble and the occasional barricade, with whole stretches of burned out countryside between. It was hard, damaged country, but it did not look as if it had been surrendered without some kind of struggle, and the idea of this struggle worried Will immensely—not from any sense of present danger, for the emptiness was old, already fading, but if you take the idea of a ruined world, who would bring a child into this?

Will thought this without judgment, despite the haplessness of his own parents. Besides, it had been different then, after the quarantines ended, when whole seasons had gone by without catastrophic weather events and there had been baseball. Even though Will couldn't quite remember this yet, not yet in actual thoughts, the feeling was there—the feeling of loss. And as he maneuvered the black car with the same forcefulness he'd assumed to drive it in the first place, easing it around the devastation of the roads and sometimes being forced cross-country along hard rocky earth, Will couldn't help but think about the people who'd fanned out there—fanned out and disappeared.

Will felt a headache coming on.

Beside him, the baby was finally asleep, and glancing over at it, Will saw again the bit of yellow drool sliding out of its mouth. Then he had a thought he couldn't stop: what if it hadn't even originated in the orange gas station where Will had found it, but had only been left there by someone else, like him? What if he did that too, just left it here, by the side of the road? Maybe the next time someone picked the baby up it would be by someone better suited to the task.

Will was thinking this when, without any warning, the busted-up, east-headed road ended at a broader south-angling highway, and soon he was sailing along again beside a little river, or stream, passing occasional farms and, every now and then, a low tourist motel. All the motels had NO VACANCY signs, but some of the farms had smoke curling out of their chimneys or men at work in distant fields. Will knew he should, but he couldn't bring himself to stop and ask directions or where he might buy gas, for how could he ever explain the baby that was with him?

Will drove for some time along this highway that followed a river that might be a stream, falling as he drove into a kind of reverie. Sometimes it seemed like a loop: hadn't he passed this exact farm before, wasn't this bend in the river familiar? Will accepted the idea of a possible loop the same way he'd accepted the car and the indeterminate baby in the zipperless sack, and even though he still had the feeling that something was missing, once he accepted the absence, his heart lifted and his inner bitterness gave way to serene new feelings of detachment.

And this is the moment—the exact moment—that the baby wakes up and the black car runs out of gas.

First, the baby startles, hiccoughing slightly as the car hesitates, chokes once, twice, then glides to a stop along the shoulder above the embankment of the river that might be a stream. Like the car, Will chokes back a little sludge of dread and then, just as arbitrarily, suppresses it, embracing his new circumstance as wholly and as un-ambivalently as, moments before, he had embraced the loop. In the absence of any kind of choice—nothing to do now but get out and walk—Will's serenity reasserts itself and, seamless as grace, he reaches over, unbuckles the baby, hoists it with a little *oomph* (it's heavier than it looks), and gets out of the car to look around.

Still, he knows it could go either way. The after that is coming—when it comes, it will come in a heartbeat. It will happen so fast.

But for now, it's not then yet, and having determined there's level ground for camping and enough wood to burn for a lifetime, Will returns to the black car to find the trunk loaded with gear. This is unexpected. There's so much of it, really—enough of this, too, for a lifetime—but the profusion does not fill Will with the same sanguine optimism that the supply of wood did, although he's not yet wondering why it's here. Instead, he is marveling at its beautiful colors—the vivid neon green of the tent and blue of the sleeping pads; the fuschia of the sleeping bags; the pure, placid white of the clever, collapsible water buckets nest; the fire-engine red of the backup feeding tank for the baby, and its little tie-dyed clump of back-up fleece.

Surveying all this—his bright richness—Will's mouth fills with something salty, instead, like happiness itself. The tent has E-Z spring poles and slender titanium stakes. The pad sucks in air with a low whoosh, growing firm and fat. The sleeping bag fluffs out of its sack to a downy cocoon. What could be better?

Inside the skin of his manly body, the skin of Will's boy hands remember the work of the camp, finding everything he needs for the night, but a fiddle for his hands and, of course, a mother for the baby. He should call it something, but what? For now, he'll just call it Baby—Baby will do.

And leaving Baby contentedly feeding, Will sets off to gather wood for a fire. But it's been raining here too.

And it turns out Will was wrong about the wood, for although there had seemed to be plenty, it's wet and mostly rotting from the inside, with all the good scrap pieces already salvaged and the trees not yet ready to fall. The damp air, too, is turning colder, which is going to be a problem—how will Will keep Baby warm or feed himself?

And suddenly, overcome with hunger—for when was the last time he ate?—Will is on his knees digging at a fungus-riddled stump and, finding the underside of it clumped with white mushrooms, his mouth explodes again, with saliva. The first one tastes of earth, almost sweet, and then Will can't shove them into his mouth fast enough, pulling them out from the base of their tender stems, mushroom after mushroom, each mushroom making him more ravenous than the last, dizzy with pleasure and the wetness from the ground soaking through his pants, and it really is cold now, but Will doesn't mind—he's eating so fast he bites his tongue and the earthy taste of the mushrooms mixes with the salty taste of his own blood, such that the astonishing sight, when he looks up, of a man and a boy on the bank above and behind them, a dun-colored van and—a *mom*!—does not even make him cry out.

Dressed in big orange fleece jacket, the man strokes a ragged beard with one hand and the boy's small head with the other, both hands stroking, mild and imperative. If he'd known he was going to have company, Will wouldn't have eaten all the mushrooms, but when he raises his hand to wave, the man—Will hates to see this—flinches. Then the boy turns and runs back toward the mom and buries his face in the green of her fleece.

And by the time Will scrambles back to his camp, the mom is already scrubbing Baby's face with a little scrap of towel and brushing Baby's tiny teeth and gums with the vigorous tip of her capable fingers. Watching the ease with which she tends to Baby's needs—the cleaning and feeding of it, the rocking to sleep, Will is wrenched by jealousy that his prior claim is no more legitimate than her natural one.

The dad, tying fish flies, has only half an eye on the boy tearing around the campground and ruining its peace and quiet.

Hey, Will calls to the boy without really thinking it through, but maybe only wanting to distract or calm him down. Let's you and me go get some water. And when the boy holds back, nah, edging closer to his father, Will adds I've got some tablets in the trunk that will make you think you're drinking Coca-Cola, and the dad says go along, and the mom, humming to Baby, paying no attention.

What's Coke, the boy says, but he's coming anyway, traipsing off with Will for an adventure, and this lifts Will's spirits enough that he doesn't even miss the thing inside him that would try to calculate the pros and cons, now that he's taken this action, of whatever in the world is going to happen next.

In this way carefree, Will and the boy head up the river, or stream, each swinging a white collapsible bucket slung over his shoulder—Will's the big one, and the boy's, the small inside one. There is something about this swinging of buckets—soon the boy's making great looping circles with his around his head—that is quietly soothing to Will. So now they'll just walk up the water a bit, beyond this shallow muck that turns out to be wriggling with some kind of larvae and skimmed with an iridescent sheen, until it is clear and running over rocks. Will can hear that, from somewhere upriver, and that's where he wants to take the boy, toward the sound of it rushing clear over rocks, but this mucky part just goes on and on.

Hey, he calls back in encouragement, hear that? I bet we find a waterfall, maybe with a pool. You like to swim?

Come on, he calls back, it's not so far now.

Later, Will will think it was maybe wrong to give the boy the idea of a waterfall and swimming like that, but maybe not, for surely the boy, being a boy, deserved a little hope. Everyone alive deserves a little open destiny of hope, he will think, even though he knows they really should have turned back when the air changed.

Will did notice the change—it was hard not to. Even though everything still looked the same as they were walking along up the riverbed, or creekbed, it smelled different, not moist and tender anymore, but old—old and dried out, and tenuous, as if it would not hold out much longer—or farther. Even at the time, Will had the strange thought that if he touched anything, a rock or a dead tree—the boy?—it would break apart and blow away into dust.

But this is the wrong thought to have, because as soon as he has it, that's exactly what happens.

When things as they are give way, Will is first alerted by a little sucking sound, not dry at all but flatulent, his foot suddenly sinking beneath—or *through*—the mud he's just been picking his way through, solid as earth. But not anymore. Just one more step and it all gives way beneath him, except that where his foot goes through, the mud forms a seal around his ankle, tough as a vacuum, and oozes in at the top of his shoe, although everything else, all the rest of his foot, stays as dry as the nothing he smells.

And then, like quicksand, the vacuum just keeps pulling at his foot, trying to drag it in deeper.

But not really quicksand because quicksand is wet and sucking—quicksand will drown you—and this isn't wet at all—*something else*.

Get back, Will cries to the boy, and he means it.

The top part of his shoe is mucky with mud, or whatever it is, but below the tight suction at the socket of the ankle, the foot dangles free and loose. If he breaks through altogether, what will happen—will he fall?

Stand back, he calls again to the boy, as if this might change things or keep the boy safe.

Will tries clenching his toes below while simultaneously pulling up above, to lengthen the line of his leg before trying, with a sudden yank, to extract it, but the foot remains firmly lodged in the empty space below. And as soon as Will takes this in, that he's really stuck, what he feels is neither fear nor dread, but just a simple feeling of regret for the ruined shoe, a feeling that starts swelling as soon as he's fixed its source. For it's not just this one shoe Will is mourning, but all the used-up shoes of his life—his worn out running shoes, and his stained Italian work loafers, and his split-soled hiking boots, and his boiled wool gray felt slippers, and his spiky baseball cleats, and his patent leather dress shoes, and his own first baby shoes with blue buttons.

All these shoes, Will remembers in what feels like the first truly tangible moment of the day, are *real*, as his foot pops out with a satisfying *phflaaapth*, and he almost tumbles backward to the dangerous ground.

Go back, Will tells the boy one final time. Tell your mom I'll get the water—I've already ruined my shoe.

But the layers of his body, or the loop of the road, or the blankness of his mind where both his logic and his memory should be, Will understands from all of this that what he really means is that this whole world is already ruined, and in the sudden slippage of this moment—which is every bit as sudden as his foot slipping through the insubstantial surface of this place—as soon as he thinks it, he remembers the baby—his Baby—the one he has left in the care of this boy's mom, and although the scientist in Will wants to reach out and rend the illusion, the man is suddenly desperate to protect the found child.

But everything, after all, back at camp is nice.

The boy is reading a book. The dad is still tying flies. The mom is making dinner. And the baby—Will's Baby—is still sleeping in its box.

That night, the mom feeds everyone hot soup out of cans, and the dad is full of advice: don't go to the stations, he says, they're all occupied. Try the corner markets—sometimes they sell gas in red gallon cans.

Will watches the others closely, looking for slip-ups or cracks in the space between them and the space the mass of their bodies takes up, even just a tiny gap that would tell him what to think. But no, everything fits together like a well-made machine, and he could even get to like it—the mom so attentive that Baby never makes a sound, although she doesn't really do anything different than he did, just inserts the feeding tube and pats Baby here and there, coos in what is meant to be a soothing or consoling way.

They say, the dad says, things will get better by spring.

Will should pay attention—he *is* paying attention. For example, what is the mom going to do about Baby's zipperless sack?

But the boy, tugging at the bottom of the mom's jacket, looks pale and insistent as somewhere a bird calls—*whoo, whoo.*

Yeah, Will says, spring.

You plan to plant? the man asks. There's still time for late crops, if you hurry.

But this idea of planting is as wrong as the layer of earth Will went through, a layer of—time? No one has planted anything in years.

Oh, Will says mildly, I'm sort of just driving around.

Now the mom's face above the smoldering fire comes into sudden focus, as she shifts the baby—*my* baby, Will is wrenched into thinking—from one shoulder to another. Even though she looks exhausted, that's not what Will is thinking. Will is thinking about the nothing underneath the ground they are sitting on now. He is thinking about the strength of the mom's hand on the arc of the baby's sturdy back, and the nothing beneath.

Hey, the man says, us too. We're just driving around too—that is, until things settle down.

Oh, they'll get better soon enough, the mom says, sighing deeply. But right now, time for bed, don't you think?

As soon as she says this, Will knows she is right—it is time to turn in. Maybe, in the night, they'll all get some sleep.

Just beyond, the creek is still making its nice rushing sound, and now there are crickets too, a kind of gentle thrumming all around. Will is just about to give in to the peacefulness of this when the woman says something to jolt him out of it.

Do you want, she says, me to watch this baby for the night? I know how it is—so you can get some sleep.

But no, that's not what Will wants. Why should he want to let her have his baby? Who would want that?

But before Will can grab the baby back and make a scene, the boy distracts them both, tugging on the mom's fleece.

You promised, he whines.

Shush, the mom says.

Now, the boy insists. A say is a promise, and you *said.*

Will turns away, embarrassed, from the small family's struggle, but all he can think now is how to get Baby back. The mom is hanging on tight. Then, for a moment, Will tries out the idea of letting her have it, maybe even joining up together—the black car in the lead, with the boy riding shotgun beside him, and the dun-colored van following behind, with the fleece mom and dad and the baby between them, all in a little caravan of waiting things out.

What would happen then? Will wonders. What would it be like to join up with them and adopt their strange tranquility—and plant?

But because Will somehow understands that to let her have the baby even just for this one night would link them all to a most failed outcome, Will rejects these ideas outright.

Maybe there is something in the back of the black car he can trade for Baby, something for the boy—a bauble or toy—maybe even, Will thinks with a little burst of hope, a handheld computer device, with games. Maybe he should just go look.

But then, at that moment, the boy surprises them all by flinging himself between his mom and Baby, demanding the mom's full attention and breast.

*Bed*time, the boy demands, his little mouth open and his white teeth gleaming, inside—and a *story*.

Ok, the mom sighs, her face going tired, but softening toward the boy, her own. Let me just get rid of this other baby. And handing it helplessly over to Will, offers her breast for the boy and begins—*once a long time ago.*

COMPANIONS LIKE HIM

AND NOW THEY are out, culled, like his trees, and taken, as he'd planned—
as *he* had planned—from the Desperate Measures Seminar, drained there of regular
hope and ambition, linked together, heart and mind, and released.

How happy he should be.

But looking at them side-by-side in the space between where they have been
and where they are going, the bottomless wash stretched out below and the dome
of the portal whitened like ash, Peter thinks the three of them are not so solid, not
so dependable as they once seemed. What if one picked the wrong car, or joined up
with the fleece family, or found the way back to the DMS compound—or the think
tank or highrise apartment, or even just the city in the rain? Anything could
happen still, for that's the way he'd wanted it—any one of them could choose a
separate destiny or path.

Trees had always been so simple—the strong ones, the viable ones standing
out with vitality markers, predictors for successful maturation, the greener
greens, the darker barks, the roots that sank straight and deep into the loamy
earth. The meanest child with half an eye could see that. But people were
not trees and from the start Peter's instincts for their natural selection were
confused. People—human beings—were in no way systematic, and from what
he had seen of Remainders, Peter sometimes worried about things like mass
and space, slippage, instability, while even in their other, more natural respects,

he often felt confounded by their most basic anatomies, their flesh and joints and neurological networks, their temperaments and hopefulness, their complex memory systems and other wretched vulnerabilities.

For one thing, they would need shoes—so many shoes—two at a time and for different functions, all the right size; they would need garments—hats—to cover their heads. What if one got sick or had a problem with an organ—an appendix or uterus? What if one had a craving for figs?

But mostly what he feels as he contemplates the six feet commingled before him is lonely—lonelier than he has ever felt; he feels bereft. Thinking this—*bereft*—a fleeting image of them in their cars comes to him, but there's something not quite right about that either, not sufficiently open-ended, not all he had hoped. And suffused with something akin to anxiety, Peter momentarily sees himself as not so unlike them—haplessly stuck in the present moment, caught up in its ravelling cusp. How—oh why—had he ever imagined that it might be different?

What had Peter wanted, when he was a boy?

He had wanted, he thinks now, to run outside and play among the others—with *them*.

But no, Peter, no, his father had insisted. Stay here, with *me*.

And so Peter stayed, studying the rubric of his father and becoming, over time, more and more like him, and so meticulous and thorough that later, when he had nothing but time—all the time that remained in the world—he'd spend it—years and years—in his planning, testing out his virus through its infinite regressions in the practice bed he'd built for it (although he could never really know what might happen when he finally let it loose) and trolling the NetZ for just the right people—people with the proper temperaments and elastic frames of mind, steadfast people of substance, tenacious and visionary, who might not just imagine a future but also embrace it.

But of all the men and women in the portal it was not so easy, after all, to choose: one good man to be his best companion, to walk fish lines and tend trees and play ball with, a partner for his complex arguments and algorithms; and a woman for the man, so he would not be alone.

And for him, Helen.

Now, the sound of them, the side-by-side breathing of bodies lying before him in the physical portal and selected for their particularities and promise— Helen's perfect hands, Will's analytical capacities and near perfect ear, his true gut instincts and muscle strength; Lyda's curiosities, her wants and words and lightness—glistens as after a rain, and although Peter has begun to suspect he hasn't understood the first thing about them, it is too late to do things any different.

For a long time after Peter's father died, after the silence of the natural world descended and Peter had moved into the primary shelter and taken his inventory and sampled the whiskey and made himself sick, after he'd imagined poisoning his own trees, after he'd lain naked in the sun and burned and blistered and peeled to this new soft skin, after he'd drunk from the creek and sifted through ashes for relics, after, finally, he'd wept, then Peter's rage went—it went all at once, leaving him hollow and empty. And it was in this new and subtle state of mind that he had at last cleaned himself up and begun, as he'd promised, to honor—to obey—his father.

And for a long time, really, he had been so good.

As regularly, as reliably as any boy could, Peter did the things his father asked, as though that might please him, even now.

But even Peter could not say what he would have done if he'd imagined there was anything to leave for—a hundred years is a long time in the life of a boy who is alone.

In later years, when the loop was over and the portal reopened to the world, Peter drifted in and out of it, half intoxicated, half consumed with his rage—for why would his father have wanted to deny him this, the companionship of others, when he had been the best boy on the compound, even later, when the compound was him?

Still later, when he had reached the age his father was when he first convened the Central Committee and slept his last nights with Peter's mother and did his last business with the outer world, that, too, would pass out of him, for in Peter's steadily increasing memory bank, these frantic days of dread and preparation had also been sour days of bitterness between his parents—his *two* parents.

You're the epidemiologist, his mother had said. Isn't it your job to fix things?

She was drinking coffee from a porcelain cup that tinkled when she put it in its saucer. Peter, a toddler, was clinging to her legs beneath the table. The legs, stripped of hair, smelled of citrus and vanilla, and of something strangely intimate, and as his father ranted about gene-splitting and wave theory projections, the legs tensed and flipped, crossing over the other. Peter lodged himself against his mother's knees.

But even then she did not say the words that hung between them: You started it, you stop it.

He did not say, *it wasn't me.*

She did not say, *it might as well been.*

He did not say, *please forgive me.*

She did not say, come, *I still love you.*

At other times they tried, his parents, to lie together in peace, the body of Peter between them only partly sleep.

It's so sad.

But don't you remember.

Oh, if only we had not had the child.

Peter detached from the portal with headaches; he detached in sweats, frantic to retain the memory that was already receding beyond what he could hold in his mind or access from his BCI, despite its considerable capacities. He remembered the smoothness of his mother's skin. He remembered her voice, low—womanly. And he remembered the smell of her violin—its old wood and resin, the guts of the strings.

But not the music, which his father destroyed. Even when he dreamed of her coiled around the body of her instrument, there was never any sound, nor did she seem entirely present, always as if she were somehow playing elsewhere and for another self, and even though her fingers and her arms would move, her feet tapping, the silence persisted around her, a gaping hole—but just look at everything she was pouring into it.

Close your eyes, Peter, breathe. And then he'd slip back into the portal, searching for—what?

Well, there had been recordings, Peter knew that. If Peter could not remember the music, he could remember his father stretched out on the sofa with his huge head cradled in the listening box, eyes closed, hands folded serenely on his lap. He could remember the look on his father's face, distant, inapproachable—rapt.

When you're old enough, his father said. Go out and play now, while you can.

Breathe, Peter, poof, Peter thought.

Later, he had searched the databases but never found any trace, not of her— his mother. In this, his father had been as thorough as he was efficient.

Still, there were times, plenty of times, when Peter believed he'd have done exactly as his father, for who could endure what human beings could do to one another, the suffering of body and spirit, the poignancy of children?

In fact, by the time he had recovered the real outer world, things had fallen into a greater disrepair than even Peter's father had foreseen. Whole continents could no longer be inhabited, with other regions filled up by the implacable Remainders, half people (among whom Peter wondered, was he to count himself?), and all the cults, the child splinter groups, the . . . shoes.

Sometimes it seemed to Peter that at the end of time all that would remain of human history would be shoes—mountains and mountains of shoes all over the world, some of them stuffed with the bones of feet, some in shiny stacks of precise rectangular boxes—shoes, and engines, and silos, and the slender titanium frames of eyeglasses, and the crankshafts of cars, and plastic bags, and mile after mile of human remains—enough to build whole cities for whomever came next—and microwave popcorn, books and sewing needles, wine racks and diamonds, dog chains, bicycles, fossilized eggs, drug paraphernalia and hospital beds, lawn mowers, zoo pens, mainframes, traffic signs, alphabet soup—all that stuff piled everywhere in stupefying mounds of rotting putrefaction. Almost more than anything, what Peter could not bear was the ugliness of this, the greed and preposterous accumulation of human waste—such that he'd begun, for the first time in his life, to understand—to truly, viscerally inhabit—the mind of his father.

For all this, Peter knew, was real.

But then he'd find himself studying lists of available flavors in brightly lit ice cream parlors, or DMS prospectuses, or menus for mates or other life choices—careers, places to live, political affiliations. He'd find himself wandering through a park full of children with small wheels attached to their shoes, or eating frozen brussel sprouts, applying fragrant ointments, watching movies in great rooms full of other people, enjoying zoos, having his teeth cleaned, making change, winding up mechanical toys, working out, being jostled by the cacophonous crush of fair or market or bus depot or airport or hospital emergency room. Sometimes animals—dangerous animals, with teeth and carnivorous instincts—roamed the streets, but sometimes musicians did too. And sometimes Peter would find himself rooting for the underdog in vast arenas where players in colorful garments enacted complex games on artificial fields, or memorizing artifacts in austere museums—a pristine urinal attached to one acid-free wall, an enormous pebble curved like the arc of a human hip and embossed with the seal of an ancient Chinese dynasty, a fragment of thousand-year-old brocade, a box filled with mysterious things.

At such times, spent and overloaded, Peter wanted none of it—and all. Sometimes Peter wanted nothing more than to remove his brain from his skull, put it away in a box, and resume entirely his life of the body. His head ached all the time anyway, the brain inside—huge—the source of this incalculable pain. It would be a nice box—like the velvet-lined case of his mother's violin or the box in the white room filled with things—but it would be dark. On the inside, it would be completely dark—no light leaking in at all, only a soft place for his brain, every bit like a natural skull, that would go on and on forever.

The cars came to Peter in the orchard. Or the idea of them did.

He'd been out there working hard, pruning back the growing branches and noting, here and there, the tiny buds that promised fruit, and this had stirred something so deep inside him that Peter, distracted and light-headed with pleasure, almost didn't notice the buzz that came with the idea of the cars, wholly formed in his mind—one red, one black—and each with timing belts and crankshafts and oil pans and windshield wipers and transmissions, two powerful cars that made noise (*vroom, vroom*) and that would dent on collision and skid out of control in the rain. Almost, he could hear them choking into gear, feel their pedals at his feet. And although there had always been plenty of cars in the fantasy modules—cars that could fly or dive into the ocean or blast off into space or careen over mountains, cars that did not need gas, cars that could zoom—Peter saw at once that these two cars were all the cars he'd ever need, for these cars—the red and the black one—were real.

You can't remember that, his father said

And then everything goes quiet because it is now—this precise moment in the orchard, where he has to stop himself from falling one more time to his knees—that Peter does remember, and remembering, finds himself back—completely and viscerally back—in the decontamination foyer of his childhood apartment, strapped into a car seat and trying not to listen through the intercom that's supposed to be off. Above him, the various nozzles and controls are painted with bright, abstract designs, and the walls of the foyer are yellow, but there's nothing cheerful about them. One of the voices is the voice of his mother, who is or has been crying. It sounds mournful and he wants to squirm away and go to her, but the seat is too small and his shoulders are scrunched down and pinched by the harness and he can't even move. And despite the static on the intercom he can make out the words. He can remember them.

The other voice is the voice of his father.

And where exactly, he says, do you think you are going?

I'm warning you, his mother says, even though it's not an answer. She's not shouting either, but that only makes it worse. No, she says, I mean it. I'm taking the car and I'm going.

I see, his father says—so which car are you planning to take?

There is something low and menacing about his father's voice, like a burned engine smell snaking its way into Peter's brain.

You can't remember that, his father said, but Peter did, remembered it all—the sudden shouting and throwing open of doors, the struggle over his car seat, the noise and unspeakable thrill of the next few moments during which his mother would throw a little plastic sheet over him and his father would position himself at the door, and Peter's mother's face, refracted many times through the folds in the plastic above him. And then they were out, shoving hard past the body of his father which had turned out, after all, to be ineffectual against the resolve of his mother, clutching his car seat to her chest and murmuring soft sounds as they ran.

Outside, splats of rain punched down on the plastic and his mother's red car waiting beside the other, the black car of his father. In the rain it looked so red, washed clean by the storm, and his mother's hair wet around her white face.

That would fall out too, like her toes from their little silver sandals, if anything his father said were true, but Peter did not know that then—would know it only later, only now, as it comes to him in the orchard, a single fragment of memory restored.

Next, Peter remembers the driving, the noise of the engine, the drenched world passing by on either side as though it were opening for them. He remembers the smell of his mother, a paradoxical odor of perfume and fear.

And he remembers that they didn't get far.

When Peter was a boy, there were times a hundred years seemed long enough, an endless stretch of time for his trees to grow and the planet to heal. But what Peter's father had not planned on (could not, indeed, even have imagined) was that, as Peter tended to his little spinning plot of healing spaceship earth, he'd draw ever nearer to the logic of his mother that would teach him to desire nothing more than what was there—a small apple plucked from a living tree, the sound of water, his own breath—becoming, over time, ever more like his own impossible memory of her and the underground people she'd taken him to, the white birds, and the man whose hands only remembered his own violin.

But, like his father's love, that would never be enough.

Now, in the portal, he moves as quietly as he can among the sleeping bodies, not yet touching them (don't touch, Peter, you mustn't) but looking—at that soft spot behind each of the ears, underneath the lips of shirts and pants, through the mass of Lyda's hair—and Will's—along the gleaming arc of Helen's skull. Looking at them, Peter examines his own toes, wriggling all ten of them a little. In the years he has gone without shoes, Peter's feet have toughened and spread, like the roots of a very old tree, and although he knows he should already be gone, he can't quite bring himself to leave yet, and so he sits, instead, a little longer with the others, abstractedly bringing his toes to his mouth to suck the soothing taste of earth, of him.

Wake up, Will.

Wake up, Lyda.

Tell me what it's like to be you.

Oh, he should leave. He should just go now.

But no, he's not going to leave because—and even though he knows he shouldn't, he's not going to be able to stop himself either—he has to touch them first. He will do this because he loves them, just as he loves the feel of them, their corporeal selves—bodies you can touch. And as much as he loves the little bald one—Helen—the one who is like him (and this, what he feels for her, Peter is certain is what love is), he still can't keep from touching the larger one—Lyda— whom he also loves. Once, Peter remembers, a small species of deer had existed that could leap ten feet into the air from a perfect standstill and land with all four hooves firmly planted on a rock the size of an infant's palm: *what*, he wonders dreamily, *could Lyda's body do?*

This thought provokes such a strong feeling in him that he closes his eyes, not daring to look at the sleeping women but only to touch them, and finally to wonder how, in all the time they've spent together in the portal, it has never once occurred to him to imagine them as separate from himself—as not-him, not-Peter—with wills and hearts and bodies and breaths all their own.

And isn't that ironic, when all he'd ever wanted was not his mother, who'd forsaken him, and not his father, who'd betrayed him, but precisely what he has now, stretched out on their separate journeys—companions like him. Which is not so different, after all, from what anyone would want—someone like the straw-haired girl he'd known as a boy, someone to touch and be touched by, someone to synchronize breath with in the night, someone with ankles and hopes and scents and words, someone, Peter thinks with a small thrill, alive.

By the time the little red car did run out of gas, drifting almost languidly to a stop, his mother had already folded herself, like a piece of subtle fabric, into the driver's seat, all the hope and daring drained out of her. The car spluttered once more and died, and in the sudden stillness Peter's mother wept.

On the outside, the rain, and on the inside, the smell of ozone and his mother's fear as they sat waiting for the black car that was coming.

When it finally did, Peter's mother reached out suddenly, but for the audio console, not him, and although there was time—plenty of time—for her to take him on her lap and hold him as fiercely as she was listening to the music, she did not. She just sat staring straight ahead and listening to the music until Peter's father appeared.

Seconds later, she was giving him back.

Too bad, Peter's father said, you chose the wrong car—the black car would have got you farther, but not even that car would have got you far enough.

For a moment, they all stood there in the rain with the music streaming around them, but when his father spoke again his voice had already been restored to the other voice, the voice Peter really does remember—the voice in the loft, and the voice in the orchard, and the voice in the litany of final instructions. In such a voice, Peter thinks now, one might yet imagine as much love as the love in the face like a moon streaked with rain.

It doesn't have to end like this, he said, as though it were a kindness—you could still change your mind and come too.

WHAT ELSE PETER KNOWS

When Peter wakes, the air in the portal has grown heavy and hot, and his hand—his own hand, as if separate from himself—has found its way not to the court reporter, where it most properly belongs, but to the poet, who stirs and flushes with the same radiance from his dream of the fir seedling that has haunted him all his life. But a body can accumulate only so much longing. Then a body—any body—has to act.

But just as it does, Will awakens from his own not-sleep, running his hands through his tangled hair and looking somehow both disoriented and alert.

Hey, what are you doing? Get your hands off her.

What, no. I didn't.

She trusted you. Then he sighs. I really hope you know what you're doing.

Between them, the suddenly male energy is charged and gratifying, and although it's the lightest of touches, Peter guiltily removes his hand. The other man—who only seems awake—is so completely present that Peter can't help but think his mother was right: what did it matter if her god were Beethoven or Bach, or Radiohead or the Beatles, or the single snowy mountain, or the sound of his very own creek, or even of the splitting of his own synth-ethic cells in his father's Petri before they were in him.

Go back to sleep, he says finally to Will. You don't know what you're talking about.

I know what's right—right is, you leave them alone.

An expletive comes to Peter's mind. Fuck, he thinks. Fuck *you*.

Will blinks, owl-like and skeptical. Just keep your hands off until they wake up. They like to have a say in it, you know.

And now he does lie back down, leaving Peter sucker-punched and crouched over the women again—over *both* of the women—who, perhaps feeling his breath or intention, turn to curl their bodies, front to back, around each other. Helen, the smaller of the two, tucks her knees to her chest as Lyda pulls her closer. They look like children now, small alien beings, with nothing erotic about them. But the moment, like all moments, contains all the moments that have led up to it, all the moments that are coming, and just as in the culvert, this suspension between two worlds—between before and after, behind and ahead, here and there—remains the single most persistent sensation of Peter's life and fills him with a sudden sense of rue and wonder.

Ok, he tells himself fighting off the little seed of doubt Will has planted to make him question, for the first time, what *they* might want. Even so, he's not quite ready yet to think the next thought: *what made him think he had the right?*

Breathe, he tells himself. *Let it come back.*

When touch comes again, it comes for the man, and there's nothing that Peter can do to stop himself from kneeling before Will and taking Will's two real feet in his hands, one foot to each hand, and beginning: *you are not me, I am not you.* The distinction confounds him, but he rather likes it, kneading the separate, long metatarsals and stubby phalanxes of Will's feet before slowly moving up the body to the ankle, the calf, the thigh. The body—the man's body—is warm, the skin a bit grainy from dried sweat, the hairs coarse and pitted at their roots. Reeling with recognition, Peter scrutinizes the body of this human male—of Will—just as he'd once scrutinized the barks of his trees, and by the time he is finished, he is weeping.

Peter does this two more times, and then because he knows they must do this on their own and find a way to accept with affection what is coming, finally he does leave, coming back to the soiled nest of pillows that is home. This takes no further effort than the thought of the idea of so doing, and yet Peter lands drenched and confused by the act.

How strange things seem here now, as though he's left a part of him behind—and, how unendurably lonesome! It seems he's been gone so much longer than he has, and it's not sweat but tears, he discovers, and *oh*, he thinks, *oh*.

In the loft—home—Peter turns briefly to review the bank of screens, where Lyda digs through beach glass and Will tends awkwardly to a colorful baby.

Never mind, Peter. Never mind.

Finally, because there really is nothing left for him to do, he goes down one more time to wait on the deck.

Peter will wait another long time now, bathed by day and night, and a feeling like satisfaction taking root at the base of his skull. He's not crying anymore, and even though it is a bad time in the history of the world, Peter thinks he might never cry again. Any man, in his same place, might have taken extreme measures; any man might have lived to regret them.

All around him, bats swoop low—real bats. And in the arc of their swooping and his final wait, Peter at last begins to take in that it never was an either/or—not the love of his father or his mother but both, and he—a small child, a toddler, with what will turn out to be a precocious memory—caught on the cusp of the irresolvable split between the two parents who loved him.

And then, from far away, he hears, faintly, what might be a violin, or maybe it's just the wind, or the sound of his own longing, or the seed Will is going to plant in Lyda, or Helen's palimpsest, or his own raw appetite for everything—a sound and its corollary thought that leaves him cool and sublime and as radiant as a moon, his BCI waxing most brightly—blindingly bright—in the very instant that the present moment catches up to him at last and a shadow passes over the sky like a promise or a hush.

SPEAKING FROM THE HEART

BOTH THE BIRD and the violin were waiting for them at what remained of the old embarkation camp—the sleeping decks and a few of the tattered yurts hidden back among the husks of mostly dead trees—each converging within hours of the other, the span of one long soupy night. Lyda arrived in the evening, just as the trees and the fast depleting sky sopped up what was left of the light like a blotter and so close to dark that she and Helen decided to sleep in what might once have been a meadow, or a clearing, making camp on an old platform, or deck. Tomorrow, Lyda told herself wearily, she'd inspect the extent of the blight and what remained of the outlying yurts, but even in that light, or no light, she could see the canvas walls were mostly shredded or gone: why would anyone have done that to what had once been people's homes?

All the rest felt strangely familiar—the sky dense with stars, the quiet brush of river gathering itself up in a long riffle from just above where they had camped to just below, the single snowy mountain that grew out of a bend of the river to the north, even the IC-era footbridge at the head of the site where Lyda now stood tuned toward the mountain like a bead. Seeing it there hurt for some reason, monumental and white, although Lyda could not fix the source of her pain.

And that's where the bird finally found her, trying to fix the source of her pain on the bridge, but because it wasn't her pain but someone else's pain—an old, deep pain—Lyda let go of it as soon as the bird swooped down, biting softly at her ear.

HellO, Lyda, the bird squawked, what took you so long?

Oh, Bird, Lyda said, with a low whistle, bird. Come here, bird, come here, you.

Not now, not now, not NOW.

HellO Bird, she tried again, how are YOU?

Just ignore it, Helen said, coming up beside her. Give it time.

And so they did, settling down in the dimming light while the bird watched from various perches. They unpacked, heated water, fluffed out the one sleeping bag they shared, debating which direction it should face—east or west. Throughout these activities, the bird perched and preened at an aloof distance in the inky darkness where Lyda could hear it making quiet clucking sounds that mimicked compassion. But it wasn't until they had finished their chores and lay together underneath the unzipped bag that it finally swooped down to join them, perching between their two heads—the heads of Lyda and Helen—where, just as they had started to drift off to sleep, it belted out a raucous lullaby.

And they woke in the morning to the sound of a fiddle.

But although Lyda felt she could recognize the music the same way she had recognized her pain the night before, or the red car waiting for her in the city in the rain, she could neither name it nor anticipate it, each strain that drifted back through the trees both familiar and not. This feeling was very strong, the notes so tangible she could almost touch them, but as the music slid into a long jazz riff, she could only recognize it after, lying there with a feeling of ah, yes, that's right—a run, a snatch of melody, something slow and melancholy, silence between notes.

Legume, she tried. *Rock, phosphorescence.*

The music was sad, especially as it mingled with the sounds of the water and wind in dead trees, the sloughing off of things—needles, broken twigs, dried tufts of moss—with a kind of crackling as they drifted down to rock, earth, deck, yurt, water, all the sounds inconsolably converging. But Lyda also had the feeling, or at least the possibility of feeling, that things might fit together soon, like the bird and car, or what might count as memory for her. And that part felt a little bit like hope.

Lodgepole; she tried *Ponderosa*. Then: *fir.*

Lyda felt ready almost for anything.

But not for the man she found playing his fiddle barefoot in the water, the most beautiful man on earth, she thought, surveying the delicate scaffold of his long spine, his mass of knotty hair, and the arch of his neck as it bent to the sound of his fiddle and water lapping at his feet.

Get out, she thought with a sudden urgency that felt alien and disconnected from her. *Get out of the water—now.*

But it was just a river, the same as any river, and he was just cooling his feet.

From behind, he looked familiar too, but like the mountain and the music, Lyda could not place him—that part of her mind somehow was missing. And although she suspected he knew she was there, he just kept on playing, absorbed by his music, which also absorbed Lyda enough that, for the moment, she failed to register the baby in the violin case, wrapped in tie-dyed fleece and sucking on a long plastic tube.

Well, not right away did she register it.

But then the music did stop, as the man lowered his bow and slowly turned to acknowledge her. In this same moment, the moment of his turning, Lyda's memory adjusted and put a name to him—*Will*—even as she was already running down the bank.

Careful, he said.

But it had been so long—how long *had* it been?—since she had been out in the world with Helen, driving the little red car up over mountains and along forest ravines where men with dogs and guns had sometimes followed, or chased them, and Helen navigating, saying turn here and turn there, as if she were a built-in GPS, and as if she could protect them from the men with dogs and guns, when sure, she had finally got them to this site where the bird was waiting, but the bird was nothing compared to Will—that Lyda wasn't careful at all.

So they hugged, breathless—*oh Lyda, oh Will*—and then they climbed back up the bank to where the violin case lay on the concrete piling of the bridge with the baby inside it, sucking, so Will put the instrument in the open lid before turning to Lyda to hug her again, the two of them so happy to burrow, just for this one minute, into the scent of the other, who smelled of memory and earth, and whose body felt sweaty, as if from sleep.

Then, Lyda *did* notice the baby, the placid diptych of it and violin—but where had he got it?

And she noticed the black car, parked askew in the old level spot where fishers used to park before angling for trout when the river was alive. The car was dusty but recognizable, unlike the baby that hardly even looked like a baby but only some deranged idea of what a baby was supposed to look like in its tie-dyed fleece, Lyda thought.

Oh, she said, Will, how *could* you?

Will stiffened, drawing away, and bent to untangle a kink in the tube. Do you mean the car, he said, or the baby, or maybe even the fiddle?

The fiddle?

Yes the fiddle—isn't it amazing? It was here, by the river, when I arrived. And anyway, what else did you want me to *do*?

Lyda shrugged. She didn't know. Be on time maybe, the feeling of hurt leaving a bad taste on her tongue. Or maybe just hold her in his mind long enough to stick with her. But Will, the mathematician, never could keep track of something so simple as time, and seeing him now, the black car behind him, Lyda felt more forsaken than at any other time since she'd found herself alone in the rain, having to choose between the two cars, or maybe since the fleece mom and her baby disappeared, or the bird. Maybe, if Will had been there too, they might have had a real choice and driven down together in the same car. Or—and Lyda caught her breath—maybe, if there had been the two of them, they'd have rejected the cars altogether and walked off together into the teeming mobs to find out what was really going on.

Ok, she said, ok. Just give me a minute. Then, more gently, let me.

And kneeling in the dirt beside him, Lyda took the tube from his beautiful hands that had just been playing the fiddle that was waiting for him when he got here in the night, and deftly inserted the mouthpiece back into the scowling O of the baby's mouth.

How did you do that? Will said, as moved by her skill with the baby as she'd been, earlier, by his with the violin.

Lyda sighed, placing one hand on the baby's smooth head and the other on Will's knee. Maybe, she thought vaguely, it only looked familiar. Maybe it wasn't the same baby at all.

What do you call it anyway—does it have a name?

But before Will could answer, he saw something move on the bridge above them—Helen—off to the other side of the river for her morning cleansing.

Oh, he said Lyda, a forceful bitterness rising in him, how could *you*?

Then, after a pause: if you must know, I call it Baby. If you call it Baby, sometimes it blinks.

At their feet, the river washed by. It would wash that way forever. The baby made its sounds—a little hiccough, a mew. Helen had disappeared somewhere on the other side of the river. And when Will touched Lyda's face—the best he could do in the way of apology—she blinked.

Ok, she said, but tell me something—where did you *get* that baby?

Shh, Will said, putting his hand over her mouth to stop her. We should go. We should just take a car—my car, the black car, it's bigger—and leave, *now*.

But even as he spoke, the words felt fatuous—how could they go? They were already here.

So they stay, this tiny band of travelers, in what appears to be the remains of an old embarkation site, shrouded by the shadow of the single snowy mountain that rises from a bend in the river. They stay, in part because they found the bird and fiddle here, but also in part because they are united by the impossibility of going back—to where? Each retains some memory of a prior self or time, but not even Helen is sufficiently coherent to hold together in the sound of the wash of this water, and by the end of the week, they will have settled into it, the soothing dailiness of camp—the airing out of beddings and the washing of dishes and clothes and themselves—that is at once both purposeful and grounding.

One thing is clear, someone lived here once, spent time—like them—in this ragged assortment of broken-down yurts with its broad central deck and discrete outbuildings for personal hygiene, and so they will live here too, at least for now. No one thinks of here as a final destination—at least they hope not.

In some respects, settling in will turn out to be surprisingly easy—both cars are stocked with various gear and supplies—Will's has an extra sleeping bag for Helen; Lyda's, a little wand for purifying water. But the aqueducts are crumbling and the outbuildings wrecked and most of the yurts uninhabitable, although two are in pretty good shape, with partially intact canvas domes and things on the inside—benches, a small table, one ample storage box—things they could use, places they could sleep, when the rains come.

If they do, Will says.

Oh Will, Lyda says.

I'll go first, Helen says, for the hanta.

Hanta? Lyda says.

The virus, Helen says—I can hold my breath the longest.

But there hasn't been a case of hanta in more than twenty years.

But Helen's already off to inspect the most serviceable yurts before anyone can stop her. First, she'll just clean out the droppings, and then she'll disinfect things, and then—won't everything be nice?

On that first night, all three of them wash in the river, scooping the cold water over each other's shoulders and rubbing each other's backs with sand. Will digs through the first abrasive layer of coarse sand to the one a little deeper, a thick and silky pocket of diatomaceous earth that he scoops up in great handfuls to rub on the women, both curved away from him and the cold. With his eyes closed, Will rubs. And then they lie down in the water to rinse themselves clean.

On the second night, Will lets Lyda sleep with Baby in her arms.

But just for the one night, he says. We don't want to spoil it.

On the third, Helen takes Lyda to a rock by the river as broad and as flat as a table and unknots her hair with an easy, graceful intimacy reminiscent of the time they spent together in the car, Helen riding shotgun and the two of them crammed so close as to practically share each other's sighs and private thoughts. If Helen shifted her legs, Lyda did too; their stomachs growled as one. And just as Helen promised, she had gotten them here every bit as precisely as if she had held a map in her lap, or head, the route marked in red to the river and the bird and the fiddle and Will and the tube-sucking Baby. Now, as she works her long fingers through Lyda's hair as subtle and quick as butterfly wings, a fluttering thrums around them and delivers them both into peace.

While Will watches from a stand of living trees, a feeling like desire rises in him with the thought—it's not a stone but a table.

Within days, Lyda will be baking.

There's plenty of wood for the oven, and once Will has repacked it with mud, Lyda sends Helen out with one of the white nesting pails to fill with berries from the thorny patches everywhere, if maybe not so dark and plump as they once were, while Lyda herself sets up in the shade to make cobblers and pies. This, too, finds its way to Will's heart, the odd domestic impulse and Lyda's languid mixing and kneading. In the heat, she wears only a thin sleeveless tee and abbreviated boxers, and her pale skin turns a dangerous pink. To the side, Baby rests in the red car's shiny toolbox, looking oddly smaller there, its body adapting to the size of its box just as Lyda's once had to hers.

From time to time, Lyda will stop what she's doing to pat Baby's head, leaving white prints where her fingers touch. Once, she tries mixing a little berry juice in the nutrition tank, but Baby spits it back at her, howling.

Sorry, Lyda coos, so sorry, Baby.

Baby blinks.

It's nothing, really, Lyda knows—a reflex. But sometimes—she can't help herself—she spins out little daydreams, simple dreams that come from nowhere and are not attached to anything, dreams of Baby walking someday, and talking, and detaching itself—not all at once but over time—from its tube and Will, to love *her* instead. Maybe, she dreams, when Baby is older, they will find a little school nearby where they can walk together, hand in hand, and where she can bring cupcakes on Baby's birthday, or at least on the day it was found.

Or she imagines weaning Baby from its tank and taking it down the river to nurse. Lyda has the strongest feeling that if she gives Baby her breast and if Baby sucks there long enough her breasts—Lyda's own breasts—will engorge with something that is not milk, but like milk, and more nutritious than anything that comes in a tank.

And sometimes, she can't help this either, she dreams of going back to find the small fleece family and give them back this baby, if it is even theirs.

But of course nothing like this is ever going to happen because Will guards it as fiercely as Lyda's parrot guards her (which, as far as Lyda is concerned, that parrot can go anywhere, sit on anyone's shoulder, nibble at anyone's ear—Lyda is generous that way—no one owns the bird, no more than they do Baby). Lyda isn't sure she understands this. There's something so stingy, so guarded and parsimonious in his attachment that gives him no pleasure at all, neither from Baby's general presence—its very being—nor from Will's own daily ministrations—the bathing of Baby's head and small slippery mouth area, the wiping down of the zipperless sack or the sterilizing of the nutrition tube and tank, the rocking and singing to sleep—none of the things that Lyda enjoys, the way a parent should—the way its mother did.

Thinking this, Lyda can't help but rue that she chose the red car—in the black car, maybe she'd have got to Baby first, and everything would already be different.

But whenever Lyda tries to help Will—show him how to prop Baby up so it can look around or hold its own tube, and doesn't he think it could use more cuddling, you can't keep a baby in a box forever—Will just gets mad, throws Baby over one shoulder, and tromps off into the woods where he sets it down next to a stump or a rock and fiddles to it for hours, away from her.

Then it is so very lonely without them.

Oh Baby, she thinks, oh Baby.

Lyda's haunted by Will's distance, haunted too by the memory of that one night he let her sleep with it, the largish baby body crooked in her loving arms the way babies should sleep in a perfect world, crooked in the arms of the one who cares for them most. Until, one day, Lyda finds herself alone with it. This *never* happens, but for some reason, Will's gone off mapping at the exact same time Helen, too, has disappeared into the ruined woods, which she does more and more these days, abstracted and remote, and making Lyda miss the old, companionable Helen, but not now. Because now it's only her and Baby and the whole hot afternoon before them.

Still, Lyda takes her time. She tidies up a bit, pausing now and then to pat Baby on the shoulder. She fluffs the pillows, arranges the shoes—so many shoes, lovely in a line, biggest to smallest—Will's, her own, Helen's, but none at all for Baby, whose tiny feet are still stuffed in its sack, so Lyda puts two little rocks there to represent the idea of Baby's shoes. And finally she takes Baby to the river, clutched in one arm, and a bucket of berries to wash in the other.

Lyda will fill the bucket with water and rinse the fruit gently. She will do this again and again, and when it is clean, she will take Baby to a spot, hidden by a welter of dead, or mostly dead bushes, and offer it her breast—one breast. Because Lyda does know something of men and rage, she will do this slyly, in secret. She will do it like the real mom did, and she'll do it when no one will see.

But despite the longing in her, Baby spits the nipple out, just like when she tried to infuse its nutrition with berries, and even though Lyda knows this sometimes takes time, time is not what she has. So she tries again to shove the stubborn little face up against her willing body, and she does this again and again until they are no longer struggling.

By the time Will finds her there, later in the afternoon, she's covered up again and crooning softly to the sleeping Baby. He comes with such a crashing through the brambles she's afraid he'll wake it up, but other than that, she feels nothing—no fear, no dread, no regret for what she's done. If there had ever been a time in the future for her when she might really have walked this child to school, maybe then she'd have something to regret. But there wasn't going to be any school for them, and as she moves to hand Baby over, Will shakes his head.

It's sleeping, he says. Leave it, for now.

Then he squats beside her and they watch the river together for a while.

Finally he says, this won't last forever, you know, and his words are as slow and as careful as they are almost tender, the freeze-dried food, our supplies. Not even Baby's nutrition will last forever.

Nothing lasts forever, Lyda says, bending over to kiss its broad forehead.

We'll have to go at some point. We'll have to decide.

Lyda doesn't answer. She's taken in what he has said—she has heard him—but what she's thinking is that in another world, the sound of the water, the smell of damp earth, how soothing all this might be. Finally, she says something that surprises them both. She says, Helen's got a tattoo.

Now it's Will's turn to pause. Fair enough, he says, I think Baby does too. You can't really see it—it's underneath the sack—but you can feel it, a hard little knob, like a latch.

I don't care, Lyda says, scrambling to get up now and go back to camp. I thought so, but I don't really care.

No, stay, Will says. You can't change anything by leaving now.

But Lyda is already up and Baby, awakened, is starting to howl. Unsure, she props it on her shoulder and pats it, too hard, in love with the solid thumping sound her hand on the small body makes, despite the latch. I don't care, she says again—you can't make me care.

What I remember, Will says, without getting up or reaching for Baby or objecting to anything at all, is numbers. All my life, I just thought that if I could get the numbers right, things would be ok. And now look what's happened.

Lyda looks back at Will, made suddenly shy by what he's said—his confession. She remembers—what *does* she remember? Almost Lyda thinks but doesn't say, she remembers something more than what's missing from her memory. Almost, she thinks but doesn't say, she remembers it's not something that is missing but someone.

But because she says nothing, Will finally gives in. I'm not going to stop you, you know, he says. You can have Baby if that's what you want. I don't think so, but go ahead, see if that will make you happy.

When Lyda gets back, Will is already straddled atop the frame of a yurt, wrapping the joists with rope. It is dangerous up there—if the wood fails, if he falls—but Will looks completely happy, absorbed in his work and singing a strange little tune she knows she has never heard from anyone but him. It's quite moving really, the sound of it somehow organic—alive. And in the wash of Will's singing it comes to her suddenly how easy it must once have been to have loved this place—how beautiful it must once have been. Watching him, for that one moment—Will on the yurt, and Helen coming back from wherever she goes, and Baby—there's nothing missing at all for Lyda. This is all there ever was and all she ever wanted there to be. It could still be nice for them here. Everything could still be nice. Lyda wants this. She wants it as much as she has ever wanted anything, even as she is struck by a certain unnatural flatness to the world, as though a membrane had been spread over everything, depleting it of nuance and reducing it to abstraction.

Hey there, Lyda calls out to Will, be careful.

For in the completeness of the moment, she's grown aware of her own body as a body in waiting, tuned in some way to this man who is working above and looking down as though she has suddenly become for him, as well, a woman in her waiting body. And when he looks down, Lyda sees it too, the way he looks at her—and then it closes up again, as tight and protective as a scar, for there is nothing free about this physical world: if Will miscalculates, up there on the yurt, he'll fall; if Lyda's body stirs, like her mother, she'll conceive.

For this reason, Lyda turns to Baby instead, steeling herself against the one thing she wants.

And Will turns back to his work.

And Helen, watching from the woods, tucks her hands deep in her pockets and, too slow, breathes. She breathes in, *breathes.*

In the days that follow, they will sink deeper into another kind of waiting that only makes them edgy and irritable.

To Lyda, it just seems so unfair. They found the parrot, Will's fiddle; they rescued Baby. Surely they're entitled to some peace. But it's not peaceful, the heat of what's rising in her, for Lyda has not not noticed that Will looks at Helen exactly the same as he sometimes looks at her. And no matter how much baking she does, how fine a model of industry or purpose she sets—how much of the tattered canvas she works to repair, stitching the rips meticulously closed with tiny even stitches, or, where necessary, reweaving the fabric itself, over and under, over and under—nothing is going to change until she does something to change it.

Maybe it's the shoes, Lyda doesn't really know, but later everything will seem to have hinged on the randomness of shoes, how one morning, they awaken to the murky light of yet another dawn to find, each of them, just beyond the pillow where they slept the night, a new pair of soft-soled shoes for camp—Will's are black, Helen's taupe, and Lyda's a brilliant red—so that now, when they walk, they can feel the earth giving beneath their feet. But in the days that follow, more shoes will appear, as if this is what they've wanted—satin slippers for Helen's tiny feet lodged in the mossy crevice of a boulder, sturdy lace-up boots for Lyda on the oven's hearth, sleek Italian driving loafers for Will.

Next, they will find, in this order: mints in a tree, one Ace bandage wrapped around a weathered stick, strings for Will's fiddle dangling from a yurt beam, fresh tubing for Baby in a rubber fishing creel, lotion for their chapped hands just downstream where they wash, two novels printed on paper and one geometry textbook, a pair of gleaming tweezers, matches, a funnel, a calendar marking the seasons but not any years, animal print blankets, cutlery, candles, and one external hard drive on the hood of the black car.

But they also lose things—Baby's favorite nipple (how Baby howls), Helen's sunscreen (Helen burns), Will's fish flies (as if there were fish), Lyda's yellow pen and favorite sock that had been drying on a branch.

There were six of Lyda's socks on that branch—six plush virgin wool socks with reinforced toes and padding at the heel and the tenderest part of the arch, all of Lyda's favorite socks (well, her only socks), so much better than the thin cotton liners she had worn before, although who needs socks, her father said when she complained that her feet were cold, if you're going to walk on this plush carpet I provide for you to keep you safe, go barefoot—one pair red, one pair blue, one pair green. But when Will brings them to her, dry, there are only five, and even though they look and look, it's clear to Lyda from the start that she'll never get that sock back—that sock is gone to the world.

Sometimes they argue, and although no one ever remembers the words they fling recklessly around, there are plenty of them, choked out from deep feelings of confusion and regret: if only Lyda took the black car, if only Will could hunt, if only Helen didn't have her tattoo. They'll agree not to argue, but then start all over again—Will washes his socks upriver; Lyda thrashes in her sleep; can't someone muzzle the bird? The light on the too-exposed deck hurts their eyes, and every single pair of dark glasses that came with the cars has mysteriously disappeared. They could really use some dark glasses now. Will blames the bird, and the bird blames Lyda, and everyone suffers from headaches.

All except Helen, who rarely speaks now.

Finally, it rains, the storm bearing down so fast in the middle of the night that everything they own gets blown around and soaked before they even know what is happening. And they run around, gathering up the things they need most—what they can't afford to lose—and shoving it into the cars before it gets ruined. Soon the cars are stuffed with wet things—sleeping bags and clothes and shoes and the fiddle and Baby and boxes for Baby and the nutrition tank and other odds and ends, such that there is no room for them, on the inside of the cars, which also stink. So they sit getting wetter on the bridge and mad at each other.

One yurt, Will mutters. You couldn't manage to finish repairing the tent for even one yurt.

But she works hard, Helen says, trying to be helpful. Look at all the progress she has made.

Rain, Will says, comes from the sky above. If you don't want to get wet, where do you start?

With the top, Lyda says, wet hair clinging to her face, you start at the top. But really, those yurts are complicated—what with all those angles and the round part of the dome, the center's hard to fix, really more like a geometry problem than a sewing project. And anyway, you could have helped—aren't you supposed to be a mathematician?

Futurologist, Will says.

Technically, Helen says, you are both.

As she says this, the modest sound of her voice, a little like the old Helen from the café and the car, triggers a memory in Lyda of the small fleece family huddled on the coast. And really, she sees now, there had been something familiar about them, the way the dad had knelt to show the boy something in the water that might have been a whale. Lyda hoped it was a whale anyway. But what she remembers now is how the boy refused to look at what his dad was showing him, bending instead to pick up and throw a stone—throw it as far as he could, like a baseball curving into space, maybe even as far as the whale, if it were a whale, if there *were* whales then—now.

But when she tries to tell the others about this small boy and the possible whale, it comes out all wrong.

What color was the fleece? Will sounds excited.

What are you talking about?

I think I know that man—that boy.

They are all shivering now, but not from cold, and you can't Lyda thinks, they're mine, thinking of the rest of that other rainy night, with her and the fleece mom in the women's bathroom, the baby sleeping between them, and their faces, crammed beneath stained porcelain sinks, close enough to be considered cheek-to-cheek, speaking from the heart.

Now, Helen moves as though to calm the shivering, laying one impossibly warm hand on Lyda's shoulder. You know, Lyda, she says, and it's almost tender, there aren't any whales anymore.

One day, that boy will be grown, Lyda thinks. One day, he'll bend, again, to pick something up from the ground, to curl his body into the folds of itself in the exact same dimensions and angles as his prior smaller self, and then he'll heave it just as surely as he'd thrown that stone into the sea when he was this boy. This older, more mature boy—this grown boy, this *man*—will so closely replicate the prior, childish curl of the boy that Lyda, seeing this, bursts into spontaneous, visceral tears—but is it a stone, or a brick, that is coming?

Lyda doesn't know that yet, for who, she thinks with a bitter smile, could know the future?

Shhh, Helen says now, *shh*.

Between them, Will stiffens, relaxes. The rain comes down. Then, for no reason, he pulls the two women—*both* women—close, as they sit on the bridge, quiet now, and wait for the rain to stop.

Some time later—no one knows how long—Will approaches Lyda doing laundry on the bank just down river. He comes on her from behind, but maybe she's singing or with the sound of the river, she doesn't hear him, doesn't even feel him behind her, bent over a t-shirt that's not even hers, but one of his favorites. Grayed from multiple washings here, in this river, the t-shirt is covered with writing in a language she does not recognize, a language of symbols. Lyda is using rocks to scrub out the worst dirt and, noticing a small tear at the soiled neck, scrubs even harder there, as hard as she can, scrubbing and scrubbing the place where the small tear is.

Oddly moved, Will watches from behind, struck not by the violence she's doing to his shirt but by the strong curve of her back, the subtle definition of her shoulders as they work. Inside the skin of the man by the river, another skin remembers, but there is something inexact about the memory, as though the body before him—Lyda's body—takes up the wrong space in either his memory or this world, and Will suspects that if he touched it—and really, Will would like to touch it now—it would not be there—*here*. The muscles of Lyda's upper arms, for example—where did they come from?

Then that, too, passes, and coming up to sit beside her, he tousles her beautiful hair and says, do you have it, too?

Lyda has to stop herself from startling, but she can't stop the deep flush that runs through her.

What? she says.

The memory thing.

Oh, she says, that—the glitch.

Then she twists the t-shirt and wrings it to a tight, dry roll, the water dripping from it onto her feet and his, which are browner than before. Pink and brown, the bare feet grip at the sand side-by-side. Have they been here so long?

I remember everything, she says—just not the way it was. I remember a box and the color white. I remember—and suddenly, viscerally, she does—*you*.

Do you remember, Will says, a table?

I told you, a box. And sometimes a vehicle, not like these cars, higher and more powerful, with room, she says . . .

For?

For all of us, she finishes, as if to say now you know, are you satisfied now?

Then neither of them says anything for a while. Lyda spreads the wet t-shirt on a rock. Will doodles something in the sand with a stick, abstract signs. They could stay here a long time, or leave right now—until Will's hand puts down the stick and lays itself on Lyda's pink foot.

It's way too hot, you know, Lyda says, for that fleece. Baby will boil alive.

But Will's hand isn't stopping. First, he squeezes her foot lightly, then the doodling starts on her, just there on the bottom of her foot. Maybe, he says, still doodling—but what is he writing?—Baby looks hot on the outside, but on the inside, his fingers curling now around the whole arch of her foot to trace the underside—softly, softly—she's as cool as the moon.

She?

Oh, who can say what it is?

Big enough for all of them, that vehicle, and someone else.

But even thinking this, Lyda feels herself relaxing, sitting back, letting her head drift toward the arc of Will's shoulder, her body inclining, at last, toward his. Already a kind of dreaminess is taking hold in which she can imagine everything different, another kind of life in an ordinary city blasted by sun and full of ordinary people attending to their daily tasks of life. She imagines waking beside Will in a bed with tangled sheets—*sheets!*—his heat, his hair, the white sun damage spots that speckle his skin. It's not so much imagination as instinct—the smell of coffee, and walking out—the two of them—to have a pastry or buy a newspaper or feed the cat. She imagines a cat, a street, trees, the sound of birds, children playing nearby in a park—toddlers on swings and boys with baseballs and bats, a bowl of goldfish.

Will's hand has moved to her shin. It's tracing lines there—up and down, up and down. If Lyda weren't looking, she wouldn't be certain he was even touching her. It's that soft, the brush of his hand.

And Lyda lets him. She lets the heat press in from all around, almost turning to him, when suddenly a thought rises up in her instead: what ever made her mother think she could protect her when look what happened to her right underneath her mother's watch.

I don't think, she says. It's not, yet—Will, this isn't right.

I remember being tested—did they test you too?

No, that's not what I mean.

But Will can't stop his hand from finding the small of her back and its completely natural dimple. I mean, he says, but then he doesn't know what else to say. It's right and not right, what his hand is doing.

Finally, he says something strange, something Lyda will never forget. He says: this is where history and geology collide.

When he says it, something shifts one last time in Lyda, like the past catching up with the future, or as though she were being shoved through a door—or a not door. And then something else opens in its place that will come to her in words and the words that come will knock her for a loop: *what kind of father would Will make?*

MERCIFUL, MERCIFUL

ONE NIGHT NOT LONG after, Will awakens from what might have been a dream to what he knows at once is a single intact memory of another night, the sucking sound of that first stagnant creek and the fleece family sleeping nearby. He awakens with the same sense of disorientation, the same certain knowledge that something is wrong. On this night, the night by the river, he lies listening to his own frantic heart and the quiet sleeping of the women on either side of the deck.

Then he sits up to check on Baby in its box, also sleeping.

But his thoughts had not been so tender, on that other night, about the fleece family—the dad's sleeping noises, guttural and indecent, and the mom with her eye on Baby. Even so, he was torn and had almost said yes. He'd almost waited out the night to say, ok, they could come with him, sailing off in the two cars together. Will had lain there in the night, thinking how it would be, like destiny itself. Sometimes, the boy would sleep shotgun beside him, his small head rolling loose on the joint of his neck. When he slept, the boy would smell sweet, and sometimes spit would slip out of the corner of his mouth. Or sometimes, he'd cry out or moan.

And at night, the boy would crawl out of the back of the van to crawl into Will's tent, curled like a dog at the foot of Will's bag.

Will imagined him curled there in the morning, his face split open with want.

Let me be yours, he would say.

But unlike Lyda, who'd got Helen, a thought that makes him bitter even now, Will had risen in that other night, stealthy as the thief he was, to siphon gas from the dun-colored van and sneak away with Baby in the night.

It's not a dream, when he wakes on the deck, but an ache—an ache, and a terrible emptiness in his hands, which lie, the long fingers of them and their blackened nails, like little animals at the ends of his wiry forearms as if waiting for something to come back to life. In the ache that is not a dream or a memory there is a round, flat rock, and all around the rock are other rocks, round rocks that border the large center stone, or maybe a labyrinth. And there's sun beating down there too.

Heat radiates from the stone, which is not, Will knows, a stone at all.

But it's not the escape he remembers but the ambivalence, sailing along in the sleek black car fueled by stolen gas. In one part of his damaged mind he had thought *that was close*, and patted Baby on its head. But because the head felt wrong—neither too hot nor too cool but yet a terrible temperature, almost no temperature at all—he had already begun to regret the capable hands of the fleece mom, which surely would have known what to do and how to do it.

Now, by the river, he wonders for the first time how much gas he'd left them. He'd siphoned a lot—enough to get here. Surely he hadn't taken it all, but how much did they need? And the thought of them stuck by that creek still, eking along with their store of cans, makes him sweat. Will's not thinking yet he should go back to see. That thought may be coming, but not yet.

Instead, another thought: *what would Peter do?*

And because that makes no sense at all, is not even a fully formed thought, just something that floats out beyond him, a thought—a name— that he loses almost before he has had it, when it's gone all that remains is this lingering, trenchant feeling of loss. Across the deck, the sleeping women stir—first one, then the other—gutting Will with a wrong, wrong feeling of displacement.

It's not so much that Helen is furtive—she's furtive, sure, but a lot of people are furtive these days—as it is that she does not entirely belong here, belongs, Will thinks, *elsewhere*, that reminds him now not so much of the fleece mom but the boy, who at least had his hope, and of whom, Will now remembers, he had, in fact, dreamed—but how could it be a dream, when it seemed so real?

They were camped, in the dream, the boy and his family and Will, too, all together on a wide, gray lake. But it's not really gray, not even the right color for any kind of lake, almost red, with ugly puce-colored pockmarks where the wind stirs it up, except there isn't any wind in the dream, only a terrible, hot stillness that makes Will so drowsy. But he's not sleeping yet, just watching, in his dreamy sleepiness, the dad teach the boy how to fish with a stick and a string. The stick is long and green—the brightest color in the dream—and the boy is both bored and impatient. He wants to swim, but not here, sweetie, the fleece mom says, that water's not clean—it's dirty.

The dried mud of the shoreline cracks open in long, brittle ripples that wriggle, like the water, as if they were alive, making Will feel disgusted with himself and the parents, for who would bring a child to such a place to camp—to fish—but just then there's a flash all along the unnatural shore, and Will sees that the boy and the dad have got something on their line. The boy is jumping up and down, anyway, and the dad is yelling, and the stick is putting up a fight. The lake smells suddenly pungent as the boy and dad bring something to the surface of the water that looks to be alive.

And for a moment, in the dream, there's a dreamy kind of happiness—the boy and dad have caught a fish, the mom will grill it for supper! But then Will sees that it's not a real fish but a garbage fish, the fish arcing up to flop in the dirt at the feet of the boy and the father, and *move*, the word rises up in Will although no sound comes out, *get away*, but now sound *is* coming out, sailing down the shoreline to the father and son, and again *move*, but too late, as the fish mouth clamps on the boy's slender ankle, the razor-sharp teeth slicing all the way down to the bone.

But maybe that really did happen, Will thinks, fully awake now and the memory of fish teeth on boy bone and the semen smell of fish so precise and overwhelming that Will knows now what he's going to do. And it is this—his new resolve to go back and get them, or at least return their gas—that pulls him from his bag and back through the night to his own black car.

Not without Lyda, he thinks.

But against the terrible urge Will has now to leave, this thought won't stop him for long—Lyda's got Helen, who does Will have?

Without even a car of her own, he'd said that first day.

You don't get to do that, Lyda had said. Helen got me here—she found the bird.

So what, you just picked her up by the side of the road, like a cat?

No, more like a Baby.

Oh come on, Lyda—but Will was really thinking, even then, of the fleece family, and how things might be different if he'd brought them too—what do you even know about her? Is she even safe?

Lyda laughed. I'm telling you, she's like a built-in GPS. You want eggs, Helen's your girl. Besides, Will, trust me—we *need* her. Then she paused, a bit shyly, before adding, besides, Helen's for me.

That was all the words she'd used, but when she used them—this was strange too—they had had the effect of draining the outrage right out of him. Will had just stood there, defused, looking helplessly at Lyda, who was small and strong and with muscles that showed in all the different parts of her body and whose words had the power to strip the inside of him completely like that. And then, he'd looked at Helen, who was even smaller, and paler, her head covered with its perpetual scarf and her elegant hands.

Now, he rubs a patch of dirt away from the car, and licking the rich mineral taste of it, lays his head in his hands, sleepless and alone in the world. The sound of the river, he knows, is the wash of the past, but however much he wants to be able to decode it—to write in the language of his symbols only he can understand—that part of it continues to elude him, and Will knows the time is coming when he's about to do the very thing he knows he mustn't, for inside the black car, as in all cars, there's a glove box, and inside the glove box, another box, and inside that box— Will has at least looked—a small handheld device, nestled in its clever hiding place. Now, Will knows, if he takes it out—if he holds it—he's going to turn it on.

What Will really should have done was tell the boy a story. If he told the boy a story, it would go like this.

Once on that long ago time all the boys—we—played a game we called baseball on green fields in parks beneath great canopies, batter up batter up batter up.

And this is the story that Will would tell because it's the one he remembers.

In particular Will remembers the mound. He remembers coiling his body, clutching the hard, round ball in his hand, cupped by the mitt. He remembers disappearing into that one moment—the exact instant of uncoiling and releasing the ball. And he remembers watching what happened after as the ball traced the arc of its unstoppable trajectory and it always still seemed that things might be ok, that this one pitch might be perfect. Will lived for that infinitesimal moment when the world would fade away and he would go with it, into the stripped-of-sound—chatter of boys, flapping of canopy, what his dad yelled—quiet. There, in that instant, Will and the skin of his tough boy body would coalesce into his one sure purpose of controlling the outcome, while what his father wanted—Will would only understand this slowly, over time—was that he, like his father before him, would be defined entirely by the elegant geometries of ball and base and boy—all this, and nothing more.

And Will hated him for it.

Will had hated, also, in this order, the shoes—the dangerous, *clackety-clack* of the cleats—the clumsiness of gear at the plate, the smack of bat on ball and probability of it coming back at him, and the flickering light of the canopy that caused shadows where shadows were not. Sometimes it would get so bad that pitchers would spin to throw out runners who were not even there, and although Will tried hard to keep track of where each boy was and what the next play should be, he lived in perpetual dread that the next game-losing error was going to be his.

They were all afraid of losing the ball in the flickering shadows of the canopy.

But Will would not tell the boy this.

Because Will wasn't the boy who lost the ball but only the boy who pitched and watched, a cry rising up in his throat for the boy who was losing the ball as it sailed out over the field off the bat—high and hard in the dark and the light of the shadows—for who could track a ball in light like that?

Always keep your eye on the ball, Will's father told him later—see what happens if you don't.

They had all blamed the shadows, but Will had the opposite feeling, as if the ball had sailed true to its mark, gone slow in the treacherous moment.

But what he'd tell the boy was how, afterwards, you couldn't get through a game without one mom or another calling time-out to ascend the ladders and repair the canopy. And these were the good times, he'd say—our moms on the ladders above us and us in the shadows below, spitting sunflower seeds at each other and doing calisthenics to keep warm. That's when we were safe, he would say—our moms making sure of that above, and us on the ground, with nothing to do. And sometimes, he would tell the boy, it would seem to us they had called time-out when nothing at all was wrong with the canopies above us, or maybe not wrong yet. It would seem to us they did this just to go up on their ladders above us, to hang out and chat a little up there, intimate and purposeful, to stop the games and what the dads yelled from the bleachers to chastise or cheer us on.

Now, it sometimes seems to Will that all he's really wanted in these long days by the river, is something like a baseball, and a canopy, above, to protect them. He's wished for a ladder and someone to climb with, for enough others to field a team, or at least a decent game of catch. And sometimes, he can't help it, he's wished there were one thing he remembers that his father told him he might cherish as a talisman or good advice.

But the girls threw like girls, and the fiddle was starting to warp from the heat, and between Lyda and Helen, Will couldn't tell which he preferred—Lyda's legs were better and she had her general cheerfulness, but while Helen, more and more these days seemed increasingly remote, he had that other feeling, as though beneath the layer he was seeing, another layer lay that he could love.

And there were still times there—not so many, but some—when none of this seemed to matter, and he could almost imagine the river *alive*. They'd have finished with their dinner—all the work of their day—and maybe Will would be playing something on the fiddle for the others who would not notice how out of tune it was, or maybe he'd just be lying on the deck in his blue sleeping bag looking up where there'd once been so many stars. Here and there, he might think, there were places in the woods where the green was coming back, and if the woods could come back, why not the river—grown green with algae and stippled with fish, why not the weather that comes from the mountain?

Why not the stars?

Why not Baby.

But in the morning, Lyda would be fussing over it, still so inert in its tie-dyed sack, and the light would be as bleak as it ever was in Little League, and Helen would already be tromping off into the woods—what did she do in the woods each day, where did she even go?

Lying there, putting consciousness off a while longer, Will would wish it was only one of them—either one, it didn't matter—Helen, whom he'd never once seen sweat, or Lyda, whose body, even from a distance, Will could sometimes smell. If there were only one—Lyda in the red car, or Helen—Helen by the stone that is not a stone—then he would not have to choose.

And then one day Helen came back from the woods with a tomato. She came cupping it in the palms of her hands, holding it before her like a promise, all red and ripe and with a little bulge of half formed seed or fruit on one side, as though it had tried—and failed—to twin itself. Split three ways, the tomato was hardly more than a taste of tomato, and when it was gone, they only wanted more.

And isn't that an odd thing, Lyda said. Before we had the one, we never gave a single thought to tomatoes.

Ravenous now for tomatoes, Will saw the first tomato as a variable—an x, like Helen herself. But solving for Helen was not going to turn out as hard as he thought, for as soon as he saw this, Will knew Lyda was wrong—Helen wasn't for her: she was for no one.

Or they were for her.

The next day, there were carrots, and after that, beets.

Soon, Lyda would be cooking up a storm.

And Will, curiosity piqued, had started to explore in earnest, although he didn't yet know he was looking for a way out, or back. Will couldn't know this yet because the food was good and it was going to be a while before he had the dream of the lake, or the one just before—or after—where it's not the boy or the fish that dies, but Will himself. But it's a gentle kind of dying, not violent, just a slow fading, or leaking through the open spaces of his body—the layers between—and someone in a clear voice saying not to be afraid. But Will isn't afraid, only anticipating something, even eager for it, and although, in the dream, he knows this idea of light is not original, he can't help but want it. *It's not really dying,* the voice reassures him—*I think you are going to like it.*

Will wasn't leaving yet when he started going off, not even so much following Helen as trying to see—to map—where they were. He went out with his compass and instruments for writing, and as much of the keen part of his mind as he had left. He went after breakfast, and he told Lyda when he was going, but even so, he was the one who felt furtive, for it seemed, in the bifurcation of his longing, either way, betrayal was his only real option.

Unless, but he wasn't yet thinking this either, he chose neither of them.

What he did not think was, walking would solve the problem of gas.

He didn't think, these old railroad tracks must go somewhere.

He didn't think, the least he could do was leave them two cars.

Three times Will tried to leave on foot.

But he didn't really know that when he first started off—he was just walking. If he put it into words, what he was doing, the words might have been that he would walk until something stopped him, or his feet blistered down to the bone, or the need for water overwhelmed him, or—impossible—a train came, which he would hop.

But really, there wasn't much time to think this because almost as soon as he left, maybe half a mile north, Will came to a massive rockslide, a mountain of slag that must date all the way back to the era of the great Western quakes. But it didn't look old, it looked new, only recently formed—no crumbling of stone, no grass or weeds or moss inching up through the cracks, not even any sign of settling or shifting, but only a sound, like the wind or deep water that rose from the spaces between its boulders and thrummed all around him.

Well, that was that, he thought.

And that was the first time.

Feeling vaguely satisfied, Will went back instead along the river, clambering over its high rocky cliffs below which green holes, murky and swirling, promised good swimming. But without any access, it wasn't until the last such pool, not so far above camp, that Will found a way down a narrow crevice that ended at a ledge still high above the river and warmed by the sun. Will stood on the ledge looking down for a while, calculating odds as a certain drowsiness began to overcome him. There were other rocks below he'd have to clear, and even though the water looked deep, as nearly opaque with sediment as it was, he couldn't really say. Besides, he was so very sleepy now, mesmerized by the soupy heat, the eddying below, the quiet brush of water, the green.

Thus, when it came—the blissful cry of boyhood cannonball ecstasy—it came as if out of the churning itself, or through the cusp of time, bringing with it a memory of leaping—the rush of wind past his face, his own throat opening in that cry, the cold fist of water exploding around him, and him—his boy body—plunging deeper, hands dragged above, legs cocked to push from the bottom and pop him back up like a cork, blasting back into the light and air—as complete and exact as any memory he'd ever had—skin of whale, man and child on the hood of his car, a vast improbable wash.

But like the deer he didn't shoot or the woman he had failed to recognize, there was something inchoate about it, and he knew it wasn't his.

Had he ever even played baseball, Will thought bitterly.

Then he jumped.

The next time Will left, he followed the railroad tracks south to where they ended at a severed trestle above a gorge so deep he could not see the bottom.

The hills to the east were too rugged for walking at all.

That left the creek Helen went up—Will had seen her—to bring back her tomatoes. And tomatoes weren't all she was bringing back now, but other vegetables as well—corn and onions and green beans and fat yellow carrots, eggplant, zucchini, peas. Helen was a veritable produce stand these days.

But, oh, was all she said now when he asked, there's nothing up there—just some falling down trailers and an old freeway culvert. But it's completely clogged up with debris—you can't really get past it, no one can. Then she said something strange. She said, up there, anyway—it might as well be the moon.

They were working on the open deck—Will untangling fish line for his new dream of fish, Helen sorting ruined tents for Lyda who had spread them around her with her various sewing tools—marking pencils, scissors, straight edge, tape measure, pincushion, tape. Intent and oddly absorbed by her work, she crouched above the remnants as though hers were the most useful task in the world.

I want to make it beautiful, she said. It's so much nicer that way.

Watching her piece it together, trying one piece, then another, working in from the circumference and slowly filling it in, Will had to hold himself back, for anyone could see she was going at it wrong. But despite what had happened in the rain, Will knew not to say it was never going to close, because he could see now that Lyda didn't care, and how, looked at a certain way, she was fitting scraps together less like a geometry problem than a map. As soon as he thought this, Will heard again the sound that had come from the rocks and himself as he jumped to the water.

Lyda looked, he saw now—happy.

Oh, she said, this one is ruined. And she held up a piece of fabric worn so thin Will could see clear through it, and with a kind of gentle logic, unraveled the rest of it, strand by strand, letting them loose on the wind until no part of the thin scrap remained.

Well, she said, as if for no reason at all, we might as well call this an Intentional Community. And then, as casually as if she had asked him for a walk, do you think we should make love?

Will would never know where the words had come from—if she spoke them, or if they unraveled, like the fabric in her hands—but they were out now, or at least the idea of them were, and Will just stood there watching her sew—the glint of the sun off the needle, the tiny holes, the thread pulling the two parts together. It would take a woman to explain this—what the act of sewing moved in Will—but Lyda wasn't talking, only sewing, in and out, in and out, puncturing and binding and working toward the elusive hole at the center of the yurt that would never be closed, like the hole in the water, or the earth, or the eye of the needle that tugs.

When Will finally looked away, what he saw was this: Helen watching him from the flat rock by the river where she had taken Baby to lull, with her fingers, into its flaccid sleep. Even at this distance, Will could see drool trailing down the side of Baby's face, glinting and metallic. But what he was noticing, instead, was Helen, absently running her long fingers over its chest, then up its neck to its forehead, then stroking, stroking its little temples—while all her attention was really on him, a not altogether unpleasant sensation, and a thought rising in him like water: *it's not a stone but a table.*

Helen the slight one, ever discreet.

Then, for the longest time, Will remembers nothing, only fragments—the Ranger, a hole or a tube in the earth, their first troubled glimpse of the ruined world after the sky had collapsed. *Merciful, merciful,* Will thinks. It must have been what he was thinking when he had climbed that first time into the buttery leather of the black car and settled in there for what felt like sleep.

And now, again: *merciful.*

And as Will falls away from the memory and moment, Helen lets him, sinking her own attention back to the sound of the river lapping up all the other sound there is, a soothing sound—like that of canopies fluttering in the wind, or stars going out in a desert night sky with a kind of crackling—and she gathers Baby to her shoulder and lets its glittering drool run out its mouth down her back. When it is empty, she washes its face with cold water dipped from the river, and by the time she gets it settled in the nearby kindling box, Will is already waiting for her.

Hey, she says, moving slowly to meet him, but he's already grabbed her by the hands—*both* her hands—and is turning them over to examine the small blue indentations at the backs of her wrists. He does this a little too forcefully, the bones of her hands crunching together with a slight crackling they both recognize.

You don't have to, she says.

But he can't not look as, holding Helen's two unnaturally quiescent hands in the vise of his one, he lays his other hand firmly on her chest, proving nothing more than that while there is a pulse there, it's wholly unrelated to the frantic beating of her now discovered heart. Will's face blanches, a slight clenching at the corner of his eyes, what might be a gathering of tears. Then he lets go, but Helen doesn't, holding out both hands so he can touch the dimples—willing him to touch them, to press one finger in each blue spot so he can feel the more erratic flutter of her own private self, even as she flattens, going dim and remote, and tiny, tiny, as though reduced to some essential element or code.

So now you know, she says finally.

Yeah, I do.

What took you so long?

And then she takes her hands away and, full-sized and opaque again, sits peaceably back on the rock like a table, crossing her legs and turning her hands upward on her knees.

No parts of their bodies touch yet.

The dark water runs to all sides of them, and more than anything, Will wants Helen to splash his face with it, just as she had splashed the face of Baby, to wash him clean too. But Will can't move—not toward the water, its cooling relief, and not toward her either.

It's not so bad, she had said, that night in the desert as, with each dying star, she had grown dimmer too, until all that remained of her naked body was a subtle shadow of itself. Not really, she had said, and—this was the oddest thing—she sounded so shy.

You bad girl, Will had wanted to joke, get back inside your computer.

I warned you, she said.

Will's throat had ached then too—it ached terribly. But he couldn't stop himself from touching the place on the back of her wrist. It didn't look bad, just a slight indentation and a dark blue spot like a smudge of ink or charcoal, and it felt fine too, like the rest of her skin—smooth and soft to the touch. But it wasn't any temperature he could feel, and the pulse, like a star going out.

Now, by the river, Will remembers making love, but in his memory, wherever they touched felt cool—or not cool, it felt absent, her touch as though no touch at all, or as though, wherever she touched him, she left little blanks, little erased parts of him.

The sex was like nothing ever before.

The sex had ripped him—his stone—from his body, and for a long time, he had hovered there, as though he might hang forever now suspended in the ruined sky, until at last she touched him again, saying gently, if you must know, we call it a tattoo.

And anyway, she says now by the river, taking off her gray scarf as if to show him her beautiful baldness for the last time, I'm not for you—I'm for him.

For the rest of Will's life, he will never remember awakening, crushed on the deck beneath the night sky and jammed among the others. He won't remember standing by the black car, the river washing by, and taking the box from the glove box, nor holding it in his hand.

Will had walked as far was he could. He had tried to leave them the cars.

For if Will remembers anything, he remembers the driving.

Not the device that was inside the box and already on when he took it out, nor the dream it was playing of him and the boy in the dun-colored van arriving at another lake, a round, blue lake in the crater of an old volcano, with a falling-down lodge where people in parkas are dancing. Some of the walls of the lodge are missing, busted open to show beds and basins inside, and in some of the beds, couples are lying together.

Don't look, he tells the boy, but the boy looks anyway, saying, why? They're only fucking.

In the dream, there's a man on the dance floor playing a fiddle, a small bald man with a soft light leaking out of him, and even though Will knows he should not be doing this, because of the ache in his arms, he goes to the edge of the platform anyway, the boy's hand clutched in his twitching large one, and now it won't be long before his leg, and it's a long one, has angled its way up onto the platform—up and over—and he's standing gaunt and awkward on the platform and hugely out of proportion to himself, like one of those long-legged birds you might once have seen at the zoo. Like a bird, then, he tucks himself into himself, and then he unfolds, graceful and deliberate, to approach the bald man with the fiddle.

Don't, Will thinks, but he can't stop himself, and even though he can't remember asking, suddenly he's the man with the fiddle, the *same* man playing the same fiddle, and in this one moment, all the low clouds around the lake lift to reveal the gathering peaks of mountains that once would have been white with snow, but not anymore. And then they descend, warm and woolly, again to close back like a blanket over all of them—the people dancing around him, and the boy's face split open with wonder, and the bald man beside him no longer leaking, and Will like a bird on the deck, and his long-fingered

elegant hands around the worn body of another man's fiddle transformed
to a jazz violin, and the night lit by the thousand moons that aren't moons,
but lanterns—or something. And even though in the dream Will's ear is
not perfect, it is close to perfect as human ears can get, as watching the boy
watch him play, Will hones himself to the point that recedes between any two
points—the note he plays and the perfect note—which marks yet another half
distance, and another, like the distance on the boy's split with wonder wide-
open face.

But it's not a dream, it's a story.

And so, what Will does: he shuts off the device.

And when he wakes up, he is already driving.

Will drives the same way he'd tried walking up the railroad tracks, or
creek, or river, or any trail off into the woods he has followed in their time by
the river. He drives with his sense of purpose restored, blindly headed, in the
black car, between here and there, between now and whatever comes next. And
it's instinct as much as sad surrender, splitting the distance by half. Although
he knows he's going to miss them, miss all of them—the one he had loved
inside the computer, and the other whose scent still somehow lingers in the
car she did not choose, making him regret that he had not taken her, as she
had suggested, at least one time for himself, had not let her love him, and him,
her— and Baby, there is nothing for it now.

Will is already going.

He is already gone.

First he heads north, up the same road he came down, back toward where
he had left the fleece family. If they're there, Will doesn't know—maybe he
should have Baby for them, but maybe he'll just bring them to it. The road looks
promising anyway—broad and mostly clear of debris and swooping up the river
valley like a promise. In the black car Will guns the engine, grinning, growing
lighter with each RPM, and so absorbed by the moment that when the rockslide
rises up before him as suddenly as the man in the rain with the child and whose
fingers, Will sees now, spelled HELP US, PLEASE, he almost cannot brake in
time—in fact spins out just a little, crushing one fender of the big black car.

Will sits there, momentarily stilled, blasting the heat to ward off the chill
of the morning and using the keen part of his brain to consider the rockslide
before him, which must—and *cannot*—be the exact same rockslide as the one

that had cut off the tracks below. It is impossible—even in the Great Quakes, nothing so massive as this had been observed—and besides, it wasn't there before, but now it is.

Then he gets out to inspect the damage. He has to beat the fender away from the wheel to make it turn, but otherwise it's not too bad. It would be easier if he had tools, but he left everything in camp.

So Will turns south—south worked, before.

All Will's life he has believed in and practiced the twin, enduring principles of abstraction and hope. Will had clutched his baseball and prayed for true aim and subtle mechanics while, high above, the mothers swayed like giant blooms, their blouses billowing with afternoon light. They had swayed and sung and stitched with their poor scorched hands, carefully mending the shrouds they sewed to protect the boys who were their sons below. Will had stood there, growing older year by year, while above him, one by one, the mothers went blind or grew fatal lumps or developed tinnitus and lost their balance. Those mothers loved their sons, but there was nothing they could do to protect them from the world that was coming.

Not one mortal thing.

In Will's mind, this was a failure not so much of love as of imagination—and its corollary logic of substitution and replacement whereby, although it was not he who lost the baseball in the light, it could have been. And if it were—Will gave himself over to this logic the same way he would later give himself over to the logic of numbers—his mother would have had no reason to keep going up. She could have stayed safely behind on earth.

Will knew, even then, their luck would not hold forever, and as she hovered sewing in the blinding light above, she grew to him, below, as dear and as distant as any other sacrifice or love.

On the sidelines, Will's dad: batter up, batter up.

On the mound, Will cupped the ball in his hand and curled his body into it, but hardly listened anymore because, ever since the boy had lost the ball and now for the rest of his life, he would understand that it didn't matter whose mother went blind or slipped—each and every living thing beneath their hapless canopy was fragile and vulnerable and doomed. Until, by the time Will's own mom fell, lovely in the dying light and slipping almost gracefully into a languid, tumbling freefall all her own, Will could only stand and watch as if he'd known that this was coming all along.

She was your mother, for God's sake, Will, his dad said. Show some respect—grieve.

But Will had already been grieving so long.

And so it was in this way that Will turned the keen part of his mind to his complex faith in the power of abstraction to exchange the thing that could be hurt—boys who lost balls and their failed moms, earth itself—with the idea of the thing so that, in that infinite space between them—the space that was no space—everything Will loved on this dear and frail planet might yet be safe.

All he had to do was crack the code.

A GOOD PLACE TO REST

THAT NIGHT, for the first time since she was a girl and had secretly implanted her bootlegged BCI, Lyda has a dream she can call her own. It begins with a swimming sensation and a tiny impossible flutter on the inside of her body, and when she gets out of the box, it is already empty. So Lyda does what anyone would do. She kisses her mother one last time, who blinks—one blink, two—and then transects the white expanse of room to summon up the elevator as naturally as if she were stepping out for milk or taking the dog for a walk.

Moments later, she's really stepping out onto the street through doors that open for her with a loud pneumatic *swoosh*, and with every step she takes she's growing lighter, almost buoyant. In the dream—but how can it be a dream when it seems so real?—she walks with purpose, a rank, metallic wind in her hair and things falling all around. A door is coming, Lyda knows, though she can't know exactly when or where it leads, no more than she can know how long she must walk through the endless rain of things.

As she walks, change is already occurring inside her—she is becoming different, not just lighter but somehow also adapted to the coming door, even as the street closes up behind her in the jumbled trash heap of the world.

When the door comes at last, it comes as a plain and natural-seeming pale pine plank door, smelling new and a little bit of pitch. Lyda stands before it waiting. The longer she stands there, the more she changes on the inside until it almost seems that she could wait forever, or until the door could be a box. This gives her such a feeling of destiny itself that when the door finally does open, swinging noiselessly open, not even the subtle quickening of her own heart and the slight sense of warning—DANGER, DANGER—can stop her from walking through to where a small bald man is waiting in an orchard beneath graceful trees. Lean as he is, he is brown as a bean, and all along he's been waiting—for her.

And when she wakes up, she's alone on the deck—no Helen, no Baby— no Will.

But Lyda doesn't notice this at first.

At first she lies a moment longer in the cusp of dream, savoring what remains of its lightness to ward off her other increasingly persistent feeling of having been adrift for a long, long time, since even before the one point she can fix—two cars waiting in the rain—has been drifting all along through a long puzzling series of misapprehensions that, like these long days by the river, or Helen herself, has left her strangely empty. The mornings are getting colder now, and Lyda doesn't want to get up, wants to stay there all day, curled up inside the extra fuchsia sleeping bag that came in Will's car. If she stayed here all day—what, would Baby go hungry, would the tomatoes rot?

Lyda doesn't think so, which is why it seems so strange that when she finally does crawl out into this exact morning, the transition from one state of being to another is as effortless and seamless and, the word comes to her, as inevitable as if she were passing through a door that was not there—from the one side of a thing, the inside, to the other, the out.

HellO Lyda, the bird calls from somewhere. How are you, how ARE you?

But there's Helen instead, seated by the fire pit and staring off across the river as though she had a plan. On the planes of her face, a vague uneasiness, but Lyda makes a quick check around, and, no, everything is fine, in its right place, at the hearth, just as they had left it the night before—the pots overturned to stay clean, their shoes in a row—with only maybe a slight coolness to the air, a tinge of weather.

Lyda raises one hand to shield her eyes—but from what?

And then she is using it, instead, it cover her mouth and stifle the cry rising like a foreign body in her.

Lyda knows that Will is gone even before she has fully taken in the blank space where the black car was—before—beside the red car. She knows it without words and her knowledge takes the form of the stifled cry and the disappearance, in her mind, of whatever remained of the dream. Helen's face, unchanged, continues staring, in its way, across the river, but Lyda can see that she knows Lyda knows, and why doesn't she say something—she should *say* something *now*. But what? For looking around more closely now, Lyda sees how particular he has been in his leaving, how every trace of Will—the black car, the fiddle, the arc of his hip on the deck next to her and its salty smell of sleep, all, she thinks—gone.

There is nothing seamless now, from their being three to their being two.

Or should she count Baby?

Then Lyda thinks it again, thinks *Baby*, is it, could he—did you *see* him, she cries out to Helen, did you see him go?

Helen looks up with the same quiet smile she reserves for tomatoes, Baby, rain.

You can't change what is, she lies outright to Lyda. No one can.

Behind them, the red car looks dusty and forlorn in its spot by the river, without its companionable twin. Looking at the blank space, Lyda fights off an urge to go to it—*her* car—and drive after them.

Oh you, Helen says, with a sudden laugh, don't worry. I've got Baby, over there in the food box, just where he left it.

He left Baby?

Well, sure he did. Didn't he say Baby was yours?

He left Baby, Lyda says again, as if trying to convince herself this is what she wants—it should be. It is what she's wanted ever since she first laid eyes on it in Will's fiddle case. But rushing over to check on Baby tucked into the food box among the stores of grains and eggs Helen's also found, there is something wrong with this victory that will keep on being wrong without Will. Without Will, Lyda thinks bitterly, everything will always be wrong.

And even though she knows her feeling is equally wrong, Lyda can't quite retrieve her prior tenderness for Baby, the need and desire it had stirred in her—before. Maybe it's petty, but what Lyda really feels, looking at it sucking from a fresh nutrition tank, is longing for her own childhood box, which if she had it now, she would crawl right into it, no matter how cramped. She would tuck her ankles up behind her neck, fold over at the joint of her hips, and slip her arms between her thighs to knot them at the small of her back. That was the best way, although there were others. She would do it. She would close the lid over herself and meet him again.

And she would say: What did I do wrong? I only wanted out, not this.

Shh, he would say, the way he did. *Shh, shh.* He would unknot her.

Come on, Helen says, and it's the old Helen, suddenly restored—the kind Helen from the café and car who knows how to find things—parrots and eggs, where they are now. Look, I've found more eggs. Remember, how good!

Ok, Lyda says, eggs. But what she is thinking is why hasn't she thought this before: oh, she says, Helen, can you find Will?

But as soon as she has thought it, Lyda wishes she hadn't, because Helen answers but not in real words but only sounds, and the sounds she does use— *shh*, Helen says, *shh, shh*—those sounds Lyda's heard before.

Then Helen adds something strange: I wish I could, she says, but it doesn't work that way.

Still, there really are eggs steaming on a platter beside the glowing coals of last night's fire, and their yellowness makes Lyda's mouth water in that old familiar way, and she looks curiously at Helen for a sign, or maybe just trying to get used to the idea of the two of them—together again. Maybe it's not so bad after all. They still have the red car and each other—and Baby. And Will has already done most of the heavy manual work they couldn't have done by themselves, and if Baby is a girl, so much the better. If Baby is a girl, they will sew tiny rings in her ears and never cut her hair, if she has hair.

After a while, Helen sighs. Ok, but there's something else.

What—what do you know?

But Helen only shakes her head, her smile going dim, and her voice, when she speaks, is low and neutral. I can't tell you about Will, she says, but one thing I can tell you is you better watch that baby. If you don't watch Baby, something is going to happen.

What do you mean, something?

I'm telling you, Lyda, you won't like it if it does.

Something, Lyda says again, almost wryly, for hadn't she once believed in a certain precision of language with which she might salvage the world?

And then she does something she's never done before, reaching out affectionately to rub the top of Helen's head as if there were hair there, but just rubbing, instead, the soft, dry skin of her glistening scalp.

Oh Helen, she says, taking the plates to wash them, you'll have to do better than that.

A time came when Lyda's body no longer fit so easily inside her box. She was lucky, Lyda knew, to be growing like that into a whole and healthy body, maybe smaller than her mother's at a comparable age, but still too big to fit inside without contortion, a time-consuming process that prevented the quick, seamless slipping into it she'd practiced as a child. It was difficult, but not impossible, and so all she could think about, on the outside of the box, was a BCI. Her mother had one once—*before*. Lyda could see the tiny scars at the base of her skull, the same light iridescent blue as a tattoo or a marriage mark. Lyda wondered if it hurt. She wondered what else it felt like.

With a BCI, it wouldn't matter how big she grew, the box would be bigger—the box would be huge. With a BCI, the box—and Lyda in it—would be as big as the world.

But of course, without a permit, BCI's were illegal, and even on the black market NETZ, hard to get. Lyda waited a long time for hers, and when it came, she wasn't sure. The device itself was smaller than she had anticipated, but not small enough, and although it emitted a low, thrumming sound, she'd carried it around for days in the fold of her pocket (for who was there to hear?), a little bit afraid.

What Lyda really wanted was one of the new synth-ethic devices you could just inject through any major vein, or even the kind you could wear inside an orifice and take out at will, but both were prohibitive on any market. Of course, there were drugs she could take—plenty of drugs—but Lyda didn't want that either. She wanted to *feel*—wasn't that the point?

Eventually, she did it on impulse, one slate gray morning. She did it working backwards with a mirror, twenty tiny sutures as sure and as evenly spaced as the ones she had practiced on all the hidden places of her body— both inner and outer thighs, between her breasts, on each bony tip of pelvis. That part felt so right. That part felt as natural, as primal, as crawling into her box when she was little.

But once she'd attached it, she couldn't bring herself to activate it. It lay there, stitched to her scalp like a threat or promise, and although it gave her headaches and left her with a mildly panicky feeling that someone (but who?) would *see*, she could not bring herself to finalize the implant, not because she was afraid—not anymore—but because somehow just the feel the tiny device at the base of her skull had already so sensitized her to the smallest thing—the brush of her mother's hand as she passed the salt and pepper, the falling of roses and eggshells outside her window, the swoosh of the elevator taking her father away and the swoosh of it returning him in the evening, the powdery scent of her mother's neck when Lyda hugged her, the boy who fell outside and who, even after all this time, could still not tie his shoes, her own toothbrush. Why Lyda should now appreciate things that had meant nothing at all before was a mystery, but for weeks, she went around treasuring each ordinary moment of mundane daily life as if it were her last and wondering if she would be the same or different, after.

During this period of uncertainty, Lyda came one afternoon upon her mother napping on the sofa, one pale hand pressed to her chest, the other hanging loosely to the floor. From where Lyda stood on the other side of the room, she could see her mother's chest rising slightly with each breath. It was shocking, really, how frail her sleeping body was, its unguarded vulnerability, and being careful not to startle or wake her, Lyda crossed the room to lay her own hand on her mother's until their breath synchronized and they breathed as one.

Then she went back to her own bed and lay down in a swirl of confusion to imagine again, but as if for the first time, her own early beginnings and everything her mother had given up for her. The BCI was wrong. It wasn't going to solve anything. She should take it out while she still could and send it back.

And then she wasn't thinking anything at all, nothing at all anymore as she felt herself flattened by a faint internal tingling or buzz, starting in her hands and feet and moving up through bones and joints toward the core at the center of her being which, when it hit, was very fast, a sudden purr, a blinding light, as the device auto-activated in her. Although it took a moment to submit, Lyda knew already she was powerless to stop the flattening of her consciousness, the dull physical suffusion taking over her slowly, slowly, along with a growing awareness of something newly separate from herself, a smell. It was neither a good nor a bad smell, but it was definitely not coming from her or her room or even her box, a sharp human smell, a smell of something living and—old— and it was coming from *outside*, like words but not words, like someone else's memories or what was going to turn out, after all, to be a kind of grace.

When something does happen to Baby, Lyda almost misses it, and for this she will carry her guilt the rest of her natural life. Helen had warned her.

Watch that baby, Helen said.

And Lyda had, she had watched Baby, as closely and as tenderly as anyone could.

But it was different without Will, and Lyda missed him terribly—the largeness of his body, at least compared to theirs, his messy hair and disparate hungers and his smells and fiddle (which sometimes it still seemed to her that she could hear, far off in the woods), even his possessiveness with Baby, or the way he looked at Helen when Lyda wasn't looking, or at her. Lyda tried to stay focused on Baby, but the space his absence left persisted, and time and again she'd find herself turning toward it instead, heart rising, then falling, like a stone. Baby was fussier too, and Lyda felt herself growing edgier and more and more detached. It was hot; it was cold. She was hungry; she was bloated. The camp was a mess but she couldn't clear her head enough even to sweep off the deck.

Until the day came that Helen returned from the woods dragging a full sack of root vegetables and handing it over to Lyda with an air of expectation. The sack smelled sour and earthy.

What? Lyda said. More?

You're supposed to boil them. Or I don't know, use your imagination—you *like* to cook.

Baby lay gurgling at both of them.

And Lyda looked down at the mound of food before her, the work to clean and cook it, and knew a time was coming when it would be too much for her and she'd say no. Who was going to eat it anyway? You do it, Helen, she'd say. You find it, you cook it. Or maybe—and really, once she'd thought of this, it was more and more appealing—she'd simply take a break and tromp off into the woods like Helen and, before her, Will.

Maybe she shouldn't have, she'll think later. Maybe, she should just have put her mind to the tasks at hand, washed and boiled the vegetables, studied up on canning. Winter would come and they should be prepared, and it wasn't so much, after all, what Helen was expecting—her gathering, Lyda's nesting. Wasn't that really a fair exchange, even without Will?

But Baby had been tied up in a little sling all morning, hanging slackly from the branches of what might have been a fruit tree, eyes drifting off to one side and the perpetual bubble of drool pooling up in the slightly parted corner of its mouth. And really, if she took a few hours to herself, she could whip up a quick stew later on, something with potatoes and those bright green beans. If they run out of kindling, if Helen finds them missing, let the rain come down, she had thought.

And anyway, with no one watching, who was there to stop her now?

And, upsie-daisy, she swings Baby off the tree and over her shoulder—let's go see what's so fascinating out there in those woods.

Suddenly, for no reason, she really is curious, for of the three of them, she alone has never even been off-site—never crossed beyond the middle of the footbridge to the other side of the river, never walked the railroad tracks, never picked a single berry from a bush. The others did it all the time. Helen crossed over and brought back her mountains of food. And Will used to play his fiddle on the other side, the strains of it drifting back over dead water and through the dead woods. He even used to take Baby with him.

But not Lyda. Lyda had stuck close to camp, the red car, things she knew. It was nice on their side, Lyda thought. Why go looking over there when it was so nice here?

Now, Lyda holds her breath the whole time she is crossing the bridge, although she doesn't even know she's doing it until she lets it out—on the other side—gasping and laughing.

Look at us, she tells Baby, we're here.

And really, except for the old railroad tracks, Lyda has to admit it's not so different, after all, on this side. Everything pretty much looks the same—dead, or at least on the way.

So Lyda takes the tracks north, not really headed for any place in particular, just enjoying the walking. The tracks go on and on. A person—the right person—could walk down them forever. But as Lyda walks, not right away but soon enough, the changing starts again in her, a kind of stirring, and she begins to notice things, maybe some green undergrowth farther back from the tracks, or here and there, a living tree.

Hey look, she cries out to Baby, a flower!

Or maybe a weed, but it's got petals and it's yellow.

But why should anything be different here, on this side of the river, sharper and more colorful—more *alive*? That doesn't even make sense.

But really, and as Lyda starts to notice other differences as well—the small scree on either side of the tracks, the trace scent of creosote, what appears to have been old power lines—something lifts in her and, incredibly, she finds herself singing. Well, it's not really singing, only half of it with words and the tune barely remembered, mostly improvised, but it's the best she can do, and it does soothe Baby, who—astonishingly—coos right along.

Lyda does not remember when she has felt so happy, and soon she is trying to walk the rails, her feet precisely placed along the gleaming steel. But Baby makes it difficult to balance, so she takes the ties—two, then one, two, then one, striking a lopsided rhythm and as alert as though a train might really blast around the bend at any moment, giving her the choice to hop its flat back and ride it away, just her and Baby.

As soon as Lyda thinks this, suddenly she hears, close behind and coming fast, what can only be the memory of a train, and quick, she bends to place her last trinket from the beach—the old metal coin embossed with an image of GOD—flat on the rail, hopping off only seconds before the first swoosh of train, and then car after car after car roaring by, and the spaces between the cars, spaces of light—spaces where nothing is. Lyda stays a long time, savoring the idea of the roar of the train, the trembling of earth and the whoosh of the wind through her fly-away hair, and when it is gone she steps back into the place where it just was, this residue of something long past. But now a cry rises up in her throat, for the flattened coin shimmers just the same in the aftermath of a real train—sharp-edged and thin as a membrane, its image of GOD completely obliterated. And as Lyda bends to pick it up, she finds it still warm from the friction of the train that was not there.

My, she exclaims to Baby, that was exciting! Just look at what that train did to my coin!

But Baby's gone quiet again—and seems somehow to be growing heavier and heavier—a ton of dead weight—and of course Lyda's been carrying it for some time now, and she's not so used to walking in the steady heat of day, such that—slowly, slowly—a soporific feeling begins to overtake her, the tracks ahead not so compelling as they were only moments before.

Well, she says, I must be nervously exhausted.

Which having said this, Lyda discovers that she is, in fact, strangely enervated by her encounter with the train, as though it has pulled up something deep inside her and left her craving only the oblivion of sleep, only just a nice spot to put the baby down, and maybe a cooling breeze off water, a good place to rest.

And this is how it happens that Lyda finds the very spot that Will had found before, the rocky ledge above the deep holes in the river, green and churning far below, where she can almost imagine fish looping in wide languid circles and maybe a sleek river otter. Lyda will never be able to say how, exactly, she finds herself here. Maybe she's wandered some time in her daze, or she's walked here directly, following a path left by Will. Not the way there, but the place, she thinks—at least it *feels* familiar. This is what she's thinking as she settles Baby in a little nest of moss, and when she stands back up—what a relief to be free of that weight—how light she suddenly is!

And that's the exact same moment—when Lyda, shed of the weight of Baby, rises into sudden lightness—that the inconceivable happens and, high above, the haze parts a little to let the sun shine down on them. For Lyda, it's a joyous feeling, and she wants to look up—to *see*—but slammed by the sudden, intense heat, can't quite. In her paisley boxers and scooped tee, her body appears brown and strong, but it doesn't feel strong—it feels sleepy and weak, the world drenched and limpid and the stupor taking hold from within, as, all around, a stunning quiet descends—no insect buzzing, no animal rustling, no gurgling from Baby—just the quiet brush of water in the channel below and the implacable heat of the radiant sun in which Lyda lies down to sleep.

First there's a man. He's not a very big man, but he is bald and he is smiling with what looks like nothing so much as a reservoir of infinite patience—in that, this man will prove to be capacious. But when Lyda, in her daze, reaches out to touch the idea, or memory, of him, he is already gone, and she would half suspect she was mistaken were it not for the hole he has left in the place where he only just was.

And then, there's a *plop*, far below, the distant, muted splash of *something happening*.

Later, Lyda will try to recall—there must have been some warning, a small burp of Baby breaking loose, or skittering of pebbles, muffled roll of fleece sack over moss toward the lip of rock. How had Lyda missed it? And then Baby falling with wide-open lungs that suck in the air but can't let it out, catching the howl of protest until—*plop*—Baby hits heavy as stone and sinks.

Plop, Baby falls.

Oh, oh, the bird calls somewhere downriver, as everything else falls back into quiet.

But not before Lyda makes her own sound, a round muted *oh* in her sleep that is not sleep, like the bird's, but the shock of it slicing clear to the bone.

Lyda won't remember diving. The *oh* comes out of her when she's already in the air without even quite rousing herself enough to be afraid, plunging down toward the green surface of the pool and the tie-dyed fleece of Baby at the bottom where she can see it clearly, as she falls, as though it were a fish, if there were fish, lying, the bright fleece of Baby, as still on the bottom of the sun-struck pool as if the river were a box instead, or someone's loving arms.

And it's not so far to the water after all as Lyda's body sails out through the space between rock and water that is only the heartbeat of time in which the body hangs suspended—in which the body *falls*—plummeting toward the glittery water which it hits with a sting and a *smack*, and then down, down through the cold churning green toward the rocky river bottom where, now— at last—she's got it by the nape of the neck or the neck of its sack—then *pop*, she pops up like a cork, bursting back through the watery froth into the light and heat and air of the rescue of Baby.

But none of this is what Lyda is going to remember, later, when she tries to tell Helen what happened, of that afternoon. She won't remember the smack of water, nor her own expert swimming remembered from the NetZ, the strength of the stroke that takes her down and down like an otter or a snake, or her own maternal instinct toward the white face of Baby staring blankly up at her through the green translucence, its small round mouth opened in a wide, shocked o. She won't remember the way the current pulls at its fleece, threatening to dislodge it or sweep it away. She won't remember how still Baby lies in a little eddy at the bottom of the pool.

Helen had warned her, of course.

I warned you, Helen will say, but it won't sound right, the way she says it now. It will sound, like Baby on the beach, choked and wrong.

Because as Lyda swims with Baby clutched beneath one arm in her lifesaving grip made firm by need, its big head propped out of the water, what she is thinking about is not so much Baby, but Will—what would Will say now? Lyda thinks a little bit proudly as she swims with Baby away from the dangerous rocks where it fell, already deepening with shade, toward the small, sandy beach a little bit upstream—there's not so much current here but the swimming is hard even so—back on their side of the river still awash in the miraculous sun.

And really, Baby calms almost instantly once they are out. It coughs a little water up and then turns its gaze on Lyda, who can't stop the love pouring out of her now because something's breaking loose in her, something powerful and urgent and alive. For who is there to stop her now?

But Helen won't be listening anymore. Helen, for the first time Lyda's ever seen, is suddenly distraught. And she's saying something, but it's all choked and wrong, how could you? Then: I warned you.

But Helen, Lyda says, who might as well be speaking to the moon.

Go away, Helen says, but she's the one who's trying to leave, and even though it is Lyda who rescued the baby, Helen's got it now, clutched under one arm while with the other she's gathering her things from the deck, stuffing her personal belongings, and Baby's, into one blue sleeping sack, her face all scrunched up with emotion. But where can she possibly go? And how far can she get in the red car when, as far as Lyda knows, Helen doesn't even know how to drive.

But dragging the bag stuffed with things in the dirt, Helen's storming off, instead, toward the most remote yurt, back behind the moss-covered boulder beneath a canopy of dead and dying tree. And she's taking Baby.

Such that Lyda finally cries out the one word she has left, cries no. No, no, she cries out, that one's got droppings.

Astonishingly, Helen turns, and when she does all the furor has gone from her face, her sudden burst of activity deflated. You think, she says, I'm afraid of the droppings?

I only meant, Lyda says, I had to do something—we were *cold*. Or not me, I had the sun on my back, but that poor baby still wrapped in its wet sack. You should have seen how hard it was shivering.

But how can she ever explain to Helen what it felt like when the fleece family disappeared, or how all she ever wanted, when Will was around, was to succor this child. I tried everything, she'll say. I laid it in the sun. I pumped its back to get the water out.

Shh, Helen will say, returned to the deck now with both bag and Baby. *Shh, shh.*

I only did what anyone would do.

And it was only just the two of us anyway, she'll think, wrapped together in the dying sun, and Baby softly hiccupping already, its soft face pressed up against my neck, the roundness of its big, baby body. Who could ever stop the love from coming out then?

But anyone could see it was never going to dry.

By now they are sitting agreeably once more on the deck, the baby stretched between them in a clean, dry fleece, and the bag stuffed with things forgotten in the dirt, the bird watching keenly from a branch above. Helen's face is still scrunched up, but calmer, and Lyda can't tell what emotion it is, or even what emotion Helen is capable of.

You weren't, Helen says at last, gazing sadly at the baby, supposed to look.

Lyda, who of course knows this now, smiles ruefully and shrugs.

Baby, sleeping now—and thank goodness!—sucks quietly, then startles, as though awakened by a dream or memory, before drifting off to sleep again, the way babies do.

Then, more calmly, Helen adds, but let's do sleep in a yurt tonight. Sleeping in a yurt will be almost like a home.

Much later that same night, after they have cleaned the yurt and moved their things and settled in, with Baby nestled in its little sack between, they will lie for a bit, side-by-side, listening to the silence of the night where once there might have been owls, or bats, their fluttering wings swooping through the tepid air, or real trains filled with passengers and freight, or living water. It had all been like that, once, even here, Lyda thinks—or especially here.

How much difference a roof makes, she says finally. It's not that much to say, but maybe it will make a little peace.

But Helen only says, there's no way you could have known.

Shh, Lyda says, but in her own voice the sound, not far enough back in her throat, is neither soft nor consoling, and almost at once she regrets it.

Maybe I should have said something.

At least we know now, Lyda says, it might be a girl. That isn't all they know, but she hopes it is enough.

I *wanted* to tell you, Helen says. You, of all of us, deserved to know.

Soon there isn't going to be anything left to say than what Lyda says now. She says, it's not really that bad, you know. I didn't even notice at first, and I was *holding* it.

But of course she is lying, and they both know it, because Lyda had seen at once—anyone would have seen—that *something was wrong* with that baby, and the shock of seeing its wrongness is thrumming through her still. It's just a baby—when it gets a little older, it'll crawl around in the dirt, it'll put things in its mouth—or *will* it? Already it cries and coos, and makes its suckling noises and sleeps and wakes, and has its whole life stretching out before it into the future—but what kind of future will that be?

On the roof of the yurt, the bird is still chattering away, but neither Lyda nor Helen can make the words out through the thick fabric walls. Between them, Baby's head a matching pair with Helen's, the both of them round and white and hairless, without even lashes or brows. A pearly thread of drool dribbles down one of Baby's pale cheeks as it startles again, stiffening in sleep.

What would Will think if he came back now and found them like this?

Of course she wasn't supposed to look—whatever was wrong with Baby, Lyda had understood, it was wronger still to look, but she couldn't stop herself from staring and staring at the shivering baby in her arms who, underneath its fleece, was—*wrong.*

And now that same wrong baby is sleeping quietly between them beneath a mound of blankets despite the stifling heat and bundled up into a fresh, dry sack that contains, like a second skin, the wrong skin of the baby inside. Lyda looked—she couldn't not—because the skin of the baby in her arms, the baby she held and succored just as though it were her own, had turned out not to be a real skin at all—not natural skin—but an artificial membrane, as thick and shiny as a scar, that covered the whole body of Baby. Almost, it shimmered, the skin. Taut and slick, it crinkled when it moved, leaving a web of white markings like crumpled waxed paper, and in the sun on the beach, it glistened. In that light, on that sand, by that river, it seemed to Lyda that if she looked hard and long enough, she'd be able to see clear through, all the way into the baby through the membrane that was not real skin to the small internal organs that might, or might not, resemble Lyda's. And then she was touching it too, the shivering skin of Baby that even now, hours later, still seared Lyda's own skin like a burn.

What was I supposed to do, she says now in the yurt, and suddenly she's crying: how many times has she picked Baby, wanting something from it, but not this?

At first, Helen lies impassively in her own sleeping bag, letting Lyda cry, until finally she sighs and sits all the way up, shaking out her hands and moving closer to Lyda. And then, this part is deliberate—she uses one hand to brush the hair from Lyda's face, and the other to rub small, consoling circles between Lyda's shoulder blades.

I did warn you, she says again.

I thought, you know, you'd be mad at me.

Above, the bird starts up in another language.

Shh, Helen says. Mad?

Will it grow? Lyda says at last.

Helen shrugs. It seems to, but it takes a long time. But really, you know, at least she stays cool. Even in that fleece, it never sweats.

Then, after a brief hesitation, she adds, you can still touch it, you know. Pick it up, put it next to your heart.

Later, when Lyda is done touching the baby, she lays her hand over the place where its heart beats with a rapid fluttering and leaves it there long enough to calibrate the rhythm. And then she hoists it back to her own chest and lets their two hearts beat together, impossibly in sync. It's a stronger, more amazing feeling than even in the bathroom with the mom or on the beach, but the baby being neither warm nor cool seems more the idea of a baby than a real baby—the idea of the space that the baby would fill, if it had mass.

You poor thing, you poor thing—it's not your fault you came like this.

What about dreams? Does it dream?

Oh, who can say what is? It sleeps, maybe it dreams—but it's not going to last forever.

And then the strangest thing so far because it is Helen who starts to cry, and Lyda who pulls her close, just the same as she did with Baby—she pulls her close and pats her on the back, until they arrive at what might amount to an understanding.

Shh, she says, *shh*, as she might to a child, but Lyda's heart isn't in it because she knows that Helen's right, and that she doesn't have the slightest idea what this means—for to Lyda it's just words, and words, she knows, will never be enough.

And it is for this reason that Lyda again turns to Baby and offers it her breast.

Awakened, Baby fusses at first, but then it does latch on—it latches on hard. Lyda presses her face to the top of its hairless head, smells its faint metallic smell, and rubs its soft membrane with her cheek, knowing the moment has come and it won't come again. Although Baby's thrumming heart is dwarfed beneath the pounding of her own, Lyda can't help that. Lyda can't help anything now but the breath she takes in and the question she is going to ask, convinced it is the key to everything.

Tell me, Helen please, she says at last: *what have you found in those woods?*

THE END OF LAYERS

DAWN COMES—either that dawn, or the next one—the sky overhead like a coarse, gray blanket, and the air has turned cool. The river washes by. It will do this forever, Helen thinks.

Sometimes Helen must have felt such a tightness in her chest, squeezed among the others and the bird sticking close, perched beside her head, picking off the stray spider or ant that crawled across her forehead—a guard bird, Will had called it.

But Helen doesn't feel guarded.

Not that.

Beside her, Lyda sleeps in her fuchsia sleeping bag, and between them, the clump of tie-dyed fleece.

The time is coming soon when she is going to get up, hoist herself out of her own sleeping bag, pat Lyda's hair—and go. The profusion of so much hair still strikes her with wonder, but after what Helen has done, she won't go any further with what her hands can do. Helen doesn't want to think about Lyda waking up, alone—there's not enough of Helen left for that much heartbreak. And anyway, it's not time for that yet—Lyda has to wake first, she has to find the empty fleece, the one red car, and the trail Helen is going to leave for her to follow if that's what she does.

If that's what she chooses.

Where did Lyda think the tomatoes came from anyway?

Well, Helen thinks, this moment has been coming for a long time now, but now that it's here, she sill lingers a little bit longer (not too long, Helen, hurry) in the yurt beside Lyda, who hadn't even wakened when Helen took Baby. It was sleeping when she did it, curled in Lyda's arms, but Lyda stirred only enough to tuck one loose hand between her breasts and smile a languorous smile. This, more than anything, Helen will miss—the langorousness of Lyda's smile—but maybe Lyda won't notice right off. Maybe she'll think Helen is out fixing breakfast, that there are eggs and Baby all clean in a cozy box; maybe she'll lie there for a moment, savoring the thought of eggs. It's such a pleasant way to imagine Lyda waking that Helen holds on to the idea of it, even as she's getting up to leave.

But although this breaks her heart for Lyda, who has put both her trust and neediness in her, Helen can't do anything about that now. And just when she was getting used to her, who is so stolidly human in her needs and desires. This thought—the thought of Lyda's needs and desires—catches Helen unaware, so she shoves her hands into her pockets to quiet the ache and tells herself that Lyda can think what she thinks when she wakes, but by then Helen will already be gone.

For who can stop her now, Helen thinks, bending down to rearrange the fleece so it looks like something's there.

And then she kisses Lyda on the forehead.

And after that, she really is going, walking one last time through the worn paths of camp, scuffling her feet so Lyda will know where to follow, and the bird flapping along behind to land on her shoulder and peck at her ear.

Oh, Helen thinks, you too?

But that doesn't stop her from turning to take yet another final look at the yurt beside moss-covered rocks where the sleeping woman lies. Maybe she should have left Baby after all—what could it have hurt? Maybe she's the one who should have left well enough alone. But as she turns, again, to the path ahead, Helen feels a certain sharpness to the air that foretells a change of seasons. The sky looks like rain, and it's cold—that baby would never have lasted in the cold.

There's a part of Helen—a large part, really—that doesn't want to be doing this, with everything pressed together and urgent, like the gray sky weighting them down. And her hands won't stop, although they hurt—ache—all the joints and the muscles and the tendons that hold them together. Mostly they hurt from what she has done, but also from the work of tracking Will. It's harder, without her apparatus, but not impossible, and these days almost anything will do—the planes of rocks or roots of trees, Baby's placid forehead or chest, the deck, her own flexed thighs—to spin the world out from her fingers and discover what comes next. Not that it's done any good for Will, who this same night has come to the end of yet another ruined road. Maybe Helen should have saved her heartbreak for him, all the roads ending like that, and Will's little hope for the future extinguished.

But, of course, Helen knows that eventually there will only be the one road left.

Helen walks quickly, if reluctantly, her own going not so much something she is doing as something being done to her, as though someone were shoving—exhorting—her from behind. Oh how she wishes it weren't, but whenever she balks, the bright bird butts its head against her temple—and they *go*.

Maybe if she'd never learned to type, Helen thinks, a tremendous weariness descending over her. Sometimes adaptations, deprived of stimulation, had been known to fail. With normal hands, who knows where Helen might have ended up—maybe in a helping profession—nurse's aid or kindergarten teacher. As a kindergarten teacher, she'd have knelt beside the children, wiping tears and noses and dispensing hugs, the neural pathways of her hands and body intact and wholly human. Out here in the world, there have been such surprising pleasures everywhere—earth beneath her feet, olallieberry pie, the idle companionship of Lyda—that the thought of real children, their hot and sturdy bodies, fills her momentarily with bliss.

Or, with normal hands, she and Lyda might have just kept on driving down that other road without ever turning inland, might have ended up in one of the vast urban centers to the south where they could have blended in. Along the way, they'd have stopped at cafés—real cafés—and eaten yellow eggs to their hearts' content, and never—*never*— succumbed to the lure of a river, this or any other.

Helen remembers lying awake much of their first night here, just the two of them, listening to its source deep inside the snowy mountain to the north, the distant sludgy pool of it behind what remained of its hapless dam to the south, and farther on, its tired sucking down its depleted floodplain all the way to its ruined bay. If she listened hard, she could hear the ancient leaping of spawning salmon, the cannonball cry of a boy, and the terrifying screech of the old, old train that had once rounded the bend in the tracks too fast. There wasn't anything left to hear after that, but Helen hears it anyway—the slow, toxic load as it worked its way downstream, killing everything in its path—skunk cabbage, newt, bald eagle, ponderosa pine, shimmering iridescent-bellied trout, river otter, five-fingered fern, polliwog, dragonfly, oak, cedar, fir.

Oh, poor ruined river, Helen thinks in her perpetual present that contained— *everything.*

This will make things easier for you, her father had said. He had meant it as a comfort. Look on the bright side, he'd said—you'll last longer.

It's time, Helen knows, although for what, not even she can anticipate. All she knows is she's been furtive long enough, and her hands ache, and she wants to stop.

Still, she hesitates before crossing the tracks, as though a train might really come, like the one she hears now—those long ago trains—as clearly as she'd once heard the sighs of dying species, or the roar of this train bearing down on her and the coin she has placed on the track just before it swooshes by in a blur of freight and metal, an atavistic rush of something powerful and prior, of something already over.

But even as she sees the coin is flattened—effaced of its image of GOD— Helen recognizes the memory as Lyda's.

The others would be better at going.

With cars of their own, they could just slip away, leaving the rest of them choking on dust. Or, they could walk if they wanted—if they chose. It wouldn't last forever, this walking. Their shoes would split and their feet give out, their tongues would blacken. But they could go a long way before that ever happened.

But not Helen, who, technically, could walk forever.

A room, Helen knows, is coming. She knows this the same way she knew what to do with Baby. But what earthly good was knowing the future, if you couldn't do a blessed thing to fix it?

And yet—so soon!—here she is at last, and there's not going to be any stopping her now, for she has arrived at the little creek that she's about to follow up all the way to where it might as well be the moon. Helen could do this with her eyes closed, she could do with her fingers—here, where the water runs shallow; here, where it pools among the green stones; here, the trailers; here, the culvert—water from deep in the earth. But she doesn't have to use her hands for this because she already has, and now she is using her body.

Following the creek, she's going to get her feet wet, and it's cold, and even hopping rocks won't keep them dry for long. If only she could skip that part of it, tromp through the woods or along the old road, walk right up to the front door to knock like a regular person—a person with pets. Helen thinks, now, a bit wistfully of her rabbit. Everyone needs a memory like that—Will's gun, Lyda's train, a mother's breast for Baby.

But Helen also remembers the pain of the tattoo that's not really a tattoo.

The creek narrows and opens up. It rushes over rocks and runs smoothly through pools, passing by an old cluster of trailers and broken down homes where people, not so long ago, had lived as far out of the world as they could get, but not far enough, and leads to the place where the froth of the water spits off the lip of the culvert big enough to let a train through but yet to squeeze so much out of a boy.

And it's not so fearsome, after all, she thinks, hoisting herself, belly first through its opening and threading her way against the strong current and away from the world. The water tugs at her ankles, bats throb above, and Helen smells something acrid. Then she trips, going down on her knees in the water, even though it's cold—icy—a little settling is already taking place inside her, a kind of calm.

There being nothing for it after all, Helen rises and goes.

Going, she'll come soon enough—there's no stopping this either—to the gone wild garden from which she's been stealing tomatoes and root vegetables, and beyond that, the cabin. But it's not really a cabin—it's far too big for that.

It's a *place.*

Trees hang low over the water; blankets of dead moss hang down from the trees.

Uh-oh, the bird says, gripping her shoulder. How ARE you?

Oh shush, Helen says. Aren't you supposed to be Lyda's bird, anyway?

But she keeps going anyway, around this bend in the creek, and another, shoved along by the unrelenting force at her back and the certain thought that it's not so far, after all, it only feels far, for already she's arrived at the burned out section of woods on only the one side of the creek, and *oopsie-doodle,* the bird says, as Helen does, at last, round the bend just beyond the burn that opens her first view of the structure up ahead—at first only the glint of the ancient aluminum roof nestled in the trees—living trees—and then the structure itself, the place like a home.

But it doesn't feel like home, not to Helen. Not, she thinks, *yet.*

Still, she knows that she is almost done now, and despite her ambivalence—her longing for everything to be different enough in the history of the world that she'd never have ended here—raised, instead, like other girls, by two parents who loved her, and a mother who might have taught her things like make-up and how to take care of her hair—Helen can't stop her reluctance from turning into a dull excitement, as though whatever happens now, at least it will be done.

And then, suddenly, how hungry she is—ravenous! Helen has been hungry, she thinks now, since the oozing olallieberry pie, since the eggs. No, Helen has been hungry her whole life.

But not for food.

Helen flushes hot, then cool. If it was just going to be about food, why bother with the rest of it? Still, a tomato would be nice now, or up there in the orchard, a thick-skinned pomegranate. Maybe being sated will not be so wrong after all, if sated is what it will be.

But the garden is just a distraction, for Helen has arrived now, almost dry, at the path that leads from the creek to the cabin in the woods that is too big to be a cabin, but yet with its hand-crafted cabinets and tongue-in-groove honey gold floors, and everywhere light coming down.

On the rail above her, the bird caws like a bird—caw, it caws, caw.

Ok, Helen thinks, letting go of the last of her regret, as the bird and all the rest of the world subsides into silence—just the rustling of wind in the trees above, the rushing of water in the bed of the creek, the soft beating of Helen's own pulse, then nothing—*nothing*—at all. Helen could breathe or not breathe, walk forever or never again. Here, she could stop; she could choose—to *be*.

But there will never be a way that she can change what she has done.

So Helen does the only other thing left: she walks up the path to the stairs that lead to the deck that embraces the world where finally she can rest for a while, on the outside looking in.

Inside, everything is covered with a fine, white dust—floors, counters, stairs, sofas. Well, that could be cleaned up in no time, that doesn't really matter. What matters—Helen can see clearly now—is the flight of stairs that leads to the loft where the milky light pools. And although she tells herself that a temptation is not the same as a choice, the light makes her dizzy.

Once she gets in she'll have to do a little cleaning. She'll clean and clean. She'll run a damp cloth over everything and sweep until the air is swirling with that fine white dust, and bats may swoop out of the rafters, but if anyone is going to stay—anyone at all—she might as well tidy up a little bit. Helen even thinks about washing the windows, but there are so many of them.

But maybe, first, she'll just take a little nap.

And it is at this exact moment that the future catches up to the present, and as Helen stands there waiting in the waning sunlight for whatever in the world is going to happen next, she tells herself it's ok just to wait. She'll just stand there on the outside looking in. And as she does, she'll think about the windows, along with the arcane principle of substitution and replacement that will determine, even now, what will happen when the two worlds converge, which begins with a sudden flap of the bird and a loud fluttering *swoosh* as it dives—dives hard—at the window, flapping the air around Helen enough to make hair blow (if she had hair), as it passes right through the glass to the vast interior of the structure, the shelter, the home, where it flies around a bit, disoriented in all that new space.

But then the bird calms, lands on the floor, hops. It hops around on the honey-gold floor—that dusty honey gold floor. It's hopping and squawking— Helen can see it and hear it—but as much as it hops and as loud as it squawks, the dust isn't moving. The bird's hopping all over it now, all around the room, and up on the table, and here and there on the stairs and the sofas, but it doesn't leave a track or stir a single bit of dust, as if the bird weren't even there.

Well, that's a good problem for Will—what kind of bird has no mass at all?

At the top of the stairs, a limpid light pools, and already the disconnections are spreading—molecule detaching from molecule, like the glass around the bird, or the syllables in Helen's head, so that the very fabric of that interior space seems tenuous and shimmering, as though what Helen really sees is not so much what's there as the spaces between. Well, Helen is looking at something, but who can say what?

Helen's just a conduit after all.

For this reason, she really is going to sit down and wait—forever if it takes that long (but she doesn't think it will)—aware only of the trackless bird on the inside, the vast silence that has entered the world, and the calm of her very own hands, cupped open on her lap and still at last.

WHAT HELEN DID

The first thing Helen did was wait for Lyda to fall asleep. This took so long. Each time Lyda seemed about to drop off, she'd stir or reach out to cup Baby's head or mumble something about Will.

Helen was starting to get nervous, because if they ran out of even this one night, she might never work up her resolve again. Or Will really might come stumbling back—Helen hadn't counted Will completely out. There were only so many roads and only so much whiskey he might have in the trunk of that black car, and then what was Will going to do?

Oh, settle down, Lyda. Hurry up and rest.

At last Lyda slept.

The next part of what Helen did—detaching Baby—was the trickiest part, because Baby, having made the connection between the breast and feeding tube, was latched on tight, wet-faced and fierce. And although Helen used her fingers to pry its suction loose as carefully as possible, Baby came off instead with a loud gurgling pop, causing Lyda to stir, words rising to her parted lips. But they were just dream words—*baby, oh baby,* or *boon.*

Once Helen had Baby in her own arms, she found she was crying—that won't do—but because she knew exactly what was coming, it was hard to stop, and she hunched in the yurt over Baby, shoulders heaving, and Baby whimpering too, little blats and bleats not unlike those of the parrot.

Eventually, when they were both calm enough, it was time to leave.

The next thing Helen did, just as soon she was safely clear of Lyda and the yurt and under the shelter of night, was strip the fleece from Baby—not because it was too hot (that baby really did not generate any actual heat of its own), but to free it up a bit, but having never been exposed to any other element than fleece, Baby's skin prickled at first. Helen was expecting this, but then it relaxed—a beautiful thing that justified her actions—and sucked in the drool at the corner of its mouth with a little slurp.

Helen tried not to look. She just slit the sack open and took Baby out as fast as she could, then tromped off with it back up the riverbank to where Lyda had saved it only hours before. In the time it was taking to get there, Helen hoped her resolve wouldn't weaken, but she couldn't tell for sure, because even though Lyda had already started, Lyda had no idea.

For example, she'd been wrong about the baby's gender—at least we know now, she should have said, it might as well have been a girl.

Helen would try to be merciful. She might have to look, but she would do it as kindly as she could—which was not that difficult because there was something beautiful, after all, about the damaged baby, whose shrunken limbs were beginning to lose their round baby shape, to define themselves as the miniaturized limbs of an old, old human being—and she would try not to hurt it. For Helen already knew that it would be a child destined to grow without changing form, only adding the layers inside the membrane, accumulating them for years and years until they could not be contained anymore.

Unendurable, she thought, as she began to stroke the baby, using the gentlest conceivable touch, which calmed Baby at once, making it less rigid and distinct about the edges. And so Helen kept it up, stroking and stroking, until at last a kind of glimmering started up beneath the skin, a pale, glowing pulse.

Astonishingly, as she stroked, the clouds parted for the second time that day, revealing not the sun but the moon, and it was a full moon—or almost full, or just waning—round and white in the night sky, with the exact same quality of light that came from inside the baby, a viscous milky light almost thick enough to touch. So Helen did. She looked and she touched, and looked and touched, as the inside-of-Baby light grew steadily brighter, until finally the baby in the sand shone as bright as the light of the moon, which wasn't light at all, and Helen knew this too, but only the reflection of a separate real light, but yet it was still growing in intensity, both in Baby and the moon, the same unearthly luminescence.

And in this dazzling whiteness Helen saw her hands—her own hands—begin to tremble.

Also, Baby had begun to look so uncomfortable, stuffed with so many layers of pulsing light. And it wasn't even as if Helen had not known this moment was coming, but still it was hard, for she'd grown, after all, attached to the baby with a kind of deep affection that she supposed must count as love.

The shaking of her hands was unexpected, but manageable, so she pressed them together to steady them, then, unable to put the moment off any longer, she laid the fat pad of her left thumb—*gently, gently*—on the tiny crease just above Baby's right eye to let a little light out, but the skin was so fragile it split like the skin of an overripe tomato. Helen just touched it, and it opened right up, and now look at all the light that was coming out—all that from one tear in the baby.

Briefly, Helen hesitated: maybe if she stopped now, she could still close Baby up, and return it to Lyda with only just a tiny mark or scratch where she'd sutured the membrane. But as soon as she thought this, Helen knew that—just like Lyda sleeping in the yurt, just like Will at the end of whatever road he'd come to with all the manliness drained out of him—there was only the one way out, and it started here on this beach with only her and the illuminated baby.

Ok, Helen told herself. And then she pressed her hands together one last time before continuing—tender but resolute, and without any more stopping. No power on earth could have stopped her now. That power was all inside Baby.

Helen tried to keep her fingers as steady and efficient as they'd once been on her apparatus. She worked quickly, trying not to tug or yank, using the same continuous pressure she had used to remove the device from Lyda. And in some respects, Baby peeled seamlessly. The first layers came right off.

But the deeper Helen went, the more delicate and challenging she found the procedure to be, harder even than it had been to get Baby off of Lyda's breast, and as she worked now with surgical precision, everything else in the world disappeared, leaving only her and Baby and what she was doing, peeling Baby like an onion or an egg. That part felt so natural, and soon a certain calm had descended over her that, as Baby grew lighter and smaller, grew deeper and more profound. Maybe Baby was crying, maybe the black car was coming—Helen didn't know, didn't care, couldn't have heard them even if she did.

But the peeling was getting harder too.

Not right away but over time. At first it was just the well of silence and Helen's steady hands, as sure and systematic now as any perfect machine—press, pull, peel; press, pull, peel—and Baby coming so naturally apart that when Helen encountered the first bit of resistance—the skin, or crust of light, or whatever it was she was peeling off not giving wholly away, clinging to another part of Baby like the stubborn membrane of a sticky egg—she hesitated, for of course she did not want to damage the baby. That was the last thing she wanted.

At the first tug, Baby did startle a little, but then settled back into the same dreamy dreaminess into which it had been lulled by the first touch of Helen, a state that was like sleep but not sleep—maybe only, Helen thought, the idea of sleep. So Helen kept on, even when she had to pry or dig, with Baby so calm and quiet now, or maybe just emitting some cooing or gurgling of pleasure, but Helen couldn't hear it, any more than she could hear her own lullaby, the singing coming out more in meaningless syllables, intended as comfort, than actual words.

There was something so utterly absorbing and soothing in what Helen was doing, and the quiet, that she wanted to draw it out forever, this exacting process, layer by layer, molecule by molecule, all the way down to the last remaining trace of the center of Baby, peeling and touching this baby forever.

But Baby, like all things, was finite.

When Helen had worked her way through the first translucent membranes to the sheer inner ones, when she had stripped those, too, and there was nothing left to strip, what she found at the center of the inside of Baby was a nest of tiny organs like the crystals of a geode, a sparkling and luminescent core. But Helen didn't understand this at first. Beside her, on the cold wet sand, all the layers of Baby lay in a crumpled heap of membrane, like a glittering shell mound. Helen could see the mound of that—she could touch it. But here, at the core, something left over—a remainder that could not be stripped or detached from its socket.

Now Helen did not know what to feel, for although she had not really let herself think it, she had at least in part been hoping for another skin somewhere deep inside the baby, a pliant and natural skin that would grow with Baby and allow her to change ages and sizes, and learn words and spelling and bookreading and beauty, in all its high and low forms, and finally someday, in another world, to fall in love and have perfect babies of her own, ignited by their own inner light. Secretly, Helen had hoped for an ending like that.

But even on the inside of her smooth baby skull, there was just another pulsing brainy light.

That was all there was, and as soon as Helen saw this, she understood that there wasn't going to be any other ending now. Dimly aware of the beating of her heart and wrists, Helen stilled her hands one final time before reaching firmly in to extract, one by one, each of Baby's tiny, vital organs, and—*tenderly, tenderly*—lay them on top of the heap of the layers of the membrane of Baby. Helen picked one up, a barely formed and infinitesimal infant heart or uterus, and held it cupped in her palm, wishing as hard as she could for this to be enough.

But despite its terrific glowing, the organ produced no heat of its own, remaining the same vague non-temperature Baby always was, and ok, Helen said at last, steeling herself for what was coming next.

Ok, ok, ok.

And because there really was only the one thing left to do, Helen acted now on both impulse and instinct, the last thing she remembered before waking beside Lyda in the yurt and leaving: Helen reached her hand out and touched all that was left of Baby—the almost solid light on the inside of her brain. And at first, it was only just that—a gentle touch—as though Helen might yet pluck this final organ out and lay it with the others. But no, it wasn't budging from its socket—it was never going to budge for her like that. So then she shoved her whole hand deep into the light that was all that remained of Baby.

Maybe that was going too far, but what else could Helen do? She put her hand in and left it there, wrist down in the light, until—*slowly, slowly*—she started to absorb it and a little glowing started in her.

Soon Helen had both hands in, cupped together in a gentle fist of prayer around what she thought must be the light of the hole where Baby's BCI attached. She left them as long as she could, glowing and trembling, and taking in as much of that gorgeous light as she could. That was how much love she held in her then.

And then she used her fingers, ever so lightly, just the slightest touch or caress, there on the inside baby to loosen this one last attachment.

Of course, she should have seen it coming—mass displaces mass. But she was too entranced by the pulsing, glowing hybrid of their bodies. And anyway, she couldn't take it back as, for a little while longer, nothing changed. The light at the core of the inside of Baby remained stable and intact, and they hovered there together, fused and whole. But finally Helen took the tip of her smallest finger and put it in the gap of the space of Baby's BCI, causing—Helen would never know quite how to put this—some subtle disturbance.

And that was that.

She couldn't stop it now—no one could. Already, the light of the inside of Baby had begun, from this disturbance, to agitate, subtly at first and then more and more excitedly until—this was inevitable—it detached and dispersed. Molecule by molecule, atom by atom, string by string, the light let go of whatever it was that held it together and drifted out into the woods that once had been alive. And this—this, diffusion—set off the rest of Baby, the glowing stones of jewel-like organs and the heap of skin and membrane—all, all of it letting go in infinitesimal bits and pieces that split apart, one by one, with small staccato pops, then spread out and ascended like little glittering glow-worms into the crackling darkness of the night.

EXODUS

UNTIL THE END
OF THE WORLD

AND THAT'S WHERE Helen is, on the outside looking in, when Peter descends from the loft, pale and disheveled, with rumpled clothes and rings of sweat around the neck and underneath the arms, his beige pants low across bare, white buttocks. Really, he's a mess, but yet kindness emanates from him and the light in the loft—the thick and beautiful light—follows him everywhere, a trail of shimmering light, and the same white dust that wouldn't budge for Bird, puffing up at his feet in little clouds of luminescence which, as he gets lower and closer, Helen can see is not dust at all, but light too—light you can touch—like the inside of Baby. Or at least there's a residue of light that has spilled down from the loft to accumulate, over time, in the center of the large room of what she sees now is a primary shelter, more like the material substance of light, if light had material—a body, the actual body that Helen knows now it does.

Well, it's something anyway—light and not light—the shimmering gauze of it a lambent corona that Peter walks right through as though it were not there but that parts around his strong, dark feet and billows up around him, striding through it toward Helen, on the outside, to open the door and let her in at last.

Come in, come in, he says in an effort to be gracious, you look bigger here. Are you thirsty? Do you want something to eat?

He's holding a square of white cloth, damp and softly napped, like flannel, and although at first Helen thinks he's going to wipe her with it, he just hands it over shyly for her to wipe herself.

On the inside the room smells old and of things that have not existed in the world for many, many years—lilac and cinnamon and something salty, like kelp, and of course, the faint metallic smell of Baby, which comforts Helen in a way she can't explain. Along the ridges of his skull, Peter's bald head, stretched to the point of translucence, throbs, each throb emitting— Helen sees this now—a little burst of that same milky light she recognizes at once as the loveliest, loneliest light in the world. Without a second thought, Helen takes off her scarf and wipes her head clean with the cloth, rubbing it softly to let this light in.

Good for you, he says. You beat the others.

It's not a race, she says, or a game.

Did I say it was a game? Who, unlike her, looks smaller, such that they seem, in *here,* to be almost the same size, head to head, shoulder to shoulder. Close up, there's something papery about him, not so much fragile as *pressed,* the layers and layers of Peter held together by the sheerest force of gravity and friction—the stratum of him, who has brought her here.

The only man left in the world, Helen thinks, who could have done so.

Peter brings her water that tastes, incredibly, of moss—it tastes alive.

Ok, Helen says. But you should know I really loved that rabbit.

The room, on the other hand, is huge—much, much larger than seems possible from the outside—a whole world of a room where a person could live an entire life—past and future—or history of the world, or time. A person, Helen thinks, would need a map to navigate this much space, with its vast kitchen to the northeast, and all the way on the other side through an immense topography of floor and light, a square of sofas arranged to face each direction of the compass. They are brown, the color of earth, and just the sight of them makes Helen want to burst into tears. How poignant they are, as though waiting for people to fill them. But oh, she is just so tired, so completely exhausted. To travel the length of this room, just to get to one sofa where she might sit, or lie, or rest, or fill the empty space of cushion and upholstery and time—that one journey, she thinks, could take her entire life.

Then Peter makes another sound, a muted exclamation, but not to Helen, who only, in this moment, wants to rest. Then again, oh—it worked!

Reluctantly, Helen turns back to follow his gaze to the place where the bird that is not a real bird has just flown through the window, again, and out beyond to the path she took not so long before from the creek where she had stood in the water and worked the pros and cons of the ever-diminishing space between there and *here*, and where even now someone else is standing looking up, as she had, at the shelter—the place, the home, the world—and its limpid glass of window and light.

That can't be, Helen says.

Don't worry, Peter says.

But no, really, she was sleeping, it's too soon—she's just after Baby. That's the only thing, so soon. I'm warning you, Peter, she's going to be mad.

Shhh. She'll be ok, you'll see.

Below, Lyda's feet must be getting cold, and Helen doesn't want to think this but she does just a little, that Peter sounds—satisfied—when he says this.

On the back of one of the sofas, the bird preens fussily, while on the outside, down the path in the water Lyda really is starting to shiver, and so it's not going to be long before she steps out of the creek and comes up to get warm. And when that's what she does, Helen sees that she's barefoot— having gone off without shoes—sees a small blossom of blood on her right big toe, sees, too, the determination that has brought her here, and something else—something ashen—even as Peter is already throwing his door wide open to the world and rushing out onto the deck to call out his encouragement: up here, Lyda, come—you're almost there, that wasn't so hard, welcome, welcome!

But just as Lyda leaves the creek bed and starts to pick her barefoot way up the stony path toward Peter calling out his welcome, there's a terrible crashing from the far other side of the house, a high-pitched screech, and then a slow defeated settling, the sound of a car door slammed, a series of low curses, and then someone's pounding on the other door—the door that faces the front path down which Peter's mother might once have walked that leads to the highway where long ago, and just as he'd promised his father, Peter had raised the black flag.

I wrecked the black car, Will calls almost cheerfully from the door, but it still kind of runs.

It's not locked, Peter calls back, come in. Then, under his breath, it really did work.

And finally—this is the best part—they're all in the primary shelter together, hugging like old lost friends, actual bodies, all their limbs interwoven, their skins shedding real salty sweat, their frantic hearts, their quick and raspy breathing. But washed by the steady miraculous light from above and the rest that leaks out from Peter, their color is improving as Peter hands them both their own white cloths to make themselves at home.

First, he says still shy, here, showing them how. Then, here.

After they clean up a bit, Peter will take them outside again and lead them back down to the creek to wash the rest of their worldly bodies. But already the outside feels different, the water, not so cold, closer to a normal temperature. One by one, they will kneel in this warmer water while Peter rubs them with sand, and then rinses away their dead skin until they are new and as white and serene as eggs.

And then they will do this for Peter.

Later, they will eat the feast that Peter has prepared over the past weeks of waiting, keeping one eye always on their progress, their anxious curiosities and confusions, their wild and disparate hopes. It's been a lot of waiting, but Peter, who's been waiting his whole life, is the most patient man alive.

Throughout this period, Peter's cooking has distracted him, for it's been full of optimism and defined by many pomegranate dishes, fruit he has laboriously seeded from the tree that has finally produced—pomegranate soup, and pomegranate salad, and elegant fillets of trout gently simmered in a stew of pear and pomegranate, and braised slivered onion with pomegranate garnish, and little dessert cups of pomegranate mousse, and sweet new pomegranate wine. This delicious feast goes on for many hours, during which Peter, whose waiting is finally over, sighs the most contented sighs of his life. If his father could only see him now, or his mother, as a certain drowsy stupor fills the room. It's the wine, Peter thinks, not yet thinking how even though everything has worked out exactly as he planned, nothing is quite as he expected.

For one thing—where will they sleep, and for how long? Two of them, being wholly human, will need a great deal of sleep, never mind food. It's a little unclear, from the wine, but Peter thinks he remembers something like three meals a day and wonders a bit distantly if the garden will be sufficient. And shoes—they will need shoes. Peter has been generous so far, but someday they will run out.

In the absence of shoes, there could be other kinds of trouble, just look what's happened to Lyda, who only that morning had wakened to the clump of empty fleece and missing Helen and gone off barefoot in a panic, damaging her toe. Peter is worried about the toe, a part of him concerned she might lose the nail. And what will happen then—will the child be born without toenails? Will this one trait run down through all the children, like the trait of human weakness, and how long can children survive in the woods, even beneficent woods, without nails to protect their toes?

Oh, they will need so many things—they will need sunscreen and catsup and emory boards, resin for Will's fiddle, paper for Lyda's poems, dental floss and birth control devices and syringes and pepper and socks and bandaids and lozenges for all kinds of medical conditions and scarves and jackets and hats and decorations and fleece and technical support. They will need, Peter thinks, shampoo.

Then it strikes him. It strikes him viscerally, for Peter, who has planned for everything, did not plan for this—their plain humanity, he thinks, their humanness. How can he ever explain one single thing—to *them*? He might as well have brought them to the moon.

But not Helen, who has found her way to a sofa, at rest at last, her knees—her perfect knees—drawn up beneath, and who looks a bit skeptical, or maybe piqued, such that seeing her there, all the breath goes out of Peter as he begins to take in how much work it is going to be to bring the world back. Unattended for weeks, the orchard is going to need watering, weeding, pruning, never mind the rest of the trees, and the fish traps will probably need to be restrung, and the solar power banks dusted, and all those tomatoes and plums and green beans and corn to be harvested and put up in jars. Lyda hardly made a dent in them, down there by the river.

And looking about the primary shelter—the place that has provided him refuge and home since the day his father died and Peter moved, as he had promised, from the outside to the inside, the place that more than anything he loves like a mother and a father and a passel of companions and best lover and teacher and friend, he sees it, for the first time, as utilitarian and a little threadbare. Peter can't remember if cleaning the sofas was one of the promises he had made to his father, but he's pretty sure they haven't been cleaned in a lifetime of sweating and gardening and watching the world go down and only himself to love.

And that's just what's on the outside. On the inside, there is so much more.

For they have all come with their own particular temperaments and talents, and Peter is beginning to understand that there is nothing in the history of their lives—in their *pasts*—to prepare them for what's coming—their *futures*. He'll have to raise them all over again and as though they were as new, as blank, as full of possibility and hope as the space at the end of the loop where coding begins.

Later, much later that first night—the others are sleeping for now—Peter, who isn't sure he'll ever sleep again, gets up to pace around the interior of the primary shelter, which no longer seems so commodious as it once did.

Feeling strangely crowded, Peter paces and paces, the thick pads of his feet soundless on the burnished floors, dispersing light, until finally he climbs back up into the loft where his little nest of soiled pillows, the depression of his own body visible among them, calls out to him Peter, *come here, come home.*

But Peter doesn't.

There's enough of him left to stand apart—stand here—staring coolly at the skin of screen where so much—and nothing at all—has come down, and where he experiences again, albeit remotely, the feeling he had as a boy in the orchard on the day the world ended, and then didn't. It's a more detached, a more desultory feeling, but as Peter remembers finding himself alone at the end of time, even though he knows he probably shouldn't, he lets himself wonder, again, what it is like to be wholly human.

Bathed by the light that comes from his screens, the same light that is him, inside and outside, eyes open or closed, Peter closes his eyes and waits just a little bit more for his father's last encryption to crack open. Peter doesn't need the computers anymore. He doesn't even need the portal. All he needs is this— his own huge BCI, and his new resolve and capacity to let it go.

When the final node of it opens at last, it's not with an image but only a sound that comes to him in the voice of his mother across the span of all this time. He wishes he could but, even now, he can't see her—can't see her on her knees, and him in her arms, and the image he's been searching for his whole life just to prove that it happened, it was *real*—because his nine-year-old face is buried in her shoulder, her violin tossed to one side and his lean boy legs throbbing from running so fast toward her whose beautiful voice forms itself into just these words and only these: *what I would say to you is just walk right into it.* And then, astonishingly: *I'm sorry.*

Then Peter does something he's never done before.

It's not a permanent solution, and it's not even anything he knows he's going to do, but there is something so imperative in his mother's words that quickly, without thinking, he powers down the computers, like anyone else, for the night. And in the ensuing darkness—a darkness without discernible dimension, just a flat, undifferentiated black—what Peter hears, again, is this: the sweet sough of wind in the trees above, the muffled sound of water in the creek below, the barely discernible hum of his own BCI, and the steady beating of his persistent heart.

After a bit, he hears something else: the sound of others breathing, the in and out of inhale and exhale like one connected body, but also separate, each separate body on a separate sofa—breath to breath—and inside even that, three other hearts beating, as regular and inevitable as their being here tonight.

Peter cannot ever remember such darkness before, but his feet remember the stairs, one stair at a time, the worn feel of them firm and familiar to his calloused feet.

So, after all, it's Peter's feet that find their blind way back onto the deck where he imagines planting himself now forever, like a tree, firmly rooted to the house his father built, and his feet slowly working their way down into the earth that lies below, sinking deeper and deeper, even as the rest of him—his brainy head and humble heart—reaches up toward the place where the stars used to be.

As long as it takes, and it could take a lifetime, Peter will stay here, growing.

And he waits. Next to watching, this is perhaps the thing he knows best how to do in his life.

Well ok, he tells himself, maybe I'll just sit here for a little while. I'll sit here on the deck and maybe they will too. He waits and waits, until:

Hey, Will says behind him, you all right, man?

And when Peter doesn't answer, Will tries again, it's not like, you know—it's just going to take a little getting used to. But the place has potential—it could really work. Then he looks up to the flat black sky and lets out a long, low whistle. Man, he says, his breath going all the way out with his words, what have you done with the stars?

In the darkness, Peter might be weeping, but it's not from sadness, more just a physiological response to the darkness. Peter's listening as hard as he can, but without the soothing hum of the computers, the rest of all this sound is almost deafening.

Poor Helen, he thinks, poor thing. And for the first time Peter wonders if she'll miss her apparatus.

The creek part is nice, though, Will says. *Waiting, breathing. In, out.* Hey I'm just trying to meet you half way.

Behind them, the door swings open again where, if there were light to see them with, both of the women would be huddled, peering from the inside to the outside and trying to find their way out. But there isn't any light, and Will can only imagine them holding hands in the darkness, clinging to each other, which makes him want to cling to them too.

Come on out, Will says, suddenly wanting this, *join* us. He wants them both outside where he is with Peter, but he especially wants Lyda—he wants her body next to his.

Shh, Lyda says, stepping out onto the deck and, holding Helen's hand, tugging her out too, moving gingerly and feeling with her other hand until it lands on the top of Peter's head. She only just touches it lightly to orient herself, but the feel of it grounds her on the inside. Or maybe, she can't tell, there's a little leaking light, but the touch itself—her hand, his head—feels charged and steadying, while Peter, who has so longed for a natural body—one with intact ovaries and viable eggs—stiffens at how carelessly she throws hers around, settling cross-legged between them and flinging her arms over their shoulders, her words careless too.

Wow, she says, what happened to the light? Lyda squeezes Peter's shoulder before adding, all that stuff that we did in the portal, that's not really real, she says. I'm not, she says, pregnant?

Not yet, Helen says. She says it so softly Lyda almost doesn't hear. Maybe she hasn't said it at all. But you will be.

Will (at least she thinks it's Will) puts his hand on her thigh, but he's speaking to Peter. So this is it, then—the end of the world?

Peter laughs. But no, it doesn't work that way.

It's not quite, you know, how I pictured it, and he doesn't sound so confident now. What about chaos, the suffering of children? What about war? Aren't we supposed to fry?

In fact, Will had always wanted it that way, falling apart over time and accidental. But so much of it, he knew, had turned out to be intentional—

the bombs had been launched with purpose; the plague genes, spliced, not swapped. Now this. Will suspects there is a certain logic here but because he can't quite find it, a feeling of competition rises up in him instead.

Shh, Lyda says again, touching him in what she hopes will be a soothing way. That part has already happened.

So what *is* this place then, anyway? What's the story here?

How dark it is, Lyda says. Can you see, Helen? Tell me what you can see.

Helen doesn't need light to see, Will says. Do you, Helen?

So now it is Helen who sighs, her breath going out and her hand reaching in the darkness for Peter's. Count your lucky stars, she says, and they all look up at—*nothing*—there's still the red car. Will didn't wreck that one. You can take that car and go. He won't stop you.

Hearing this, Peter startles, surprised, even pained, that she would say so, but of course she is right—they are free to go, if that's what they want. But the thought of them leaving—so soon!—fills Peter with an unfamiliar urgency and makes him expansive again.

No, stay, he wants to tell them, but it doesn't work like that, either, because it's not up to him. Besides, even just the thought of trying to explain everything he's done to arrange—*all this*—is so exhausting that it suddenly strikes him how easy it would have been, before, for someone like his father to have found someone like his mother—if that's what he wanted, if he had tried. And because it takes them being here for Peter to begin to understand this, his throat aches too much to say anything at all.

It really does hurt, but that's at least in part from all the talking at dinner—as much from what he has already said as from what he is going to say. That part is coming, and it's physical—an actual physical ache that knots the longing up inside and renders him, paradoxically, speechless.

But what do they expect him to say anyway—welcome to your new Intentional Community, your own little spinning plot of spaceship planet earth.

Warrior, Lyda says, who, compared to Helen, is huge in person—an Amazon to Helen's little Etruscan—*light, pomegranate, rock.*

I still don't get it. Despite his muscularity, the edgy force of it pressing relentlessly outward, Will is almost whining from his inability to fully parse the moment.

You're not supposed to get it, Helen says, not like that. That's not what Peter wants.

Tell us, Helen, Lyda says, accidentally bumping Peter's thigh with her gigantic knee. What *does* Peter want?

Almost that breaks things loose inside him, but not quite, and as he and Helen sigh the very same slightly exasperated sigh, it breaks inside Lyda instead, who gets up suddenly to walk—walk fast and with resolve—over to what she imagines must be the outer edge of deck, down being so familiar to her that, despite the darkness, she stops herself in time—one more step and she'd have been the one falling forever. Standing there at the edge of what must count as the world for her now, Lyda feels poised and completely absorbed by the abyss she can't even see. But it's deep, she knows. How far down does it go, anyway? And she rummages around in her pocket to find one last shard of beach glass so smooth and worn that she almost hates to part with it, but yet hesitates only briefly before letting it go.

Don't do that, Peter says.

But Lyda's not listening to him just now. She's listening to the falling—listening and listening and listening. Wow, she says after a bit. It's not, I mean, Peter—this isn't the bottomless wash?

More like a spiral or a whirlpool, Will says.

Shh, Helen says. It's just a metaphor.

Or, Will says, the center of an elusive circle.

But even as Lyda takes in the absence of sound of the shard not landing, the others rise together with a faint rustling to join her at the edge of the world. One by one, they settle there, sitting themselves on the lip of deck and dangling their many legs over—all eight legs hanging down together like the appendages of a single organism swinging back and forth every bit as if the distance between them and the rocks below which, cupped as they are in the fist of total darkness, they can't begin to fathom, is no longer any real concern of theirs.

It's safe though, they're pretty sure of that. Right now where they are, they are all as safe as they could ever be.

You know, Lyda says, nestled happily between Helen and Will, after I attached my BCI, my box got big again. For so long it had been so small I hurt things—my shoulders, hips—just getting in, but suddenly it was huge all over again and everything fit—not just my body, but the rest of my stuff—the maps and the suture repair kit and emergency recharger, troubleshooting tips in many different languages, my pen and paper and adaptor and all the notes

I kept on his—your—coordinates. Everything was there—all my ideas. She pauses, only briefly, before turning toward what, in the darkness, she hopes is Peter. But you knew that, didn't you? You planned it.

What Lyda really wants to say, the thought that comes to her obliquely, the question she can't quite frame yet—then she does: did you plan my father, too?

Oh Lyda, *shh*, Helen says, putting one small hand on Lyda's bent back. Peter's portal, she says, works in mysterious ways.

Wow, Will says, letting out a low whistle. You had a BCI? And your father found it?

By now Lyda wishes she had never started, because it wasn't so much that her father had found it with his meaty hands, the way he found everything else, as that he'd been about to, the only thing, she thinks, that was her own.

That wasn't all he found, she says finally, the numbness lasting even now.

But what does all that matter? Peter says, before adding softly, *what I would say to you is walk right into it.*

Like you gave us any choice. But really—Will sounds better now, almost wry and not so bitter—I didn't know she had it in her.

But Lyda has stopped listening again to all this—noise—and just as she'd once listened from the inside of her box for the echoes of the outer world or the slow, pneumatic swish of her father coming home, is listening instead, and acutely, for something inside her. Lyda does not possess Helen's extraordinary hearing, or even anything close to it, but she has her human body, which she turns again to Peter, this time with a question. It's not so much a sound, inside her, not even a touch, what she feels—not a pulse or a flutter, but a cell, or a clump of cells dividing. Lyda cannot hear them but she can feel them, or at least she can feel the idea of them splitting, and whether it's slow or fast, it will be relentless, this division, Lyda does know that, while with another part of her mind she is desperately trying to remember what she left in the box, what careless detritus, what trace of Peter might still be there for her father to find.

And now again, unmistakable, the thing inside her stirs, not yet human, but with the full potential of becoming so, and as her heart, in her body, opens up to receive the body in her heart, it meets—it can't not—the certain skepticism of her mind.

You said, she says to Peter, we were safe in the portal. What we did—you promised I couldn't get pregnant.

But it doesn't matter anyway, because Lyda also knows that even if it's not a real baby, there's nothing she can do to stop it now.

Slowly, Lyda also begins to be aware of Helen's hand on her back, rubbing small consoling circles, and Helen saying, *shhh, shhh*. It's ok, she says, giving Lyda's own words back. And she laughs. But not even Peter, she tells Lyda as if to reassure her, knows how long it's going to take. Tell us, Peter, please: how long will such a zygote remain a tiny zygote? Or is Lyda going to grow old, with just the idea of it nestling inside her?

And when Peter doesn't answer, Helen moves her remarkable hand to squeeze one of Lyda's supple ones firmly, imparting a feeling of calm. Be glad, she says, for a body that still works like that—at least you'll grow old.

At this, Lyda notices something else, unexpected but familiar, a bit like light—light touching her, but from the inside. It's the strangest thing, there on the deck in the darkest imaginable night and all out of words, but yet her body—Lyda's own body—starts to relax. It seems now she's been holding out against Peter from the moment she first walked through the door, or entered the desert, or the red car, or the hole in the earth or lava tube or burrow, but as this new serenity takes over, beginning on her face—if anyone could see it—with a look such exquisite gratitude, Lyda understands now—she *feels* it—that this light, all the light, is coming from the inside of Peter.

Begin, she tells herself, with just one breath. There will always be another—breath, touch, layer, word—the idea of a word. A person could get used to such a feeling, unfolding in the present moment, this raveling. If Lyda were thinking in thoughts, what she'd think was that's what story is for, to stitch them together, one to the other—to earth, history, time, matter—story that keeps things from flying apart, like the skin of the missing baby. But just thinking of Baby makes Lyda wish someone else would talk now.

On Lyda's hand, the hot and gnarled knot of sinew, bone and artificial nerve that is Helen's, stiffens, flushing with heat. Peter was different, for what his dad had done to him, he'd done out of love and hope, cloning the synth-ethic cells from Peter's own body and then painstakingly adapting them so that, long after the father was gone, the boy would be perfect and every bit as natural—as real—as any living boy—only better. Love could do that, Helen knew from the instant she first saw him in the courtroom—saw his perfect head, met his perfect gaze, understood his perfect logic and mind, but now she also understood with the force of things breaking open inside her that, just as his father had done that for him, Peter had done this for her.

Helen's own process, she reflects, is so different, never happening without little jolts of something, small electric charges passing through her. The sensation is not without pleasure, but it is still, in part, mechanical. Things pass through her, going in and coming out again the same—and *different.*

But not Peter, who, technically, could change the world with a thought, or a gaze.

And now his head—the round, smooth orb of it, and the pulsing blue lines where the plates fail to close, and the gaze from inside, and inside the gaze— Helen feels herself pulled toward him as she had that first time in the courtroom, as though into water, the loveliest and the most poignant on earth, becoming, in this moment, again and wholly his.

Don't you see, she wants to say, but it's still too dark to see anything at all.

Well, Will says, settling back and throwing his arms companionably around the others, while you were getting drunk and he was cooking, I went upstairs to look.

Oh, Will, Helen says. She says it with the strangest sound, something that might be a giggle or just a barely suppressed laugh. Don't be so literal, she says. It wasn't Peter messing with our minds, but everything else—the *world* messed with our minds.

Did I say he messed with our minds?

Not yet, but you were going to.

No, listen. You too, Will tells Peter, who is smiling in the dark. I mean it—I went upstairs, I *saw* what you've got there.

And then there's a silence, a new small strain, until Will tries again.

Ok, you want story, here's a story for you: in the early days of atomic development, no one really knew what was going to happen. Between what they thought that bomb would do and what it might do, well, that was all still theory. Some of the scientists thought it would go off the way it was supposed to, just in time to save us, but others—not so many, but enough—were convinced that splitting even one single atom would ignite the very atmosphere of earth and blow us all to smithereens.

After a pause, he adds, I really hope you know what you're doing.

At this, Lyda laughs. Try to look at the bright side for once—we're going to need that kind of guy around.

Then she sighs a huge contented sigh, placing one hand on her belly and swinging her legs in the darkness.

So ok, if the stars are really gone—isn't there some actual science to this, gravity or something? Like, wouldn't things collapse, or fly apart? So I'm pretty sure, she says a bit dreamily, we're safe here, for now. Aren't we, Peter?

Peter says, Helen says, that's what grace is.

And anyway, Lyda says, that thing about the bomb—isn't that more or less what happened?

Between then and when the darkness somehow begins to lift, no one has anything else left to say, so they sit in their silence, dangling their legs, their hands intertwined with each other's. They could go on this way forever but it's not going to take that long because the glimmering has already begun—not real light yet, but more like the idea of light, or its anticipation—some small illumination on the verge of coming back into the world, or as though a tiny tear has been rent in the fabric of its darkness.

Suddenly, Lyda calls out, wait, there's one thing I forgot.

And she stands, a bit stiffly and, before anyone can stop her, takes a final breath and steps off into the darkness as though slipping right through the window, like the bird, of the high white apartment and into that other world where things still fall. And there's the boy already, bent over his shoe, hapless and falling forever, and not even looking at her, but yet waiting. All his life he's been waiting for her. And Lyda, who has grown so completely beyond him by now into her strong, lithe body on the cusp of womanhood and another body maybe forming inside her, the way bodies do, latches on to him now, timing things so precisely that they fall together, face to face, and finally she can touch him—she can help.

At that exact moment, he looks up and grins, trusting her at once.

First, Lyda tells herself, she will help him tie his shoes, just a small, maternal gesture—*loop the rabbit ear here, the rabbit ear there, pull that one through, oh you're so good and smart.* And then she will send him off to play.

But it is so nice, when she's done, to get back to the deck where, no one is quite sure yet, but something is different about the light—a kind of softening, maybe—and at least the others smell familiar. Lyda will rest now, with them—they'll all rest together.

By the time Peter finally begins no one is quite sure how long it's been that they've been waiting on the deck for exactly this to happen. When it does, it is without any sound, but only light—or *lightening*—as though the sound of Peter cannot quite be recuperated yet. But finally there's enough light to see that Peter's talking, he's telling them a story—his story—his mouth going a mile a minute but no words coming out, or words they can hear. Words falling, Lyda thinks, into a bell of perfect silence—are they deaf? But then Helen says, *shh*—and Lyda hears *that*.

But that's ok, because Lyda can see something else starting to happen—anyone could see that. And so Lyda touches the deck with the flat of her palm to steady herself, swinging her legs again freely in the space beneath the deck that is growing, even now, wider and darker.

That can't be.

On the deck, it's getter lighter, but in the space below, looking down into it, her feet just disappear into the black, the ends of her own legs—her feet—as though detached from the body—her *body*—on the deck.

People, Helen says so quietly it's hardly even speech at all, can get used to almost anything. But how would you feel if you were the last man on earth?

That's the sort of thing that never happens, Will says.

It happens in a million homes, a million times a day, Lyda says

This one's not a metaphor, Helen says in her steady, quiet voice. That's not what it is.

Beside them, Peter hasn't let up, and now they can all see the undeniable edges of palpable light—light they can touch.

Hey, Lyda turns to Peter, where are we anyway? What *is* this place?

And then, finally, Peter does make a sound, not a word so much, hardly even human, but yet the first truly human sound he has made in more than a quarter of a century, and as everybody turns to look at him, they see that whatever light there is, is coming from him—from the seams of his skull and the round open o of his mouth, all of it leaking from *him*.

But at least they can see now.

And they can see, Lyda can see—they can all *see*—because of what has cracked open in Peter—because of what is coming out of him, who's talking freely now—talking to them. Still, it's not anything coherent that is coming out, not so much words as raw meaning, cracked up and raspy—or not even that, more just the idea of the cracked-up sound, something that has never yet existed, and it comes in the shape (if it could be said to have a shape) of long luminescent strands of *something* spinning out from the back of Peter's throat, a braid or a rope, some unearthly element that has neither sound nor light, neither corpus nor its absence—but both.

Spellbound, Lyda thinks: this is what language would look like if language had a body.

Helen thinks: he is peeling himself from the inside out.

Will thinks: I *knew* it. Then he thinks: I can't watch.

But in truth, all three of them are completely mesmerized by what is coming out of Peter. Beyond them, the world remains pitch black, but here on the deck, the little pile of shimmering stuff spinning out of Peter has grown bright enough to illuminate the simple circle of nothing else but them. Now, watching is all that any of them can do as Peter keeps on spinning. Sometimes it seems translucent, as though infused with its own internal light, but sometimes it seems viscous and fetid. And it doesn't come from his tongue, or even just his mouth, but from deep, deep inside, and as it comes out, long coils of it spin around him, like a cocoon. But it's piling up around them too, accumulating form and heft and friction, until the pull of gravity spills it over the deck and into the void below, alternately threatening to pull Peter over the edge or, the way it's piling up so fast below, to fill the void and overtake or engulf them. Sometimes, it wafts easily out of his mouth, weightless and drifting, but at others it's expelled from him, as though Peter were gagging on the actual organic material of the inside of him.

To Lyda all this is so amazing that she almost doesn't notice Helen touching the pile of material growing around them, streaming down over the edge of the deck and into the nothing below. Should Helen be doing that? But Helen, closer to the bone of it, can't stop herself from reaching out to touch the beautiful stuff—for it is, it is just so amazingly, so breathtakingly beautiful—what is coming out of Peter's mouth. She touches it with her hands.

Hey, Will says during a pause in Peter's story. Show me how you *do* that.

But Peter just looks at him quizzically and starts up again, the stuff bluer now, like ice, or alternately hot, then cold, then no real temperature at all, like Baby, or just the idea of temperature, of light, of color.

And then Helen does the strangest thing. Peter has his eye on her—he is watching her. But the others, dazed and ecstatic, almost miss it, but Helen has eyes only for the light, which she already *knows*. And because Helen already *knows* it, she knows what to do: she puts her hands all the way into the light, and once they are in, she takes off a finger. Then another. She starts with the index finger of her left hand, although she could just as easily have started on the other end, all Helen's fingers being equal. There's a little popping noise of each finger breaking off, and then a tiny sucking as she tucks it deep inside the pile of stuff that Peter continues to expel. There is so much luminescence being made by Peter that it's difficult—almost blinding—to watch her do this, remove all her fingers, but Helen isn't doing this in order to be watched. And it takes all her concentration anyway, for it is a delicate operation, locating the exact place at the joint to bend back and crack open, then quickly twisting it off with a sharp, discreet yank.

Hey, Will says, don't do that.

But Peter just keeps on disgorging his stuff, and Helen just keeps taking off her fingers, each so absorbed by what needs to happen that only Lyda notices the light coming out of Helen's open finger socket is almost the same as the light on the deck, or the stuff from Peter, a little luminescence leaking out of Helen, too. The light crackles a bit, but that's the only sound there is, not even the rush of creek below, as Helen sucks each empty socket briefly before stuffing it closed with some small bit of Peter's light until no one can tell his light from hers.

When Helen gets to her second hand, the procedure is more difficult, but Lyda knows better than to offer to help. Helen has to use her mouth now, placing each finger delicately in between her teeth, and then biting down and pulling—pulling hard. The first one is the most difficult, but once she gets the hang of it, it goes quickly enough—beginning, on this hand, with the little finger, then finger after finger until, finally, the thumb.

At last it is over. Helen's fingers are gone, and Peter has expelled all of whatever it is that was once inside him. But he doesn't look deflated—he looks, instead, replete. Without fingers, Helen's hands are not nearly so hot.

But already another strange thing is beginning to happen: the material Peter has expelled is stirring a bit far—far—below where their feet still hang. It stirs, then ripples, just a gentle roll at first, but then more and more agitated, gathering momentum and intensity until it's almost violent and little crackling sparks are flying off all over, causing tiny rifts inside it, dark spaces that widen into fissures as, bit by bit, the stuff itself starts to come apart, like the light of Baby before it or the thread of fabric Lyda once unraveled on the deck, and disperse into the darkness still around them. And as it does, one by one, Helen's fingers fly off, too, until all ten of them are hanging like stars above, and then another light comes down to join the roiling light below, releasing, when the two lights meet, such a blinding radiance that for a while no one can see anything at all.

When it clears, what remains turns out, after all, to be the shadowy world of any day's dawn, and each of them blinking like bats. But there it is—all the old familiar world, every bit of it still there (save for Helen's fingers), and in fact—because this is what dawns do all over the world—it's getting brighter and brighter, earth turning itself, as it has always turned, in its dogged daily spinning and thankless steady orbit around the sun and through the galaxy and time.

It's going to be another soupy day.

But when Lyda looks up, the sky instead turns a brutal shade of red, then an equally brutal black, with storm clouds gathering along what looks to be the backbone of the world. This almost never happens. This lies in the category of the flat-out miraculous—actual *rain*.

Looks like rain, Will says.

So it does, Lyda says.

Looks like it's going to be a doozey, Helen says, slipping the nub of her cooling hand into the socket of Peter's waiting palm.

Let's go in, Peter says, and finally his voice comes out clear and true, if maybe a little tired. Who wouldn't be tired, after all of that? Still, it's an ordinary man's voice saying ordinary things, what any man might say, just plain common sense.

So he says it again: let's go in, out of the rain.

And then, because it really is starting to rain, a real downpour—cats and dogs—that's what they do.

KATHARINE HAAKE'S prior books include three short story collections and a hybrid novel, *That Water, Those Rocks* (University of Nevada). Her work has appeared widely in such literary magazines as *One Story, Witness, The Iowa Review,* and *Crazyhorse.* A regular contributor to scholarship in the theory and pedagogy of creative writing, she is also the author of *What Our Speech Disrupts: Feminism and Creative Writing Studies* (NCTE), and teaches at California State University, Northridge.

TITLES FROM

WHAT BOOKS PRESS

POETRY

Molly Bendall & Gail Wronsky, *Bling & Fringe (The L.A. Poems)*

Kevin Cantwell, *One of Those Russian Novels*

Ramón García, *Other Countries*

Karen Kevorkian, *Lizard Dream*

Gail Wronsky, *So Quick Bright Things*
BILINGUAL, SPANISH TRANSLATED BY ALICIA PARTNOY

FICTION

François Camoin, *April, May, and So On*

A.W. DeAnnuntis, *Master Siger's Dream*

A.W. DeAnnuntis, *The Mermaid at the Americana Arms Motel*

Katharine Haake, *The Origin of Stars and Other Stories*

Katharine Haake, *The Time of Quarantine*

Mona Houghton, *Frottage & Even As We Speak: Two Novellas*

Chuck Rosenthal, *Coyote O'Donohughe's History of Texas*

MAGIC JOURNALISM

Chuck Rosenthal, *Are We Not There Yet? Travels in Nepal, North India, and Bhutan*

ART

Gronk, *A Giant Claw*
BILINGUAL, SPANISH

WHAT
BOOKS
PRESS

LOS ANGELES

What Books Press books may be ordered from:
SPDBOOKS.ORG | ORDERS@SPDBOOKS.ORG | (800) 869 7553 | AMAZON.COM

Visit our website at
WHATBOOKSPRESS.COM

CPSIA information can be obtained at www.ICGtesting.com
Printed in the USA
BVOW040106060313

314714BV00002B/64/P